2024

Patricia J. Free

This book was given to me by Sherry Murphy Holland Her Daughter Jenny Haley is the author + my friend

Sherry You been my dear friend for many years

THE RED ROSE

JENNY HALEY

DEDICATION

For Jonah.

CONTENTS

BAILEY ROSE, M.D. SERIES

CHAPTER ONE

Bailey Rose slept like the dead that night, waking with a start as the morning sun bathed the bed. She did not even remember falling asleep, and vaguely recalled Gacenka mentioning something about special tea to help her rest. She smiled wistfully; the wise, beautiful mother of the man she loved had been nothing but loving and solicitous to her, even though she must have known that Bailey had been with Jacob, in his bed, behind closed doors. Bailey was no good at duplicity; she was certain that her glowing face had broadcast the truth just as surely as her swollen mouth and tangled hair.

She curled herself around the pillow, imagining it was *him* she was holding. *Him.* The thought of never seeing him again after today sent horrible waves of anxiety coursing through her body.

She glanced at the clock. It was four minutes past seven. She watched the second hand make its long journey around the face; surely this clock must be slow. Sixty seconds felt like ten minutes. She hid her face in her pillow, willing time to go faster, faster. She breathed deeply, imaging her patients, Gabby, her clinic. Instead, his face filled her mind. He smiled at her with that one damn dimple. *Get out of my head,* she whispered. When she thought she had successfully passed a true ten minutes, she turned her head to peek at the clock, testing herself.

One minute had passed. *One.* One more minute in her life that was to be full of perhaps millions of moments like these.

Already, it was an exhausting, pointless task to pass every minute of her life without him. She tried to imagine a whole day of this, knowing she would not see him, talk to him, touch him. A whole week. A year. A lifetime without Jacob Naplava, the boy she had fallen in love with fifteen years ago at the tender age of twelve—the boy who was promised to someone else.

She felt the dark wing of a depression unlike anything she could have

1

envisaged brush across her. She thought she understood now why people took their own lives; the despair was truly all-consuming. She allowed herself to sit on the precipice of it and dangle her feet. Perhaps she could go home and just curl up in bed, refusing to eat or drink. It would only take a few weeks. But that would be so very cruel to those who loved her. It would be better to disappear, perhaps with some sort of note about seeking adventure. She would find a tropical island, and when she arrived she would shed her clothes and swim naked out into the warm, blue water. She would pretend that Jacob was with her, by her side; the water caressing her skin would be his hands skimming over her body. She would swim as far she could go—which would be about three feet beyond the point at which she could touch, since she could not swim—and let the water fold her up. It would fill her eyes and mouth and she would let it; she would breathe it in, the watery salt and silt, and it would be horrible and painful for only a moment or so, just like it had been in the creek when the Vodnik tried to drown her. Then the smudgy black dots would appear around the periphery of her vision, eventually crowding everything else out until her world was a silent and shadowy nothing. The pain would vanish, wouldn't it? Wouldn't it?

No. She did not believe that it would. She had seen death, over and over, and she had observed it to be more of a passage than an ending. Shedding the corporeal was no guarantee that she would cease to need him, mourn for him, long for him.

And she believed in God. She had spent her teenage years raised by *nuns*. What would Jesus think of her drowning herself? Or of curling up in a bed, starving herself? She had begun praying when she was twelve years old, the moment after she shot Senator Hawk, the man who had caused her mother's death and who desired a young girl in the most depraved way imaginable. She had begun praying as though Jesus was a father to guide her. Her eyes shifted to the Bible on the bedside table. She had placed it there the night before after pushing the bed back into place, protecting the carving that was Jacob's and her secret alone. She reached for the leather book now, longing to be comforted. She opened it, murmuring a prayer to direct her to the right verse. *Surely God is my salvation; I will trust and not be afraid.* The words shone forth, and she repeated them. *I will trust and not be afraid. I will trust and not be afraid.*

She closed the book and felt a peace steal over her. Yes, the pain was still there, and even the dread, but *life* was there, too, and hope. She would get out of bed, wash up in Jacob's wonderful bath, and join the family for breakfast. She would move forward, one moment at a time. She would go to Philly—briefly—and travel on to Ireland, in secrecy, and pray to be led down the right path.

Jacob did not sleep that night. Not one damn wink of sleep. He paced.

Back and forth, back and forth, his hands clenched into fists. Five times he left his room and headed down the hall to hers. To his old room, where she slept in his bed, without him. Five times he stopped at her door and retreated, muttering imprecations to himself. The final time, he braced one hand on each side of the doorframe, head hanging low, and almost gave into the grief that was building like a tidal wave within him. *Think. Think. Think.* There had to be a way for them to be together without him losing the baby. What would it take for Caroline Vogler to allow him to be a part of the baby's life? Money? No; she had plenty of that. She wanted *him.* He suspected she wanted an up-and-coming political star, to be brutally honest about it, but he also intuited that she loved him in her own fashion.

The idea came to him at half past three o' clock, the absolute dead epicenter of night, his head fuzzy and spinning with fatigue. Nobody knew Caroline was pregnant except his parents and Bailey. Well, Marianna, too; he had forgotten about that. He would ask Caroline to postpone the wedding, using the quarantine as an excuse, since it had so greatly delayed the campaign. His mother would accompany Caroline on a trip abroad to visit family back in Moravia while he stayed home to campaign: surely no one would frown at that. She would give birth there, no one back home the wiser, and Gacenka would bring the baby home, claiming it as a distant, orphaned relative. Caroline didn't want the baby anyway: she was terrified of her father finding out the truth. After a time, Jacob would break his engagement with Caroline, marry Bailey, and together they would adopt the baby!

He was elated for precisely ten seconds.

I must be losing my godforsaken mind. Caroline would never agree to it, not for any amount of money in the world, and she was much too bright to be deceived by such a moronic plan.

Why the hell can't she just disappear after the baby is born? What if she did *disappear?* Jacob knew all manner of men. It was a simple thing to make someone disappear; it could be done quietly with no way to trace the act back to him.

And it was at that moment, when his thoughts began to turn dark and desperate and wicked, that he knew it was time to get on his knees.

At first he prayed for a way to Bailey. *Please. God. Let us be together. I can't live without her. I can't. I don't want to.* It was not even a prayer; it was more of a supplication. His cheeks were wet and his stomach was in a knot. No relief came. *What do I pray for, then? Help me.* He pictured her in her room, in his bed. Was she crying, too? Did she feel as desperate as he did right now? Was darkness crowding her soul—this horrible, panicked sensation? Oh, God, he hoped she wasn't suffering like this.

So he prayed for Bailey's happiness. He prayed for the strength to do the right thing, whatever that was. He prayed for patience.

When his chest loosened and he found he could breathe again, he got up and went to the front porch, stealing quietly through the house, not even pausing at her door. And he sat on the swing, arms crossed over his chest, waiting for the sun to rise.

CHAPTER TWO

Breakfast was every bit as excruciating as she expected it to be. She arrived late, putting off entering the dining room as long as possible. She had dressed in her eggplant-colored sport dress with the hidden trousers; her hair, still wet from her bath, was plaited into a simple braid. As she approached her customary chair, Jacob rose from his, their eyes meeting, and in his expression she saw love, loss, and desperation. Her breath stuck in her throat and her eyes stung. She would never make it through this meal. But he flashed a grin and made a little joke—how did he do that, make her smile even on this miserable day?—and pulled her chair out for her with a little bow.

"The lady deigns to join us," he announced, making a flourishing gesture with his hand. "The seat of honor for you, our savior this past four weeks. We owe you everything, Dr. Rose."

The others laughed and murmured their agreement, and Ginny sprang from her chair and gave Bailey a grand hug, wrapping her arms around Bailey's waist with such force that she knocked her off balance.

"Don't go, Bailey!" she begged. "Can't you put us in quarantine for another four weeks? We can get Franz sick with the diphtheria, can't we?"

"Ginny, hush," scolded Gacenka, while Franz had a few more choice words to say.

"I'll miss you too, Ginny," Bailey managed. If she carried through with her plans, she would never see any of them again. A stone settled in her heart and dragged the smile from her expressive face. Jacob noticed and extricated Ginny, ordering her into her chair, and seated Bailey solicitously. He pushed in her chair and squeezed her shoulder, his hand lingering, caring nothing for who saw or what they would surmise.

She looked up at him and met his gaze. "Thank you," she murmured, and covered his hand with hers, and there they remained, frozen, eyes locked,

5

as the family looked on. Eveline smiled behind her hand, delighted; Franz stared, amazed and confused; Ginny gasped and clapped her hands twice until her mother shushed her.

Finally, he lowered himself into his chair, clearing his throat and avoiding his family's gaze. "I'll say grace," he announced, and took Bailey's hand under cover of the table, lacing his fingers with hers. He squeezed tight, and she returned the pressure.

He held her hand the whole meal; he wouldn't let it go. Somehow he managed his utensils with his left hand; they avoided anything that needed cutting. But they did not let go. Gacenka watched, her heart aching for them. Franticek frowned, deep in thought.

It was under cover of one of Ginny's boisterous arguments with Franz that Jacob leaned to her and whispered, his voice raising goose bumps on her arms. "Will you walk with me after breakfast?"

She shook her head. "No, I better not."

The pressure on her hand increased.

"You will," he said softly.

She looked at him then. "You can't order me around," she snapped, deciding that perhaps anger was the best route. What she really wanted to say was *Yes, Jake, let's find a green meadow.* Her gaze traveled to his lips. She noticed that there was a tiny red mark on the lower one, just a bit left of center. She wondered if her teeth had made it.

He smiled. "Okay. If you won't walk, we'll talk here. Rosie, I know what you're thinking. You're going to go to Philadelphia and then you're going to sneak off somewhere far away without telling anyone so I can't find you. Where are you going? Ireland, I'll bet. You want to go there. Am I right?"

Her eyes widened and her mouth fell open, dumbstruck. "How did you— how on earth?" Her head spun. Her well-laid plan—the only damn plan she had—had just been neatly dismantled!

His smile grew wider. "Sometimes I think we're two parts of the same whole, do you know what I mean? Don't forget that. I'll spend a lifetime tracking you down if you leave."

The argument between Ginny and Franz grew louder, with Eveline chiming in for added confusion. Gacenka's voice was on top of it all. But Franticek sat quietly, studying his son and the dark-eyed young woman beside him, who looked as though she had just been whacked a good one on the noggin.

"This doesn't solve anything," she whispered.

He shrugged and sat back. "I need more time to think, but don't run, Bailey."

She gave a sharp tug on her hand but he refused to relinquish it. "I can go anywhere I want!" she hissed.

"So can I."

"No, you can't! You have a campaign to win and a wedding to attend!"

He leaned forward again, his face a scant three inches from hers. She wanted to kiss him so badly she bit her own lips. "Rosie, please, just be a little patient. Trust me, okay? Don't be afraid."

I will trust and not be afraid. The very same verse from Isaiah she had found this morning. She shook her head in disbelief. "What exactly *are* you?" she whispered. "How do you read my mind?"

In reply he touched his heart with his fingertips and then touched her own heart, his fingers burning her flesh and sending color leaping to her cheeks. "Two parts of a whole," he repeated. He withdrew his hand though he longed to keep it there. His jaunty manner was gone; he was worshipful now, and she found herself struggling to breathe.

She suddenly realized the table had gone quiet. Five pairs of eyes were on them.

"Are you two fighting?" piped Ginny, and Eveline kicked her under the table. "Ouch!" the little girl yelled, and the children began to bicker again, the strain of the quarantine and the excitement of leaving the house making them fractious.

"That's it! Everybody up! We have family meeting us in the yard in ten minutes!" Gacenka shooed them away, keeping Eveline to help clear the table and ordering Bailey outside with the others to await the wagons.

Bailey made her way outdoors, Ginny dragging her along, relishing the warm, sunny September morning, aware all the while that in the span of an hour she would retrieve her belongings and board a wagon for the train station in Boerne. Would Jacob come with her? Of course he would. He would probably insist on sitting in the same seat. Would he hold her hand? Would he whisper in her ear, promising to search every corner of the earth if she dared to flee? *Dear God, what was she going to do?* She felt hysterical laughter building. It was an impossible situation, and Jacob had clearly lost any ability to think rationally. She should have never told him she wasn't marrying Thomas. She should have never let him kiss her again.

And even as she thought it, her eyes met his and she wished for it all over again.

The wagons began to pull in: Bailey had left a note on the porch several days ago announcing the last day of the quarantine and asking for *one* wagon to take her to the train station: she had expressly asked that the rest of the family exercise caution and stay separated for a few weeks more. The return note, penned by Johann and addressed to Jacob, had been short and to the point. *Fat chance. We're rounding up the gang; just try to keep us away. We'll bring the wine and a fiddle. Let's dance! P.S. Jacob, have you behaved? I hope not, little brother.* Jacob had read it and immediately passed it to Bailey, who had blushed like a schoolgirl and bolted from the room.

And here they all were now: Johann and Lindy, Marianna and Miguel, Joe and Clarissa, and Anton, hand-in-hand with Mayflower, doting over her. At least none of them had brought children. Bailey beamed at them and felt her spirits rise. Kube wasn't far behind, pumping Jacob's hand and looking sinewy and dangerously attractive. *A cowboy for Hope*, mused Bailey, delighted with the idea of matching her newly-found sister with Kube, and then remembered that she would likely never be back here to orchestrate that meeting. Forget Ireland: she would have to travel somewhere remote, like Timbuktu. Timbuktu! Did she even know where that was? Africa, perhaps the Sahara? The hysterical laughter threatened again.

And then the answer came to her. She must marry. She wouldn't marry Thomas—that would be deceitful. Maybe she could find another heartbroken soul and they could cobble together a life of sorts, with all cards on the table. She would get married as quickly as she could, to a man in Philadelphia; surely Hope and Cordelia could find her a man. She would have a baby of her own, and when Jacob came for her she would show him how happy she was without him. Only then could he have the life he was supposed to have, with a little Moravian wife and a beautiful child, an important political office, and the chance to make a difference not just here but maybe even as a governor or senator. None of that would happen if he stayed with her; he stood to lose everything—especially his own child. But he would not follow her if she were married, and especially not if she were to start a family of her own.

The thought of lying with another man made her absolutely sick. She would never love anyone else, ever.

She moved toward the family that she loved, embraced by one after the other, a mug shoved into her hand and a toast made to her healing powers. She learned that Mayflower's given name was Alice, and she hugged her close, whispering congratulations, for Anton was clearly in love. She was passed around from one family member to another, but somehow Jacob was never far from her side. Did everyone notice? How could they not? She found she didn't care. It was their last few moments together, wasn't it?

When she found herself hugged tightly in Marianna's arms, the tears welled. "Oh, Mari. I wish I could talk to you," she choked. Marianna held her at arm's length and looked at her gravely.

"What happened between the two of you?" she asked bluntly. "Jacob is following you around like a detective and you look like your best friend died."

Bailey laughed, swiping her eyes, and nodded. "He *is* following me," she confided.

The man in question appeared out of nowhere, leaned in and whispered "Damn right." He winked at them and backed away, putting one finger to his lips, then joined Kube and his father on the porch. The women stared after him, Marianna grinning and Bailey shaking her head helplessly.

"What the hell is going on, Bailey?"

Bailey sighed and watched him watching her. "We want. We can't have. Nothing has changed, except I've decided not to marry Thomas, which I never should have told Jacob."

Marianna draped an arm around her shoulder and pulled her close.

"I'm so sorry. What can I do?"

Bailey shook her head mutely. "Nothing has changed. There's nothing to be done."

Marianna gave a snort. "Does Jacob know that?"

"He's lost his mind," muttered Bailey.

"I wonder what pushed him over the edge!" Marianna smirked and elbowed Bailey. "I want details, young lady. I have to confess: we have a pool going. Jacob and Bailey trapped together in the same house for a month; oh, mercy!"

Bailey gaped at her. "A pool? Like a *bet*?"

Marianna made a sheepish face. "Well, yes. It was Johann's idea, of course. And I'll have you know that I bet on the side of your virtue." Bailey continued to stare, speechless. "But I hope I lost, I really do," Mari whispered.

"Was the bet for a homerun?" Bailey asked wryly, and Mari shrieked, causing Jacob's head to whip around. Fortunately, he was out of earshot.

"Yes! That was the bet! Oh, Bailey! Did you…"

"You won," she said shortly. "But only perhaps by the grace of your mother knocking on the door."

It was Marianna's turn to drop her jaw, and Bailey left her there and hurried away to find Ginny, laughter bubbling up within her as she walked away. Could this morning be any more surreal?

Someone had produced the promised fiddle and Ginny wanted to dance, so Bailey allowed herself to be twirled around the yard with the other couples, laughing in spite of the turmoil in her heart. How she loved this big, irreverent, warm, loving family!

They danced until the merry sounds of the fiddle suddenly petered out, much to the dismay of the small gathering. "Hey, Carlos! Fire it up, man!" yelled Johann.

Carlos the fiddler simply pointed with his bow, and everyone turned to look. Approaching from the east was a black covered box wagon, and as it drew closer, it was obvious that it was a police wagon. They all watched silently, sharing questioning glances, as the conveyance, pulled by two black horses, made its final turn into the yard and came to a halt.

"Which one of you is it this time?" bellowed Kube. "Santiago, have you been thievin' in Austin again?"

The man in question turned pale, and Kube groaned. "Geesh, boss, I'm sorry about this," he muttered to Jacob.

"Maybe it's something to do with the quarantine," Jacob offered. Bailey's heart fell: already they had learned that four additional families were in quarantine, with two confirmed deaths of children under the age of five. Maybe they were coming to fetch her, but why bring a police wagon? Or could they be carrying out orders to quarantine them again? At this thought she felt a soaring hope, even though she knew she was being irrational.

A squat man with an improbably curly mustache exited the wagon with a good bit of trouble, yanked fussily on his dark blue wool sack coat that reached to the middle of his fat thighs, and straightened his navy blue cloth cap that featured a wreath enclosing the word "Policeman" on the front. Only then did he look up, his close-set, squinty eyes scanning the crowd. He cleared his throat officiously.

"I am seeking a Bailey Rose," he announced, his voice somewhat nasally but clear and piercing. An absolute hush had fallen over the family, and Bailey stood, clutching Ginny's hand.

She raised her free hand. "I am Bailey Rose," she said in a controlled, low voice that belied her nervousness. Something was terribly off about this. Why hadn't he just asked for the doctor if he was escorting her to another quarantine?

The officer swiveled his gaze to her, and then immediately to the Naplava boys, who stood in various positions on the porch and in the yard. This could get tricky if she meant something to them. He took two steps backward without removing his eyes from the crowd and tapped on the wagon with his billy club. At once, two burly officers emerged, clubs drawn, and flanked the first officer.

Jacob was off the porch and by Bailey's side in three seconds; he leaned down and whispered something in Ginny's ear, and she scampered off to Gacenka. Bailey stared at Jacob, the blood draining from her face. *What is this?* her expression beseeched, but he just smiled and shrugged, placing a protective hand on the small of her back.

The first officer approached Bailey, his men close behind. "Bailey Rose?" he barked.

She nodded dumbly.

"That's *Dr.* Bailey Rose," corrected Jacob, his voice icy although his expression was pleasant. "If you're fetching her to tend a family, the least you can do is show some respect, Turner."

The officer's tiny eyes locked onto Jacob's. "Ah, Jacob Naplava. It's a pleasure to see you again. I'm happy that you've come through this illness unscathed." The man bobbed his head, obviously a bit in awe of the young rancher cum mayoral candidate. But just as swiftly his smile vanished and worry etched a line between his unruly brows. "Mr. Naplava, I'd advise you not to get involved in this."

Jacob's expression turned to stone. "Get on with your official business, whatever it is," he ordered.

Officer Turner stared at Jacob, clearly dismayed. *Just my shit luck to have to arrest a friend of Naplava's. He'll have me demoted to street sweeper by the end of the week.* But there was nothing for it: he was the lead officer and he had a job to do.

"Bailey—Dr. Bailey Rose," he quickly amended, glancing at Jacob for approval. Jacob stared at him with blood in his eyes. "You are hereby under arrest for the murder of Senator Adam Hawk. You shall relinquish all weapons and accompany us to the Bexar County Jail."

There was a beat of disassociation in which Bailey was certain she was going to finally let loose with unrelenting hysterical laughter. Her mouth opened and she waited for the sound of her own insane mirth, but it never came. Instead, there was silence. It was a frozen silence; nobody spoke, nobody moved, nobody breathed.

And then everything happened at once.

The two thugs behind Turner stepped forward and reached for Bailey; she saw a flash of handcuffs, and the sight of them finally prompted a sound. "Jake?" she choked; it was halfway between a word and a cry for help. Her voice was guttural and not her own. It was the sound a drowning person makes.

"Like hell you will!" Jacob growled, and stepped in front of her. "She's not going anywhere."

"Mr. Naplava. Please, move aside."

Jacob leaned back and whispered in Bailey's ear. "Get up on the porch until I get this straight, okay? Stick by Ma."

She obeyed, her legs rubbery and face ashen. She reached Gacenka, who gave her a nod of assurance and pulled her close, her arm around her waist.

In the yard—in a mere instant it seemed—the Naplava men closed ranks: Franticek, Anton, Johann, Wenzel, Joseph, and Miguel formed a wall behind Jacob, all wearing his stony expression. Bailey's throat was thick with gratitude. They were protecting her; all of them!

"Now boys, we don't want any trouble," began Turner in a soothing voice. "This doesn't concern you."

"Anything that concerns Dr. Rose concerns us," corrected Jacob. "And she's not going anywhere."

Turner swallowed nervously, sweat beading his brow. He gave a slight motion behind his back and the officers put their billy clubs away, placing their hands on their holsters instead. Bailey saw the movement and understood what was going to happen. A wave of horror rolled through her belly.

"Mr. Naplava, I have here an arrest warrant for Dr. Rose," began Turner again in a placating voice. "It's all proper, signed by Judge Cappas. It's legal, with all due respect. See it right here, look it over, why don't you? Calm down now, and look it over with your own eyes." He reached very slowly into his pocket and withdrew a packet of papers wrapped in a leather pouch, handing them over to Jacob, who stood with his arms still at his side. Jacob glared at him, unwilling to acknowledge even the possibility that these men would be taking Bailey anywhere.

"Please, Mr. Naplava. Look it over."

Jacob finally moved, snatching the papers from Turner's hand. "I'll look, but you're not taking her," he snarled.

Time stood still again as he read the warrant with his keen eye. Bailey began to shake: her entire body was trembling, even her teeth were rattling together. *This cannot be happening. No, no. Oh please, God.*

When he was finished, he threw the document to the ground.

"This is beyond ludicrous. From these dates, you have her committing the murder when she was fourteen years old. Fourteen!"

Twelve, thought Bailey dully. *I killed him when I was twelve.*

"What's your point, Mr. Naplava? There is no statute of limitations on murder, and you know as well as I that fourteen is plenty old enough to be held accountable for adult crimes."

Jacob shook his head and took a step toward the officer. The two officers behind Turner unfastened their holsters with a flick of a finger, and Bailey gasped. *They're going to kill him. They're going to shoot him dead, and maybe some of his family, too, and it's all my fault.*

"I have to take her in; you know that, Jacob," reasoned Turner, his eyes darting to the men behind Naplava. He was horribly outnumbered and there was no doubt in his mind that at least some of these men were armed. "You can see her in jail and fix her up with the best attorney. Hell, you can defend her yourself!"

No! Bailey clutched her stomach in fear. He could not defend her; it would be the end of his political career—maybe the end of his ranch, too, if his reputation was ruined defending a murderous child who grew up in a whorehouse. A child who had killed a United States Senator!

"You're not taking her. If you want to try, go ahead. I guess you'll have to kill me first, though," replied Jacob calmly. "You'll be slopping shit in the streets for the rest of your career, you know." He stepped on the warrant and ground it into the dirt.

"Naplava, this is your last warning. Step aside."

Jacob stood as still as a tree, tense and aware.

"Are you armed?" asked Turner.

"No," Jacob replied. "Your men will have to kill an unarmed citizen."

"They won't kill you," corrected Turner, sweat pouring down his face. "They'll just shoot out your knee caps."

"Do what you need to do, and I'll do what I need to do." Jacob stood calmly, mentally assessing his chances. He knew Johann had his gun; he always did. Kube was packing, no doubt about that, and Miguel. He doubted if anyone else was. Anton couldn't hit the side of a barn.

"Are you boys armed?" Turner raised his voice, never taking his eyes from Jacob. "Throw 'em down now and save yourself. You don't want to get shot through with your women watching. I know a few of you are packing. Johann, you always carry. Throw it down."

"How 'bout I point it at your head instead?" returned Johann immediately. Bailey's eyes flew to his wife, aghast, but Lindy's expression was defiant.

"And what about you, cowboy?" asked Turner with insolence. Kube grinned.

"Well, officer man, I don't give a damn whether I live or die, and I can draw on your men before you can say *fat blue pig*."

And he did just that. The verbal play was over before Bailey could fully grasp what was happening: Kube's pistol was pointed at Turner's head; Johann's revolver was aimed at the officer closest to him, and both officers had Jacob dead square in their crosshairs.

"No!" Her anguished cry rent the air; it escaped her with no conscious volition. She stumbled down the porch stairs, shrugging away from Gacenka's grasp. "No, Jacob! Stop, everyone! Put your guns away! I'll go! I'll go!" She pushed her way through the wall of men and planted herself in front of Jacob, facing Turner. "Put your guns away and I'll get in the wagon."

"No, Bailey, Jesus! I'm not letting them take you!"

She turned to him, suddenly calm, desperate to show him that she was unafraid. She put her mouth to his ear. "Jake," she whispered. "I committed this act. I did. I never told you. It was that horrible day. That's why I couldn't come back to you. Let me go with them, okay? I don't want—*this*. I don't want anyone to get shot! I couldn't live with that."

He turned to look at her, his expression tortured. "But I can't let them—"

She grabbed his chin and turned his head so she could speak into his ear again. "You have to let me go."

You have to let me go. In every way conceivable.

He grabbed her hands, forcing her to stay rooted to the spot, and glared at her for long, silent seconds as the tense drama paused obediently for them. Finally, just as Turner was about to lose his patience and Kube's trigger finger began to itch something horrible, Jacob gave a terse nod.

"I will get you out. I'm going to defend you. I've got a man who's the best there is, and he'll help me. I *swear* to you, Bailey. It'll only be a few short—weeks—okay?" His voice broke on the word *weeks* and Bailey suspected that he was being overly optimistic.

She smiled at him and stroked his face; just one pass over his beautiful features, but enough to make him close his eyes and press into her palm. Her eyes filled with tears. She would never let him defend her or get his name sullied in any way. But he didn't need to know that yet.

"All right then, Miss—Dr. Rose. If you'll step this way, we will proceed with as much dignity as possible," Turner muttered. He nodded at one of the men, and Bailey found herself yanked roughly ahead, her wrists painfully manacled with the handcuffs.

"You don't need those," shouted Jacob, pulling her away from the officer. "Take them off!"

"Mr. Naplava, step back, please," Turner began. Johann pulled gently on Jacob's arm.

"C'mon, brother. You heard what Bailey said. You're not helping her this way."

Jacob felt the loss then: it was the edge of a sharp, swift knife, cutting her away from him. And it felt just like the goodbye they had fifteen years before. He pushed at Johann and reached for her, only to find himself pulled back by Wenzel this time.

Wenzel managed to restrain his much stronger brother by the elbows only long enough to whisper in his ear. "Tell her," Wenzel said. "Tell her now. It's time."

Jacob lunged toward Bailey, who had been dragged halfway to the wagon by this time. He shoved the guard to the ground and the other officer gave a roar of disapproval.

He reached her and grabbed her hand. "I love you, Rosie." he choked. "I love you!"

The other goon brandished his billy club and laid it across the side of Jacob's skull, and all was black.

CHAPTER THREE

She could stand the heat. She had lived in south Texas almost her whole life, after all. There was no breeze in her stifling cell—not even the promise of one, but if she tied her hair up, removed her shoes and stockings, and sat very, very still, she could overcome the heat faintness that was swiftly conquering so many of the other prisoners.

She could stand the claustrophobic confines of the cell. The thirteen foot by seven foot box with bars on the tiny window was much more spacious than her room under the porch at Ft. Allen. In fact, when she curled up in a tight ball on her bed—three planks covered by a thin, stained mattress—she could imagine herself to be a girl again, hiding from the chaos of her life, reading from her big book of Shakespeare by the light of one candle.

She could stand the loneliness. She could close her eyes and move her hands slowly in front of her, reliving the moment when she touched Jacob and saw way down deep into his soul; just as she had promised, the moment retained absolute clarity.

But there were things that might drive her mad. The sounds and smells were the worst offenders. All day the women in the female wing of the Bexar County Jail—located on the second floor of a three-story limestone building on the corner of Commerce and Camaron—shrieked and cried, fighting each other and shouting for the guards. Heads were banged against bars; the contents of stomachs were emptied onto the floor, and the smell of urine and offal was unrelenting. Drunken singing and the foulest of language accompanied each hour of the night. Always there was someone moaning and crying and begging for water—lost wretched souls absolutely bereft of hope. Of the thirty cages in the Bexar County Jail, there were only five for female prisoners, and as far as she had been able to tell, about fifteen women were crammed into four of them. She alone had a private cell. Jacob; of course he must have had a hand in that. She felt guilty but was profoundly grateful: many of the women were from the Row or one of the cathouses or saloons, and as the officers paraded them by her cell, she would hide her face, ashamed, hoping that no one would recognize her.

She had been here for twenty-four hours, and she still could not quite believe how swiftly her life had changed.

After the beast with the club had knocked out Jacob, she had struggled in vain to get to him, frantic to ensure that he was still alive, but it was no use. The officers had picked her up bodily and thrown her in the wagon amidst yells of alarm and rage from the family; her face had smacked against the hard edge of the seat, causing her vision to dim for a moment. They bore her away in the curtained wagon before she could even turn around for a last look.

I love you, Rosie. I love you. The words had reverberated through her, echoing again and again, and still echoed as though he were speaking them anew every moment of every day. The words had changed her; had changed everything, just as she knew they would. She had begun living at that very instant; she had felt herself open like a bloom, every part of her, and joy and desire and excitement and strength and goodness had rushed in, filling every fissure, forming her into something better than she ever thought she could be. And the expression on his face when he said them—*oh!* She had recognized it! It was the expression he had worn on the day long ago, when they were children. When they had danced with Wenzel by the creek and lay on its banks, the trees spinning above them. He had reached over and touched her lip and said *Rosie* with the entirety of the world contained in the blue irises of his eyes. Now she understood: he had meant *I love you.*

It had been yesterday, only *yesterday* when she had touched him for the last time, when his fingers grasped for hers as she was dragged away and he was struck down. Had Johann then drawn his gun? Had Kube jumped to the defense of his boss? Had men perished in a gunfight—or, God forbid, women? *Was Jacob even alive?*

The ride to the train station in Boerne had been wild and fast: before she could come to her dazed senses, she was being pulled roughly from the wagon. They had yanked a hood over her head and she had wondered if they were going to shoot her right there and just be done with the expense of a trial. But they merely growled something about not letting a murderous whore like her cause a public scene, and dragged her up the train steps, pushed her into a seat, and sat with her, knees to knees, refusing to remove the hood. The journey from the train station to the jail was much the same: she was hooded, pulled, and shoved until she found herself in a windowless office, seated in front of a clerk with bulging eyes and a drooping mustache. He silently held out his hand, and when she hesitated, confused, the goon beside her unlocked her handcuffs and ordered her to present her hands to the clerk. The man, his face growing sterner by the moment, removed

Jacob's ring from her finger, and she gasped and gave a small sob before she could help herself. The police officer barked at her to shut her trap, and she bit her lips savagely to hold in her emotions.

"Any other jewelry or personal items?" asked the clerk in a bored tone. She had shaken her head numbly.

"We collared her on the front lawn. We'll have JoAnn frisk 'er, though I wouldn't mind doin' it, if ya' catch my drift." The two officers laughed uproariously while the clerk looked on dispassionately. Bailey was certain she was in a hellish circus of the absurd.

Her wrists were shackled again and the hood was yanked over her head, and by the time she could see again she was on the floor of her tiny jail cell, her wrists bloodied from the cuffs. JoAnn the matron came along in a few moments and pulled her roughly to her feet. "Turn around and put 'yer hands up high on the wall," was all that she said, and then commenced with a thorough patting down. Bailey's eyes stung with humiliation as she felt the woman's hands on every part of her. It was over in a few moments and the woman left without another word.

All that day she had suffered alone in her cell. When the guard brought her moldy bread and watery soup long after the sun set and her cell had turned black as night, she asked when she might be able to talk to someone, and he had taken pity on her.

"I'm not supposed to say anything, Ma'am, but there's been a whole slew of folks trying to see you."

"There have been?" Her voice was trembling and she felt tears well in spite of her best efforts to be brave.

He nodded enthusiastically. "It's the truth. That fellow that's running for major—Naplava's his name—he's been at the clerk's desk all day. He started back here to the cell block on his own and they had to have Billy come out and threaten to lock him up! He's still out there, rantin' and a ravin'. And another fellow—a tall fellow with a tall woman—whoo-hee, she's a looker. They're waiting to see you too. And a nun! Gosh! What a crew! But Sheriff McMurray gave orders to the clerk: he won't let none of them back here yet."

Bailey had laughed and hugged herself. Jacob was fine! And he was here, fighting to see her! She couldn't let him, of course, but just to know it made her dizzy with joy. And Thomas and Gabby, and Sister Anna!

"When might I see them?" she asked in a small voice.

The guard gazed at her, his face full of pity. "Gosh, I don't know. I'll find out, I promise. I promise, okay?" He had lumbered off quickly, and only after standing for sixty minutes, clutching the bars so tightly her knuckles turned white, did she realize that he wasn't coming back. She had spent a sleepless night curled on her bed, fighting to stay lucid in the stifling heat, battling the demons of fear and depression. Her cheek throbbed where the seat had struck it and she longed for a cool wet cloth.

17

But in the morning, with Jacob's words repeating like an intonation in her mind, she had decided that it was all for the best. She had shot and killed Adam Hawk fifteen years ago. She could have just as easily walked away. She was guilty, and that is what she would tell the judge or jury, no matter what her lawyer told her to say. She would spend her life in jail or be put to death, and Jacob would carry on. He would marry the mother of his unborn child, become mayor, and change the world someday. His children would change the world, and their children, and theirs. He was a great, great man— not just because she loved him, but because he was touched by some kind of unknowable, incredible, magical goodness—and he needed to have a powerful place in this world, unfettered by scandal. She could give him that much.

A silent, glaring, female attendant dressed in wrinkled black cotton and a black cap brought her bread and cheese for breakfast, a washbasin, a sliver of soap, and a lukewarm pitcher of water. Bailey pushed the food away and cleansed herself the best that she could, carefully taking the eggplant sports dress off and sponging quickly. The dress was soiled and she attempted to wash parts of it, too, draping it over her bed to dry. She unbraided her hair and combed through it with wet fingers, re-braiding it and securing it with shaking hands. She used the basin to relieve herself, pushing it as far away from herself as possible when she was finished, feeling tears prick her eyes.

And then she sat perfectly still in her shift and drawers, facing the wall. So this was to be her life now. She had murdered a man who belonged to a powerful family. She would spend her life in a cell like this, or, mercifully, be executed. She wasn't afraid to die; in fact, she would prefer it to an existence such as this. She had already seen the trap door in the ceiling just a few feet down from her cell, and she knew the process by listening to the murmurings of her patients over the past months. A prisoner to be hanged was led to the third floor, made to stand on the trap door with a hood over his head, and the lever was pulled. The doomed soul would fall to the second floor, hopefully with a broken neck and instant death, or twist on the end of the rope until the job was done, the inmates on the second floor looking on. She closed her eyes and imagined it. Would she cry? Beg for mercy? Would she faint before they could put the noose around her neck? She didn't think so. She would close her eyes, just like this, and let her mind and soul fill with him. His face would be the last thing she would see: she would take the image with her, peacefully.

Jacob could move on without her; she didn't want him to spend the rest of his life trying to see her as she rotted in prison. How ungodly horrific that would be for both of them.

She stood occasionally to shake out her dress, and when it was reasonably dry, she donned it again, hating the heaviness of it, but putting her chin up and setting her jaw. But at some point, bravery began to devolve into resignation, and resignation shifted into misery and despair. By late afternoon, after ten hours of no human contact, food, or water, she lowered her face into her hands to weep.

"Miss?" The voice was hesitant. "I mean, Dr. Rose?" Her head snapped up; it was the guard from the night before.

"Yes?"

"You can see one person now, Dr. Rose. The chief says to allow you to see one person only. Follow me." And just like that, he produced an enormous skeleton key and unlocked the bars, gesturing for her to come forward. She stood and realized that she had been sitting in one position for far too long; she stumbled and went down hard on one knee, and a cry of pain escaped her.

The guard rushed into the cell to help her up. "Oh gosh, Miss. I'm sorry about all this. You seem like such a peach." He grabbed her elbow and helped her up, his homely, pock-marked face twisting in sympathy. "I have to cuff you again too, dang it." He produced the dreadful handcuffs and she held out her hands obediently, shrinking from the feel of them against her bruised, chafed wrists, but he put them on so loosely that she could have easily slipped free.

"Won't you get in trouble?" she whispered.

He winked at her and led her out of the cell. They made their way down a long hallway, and as she walked by the other cells, the women reached through the bars and called to her.

"Here, sugar! Be my cellmate!"

"Well look at that precious thing. C'mon, Miller, let us teach her a thing or too!"

"Welcome to the Shrimp Hotel!" The Spanish word for shrimp was *camarón*, just like the street on which the jail was located. Being a "guest" at the Shrimp Hotel was something she heard about quite often from her patients. And now she was among their ranks.

The guard growled at them, hitting the bars with his club and making contact in a few instances, bruising a few fingers along the way. "Shut up, why doncha, the lot of you?" he yelled. "If you want yer supper, that is." The women finally quieted, and they proceeded down three more hallways before entering a small, sparse room with two chairs. He gestured toward one of the chairs and she sat gratefully. Her legs were so weak.

"Now who will it be?" he asked abruptly. "Chief says you can see one person. Mr. Naplava's still here and beggin'—demandin'—to see you! And that tall feller. The good-lookin' lady went home. 'Pears she's expectin', so she's probably tired, I guess. And the nun went home but she said she'd be back tomorrow. So pick one, and make it snappy." His words were rough, but his eyes were kind and he smiled at her warmly with his yellow, crooked overbite.

Oh, how she longed to see Jacob, to bury her face in his shirt, to feel his hands in her hair and his strong arms around her. To breathe in the scent of him and see his ubiquitous grin. But she must not. She must not let him be a part of this.

"I will see the tall man, Thomas Eckles," she said in a barely-there voice, and the guard nodded and left, shutting and locking the door behind him.

She scarcely had time to smooth her hair and run a hand nervously over the front of her dress before the door opened again, and in walked Thomas, followed closely by the guard. His face as he saw her told her all she needed to know: shock and dismay, followed by abject pity.

"God in heaven! What have they done to you, Bailey?" He rushed forward, but the guard reached out and pulled him roughly back.

"Now look here. I already explained this to you, Reverend. There'll be no touchin' or contact of any kind with the prisoner. You sit there." He pointed to the other chair, which was situated in the opposite corner from Bailey. And then Miller stood by the door, his arms crossed over his chest.

"Might we have some privacy, Mr. Miller?" Bailey asked in a quiet voice, but the guard shook his head.

"Sorry, miss. I have to stay for this feller's protection."

Bailey flushed deeply. Of course: she was a murderer, after all. She might kill Thomas with her bare hands, if she was of the mind to.

She dared a glance at Thomas, her dear, beloved Thomas—the man who was still her fiancé, although she had already decided to break that bond before her arrest—and was dismayed to see that he was still staring at her with an expression of astonishment and despair. He took in her deeply bruised cheek, swollen with an ugly red and purple welt; her disheveled appearance, and her thinness. Almighty God, she was so thin and pale!

"Bailey, my dear, are you—I'm so sorry," he began, his voice breaking, and he was abashed to feel tears fill his eyes. "What have they done to you?"

She straightened her shoulders and attempted a smile. "I'm fine, Thomas. I really am. I hit my cheek in the wagon when they fetched me from the Naplava ranch. I'm just hot and tired; that's all."

He tried to smile in return. "All right," he said miserably. He was utterly at a loss. He hadn't expected her to choose to see him, and neither had Jacob. Jacob's face had fallen when the guard came out and pointed at Thomas, but he had come forward and gripped Thomas's hand.

"Please, Reverend. Please make sure she's okay. Tell her I'm here, won't you? And that I've hired J.T. Cunningham, the best defense lawyer in Texas; hell, in the southwest! He'll see her tomorrow; he's traveling from Austin. Tell her to hang on until tomorrow, okay? And give her my—" here he had gulped, reddening, but refused to look away.

Thomas had nodded and smiled kindly, gripping Jacob's hand firmly. "I'll give her your love," he had said in a low voice.

Jacob had simply nodded, and Thomas had thought he never in his whole life long had seen, or would ever see, such a look of love and devotion in a man's eyes. Clearly something profound had happened at the Naplava ranch, just as it had happened at St. Ursuline's refectory between him and Gabriella Flores. Dear God in heaven; he, Thomas, a man of the cloth, was in love with his fiancé's best friend; he couldn't possibly tell her that, could he? Not now.

"Bailey," Thomas said, clearing his throat and glancing at the guard. "Jacob Naplava is still waiting out there. He hasn't left since he got here yesterday. Says he won't leave until you see him."

He watched for signs of reciprocation of the love he had seen shining in the young man's eyes, and yes, there it was—just a flash before she could disguise it, but blazing forth for one imprudent moment. He smiled.

"I can't see him," she murmured.

"Why ever not?"

She shook her head miserably. "He can't associate with me, Thomas. Please make him understand. He'll lose the election. He may lose his fiancé. He could lose everything. This is huge, Thomas. A huge, huge scandal, don't you see?"

He gulped: she didn't know the half of it. Her arrest had made not only the San Antonio papers but those in Washington, New York, Boston and Chicago. Gabby had collected all of them and was probably at home grimly poring over them this minute. The headlines were all the same: "Child Prostitute Arrested for Murder of United States Senator!" Not until one began reading was it made clear that a young woman had been arrested for a crime committed fifteen years ago. The press had convicted her already, reveling in the sordid details of a love triangle between a celebrated salon woman of ill repute, a senator, and a trampy girl.

"Jacob said he has a man coming, a lawyer, the best there is. He'll be here tomorrow and the whole mess will be straightened out when you get your day in court."

Bailey smiled and shook her head. "I don't need a lawyer, Thomas. I'm guilty, and that's what I'm going to tell the judge."

Thomas stared at her dumbfounded. "No!" he finally erupted. "I don't know what happened that night, but I can guess, Bailey. You were protecting yourself. You were justified. And that's the night your Mama disappeared! She was the woman in the room, wasn't she?"

Bailey glanced at the guard and discovered that he was listening with undisguised fascination.

"Thomas, please," she said in a low voice. He looked at the guard and cleared his throat.

"You must see the lawyer. And you should see Jacob, too. I really don't think he'll leave until you do."

Bailey reddened and swallowed thickly. Now was the time to tell him; her heart pounded and she felt tendrils of dread curl in her stomach. "Thomas," she whispered.

"Yes?" He was pulling on his earlobe anxiously, and Bailey was charmed all over again by his quiet brown eyes and boyish curling hair. He was such a kind, endearing, appealing man. Why couldn't she have loved him?

She took a deep breath and said the words before she lost her will. "I can't marry you."

"I know, dear," he answered gently. "I took one look at Naplava's face and pretty much knew. He sends you his love, by the way. He loves you, Bailey, in case you had missed it."

"I'm so sorry," she choked. "I never meant to hurt you. I'm so sorry." Tears coursed down her cheeks and she made no move to wipe them away.

Thomas jumped up and moved toward her, meaning to comfort her—she looked more pathetic than he could have imagined—but the guard halted him with the tip of his billy club and pointed back to the chair.

"One minute left," he barked, but he didn't mean it. This was better than the matinee at the White Elephant Playhouse!

Bailey looked at the guard in dismay, then back to Thomas. "I'll understand if you hate me right now."

"I don't hate you!" He sat, regarding her with a kind, steady smile. "Do you love him, Bailey?"

She sobbed once and then nodded. "I do. Oh, I love him, Thomas. I've loved him my whole life." Her voice was ragged and raw. "But he's for another. Not to mention the fact that I'm in jail for murdering a senator!"

"I'm glad you love him. Love finds a way. Don't give up Bailey." The words sounded trite, even to his own ears, but she smiled at him kindly.

"Thank you for being so understanding."

"I have something to tell you, too," he blurted, unable to hold the secret to himself any longer. "It seems I have found love, too, in a most unexpected place."

Both Bailey and the guard looked at him in surprise.

"What? What do you mean?"

He cleared his throat anxiously and gave his earlobe six successive tugs. His Adam's apple bobbed a few times and a bead of sweat appeared on his forehead.

"Get to it, man!" the guard admonished. This was getting good!

Thomas nodded and looked at Bailey beseechingly. "Bailey, I'm in love. I'm in love with Miss Flores."

The words dropped into the stifling space like a bomb, sucking every last bit of air out of the room. Bailey stared at him, stunned. There was a thick silence as the precious seconds ticked by. And then a smile broke over her sad features—a beatific, exultant smile. Of course! How extraordinarily dense she had been not to have seen it! Thomas's blustering and anger around Gabby, Gabby's over-protectiveness of "Tommy," and the intense, passionate energy that dictated their every encounter. Of course they were in love!

"Oh, Thomas! Yes! I think I must have known that, deep inside. I would have seen it immediately if I hadn't been so wrapped up in my own little dramas. You love her! And she loves you!"

Thomas's own features were transformed by relief. "Yes, the feelings are *quite* mutual," he mumbled, his face flaring.

I'll bet he kisses her the way I wished he would have kissed me, once upon a time, she thought. But there was no jealousy or regret in her heart: she was ecstatic for them both. And the thought of kissing brought up another image: one of her and Jacob rolling around on his bedroom floor like two wild things. She felt a flash of desire. How incredible that her body could react that way even in these dire circumstances! She was in prison, awaiting the gallows, no doubt, and she was thinking of Jacob Naplava's lips!

"I'm so very happy for you both. I really mean that. Take good care of her, do you promise? And send her my love. Tell her how delighted I am for her."

He frowned; this sounded like a goodbye—a permanent one.

"Of course I will. But you can tell her yourself; she'll come back tomorrow, and she wants very much to see you."

Bailey nodded. "That's good. I love her so much. I love you both; you're my family, you know. Raise that baby as your own, won't you? And have lots more! She wants to open a restaurant; don't her dissuade her, Thomas. Oh! The ring! I put the betrothal ring you gave me in my tin beside my bed. Please give it to her, won't you? It was meant for her finger. You know, I'll bet you were thinking of her when you bought it. It was always just too—too *much* for me, you know?" She was speaking quickly, urgently.

"Bailey, stop! We'll see you again tomorrow." His voice had a tinge of desperation now.

She nodded miserably, not daring to speak. She was going to hang for the crime she had committed, and she didn't think she could bear to see Gabby, or even Thomas again after this. And especially not Jacob; my God, that would be *unbearable*. Goodbyes were ghastly things. Better just to fade away than to face the ones she loved knowing it would be the last time.

The guard took her away then, sensing that the juice was over and done with, and Bailey stumbled back to her cell, curled on her cot, and imagined dancing at Gabby's wedding.

CHAPTER FOUR

Jacob took one look at Thomas's face and thought that maybe—just maybe—this, after all, was the worst day of his life. There were other strong contenders, but Thomas's despairing look made Jacob's heart shrivel into a cold little raisin.

"How is she?" he croaked. His head throbbed where the son-of-a-bitch pig and clocked him yesterday with the club. He hadn't slept for two days straight; he had spent last night either standing at the clerk's desk, demanding to see Bailey, or in heated conversations with Judge Beckett, ordering him, *pleading* with him to release her to his custody. All to no avail. The one thing he had managed to do was to ensure that she had a private cell—that had been accomplished with a hefty contribution to the Texas Rangers Company B, of which Sheriff McMurray's brother was a proud member.

Thomas took him by the elbow and led him away from the clerk's desk to stand in the sunny window at the far corner of the lobby. "I'm not going to lie, Jacob. She's in rough shape. Looks like she hasn't eaten or slept for a while, and she's got—well—she's got quite a big bruise on her cheek."

Jacob's eyes bulged and he yanked his elbow away from Thomas. "I'll kill that motherf—"

"Naplava! You're not helping her!" Thomas said sharply, grabbing the young man's arm again. "Listen now. She's resistant to meeting with your lawyer friend. She wants to confess and have it be over with."

Jacob stared at him, his face draining of all color. "Thomas—my God, she can't do that! She'll—hang—for sure." The words were an abomination in his mouth. Cold fingers of fear gripped his vitals and he thought he might throw up.

Thomas regarded him. "She's worried about you, my friend. She's afraid you will give up everything to defend her; that you'll ruin your chance for election, lose your ranch, lose your fiancé. And your child."

24

Jacob looked at him sharply. "So you know everything."

"Yes, I do. Gabby told me about the baby coming."

"I don't give a damn about any of that. I don't care about anything but her." He launched himself back toward the front of the lobby, intending to walk—*run*—straight past the clerk, the armed guards, and force her to talk to him. He had to make her understand.

"I know how to make her change her mind!" Thomas shouted after him.

Jacob stopped, his back still to him, every muscle straining forward. *Go! Stay and listen. Go to her! Stay and hear what he has to say. He loves her, too.*

Slowly he turned and faced Thomas. The man was framed in the sun from the window, giving him a glowing, haloed effect, and Jacob squinted and rubbed at his eyes, convinced for a brief second that he was seeing an angel. He sighed, shoulders slumping, and made his way back to Thomas.

"How?"

"Miss Flores can convince her to talk to the lawyer. She has a very special—influence—on Bailey. I can't explain it, but she has a way of cutting through all of the..." He paused, groping for a word that he couldn't quite say.

"Bullshit?" Jacob provided.

"Yes. That. She will make her understand, I know it. But I don't think Bailey will agree to see her; that's where you come in. See if you can get McMurray to *make* Bailey see Miss Flores. I'll do the rest."

"Consider it done."

The two men regarded each other silently for a moment. Jacob finally found the words he needed to say. "Thomas, I'm sorry about—well, dammit." He paused and swallowed, staring at the floor, and then finally met Thomas's benevolent gaze. "I'm sorry about falling in love with her. It happened when I was a kid, and well, I just never got over it. I thought I let her go, but I didn't. I can't." He was abashed to feel tears pricking his eyes.

Thomas grasped Jacob's hand and shook it warmly, over and over. "It's okay, good man. It's okay. Bailey and I weren't meant for each other; you might as well know that I intend to ask Miss Flores to marry me."

Jacob stared at him, mouth falling open, caught completely off guard. Thomas laughed. "That's about the same expression I got from Bailey just now!"

Jacob recovered and gripped Thomas's hand more tightly, pumping. "Congratulations! I sure didn't see that coming, but congratulations, Reverend!"

Thomas nodded and smiled. "And she told me about you, too, so let's just get the awkwardness between us over with. We need to work together."

"What did she tell you?" Jacob ventured, his heart pounding.

Thomas hesitated. "Well, I gave her your love, as promised."

Jacob gulped and nodded, waiting for more.

"I think I better not say any more. It's not for me to say," Thomas finished gently.

Jacob felt like a schoolboy waiting to find out if his crush returned his affection. But his heart fell: surely, if she had declared her love for him, Thomas would have shared that. She was not ready to trust him; she had never revealed her life as a child prostitute; she had never told him about the murder of Adam Hawk, and she had never told him she loved him. She wanted to let him go.

He nodded again and gave Thomas's hand another shake, forcing a smile.

"Okay, then. I'm off to donate more money to the Rangers." Thomas bid him goodbye and Jacob moved toward the door, numb with disappointment.

Bailey spent another miserable day and night in her cell, forcing herself to eat the rancid food. She was made to relinquish her eggplant dress—it seemed like another lifetime ago when she had bought that dress anticipating a night out with Thomas—and she was now dressed in prison garb: a dreary, shapeless gray cotton dress that was so large it made her look like a lost little girl. And that she was: a scared, lost, little girl, curled up on a cot, staring at the wall, hour after hour. When the long, noisy night had passed—her third in the Shrimp Hotel—a new guard came to her cell, a squat, powerful-looking troll with yellow, tufted hair and a deep scar between his brows, cuffing her tightly and ordering her to walk down the hall to the same room where she had met with Thomas.

"Where are we going?" she finally asked, swallowing the lump of fear.

He glowered at her. "Shut up, bitch," he snarled. "You don't talk to me unless I tell you to. I hope you hang for what you did, and I don't care if you are a doctor now. That's not natural, nohow. No *woman* should be doctorin'. You one of those man haters? I guess so! I'd like to see you try to get a jump on me like you did that poor sap Senator!" He gave a powerful tug on her cuffs and she felt them cut into her wrists. She pressed her lips together to keep from crying out. "He probably would have been President of this here United States if you hadn't offed him! Did you know that? That's what they're saying! You'll be takin' a walk upstairs soon, if you catch my meaning, and it couldn't happen a second too soon. This here jail has turned upside down 'cause of you." He laughed, and thick, white spittle pooled in the corner of his mouth. She looked away, sickened by the sight and sound of him.

He pushed her into the small, stuffy room and pointed to the chair in the corner.

A few moments later, the door opened again, and there was Gabriella Flores, in all of her towering, dazzling glory. She was so striking that Bailey's breath stopped in her throat and tears came to her eyes. She tried to think of just the right word to describe the transformation, and then she had it: Gabby had been *healed*. Her expression was soft and open and her eyes were clear and tranquil. The bump in her belly was larger, and her hands rested naturally there, cradling her unborn baby. She was almost to term now, in Bailey's estimation. She had wanted to deliver Gabby's baby: the thought of missing the birth brought tears to her eyes. Gabby's glossy black hair was now long enough to be gathered loosely high on her head in a small Grecian coiffure, wound around with a blue ribbon to match her gown.

"Gabby! You look—majestic!" Bailey breathed, laughing.

"Well, you look like shit," Gabby returned evenly. She took a step toward Bailey and was stopped by a baton on her chest. She put one finger on the end of the baton, moving it away from her body, refusing to even look at the guard as she did so.

"If you touch me again with that stick you will be dead by this time tomorrow. I know just the people to do it, and I will do it." The threat was delivered calmly without so much as a glance at the scowling man; he opened his mouth to protest, thought better of it, and closed it again, his face beet red with anger. Bailey squelched a laugh and felt a surge of love for this indomitable woman.

"I've missed you," Bailey choked.

"And I've missed you," she returned gently.

"Are you feeling well? Is the baby ready? Who will deliver?"

Gabby laughed. "So many questions! The baby is wonderful. Karl Schwartz will deliver me if you are not out of here yet."

"How—how is the clinic? There are so many patients I'm worried about…" There were several patients she had been treating for serious illnesses, and a few women she felt as though she had almost convinced to leave the cathouses. She hadn't laid eyes on those patients for over six weeks!

"The clinic is stumbling," admitted Gabby candidly. "Karl is doing the best he can, but the women miss you. Many of them refuse to be treated by a man now. I would say that we see maybe five patients a day, on average, instead of our usual twenty or thirty! You are *needed*, Bailey."

Bailey's shoulders slumped. She wasn't sure what she had wanted to hear: that the clinic was doing brilliantly without her, or that it was not! She felt a keen longing to return to those desperate women and children, and she groaned and dropped her face into her hands.

"We don't have time for that, so let's cut to the chase," Gabby snapped unexpectedly. "You are going to stop with the martyr act and see the lawyer today. You are going to tell him the whole truth and let him defend you."

Bailey shook her head. "No, Gabby. What's the point of that?"

"The point is to live."

Bailey shrugged miserably. "Maybe I don't want to live," she said in a small despondent voice.

"What did you say?" Gabby's voice was a sharp blade.

"You heard me."

"Oh, I see. You want to die. Okay then. I certainly have been in that place myself. I will send a telegram to your sister and aunt and let them know. I will tell Sister Anna, too. And don't worry about all of your patients; they don't need a woman doctor at all. You're right. You have nothing to live for." She rose in a grand sweeping motion and gestured to the guard. "I am finished."

"No!" gasped Bailey, rising from her chair. The guard flicked his holster and put his hand on the butt of his pistol.

"Stay in your seat," he ordered.

She sat. "Gabby, don't go yet."

The woman turned to her, raising an eyebrow. "What more could you have to say? You have made up your mind, and now I have to go and sweep up the mess you leave behind. You are being selfish. You think you're making it easier for everyone, but you're not. Death is easy, Bailey. I've held it in my hands so many times. It's as easy as stepping behind a curtain. But the easy thing to do is never the right thing. Never."

She took a step toward Bailey, arms on her hips, the guard wiggling with displeasure but unwilling to test her. He knew who this woman was: she was—or had been—the highest-priced whore in town. Paradoxically, that made her powerful. She had many, many potent friends in this city, city officials and rich businessmen, and the wickedest of criminal bastards, too. And now she was hooked up with that Reverend Eckles goat; he was a big-wig, too.

"If I go through a trial, *someone* will be ruined. In many ways." Bailey carefully omitted Jacob's name: this guard was the kind who would run to the papers and sell a story. "I can't bear the thought of it."

Gabby regarded her tenderly, shaking her head. "*Mi amiga*, if you hang, *someone* will die soon after, either by his own hand, or drinking himself to death, or by some other means at his disposal. I don't know much, but I know men. If you love him, you need to keep yourself alive. Do that for him if not yourself."

Bailey stared at her, despairing. She had considered her decision to confess and accept her capital punishment as a gift to Jacob; a way for him to be distanced from her and for this whole mess to resolve quickly so he could move on with his life, much as he would have done if she had disappeared to Timbuktu. But could Gabby be right? Would he really— would he want to die without her?

I would want to die without him. And isn't that ultimately why I'm doing this? Rather than facing a life without him, I'm choosing to die; it'll be easy for me, over in an instant, or a few moments, at the most. Imagine the horror for him. I'm putting myself first, when all the time I thought I was doing this for him.

As the epiphany dawned, she lowered her face into her hands and wept for the first time since she had been jailed. Her entire body heaved with the pain of it. She cried for Jacob, who may at this moment be deciding how to end his own life, if it came to that. She cried for herself, because now she realized that she would try to live, and Gabby was right: it was infinitely more difficult and painful than the decision to die. She was choosing uncertainty and fear and a lifetime without him, knowing he was wedded to another, watching his child grow, watching his family increase—watching the clock ticking interminably through every pointless moment—she was choosing *that*, God help her.

"I'm going to comfort her. Stay where you are," she heard Gabby order quietly, and then she was in her friend's strong arms.

"Be brave," she murmured, kneeling before her and holding Bailey tightly, straining to transfer strength and conviction to her best friend, her sister. "I want to say to all the people who love you, 'Bailey Rose is brave and strong, and she chooses to live'."

CHAPTER FIVE

Alice Barnes knew the city intimately, like a lover knows every freckle on the skin of her beloved. The city was her lover. She had slept in most every alley; she had worked every street; she had thieved from every corner stand. She could slip through the metropolis undetected in the middle of a bright sunny day. Even though very few things could surprise her any more in this life, she was always astonished at the way a child—especially a destitute male child—was utterly invisible to most people. She had masqueraded as a boy every moment of her life on the streets that she had not been whoring, simply as a matter of survival.

Anton had not yet been summoned by Caroline to do her wicked bidding—Alice assumed she was distracted with the arrest of that wonderful Dr. Rose. Boy oh boy, did *that* whole deal smell rotten to Alice; Caroline *had* to have had a hand in it—and she found it a perfect opportunity to begin her detective work. She paid a delighted young newsie five whole dollars for his raggedy garb; she yanked him right into an alley and made him strip down, then handed him a bag of new trousers, shirt, socks and shoes along with the money. He had swiped at his eyes with gratitude and ran away before she could see him cry. And then she slipped into the streets as a grungy ragamuffin, vanishing into the city like a wraith. Within an hour she had in her possession a bicycle, which she had pinched from a sorry yack who had parked it for just one moment too long. She felt bad about that and vowed to herself that she would make up for it somehow, even if he had been wearing diamonds on his timepiece. At least she hadn't palmed the timepiece; *that* was something.

An hour later she showed up on the doorstep of the Vogler mansion in the ritzy King William District—known to the rest of the population as Sauerkraut Bend, thanks to the plethora of wealthy German businessmen who had constructed mansions here—with an envelope in her hand. The three-story limestone home with the mansard roof was a sight to behold! The walkway was lined with palm trees, and she had heard there was a swimming pool in back, fed by the springs and flanked with what they called the "river house." How she longed to see it. Well, maybe another time. She rang the bell and waited, hat pulled down over her eyes and a boyish slump to her shoulders.

"Oh," said the butler who answered the door, looking at her and wrinkling his nose. "Around back to the kitchen for scraps. I suppose the cook can help you out. Or go to the servants' quarters if no one answers."

"No sir," replied Alice gruffly. "I don't want no food or nothin'. I have a message for Caroline Voggler." She mispronounced the last name on purpose, swiped the back of her hand across her nose, and was quite pleased with her performance. She made a smashing boy.

The butler held out his hand imperiously, but she backed up a step and shook her head. "Oh, no sir. The man told me to hand it to her direct-like."

The butler frowned deeply. "What man?"

Alice tapped her chin with one finger. "I dunno, I guess. Wait a minute. Some funny last name. Diplava or somethin' like that."

The butler grew still and an expression of alarm crossed his face. "Was is *Naplava?*"

"Oh yeah, yessir. That's it, by gum. He was an ace, too."

"You must give it to me!"

Alice shook her head again stubbornly. "Nope. Nothin' doin'. He paid me a fin and told me to put it in 'er hand myself."

"Well, that's quite impossible. She's not here."

"Where is she? I can deliver it. I got m' wheel in the bushes." She jerked her chin toward the shrubbery, where the front of the bicycle was plainly evident.

The butler looked considerably more nervous and less starchy than he had when he answered the door. He could only imagine the wrath that would be visited upon him if Miss Caroline found out he had delayed a message from Jacob. She hadn't heard from him but one time since he'd been in quarantine, and that was a terse telegram. Naplava hadn't even contacted her after he was released from quarantine; rumor had it that he was camped at the jail, trying to spring that woman doctor who killed the senator. Miss Caroline was literally pulling the house apart, room by room, waiting for him to come.

He glanced nervously inside the house and considered his options. He could forcibly take the message from the boy—he didn't much like that idea; the boy had the hardest eyes he had ever seen—or he could take the boy himself to Miss Caroline. He didn't want to entertain that idea, either: if it was bad news, he wanted to be as far away as physically possible from Miss Caroline, who was known to throw knives. That left one option.

"She's at San Fernando," he snapped, and melted back into the house quickly. The door clicked shut with finality, and only then did Alice let the smile break over her face. So easy!

A brisk twenty-minute ride later and she arrived at the Cathedral of San Fernando, a massive, gothic church over 150 years old right on the Main Plaza. She'd never been inside, but she found, once again, that a waif is indiscernible from his surroundings, and she slipped right in, unnoticed. The dark, cool interior was heavy with the smell of incense and wax, and when her eyes adjusted, she had to stifle a gasp of appreciation. The bones of the Defenders of the Alamo—Davy Crockett, William Travis, Jim Bowie and others—were enshrined in a sepulcher here, in front of the railing near the steps at the altar. Two side altars, one for Our Lady of the Guadalupe and the Virgin as the patron saint of the Canary Islands, were each surrounded with meticulous paintings that Alice wished she had hours to study. The cream-colored ashlar blocks of limestone rose above her in an arch for 180 feet, and she leaned her head back so far to gaze at the ceiling that her cap fell off. She retrieved it quickly, jamming her hair underneath and looking around furtively to be sure that no one noticed.

The sanctuary appeared to be almost empty: only two old women veiled in black sat huddled in a pew near the front of the expansive church. Where would Caroline be? What would she be doing here? Perhaps changing her wedding plans? She was supposed to have married Jacob just a few days ago, on the final day of the quarantine, Alice recalled Anton saying. Caroline was no doubt re-organizing the arrangements, but where did one do that in a church? There could be dozens of hidden offices here; how would she ever find her? She couldn't just ask; she'd be thrown out on her arse.

She had just resigned herself to waiting outside when her gaze lit upon the two women again. What had made her think they were old? Their costumes, perhaps: they were both garbed in black crepe with mourning veils. They were so close their foreheads were almost touching, whispering together. As Alice watched, one of the women began to rise but was pulled down again with some force by the other. She stared, the skin prickling along her scalp; the forceful action was completely out of context in this peaceful setting. The woman who had pulled the other down suddenly looked around the church furtively, but Alice had situated herself so well in the shadows that she was sure she had not been seen.

Ever so slowly, after moments of silent waiting just to be certain, she sunk to her knees and commenced to crawl along the floor, approaching the rows of pews. If she was spotted, she would simply claim she had dropped a coin; no one would question the need of an urchin to track every coin possible. She was small enough to be able to squeeze under the pews, and she made her way forward like a snake, slithering along the cold floor, pausing every few seconds to ensure she had not been seen or heard. Finally she was under the pew directly behind the women and could clearly hear every word. What she heard confused and intrigued her.

"Mrs. Hall, please! I want to tell Frank! We shouldn't keep secrets from one another!"

"Absolutely not! You will not tell him!"

"I don't understand why not. He already knows I'm done with whoring."

At this, Alice clapped a hand over her mouth to stop a gasp. Whoring? The younger-sounding woman used to be a prostitute? She was dying to get a look at her now; if she had worked in one of the parlors or hotels, Alice would know her for sure.

"Look, my dear. It will be so much easier if you just tell him that you want some time to make yourself—*clean* for him. Clean and worthy." At this, Alice rolled her eyes and wished she could jab one of her grimy fingers into Mrs. Hall's eyeball. "Tell him you need six more months apart, and then if he feels the same way about you, you will be honored to marry him. Don't make yourself so available! Knowing he'll have to wait for you will make his love all the stronger."

There was a silence as the girl apparently pondered the words.

"And might I remind you, I have paid you one thousand dollars to keep this contract private."

At the mention of the sum, Alice had to clasp a hand over her mouth again. A *grand*? What in the hell could an ex-prostitute—one who sounded like a teenager—possibly offer that was worth one thousand dollars?

"Not to mention the additional one thousand you will get upon delivery, along with the five hundred for your friends. Unless you want to back out of the deal. That's entirely fine, although I can't tell you how disappointed my husband and I will be. I will just need the first payment back, please."

There was an ominous silence.

"I can't pay you back just now," the girl ventured.

"Oh, I see. You have spent it already, is that it?"

The girl must have nodded, because Mrs. Hall made a sympathetic sound.

"My dear, that is perfectly understandable. You deserve that money. Spend it! Get ready for your wedding and your beautiful marriage! If you want to enter society, you must look the part. Why, that is most of the battle; believe me, I know! Make your man proud of you."

Alice stuck her tongue out savagely at the horrible Mrs. Hall.

"Yes," came the small voice. "I guess you're right. I'm sorry, Mrs. Hall. We're square, I promise."

"Very well. Have you been well, Honey?"

"Yes. Everything is fine."

"Good. Wonderful! Then I will see you back here next month." There was a pause and some shuffling noises, as if the women were gathering items together and preparing to leave. Alice used the opportunity to slither all the way back to the shadows at the rear of the church. She could no longer hear what they were saying, but now was her chance to get a good look at their faces. She positioned herself behind a large stone baptismal font, peeking out as they strolled by. She was disappointed: the taller woman, the one she presumed to be the younger woman, was still completely veiled. She did see that the girl had blond hair, a lovely golden color. The smaller, older woman's face was also concealed; her hair was dark and puffy and she had matronly wide hips and a bit of middle-age bulk to her. Her hopes fell: here she had been spying for nothing; meanwhile, where could Caroline Vogler be? Had she come and gone already? She could go inside and have another look, but the prospects seemed dim. Better to make her way back to the Vogler mansion and hope that Caroline would head out again soon. She was dying to catch her diddling one of her beaus. Anton couldn't be the only man she was sniffing after. If she could catch her in the act and prove it—maybe by blackmailing some sad sack Caroline was screwing—she could get the wretched woman off Anton and maybe away from Jacob as well.

She slipped from the church behind the women, unseen. The younger woman left on foot; the older woman waited for less than moment before a hired hansom cab pulled up. Alice was close enough to hear the address she issued to the driver, and her heart began to pound wildly. "509 King William," she snapped, and Alice was shocked to hear Caroline Vogler's unmistakably haughty and well-modulated voice emerge from the middle-aged, fat matron with dark hair. *509 King William. God in Heaven, that's the Vogler address!*

As soon as the cabriolet began moving, she ran to fetch the bicycle from the shrubbery and was on her way, easily keeping pace with the horse. Her mind was whirling: was this Caroline Vogler? If so, why was she in disguise? Well, that was a dumb question: obviously she was paying the other woman to deliver something very illegal. What on earth could be worth that much money? What would a very young ex-prostitute be able to procure that would bring that much dough? Two things immediately came to mind: jewels and artwork, both of which were easily accessible and plentiful in the best of the city's salons. Hundreds of thousands of dollars' worth of jewels and artwork were present in every self-respecting "boarding house," especially Ft. Allen, the Purple Pansy, and the Gilded Lily. Could the girl be fencing goods like that? It was an incredibly dangerous prospect: every parlor had armed guards who weren't afraid to use deadly force to protect the property. Maybe it was one incredibly valuable painting or just a few jewels; that would be more likely. But why on earth would a very wealthy woman like Caroline Vogler care about purchasing stolen goods? It just didn't make sense. And what was this about a delivery? There must be something awesomely valuable being shipped or smuggled, something that Caroline needed. Maybe a certain drug? She had heard of a new drug that was spectacularly expensive and hard to find; only the wealthy could afford it, but she couldn't recall the name of it. Could Caroline be addicted? That would certainly explain her erratic behavior, and judging from her behavior with Anton, she was familiar with hallucinogens! Yes, maybe that was it: it explained an awful lot.

She stopped well short of the estate and shoved the bike into a huge rose bush, then commenced to stroll casually down the street, hands in pockets, whistling and spitting with remarkable accuracy. She glanced at the house as she walked by and saw Mrs. Hall disembark from the carriage.

Only now Mrs. Hall wasn't a frumpy, middle-aged brunette. She was a platinum blond with a curvaceous figure and expensive, fashionable clothing. She leaned close to converse with the driver, jerking her head toward the back seat, then paid him with what looked a substantial roll of bills—paying him to keep his mouth shut about the transformation, no doubt—and swept into the house without a backward glance. The driver sat and counted out the bills, a look of wonder on his face, and Alice the street urchin walked right up and hopped into the cab.

"Give me a ride, mister?" she said jauntily, her voice rough and boyish and teasing. The man started and whipped around, scowling, and then chuckled at the jaunty look on the boy's face.

"Aw, go on, out with you now," he growled good-naturedly.

"Need anything, coachman? Can I brush your horse or fetch a pail of water and oats?"

"Naw, go on," the driver repeated. He reached back and nudged the boy with the butt of his whip.

"Gee, I could use a bit or two," persisted the grinning boy. The driver frowned and poked him again, harder, and the boy swatted at the whip. "All right then, let off, old skiffer." She sprung athletically from the cab and sauntered away, glaring back and spitting contemptuously. Then she turned away from him to hide her wide smile, for she had seen what she needed to see: a dark wig, wads of cotton for padding, and a dark crepe cape and lace veil.

Her mind worked on it the rest of the day, but nothing fit together. She berated herself for not following the younger woman, but how was she to have known? How could she find her? Caroline had said that she would see her in another month: that would be too late.

She had to find her.

CHAPTER SIX

On the fourth day of her incarceration, Bailey arose with a jolt: standing above her and gently shaking her shoulder was yet another jail attendant, an older woman with wide shoulders, black hair streaked with gray, and steady, kind eyes. "Dr. Rose?" she said softly. "Dr. Rose? It's time to get up now. You are moving today, lucky girl!"

Bailey sat up and rubbed her eyes, disoriented. The sun was slanting through her tiny barred window: what time was it? For a moment she couldn't even remember what day it was!

"I'm sorry, wh—what? Can you tell me what time it is?"

"Why yes, it's a half past nine in the morning. The sheriff has ordered that you be moved."

"Moved?" Bailey stood and swayed. She *must* eat today.

"Yes. You are going to be housed in a room at The Vance House." The matron snuck a peek at the prisoner and grinned to see the shock register on her face.

"The Vance House! But why?" The hotel was located just a block south from the courthouse across Nueva Street: formerly used as an army barracks, it was now a well-appointed two-story limestone Greek Revival establishment with a flat roof, six square columns, and an ornamental iron railing at the front and the rear. She pictured it in her mind and marveled that she may actually be going there, away from this cage. She didn't dare believe it. "I don't understand," she stuttered again, frozen in place as the matron cleared away the untouched dishes and wash and refuse basins.

"Well, I can't say much, but you've caused quite a ruckus at the courthouse. Newspaper men crawling all over at all times of the day, hoping to get a glimpse of you. The ones from New York are the worst, treatin' us like back-country simpletons. We just can't function properly, you know." She turned to pull something from her wheeled food cart as Bailey looked

36

on, her jaw agape. Newspaper men? *New York?* This whole scandal was clearly much, much bigger than even she had anticipated. She felt her stomach clench and she bent over with the pain.

The matron jumped to her aid, lowering her back onto the makeshift bed. "There's a good girl. Here; drink this coffee; it's fresh and hot. Eat these, too. You just need some food and rest and you'll be right as rain. I know you ain't been eatin' a thing, and you got to eat, startin' today, you know?" Bailey nodded numbly, gulping coffee and obediently eating the proffered biscuits slathered with honey.

"Now, Dr. Rose, I'll be back in five minutes with some garments for you; then we'll make our escape." She winked at her and Bailey allowed a smile, her weary mind whirling with questions. She must be a national sensation—well, of course she was, now that she thought about it more clearly. An old, unsolved murder of a young, handsome, up-and-coming senator, with the killer suddenly unearthed, and she was nothing less than a young daughter of a prostitute! It was titillating, to say the least.

She closed her eyes and leaned her head back on the wall. No doubt she would meet with her lawyer today—the fellow Jacob had secured for her, according to Gabby. What would she tell him? If she just said, "I'm guilty and that's how I want to plead," would he let her? But she couldn't do that; she had given Gabby her word. She would have to tell him the whole story and let him decide the best course of action. The thought of telling the story to a stranger made her head pound and sweat bead on her brow and palms.

When the matron returned, Bailey had finished her coffee and biscuits and was pacing nervously. When the woman fished around in a garment bag and brought forth the promised garments, Bailey gasped, and then laughed. "Of course," she murmured, taking them and shaking her head in disbelief. "You must disguise me or we'll get mobbed when we exit."

"Indeed," the matron replied, chuckling. "I daresay nobody will be lookin' for you in *this* getup."

"And what's really funny is that I was raised at St. Ursuline's," Bailey laughed again, for she was holding a nun's habit, complete with a wimple and hood!

The woman nodded. "Well, don't I know it! A Sister—Sister Anna, I think it was—brought this over last night after speaking with your friend, that Naplava fellow. It was all his idea, moving you out and giving you a more comfortable place to say. Now isn't that nice? He seems real concerned about you, dearie."

Bailey turned away to hide her smile. Of course it was Jacob who had orchestrated this; who else?

"Now do you know how to put that on? Do you need help?"

"Oh, yes, I know just what to do," answered Bailey softly. "Thank you."

"All right then. Here's a clean basin with warm water to wash up. You'll be happy to know that you can take a bath when you get to the Vance House; what do you think about that! They have a bathtub with indoor plumbing, a few on each floor, if I remember it right."

She departed and Bailey dressed swiftly, her hands shaking with excitement. She was leaving! She was breaking free from this horrid place with the wretched food and hellish noises and oppressive heat. She could bathe so she wouldn't shame herself before a great man of the law; she had been worried about that. And was it possible—could it be that she would see Jacob today? He had mentioned that he would be part of the defense team; that was a horrible idea, wasn't it? He should keep himself as far removed from this as possible if he were to have any chance at all to get elected. Surely his friend, the brilliant defense attorney, would know that. If asked, she would deny him the chance to see her, just as she had done up to this point. But maybe she would not be asked, and he would just be there, smiling at her, his eyes full of devotion. Her breath came faster, just imagining it. Oh, to see him again…

The matron came to fetch her a short time later and gave her instructions: Bailey had been widely reported to be a slim, boyish, un-corseted red-head with dark eyes. Bailey blushed at the description; honestly, did the whole world need to know that she was flat-chested and didn't wear a corset? If she kept her eyes downward and head covered with the hood, she would not be noticed. The matron padded the habit with a few extra bits of cloth until she was adequately busty and plump, and Bailey snickered as she looked down to survey herself.

"I wouldn't even recognize myself!" she admitted. "You have definitely made me more—blessed!"

The matron laughed in appreciation. "You're not the first person I've disguised, my child. They put me in charge of making sure witnesses stay safe, and I've become quite the costume master."

They left the jail cell and proceeded down the hall, Bailey's heart pounding. The hallway was strangely quiet this morning: there were no jeers or calls, and she realized that the prisoners felt free to harass her in a way they never would a nun. They navigated through three long hallways and past the scowling guards, past the clerk's desk into the lobby, and here Bailey gasped and stopped. The expansive lobby was filled with newspaper men! Men with new-fangled cameras, notebooks, puffing away on cigars, murmuring to each other, draping themselves across the furniture, pestering the clerk's staff. There were even men asleep on the floor in the corners! There were dozens of them, and many of them turned to look at her with interest, bored with the interminable wait. She dropped her chin to her chest immediately, hiding her face, her heart pounding.

The matron turned and gestured to her. "Come, Sister," she said softly. "We must get you back to the abbey."

Bailey nodded and followed the matron obediently, her legs shaking.

"Hey, sister. Who were you here to see? Were you praying with Dr. Rose? We know she was raised by nuns—were you one of them? Do you know her? How is she? Is she going to plead guilty? They've got her dead to rights, don't they? Will they go easy on her since she was just a kid? What does Jacob Naplava have to do with this? Are they lovers? Did she say what it was like being quarantined with him for a whole month? Were you hearing her confession?" At this last comment there was uproarious laughter. "Isn't he supposed to be marrying that Vogler dame? I heard the wedding was postponed—when are they getting hitched? Does he have the judge in his pocket? What do you think his chances are for election now, Sister? Not so good, or even better?"

The questions came one after the other, on top of each other, the men pressing her from all sides. She smelled rancid breath and sweat and cigarette smoke and she thought she would retch, right there on the floor of the lobby. Her face was flaming, her eyes wide with shock. Lord, oh Lord, the things they were saying about Jake! Her Jake! He was sullied now! All because of her.

The matron yelled at the men and pushed her way through, creating a path for Bailey, who was by this time stumbling and tripping on her robe, her eyes blinded with tears of disgrace. They finally pushed their way through the door and the matron immediately led her up into a hired cab, and before Bailey could get her senses about her, they were setting off at a break-neck pace, leaving the newspaper men behind, some of whom were frantically trying to hire a rig or find a horse to follow. A few comically ran after them for a few blocks before giving up the race.

"Where are we going?" whispered Bailey.

"Well, I figured we'd need to lose those idiots first. We can't let them see you walking into the Vance House, now, can we? So we'll just drive around for a spell."

A spell was three hours. For three hours they drove around the city, winding up one street and down another, even stopping once to change carriages, the second one white and pulled by two horses; notably different from the first. The matron slept most of the time, and Bailey sat ramrod straight, staring at her hands and suffering in the sweltering heat. The lengths to which they were going to keep the press away were terrifying.

This was all so very much bigger than she had ever imagined.

Two hours after she arrived, at last, in her room at Vance House and had a long cool soak in the bathtub that was so sweet it brought tears to her eyes, she was dressed in another drab gray garment and ready to meet with her lawyer. She had braided her clean, wet hair and tied it in a knot at the end; prisoners were not allowed hairpins or ribbons. She looked in the mirror and despaired: her face was thin, making her dark eyes look jarringly enormous, and there were dark smudges beneath them. The bruise on her cheek was fading to an ugly mustard-yellow hue. The matron—Mrs. Knittle was her name—had given her instructions to wait in her room; the meeting would take place there. A guard was stationed outside of Bailey's room to prevent escape, and the window had been fitted with temporary bars. "Just so you don't get any ideas," the guard had snarled, puffing his chest with self-importance at being the given the job of guarding the Red Rose. That's what the papers were calling her, according to Mrs. Knittle, who had shown her the front page of *The New York Times* once she had Bailey settled in her room.

"I guess 'cause you were from the District back then, you know? And you've got that red hair. You know how those newspaper fellers are. Always looking for some silly nickname." Bailey's face grew red with anger, giving her nickname even further credence. She was appalled at the name. It sounded like a brothel name, the implication being that she had been a child prostitute. She had never even considered that people would presume that! For the first time, she wondered at the version of events the papers were reporting.

She sat stiffly on a chair, wringing her hands. The guard had been ordered to drag in three extra chairs and a table; the room was cluttered now, the extra furniture jammed around the foot of her bed. When the tap on the door came, she bolted from the chair, knocking it over, and she felt a pang as she remembered Jacob sending his chair careening when they met at Thomas's church. It seemed so long ago!

"C—come in," she choked, her voice thin and reedy. She cleared her throat and thrust her chin up a notch. *Get it together!* Gabby would be smacking her in the head if she could see her timidity and fear. She made fists and shook her arms a few times, bolstering her courage. "Come in please," she repeated clearly, and was pleased to hear that her voice sounded firm and calm. Firm and calm. That's what she must be. *Trust and do not be afraid.*

A young man entered the room: he was pleasant-looking, with dark chestnut hair and closely-trimmed whiskers. His brown eyes twinkled as he saw her. Following him were two older men, one a portly man with white, wavy hair and crooked teeth, and the other a tall, sturdy looking fellow who bore a striking resemblance to Abraham Lincoln. Bailey did a double-take and was certain that this man must be the lawyer Jacob had arranged for her. She had Abraham Lincoln on her side; how could she possibly lose? She stifled the ubiquitous nervous laugh—*always*, she was a step away from a hysterical giggle when she was anxious—and shot her hand out at the closest man, the first young fellow.

"Hello. My name is Dr. Bailey Rose," she said smartly, standing tall. The young man's eyebrows shot up, pleased at her spirit.

"Why hello, Dr. Bailey Rose! I've been looking very forward to meeting you! My name is J.T. Cunningham, and these are my colleagues, Franklin R. Mooreland," he gestured to the man with white hair, and she shook his hand, "And William Henry Flanders." She shook Abraham Lincoln's hand and tried not to stare, but she failed miserably; the awe broadcasted clearly across her transparent features.

"I know it, he looks just like President Lincoln, doesn't he?" J.T. Cunningham smirked, and William Henry Flanders laughed good-naturedly.

"Don't worry; I get that all of the time," he responded with good humor. "I believe Lincoln was a hair taller, but I'm pleased to be compared to the greatest of our leaders."

"In my youth, I looked just like Charles Coghlan," Mr. Mooreland interjected, and then looked offended as the other two men guffawed. "Well, I did, wouldn't you say, Dr. Rose? Do you see the resemblance?"

"I really couldn't say, Mr. Mooreland. I have never seen Mr. Coghlan perform. You do seem to resemble him from what I've seen in the dailies," she added hastily, seeing his crestfallen look. The chubby man looked nothing like the suave, handsome actor.

They all chuckled and then Bailey sat, realizing they would all continue to stand until she took her place. Once they were all settled, the men began unbuckling leather portfolios and bringing forth important-looking documents.

"Now, Dr. Rose, let's not waste any time. You understand that—"

"I beg your pardon, Mr. Cunningham," Bailey interrupted, confused. "I'm so sorry to stop you, but—are you—to be my lead attorney? What are your roles?"

"Oh yes, of course! I beg your pardon. I am your lead man, Dr. Rose. Mr. Mooreland here is quite the expert in chasing down witnesses, and Mr. Flanders is of critical importance when it comes to aiding me in crafting my cross-examinations."

Bailey stared at him, somewhat flummoxed. He was so *young!*

"Thank you," she finally muttered.

"I attended law school with Jacob Naplava; did he tell you? I've practiced in Austin ever since."

Abraham Lincoln leaned forward and tapped his quill pen on the table for emphasis. "He won't blow his own horn, but this young man is the most revered defense attorney in the state of Texas. Don't let his age fool you, Dr. Rose."

She nodded appreciatively and felt herself relax. She already felt comfortable with these men; what more could she ask for? And she trusted Jake completely. *Where was he?*

Mr. Cunningham regarded her keenly for a beat and then adjusted a pair of spectacles on his nose, peering at her. "You may wonder where your friend Mr. Naplava may be today. Well, I'll tell you, you did the right thing by refusing to see him, Dr. Rose. The right thing for *you* mainly!"

She looked at him, startled. "I didn't want to see him because I was afraid it would ruin his chances of getting elected." Not to mention ruin his chances to marry the mother of his child!

Cunningham nodded, stroking his chin. His bright eyes were snapping, shifting, and she could sense that this was a man of formidable intelligence. "I don't know about that yet. The newspapers have been brutal on you, but we've been casually nosing around town today, Dr. Rose, and I will tell you that most of the folks we've talked to are very sympathetic to your plight. *Very* sympathetic indeed. Having a powerful man about town connected with your case may work against you, though; there may be a perception of unfair advantage, and we don't know as of yet if the jurors we select will be Bexar County citizens or not. We may cast a wider net. If they are, though, we need to keep everything on the up and up. So I told Jacob to keep his distance."

The Charles Coghlan hopeful snorted. "We just about had to lock him in a cell at the courthouse to keep him away. That boy can make a bit of trouble, I should say."

Mr. Cunningham smiled affectionately at the description of his friend but did not remove his eyes from his client's face. "Dr. Rose? Let me ask you a question. If I were to ask you how you wished to plead, right now, what would you say?"

"Guilty," she replied without hesitation.

There was a silence that lent gravity to the stark words.

Cunningham nodded. "All right. I appreciate your honesty. Now let's shift gears a bit. I need to inform you that the grand jury has returned a true bill. Do you understand?"

Bailey nodded, her heart falling. "Yes," she murmured. "I am to be indicted."

"You already *have* been indicted."

"And what is the charge?" she asked, dreading the answer.

"I was hoping for manslaughter, or second degree at the very most. The district attorney—Augustus Jennings is his name—is absolutely delusional to think he can prove premeditation. But the charge is murder in the first degree."

"Punishable by death," finished Bailey, before cowardice stole her voice clean away. She gulped but kept her eyes trained on Mr. Cunningham, and to his credit, he did not blink or look away. He merely nodded again.

"Yes, but over my own dead body, Dr. Rose. We will have an excellent defense, and Jennings is an idiot. He won't be in office for much longer. Before I launch into all that, the fellows and I need to hear your story. Can you tell it?"

He spoke so quickly, without any prelude whatsoever, that she was taken aback.

"My story?" she repeated dumbly.

"Yes, start at the beginning and leave nothing out, if you please." He nodded briskly at Mr. Flanders, who readied a note pad, his pen hovering above it expectantly.

She swallowed once, twice, and tried to think of where to begin. "Well, that evening I had gone to the Gaslight—"

"Oh no, excuse me, Dr. Rose. All apologies; I haven't made myself clear at all. I need you to start from the very beginning. Of your *life*."

She breathed a huff of laughter, astonished at the request. "What?" she finally managed.

He smiled kindly. "I know it sounds utterly insane. But I have learned that important things are missed when an attorney asks a client to account a story at a point too late to be of value. So it's best just not to leave anything out. We might as well start with Day One, right?"

She glanced at the other two, open-mouthed, but they just nodded and smiled. "Dr. Rose, allow me to fetch you a coffee and a pillow for your back," said Mr. Mooreland kindly, and before she could desist, he had slipped away.

"Really, Mr. Cunningham, I'm sure I don't know where to begin."

"When were you born, Dr. Rose? What was the date and location? What were the circumstances? Who were your parents?"

She flushed. "The circumstances were less than ideal," she murmured, embarrassed. "In fact, I just learned about them myself a few short weeks ago."

Mr. Cunningham smiled and stretched back, hands behind his head. "Tell me the story of Bailey Rose."

And so she began, haltingly at first and then gathering steam as the young lawyer asked astute questions in his kind, unassuming voice. He expressed sorrow to hear about her father's death in battle, and offered shining words in regard to his bravery and skill. When she told him about being born in a brothel, one eyebrow quirked.

"In a brothel?"

"Beg pardon?"

"Do you know if you were actually born inside Ft. Allen, or were you born in a hospital? A doctor's office? A midwife's home?"

Bailey did know the answer to that question, surprisingly enough. Her mother had told her one day when she mentioned she had been helping Gabby's aunt deliver babies. "A midwife delivered you, too," she had said, stroking Bailey's hair in a rare moment of lucidity. "I'll never forget her name. It was Theresa Cazella. She was from Italy! She didn't speak much English, but she was so very kind, and she was skilled, too. She took good care of

43

me." Her mother had a wistful expression: perhaps it had been the last time anyone had taken such solicitous care of her.

"That's fantastic!" Mr. Cunningham exclaimed. Abraham Lincoln scribbled furiously. "Many midwives are wonderful at keeping detailed records of births and even registering them with the city. And you say that was the fifth of February, 1864?"

"Yes."

"So you were twelve years old at the time of the death of Adam Hawk?"

"Yes."

Mr. Cunningham frowned briefly but said nothing. Naplava had told him she was fourteen. Not that it made much of a difference: he wasn't gunning for the infancy defense anyway, and she would be at the outer edge of it at age twelve nonetheless—it wouldn't fly with a jury. But the discrepancy bothered him. He would need to look at the birth record if there was one.

"Go on, Dr. Rose."

And so Bailey recounted the story of her own life: her miserable existence at Ft. Allen, her mother's addiction, her experience living under the porch, her beatings from Blanche, running the streets with Gabby and Juan, her grueling job of cleaning the brothel during the day. She told the story of attending the German school for one day and meeting Jacob, then being molested by Otto Bichenbach. At this point Mr. Cunningham leaned forward and briefly covered her hand with his own.

"I'm sorry to make you recount these painful memories," he said, his voice sincere.

"Oh, you haven't heard anything yet," Bailey said with a tight smile. She went on to describe Jacob's rescue and her precious two days at the ranch, but when she got to the part about going down to the creek to wash off after the tecolé fight, she paused. A pulse pounded in her head. If she left out the Vodnik, how would she explain it later, when she had to tell about the night in question? Should she leave out the whole supernatural story? These men would think she was crazy! She stared at her hands, gripping them together with force as she remembered the horrible, guttural man/woman voice and the tremendous yank on her hair.

"Dr. Rose, please, don't leave anything out," said Mr. Cunningham softly. "And let me say, anything and everything you tell us in this room will remain absolutely and utterly confidential. We will not share it with our wives, our friends, our colleagues. We will never, ever utter it. If the information is necessary for your defense, that's a decision we will make together."

She took a deep breath, staring at him, miserably conflicted. "Okay," she finally whispered. "What I'm going to say next is going to sound crazy. But you may think it's important later on. When I was bathing by the creek, lying on my back with my head in the water, someone said my name. I couldn't tell if it was a man or woman, but now I know it was a man. He ordered me into the water. Then he pulled my hair, hard, and in I went. I almost drowned: Jacob saved me by pulling me out and forcing the water out of my lungs. I think—I *know*—it was a Vodnik."

"A Vodnik?" repeated Mr. Cunningham. His expression was confused but not condemning.

And so she had to explain Jacob's story that he had relayed to her on the wagon trip to the ranch. She felt her face flame.

"Dr. Rose, you were only twelve; could you have misconstrued the situation? Could someone have been in the water and pulled you in, meaning to attack you? It could have been anyone: a tramp, a child molester, for example. You were a pretty young girl with no clothes on, your protector out of sight."

She nodded. "Yes, of course, I've thought about that. But I didn't see anyone, and my head was out of the water for a time while I struggled; I would have seen someone! And I met him—the Vodnik—again, later on."

"Okay, fair enough. You were right to tell us; go on, please." Really, the man was unflappable.

So she talked on and on, including everything except mention of Wenzel's extraordinary gift, and of course, the kiss with Jacob on the wagon ride home. It was a moment she held in safe haven; it was inviolable and would remain so, as would any other mention of her intimate moments with him, she sincerely hoped.

She recounted her parting from the Naplavas in the plaza and her journey back to Ft. Allen to speak with her mother. When she related her conversation with Lola, he made her repeat it five times, the first two times without interruption, and then the last three with keen questions that helped her to pinpoint details she had forgotten to tell.

"Is Lola still at Ft. Allen?" he finally asked, holding his breath.

"Why, yes; in fact, she's the only girl still there from my time there," replied Bailey. "Will she be a witness, do you think?"

"Oh, yes, Dr. Rose. I can't tell you how fortunate this is. And is Blanche still the Madame at the establishment?"

Bailey nodded. "She won't speak to me or see me, but she is still there. I don't know if she'll testify, though. I think she truly hates me."

"Yes, she will testify," offered Mr. Mooreland cryptically.

"And now, go on, Dr. Rose," said Mr. Cunningham, not wanting to lose the momentum.

She told about running all the way to the Gaslight Hotel, walking in the front door, and being stopped by the doorman.

"Did he tell you his name?"

"No, I'm sorry, he didn't. But I told him mine."

45

"Well, *I* can tell you his name," responded Mr. Cunningham unexpectedly. "His name is Rufus Jones. He's a key witness for the prosecution."

"Oh," said Bailey in small voice. "Of course: he's the person who knew I was looking for my mother."

Mr. Cunningham looked at her sharply. "He knew you were looking for your mother? You told him that, exactly?"

She nodded, thrown by his intensity. "Yes."

"Tell me exactly what you said to him and what he said to you, and what happened next."

She told the story seven times, Abraham Lincoln's pen flying, Mr. Mooreland's fingers drumming faster and faster on the table, and Mr. Cunningham's acute eyes snapping. She recounted walking up the stairs to Room #226 and the horrible feeling of dread upon discovering that the nice doorman had not accompanied her. And then she told the story of opening the door and every atrocious, aching, nightmarish moment that followed. The immediate act of being thrown to the floor, of seeing her mother dead on the blood-stained bed, of fainting, of waking tied with her own sash to a chair, with needle marks in her arms and drugs in her veins. Waking to find a grown man sitting on the floor in front of her, his pants unbuttoned, needles and a bottle of whiskey and a gun at his side. The story of freeing herself and picking up the gun and the way it felt cold and solid in her hand. Of her conversation with the weeping man who was suddenly human and pathetic; of his apology for the shooting of her mother when they had struggled for the gun; of his admission that he was a monster and that he would come for her and possess her, body and soul, as soon as he could stand and find more drugs to fuel him. About how he begged her to shoot him. About how he asked for her forgiveness and she gave it to him. About how she could have walked away, but didn't. She didn't walk away.

The room was silent for a long, long time, and Bailey could have sworn that Abraham Lincoln wiped away a tear.

Mr. Cunningham cleared his throat, and for the first time, appeared to be at a loss. "My dear Dr. Rose. I can't describe how sorry I am for the loss of your mother and for the action you were forced to take."

"You mean—you think I did the right thing?" she asked in a small voice. Her heart was racing painfully now.

He looked at her incredulously. "You are twelve years old and enter a room, you are struck across the face and thrown to the floor, see that your mother has been shot dead, you lose consciousness, are tied up and injected with drugs and told that you will be raped as soon as he is physically able, you are asked to end a miserable, rotten, sick life, and you're asking if you did the right thing?" He shook his head and gave a humorless laugh. "You did the *only* thing you could to survive. You were a remarkably brave and level-headed girl. No jury would ever convict you!"

For a great man of the law to exonerate her, even if the courts did not, was a profound, pressing weight lifted from her chest. She suddenly felt as though she could breathe again! She gave sob and buried her face in her hands, feeling both Mr. Cunningham and Mr. Moorehead patting her shoulders consolingly as Mr. Flander's pen continued its never-ending scratching. *He must be carefully recording notes of my weeping,* she thought inanely.

She got herself under control and peeked at Mr. Cunningham, who had sat back in his chair and was regarding her with his usual intensity.

"Dr. Rose, I need you to tell the hotel part all over again, and I'm going to ask you some questions, all right?"

She nodded, and for the next two hours he asked questions that were so detailed that for as intelligent as she was, she had no idea what he might possibly do with the information she was giving him. What did it matter, the color of Adam Hawk's eyes? Or the style of her mother's stockings? And when he finished with his questions, he asked her to tell the rest of her life story! She had to recount her years at St. Ursuline's, her time in college and medical school, the opening of her clinic, her relationship with Thomas, her re-acquaintance with Jacob and the trip to his ranch.

"Were you intimate with Jacob? I'm so sorry, Dr. Rose. I know this is uncomfortable."

"I don't understand why you need to know that." Her voice was clipped.

"I have to anticipate issues the prosecution will raise. Your character will be examined minutely. Now you said had a beau in New York, but you were really just friends, is that correct? Just a few kisses?"

"Oh, mercy," muttered Bailey. "Is this really necessary?"

"I'm sorry, but it is."

"Well then yes, Ben and I were friends. He asked me to marry him but I did not return his affection in that way."

"Now you told me all about your trip to the Naplava ranch. You spent a considerable amount of time alone with Jacob as you were riding the range, and you said there was a dance as well. I'm sorry I have to ask." He let the question hang, and Bailey felt her entire head consumed with a red hot flush. *I must look like a lobster right about now.*

She cleared her throat. "There was an incident in a barn during the dance."

"An incident?" Cunningham's voice was pleasant and professional, but she couldn't help but to feel violated.

"Jacob and I—we—oh, for the love of the Lord God above! This is *private*, Mr. Cunningham. The most private and precious thing in my life!" Well, she hadn't meant to say *that!*

"I'm so sorry," he murmured. "Try to think of me—of the three of us—as a machine, Dr. Rose. Your defense machine. You just need to feed in information so we can process it. Whatever is not useful will be disposed of. I don't know if it will make you feel any better, but the fellows and I have heard anything and everything you could ever imagine, from folks in all walks of life. And each one of us have had intimate encounters in our own lives as well. We are not here to judge you, Dr. Rose. I think it's safe to say that we all like you tremendously, and are in awe of your achievements as a physician. Not to mention the fact that Naplava is one of my best friends, one of the very finest men I know. If I were a woman, *I'd* be in a barn with him."

She couldn't help but laugh—they all did—and she felt a little better after his speech, although she still dreaded what she would say next.

"Okay. We—we kissed and held each other passionately. We spooned, I guess you could say."

"Did you consummate the relationship at that time?"

"No." Her chest felt tight and she found herself wanting to cry.

"Thank you, Dr. Rose, and I am truly sorry. Now you can see another reason why Mr. Naplava was not permitted to be here today. I would have been on the floor at this point, with a boot on my throat."

They all laughed again, and Bailey found the tightness releasing.

And then she was compelled to launch into the story of her trip to Pennsylvania and everything she had discovered there about her family. She repeated over and over the story of her grandmother's shooting and her mother's abduction and eventual abandonment of Hope and her departure to San Antonio. Mr. Cunningham nodded gravely, his eyes closing in sympathy, but then snapping again as the disparate pieces of Bailey's defense came together in his mind.

"And when you arrived back home, you were almost immediately called to the Naplava ranch, correct?"

She nodded. "Anton came to fetch me, but I traveled alone by train. I diagnosed the older girl, Eveline, with diphtheria, as well as her father. And then the younger girl, Ginny, contracted it, too. She almost died." She recounted the dark days and nights and her efforts to save the child's life.

Cunningham shook his head in wonder, and the faces of the other two men reflected his look of awe. "What a gift you have, Dr. Rose. The family is indebted to you: first Joseph's wife and baby, and then the other children and Elder Naplava. My, my."

She colored. "Of course they are not indebted! They are like my family, Mr. Cunningham."

He nodded in sympathetic understanding, then stared at his clasped hands, wondering how to ask the next question and dreading having to do so. She seemed like such a fine young woman to have come through every hardship in her young life, and now she had to suffer the trauma of this trial and the indignity of his invasive questions. It was the aspect of his job that he cared for the least.

"Dr. Rose," he began with a sigh. "I'm dreadfully sorry to have to ask this again..."

She held up a hand. "Jacob and I were intimate on the last night of the quarantine," she said quickly, to get it over with. She could see that he was almost as discomfited as she. "But we did not consummate our relationship."

"I'm sorry," he muttered again.

"It's quite all right. What's next, Mr. Cunningham?" She suddenly felt interminably weary. "Do you want to know about when the deputies came to arrest me?"

"Why, yes, that would be helpful." He cleared his throat and hoped that she would hold up this well in court. She was extraordinarily composed.

She told it, leaving nothing out, and he asked surprisingly few questions. A suspicion began to form in her mind. "What happened to those officers, do you know? Will they be reprimanded?"

He snorted and the other men snickered, too. "All three of those men have lost their badges."

"Oh, no, did Jacob..."

"Jacob still has a goose-egg on his skull from that moron," interrupted Cunningham. "He's lucky to be alive. Those men did not follow procedure. In fact, the sheriff ordered them to arrest you at St. Ursuline's upon your return from the Naplava ranch, but the men took it upon themselves to take the Boerne train, commandeer the Boerne police wagon, and ride out to the ranch as if they were collaring Jesse James himself. Delusions of grandeur, Dr. Rose."

There was a silence as the image of Jacob declaring his love for her flashed into her mind: his choked voice, the touch of his fingers on hers, the adulation in his eyes, and then the club descending across his skull before she even had a chance to open her lips to respond. Unbeknownst to her, every emotion was displayed on her expressive face as she remembered: surging love, shock and horror, and grief. The men watched, fascinated, until Cunningham shifted and cleared his throat again.

"Dr. Rose do you understand what will happen next?"

"I assume that I am to be arraigned."

"Yes, tomorrow. At the arraignment you will be asked for your plea, and I advise you to plead not guilty."

"You do?"

"Absolutely. We can build an excellent case of not guilty by reason of self-defense." He paused to allow the gravity of what he had said sink in.

"But I could have walked away," she finally managed. "I could have walked right through the door."

Cunningham was already shaking his head emphatically. "Really? Think about that, Dr. Rose. You were struck by Hawk before you fainted, and while you were unconscious, you were bound and drugged. That in itself is reason enough for a justifiable homicide. And then when you awoke, Hawk told you, in no uncertain terms, that once he was able, he would come after you and assault you."

"But he was incapacitated. I saw with my own eyes he could not get up off the floor."

"For how long? Did you know the exact amount of time it would take for him to recover?"

"Well, no…"

"Two hours? One hour? Thirty minutes? Five minutes? One minute?"

She nodded. "All right. I follow your logic. But didn't I have a—what do they call it—"

"Duty to retreat? No! Certainly not! And that has been firmly established in precedent, especially in the state of Texas!"

She shifted in her chair, agitated, her fingers drumming on the table. "But how do you prove all of that? Everything that happened? I'm the only one who survived that night!"

Abraham Lincoln leaned forward and placed his big, wrinkled hand on top of hers. "Leave that to us, Dr. Rose."

"As we build your defense, we will be meeting with you regularly," added Cunningham. "Don't worry: you're an important part—the *most* important part—of this team." He began to shuffle his papers together. "Tomorrow, you have one line to say. 'Not guilty, your honor.' That is all that will be required of you. Judge Samuel Simmons—Speedy Simmons, they call him, and you'll see why—is fair and honest. We're lucky to have him on the bench." He looked up at her with a smile and a twinkle in his eye. "Let's hear you say your line."

Bailey cleared her throat. "Not guilty, your honor," she repeated dutifully. Her voice was thin even to her own ears.

He paused in his shuffling, straightening to frown at her sternly. "Dr. Rose. You are *not* guilty. I believe that with all of my heart. *You are not guilty.* Now say it."

"I'm not guilty." Her voice was stronger now; she was somewhat awed by his passion and only hoped she could live up to it.

"Do you wish he would have lived another day to track you down and take what he wanted from you?"

She stared at him, shocked into silence. She shook her head dumbly.

"Listen to what Augustus Jennings will say. 'You were just a throwaway child, anyway, right? A powerful, important man like that: he should have been allowed to indulge in his harmless little habits.'"

"Harmless habits?" Her voice cracked.

"You were probably already a whore anyway, so you had no right to defend yourself. You put yourself into his hotel room, and you should have just stayed in the room and let him do what he wanted to do. What's the harm in it?"

She squeezed her eyes shut and covered her ears with her hands, shaking her head. "Stop it! Stop!"

He forced her hands down. "Girls from brothels don't have any right to defend themselves from respectable men. You went to that hotel room for an obvious purpose. You wanted to seduce him. It's obvious! You *are* guilty!"

"No! *I am not guilty*!" she yelled.

She stood and shoved him, hard, and he stumbled back, caught by the quick-footed Mr. Mooreland. Her hands flew to cover her mouth as Mr. Cunningham was set aright again, smoothing his rumpled jacket front. "There! Now there! *That's* the certitude I want to see and hear, Dr. Rose! You want to live, don't you?"

Gabby's face loomed in front of her then, and Jacob's. "Yes," she whispered. "I do."

CHAPTER SEVEN

Cunningham had stressed the importance of appropriate attire to solidify her image as a professional, up-standing citizen, and a new costume had been delivered: a lovely ivory shirtwaist to be worn under a tailor-made jacket in shades of brown, and an elegant, matching brown bell-shaped skirt with pleats in the center of the back. Ivory gloves and brown leather calf boots finished the ensemble, and he had even provided a full petticoat, camisole, and an item that made Bailey blush intensely: a bust girdle! She stepped from her bath and regarded herself forlornly in the vanity mirror: she wasn't too sure that she would even need that type of support! She used to have curves before the quarantine and her arrest: maybe someday she would have them again. The costume was curiously missing a corset, an item without which most conventional women would not consider leaving the house. If Cunningham had purchased the outfit, it was an uncharacteristic oversight, but maybe he knew little about women's underthings. She dressed quickly and gathered her hair into a knot on the top of her head with a puffy bouffant surrounding it, disliking the style but understanding the importance of playing the part. And this would likely be the last time for several weeks she would be able to dress in something other than gray, itchy prison garb.

Cunningham and his fellows arrived at nine o'clock sharp, and as he handed her into the carriage under the scowling regard of the ever-present guard, she thanked him for the clothes. "These things are lovely. You have many talents, Mr. Cunningham!"

"Oh, you wouldn't have wanted me to choose your costume!" he chortled. "Yesterday after we met, I called for your supporters and we all had a nice sit-down meeting."

This explained nothing, and she quirked her eyebrow at him curiously. He waved her in with a smile, and it wasn't until they were all settled in the covered carriage that he elaborated.

"As you can imagine, your friends have been *very* interested in news about you, Dr. Rose. Yesterday evening a good-size group of us had a nice dinner at St. Ursuline's: Sister Anna was there, and Reverend Eckles, Miss Flores, Mrs. Hannah Birchwood, Anton Naplava, Miss Alice Barnes, and, oh yes, Jacob Naplava."

She was unprepared for the effect his name had on her senses: a surge of adrenaline flooded her body, and for a moment she found it difficult to speak.

"They were all there for me?" she asked in a small voice.

"Of course! I let them know a few minimal details about our defense plan, how well you look and your excellent frame of mind—you know, that sort of thing."

She nodded mutely.

"Mrs. Birchwood insisted on shopping for your costume: she told me she knows just what would suit you. I hope she wasn't too far off the mark. You look—well, wonderful, if I might say it." He cleared his throat, a bit embarrassed, and his glance darted to Mr. Mooreland and Mr. Flanders, who were nodding enthusiastically. They were all a bit intimidated, in fact, by the transformation: Dr. Rose was an unexpectedly beautiful young woman. Cunningham recalled the besotted look on Jacob's face the night previous and suddenly understood it keenly.

"Please give her my sincerest thanks," she murmured. "The clothes are lovely and I'll pay her back just as soon as I can."

Cunningham waved one hand dismissively. "No need for that. I believe the clothing was sponsored by a friend of yours." *A friend.* Jacob, no doubt, and she colored to her roots. "Speaking of that friend…well, shoot, how can I put this clearly? Dr. Rose, I let your friends know they are welcome to visit you during your incarceration, with the exception of one. As we discussed yesterday, I just don't think it's a wise move for Jacob. I don't know yet how an association with you will affect the outcome of your case in the eyes of the jurors."

"Not to mention how it will affect his election," she added.

He shrugged. "While I care about that on a personal level, the path of his political career is actually not my focus or concern. *You* are my one and only concern. So I have instructed him to stay away, and I sincerely hope he will honor my wishes."

She nodded glumly and turned to stare out of the window. So she would not see him for weeks, and in the meantime, he would get married. *Married.* While she sat in a hotel room and waited to live or die. The prospect of not seeing him for that length of time—maybe never again—caused her shoulders to slump and her chin to fall. Cunningham glanced at his colleagues worriedly.

As the carriage approached the courthouse she realized that the time of her arraignment was public knowledge, for there stood the cluster of reporters: all of those horrible men in rumpled suit coats and stained vests and bowler hats, holding tiny notebooks and pencil stubs, furiously scribbling descriptions of her every move, fumbling with cameras, and sketching her likeness as she was handed down from the cab by Mr. Cunningham. Flanders and Mooreland flanked her immediately, and Flanders' likeness to President Lincoln momentarily distracted the weary men. "Hey, now! Abe! Care to address the crowd?" Flanders played along, stopping to chat with the horde while Mooreland and Cunningham hurried her forward at a break-neck pace. Before she knew it, she was inside the lobby and rushing down a wide hallway to Courtroom Number One.

The arraignment was astonishingly brief. There was no one present save the lawyers, Bailey, the judge, two guards, a clerk, and a stenographer. Judge Simmons was a rotund man with salt-and-pepper hair that stuck out from his skull in random, wiry patterns. He wore enormous muttonchops, white and bushy and thick, and Bailey found, to her horror, that she could not take her eyes off them.

As soon as they were all seated, the session was called to order and she was asked to stand again. Cunningham stood with her and offered her a bracing smile. *Not guilty, your honor,* she whispered to herself.

"Dr. Rose, you are hereby charged with the crime of murder in the first degree of Senator Adam Hawk on the night of the twentieth of May, eighteen hundred and seventy-six, a crime punishable by a sentence of life in prison or death by hanging. Do you understand these charges?"

"Yes, your honor." The words *life in prison* had struck a chill in her heart, much more so than *death by hanging.*

"How plead you?"

She took a deep breath, and before she could even form the words again mentally, out they flew, her voice strong and full of conviction. "Not guilty, your honor!"

She thought she had performed magnificently, and was a little let down to realize that absolutely no one in the courtroom seemed the least bit surprised or impressed by her pronouncement save Cunningham, who beamed at her. Jennings, an angular older man with a completely bald head and a thin, gray mustache, was jotting notes and displayed not a flicker of emotion. His team was likewise unresponsive, looking through papers or staring at the judge, seemingly bored.

"Very well, let the records show that the defendant Bailey Rose pleads not guilty. And now for the matter of bail."

Jennings rose with an unexpected speed and his sharp, nasal voice cracked through the room. "Your honor, the people of Bexar County respectfully request that bail be denied. The defendant has committed a capital offense and furthermore is clearly a risk for flight, as she has demonstrated a habit of frequent travel within the past few months."

"The defendant has been *charged* with a capital murder offense," corrected Simmons grumpily, glaring at Jennings. "The trial hasn't started yet, Augustus. Approach," he snapped, gesturing at both Jennings and Cunningham, and Bailey was left to conjecture as the three men murmured together. After a few minutes the attorneys returned to their seats.

Cunningham leaned over to whisper in her ear: "I'll explain later."

"Bail is denied," barked the judge, and Bailey's spirits fell. For one brief moment she had hoped that she would be sleeping on her cot at St. Ursuline's that night and returning to her clinic the next day! She didn't know if they would have allowed her to work, but just the prospect of it made her feel more normal, not like such a *criminal.*

"Your honor, one more point," whined Jennings. His adenoidal voice was incredibly grating. "The defendant enjoyed a stay in the Vance Hotel last night. Why a—*person*—charged with a capital offense is not sitting in a jail cell is beyond my ken. The citizens of Bexar County respectfully ask that the defendant be immediately returned to the Bexar County Jail." He sniffed disdainfully and sat down, his nose twitching, clearly expecting the judge to agree with him.

Judge Simmons glared at Jennings and then glared at Cunningham, allowing no more than five seconds before he erupted. "Well? Cunningham? Speak up."

Cunningham flushed and stood. "Your honor, we would be happy to recommend that the defendant be returned to the jail. I believe the sheriff moved Dr. Rose due to the fact that there are a few dozen reporters *living* in the lobby of the courthouse. They have already had scuffles with the guards and are pestering the receptionists around the clock. We fear that the defendant's right to a fair and speedy trial may be compromised due to the relentless and unchecked efforts of the press, not to mention the disruption to other activities in the courthouse unrelated to this case. Until such time as the dignity and efficiency of the courthouse and jail can be secured, we feel that the defendant should be moved frequently to evade the newsmen." His speech was quiet and respectful, but when he implied that the judge's courthouse was insecure and—even more grievously—that a *speedy* trial was in jeopardy—Simmons' eyes widened and his muttonchops quivered with indignation. Bailey stared at them, absolutely entranced.

"I had no idea; I've been out of town until late last night. No idea, dammit!" His voice thundered through the empty room and his muttonchops vibrated in fury. "Guard!"

A young man stepped forward, his face pale. "Yes, your honor?"

"Get me Sheriff McMurray! I want him in my chambers immediately!"

"Yes, your honor! Right away!" He scampered away, his footsteps echoing in the vast courtroom.

"Discovery three weeks from this date!" barked Simmons. He banged his gavel, heaved himself from his chair without another look at anyone, and stomped through the doors in the back of the courtroom into his chamber, slamming the door.

"And that's Speedy Simmons!" laughed Cunningham.

Bailey regarded her young attorney with a flummoxed expression. "That's it?"

"Yep." He scooped papers into a leather case and offered his hand. She stood, still frowning.

"But why was I denied bail?"

"Simmons wasn't going to budge on that." He glanced at her dismayed face. "It is exceedingly rare that a judge will grant bail for a capital offense. I could have fought Jennings, but I didn't want the public perceiving that you have special privileges, and I don't want to antagonize Simmons."

She nodded glumly and they made their way out of the courtroom and down the wide hallway. "What happens now?"

"Well, you'll go back to Vance for now, but I suspect those reporters will be cleared out of the courthouse by this afternoon."

"So I'm going back to jail."

His brow crinkled and his grip tightened on her elbow. "I'm afraid so. I'm sorry, Dr. Rose. And Naplava is going to nail me to the wall when he finds out," he added under his breath.

She straightened her shoulders. "That is fine, Mr. Cunningham. It's better that way, right? To avoid that whole privileged status issue?" She smiled at him bravely and winked.

He felt a surge of admiration. "Yes, it's better. I'll make sure you have your own cell. And it won't be long before you're out of there forever. I have a good feeling about this case; I like the way Simmons was looking at you, and Jennings is over-confident, which means he's going to get sloppy."

Before he could expound they were in the lobby and the horde descended.

CHAPTER EIGHT

Gabby was wide awake at midnight, propped up like a beached whale in her cozy room at Harding House, trying to read Ibsen's *Hedda Gabler and Other Plays* but fighting to stay focused. She had plucked the book at random from a shelf in the well-stocked library, hoping to read herself into a stupor, but the baby was wide awake and kicking her high in her ribs with gusto. She sighed and lifted her nightgown, watching her bare, distended abdomen undulate likes waves in the ocean. It was captivating right up until he punched her somewhere in the vicinity of her bladder; she groaned and rolled onto her side. "Hey there, T.J., how about a little nap?"

T.J. *Thomas Juan.* She had already decided it was a boy and he would be Thomas's namesake, as well as her brother's. She hadn't told Tommy that yet because he hadn't proposed.

He hadn't proposed.

She knew he loved her. He was affectionate both in action and words, and he was beyond solicitous. He had written her achingly beautiful love letters and poetry; he really was quite a talented writer. He told her every day—multiple times a day—that he loved her. He kissed her tenderly and passionately; oh, the passion was there, all right! But the words she had been longing to hear had yet to emerge from his lips.

T.J. stilled for a precious moment and she sighed with relief, her eyes drifting shut. Tommy had confessed to Bailey, and everything on that front was smooth and clear: her dear friend was and forever would be in love with Jacob Naplava, for better or, more likely, for worse. So what was Thomas waiting for? For the trial to be over? It would be two or three months, according to Mr. Cunningham, and maybe longer. She would like for Bailey to be present at their wedding; there was no question of that. But he could *propose* now, couldn't he? Was he afraid to show the world that he loved her? Was he having second thoughts? He would surely lose his position in the church when—if—he married her. They had already spoken about it: he wanted to concentrate his efforts on Harding House and perhaps pastor a small church, but maybe that prospect didn't seem so attractive now. He was very highly regarded and well-known in this city: did he want to relinquish that reputation? For he would become the object of intense gossip and ridicule, marrying a pregnant ex-prostitute.

She felt a tear well in her eye and escape down her cheek, quickly joined by others. She hadn't cried since she was fifteen years old and was sold by her mother. But she gave into it now, blaming the pregnancy, Bailey's uncertain future, her fear of childbirth—anything except the true cause, her anxiety that her dear, dear Tommy was slipping through her fingers.

The knock came so softly that she didn't hear it over her sobs at first. By the time it registered, the door was already opening.

"Miss Flores? I mean—Gabriella?"

Oh, *díos mío*! It was Tommy!

She clutched a handful of the soft quilt and dragged it across her face, frantically blotting her face. The book slid to the floor with a bang.

"What on earth—what's wrong?" His voice raised gooseflesh along her arms. He had no idea how much she loved him; she could never make him understand, could she?

"Oh, Tommy! I love you so much! But I don't have the right words for it." She sobbed out the last few words and he was on the bed, dragging her into his arms in an instant.

"Those *are* the right words, my angel." He dried the rest of her tears and kissed her face where the wetness still remained. She allowed it, reaching for him hungrily and pulling him closer, and before they knew it they were pressed together, full-length, her leg wrapped around his hip, straining toward him. His hands slipped inside her gown and stroked her swollen breasts; he had never done that before. She shivered in appreciation and pressed closer.

"Ah, Gabriella, I can't wait," he breathed.

She stilled, her heart thumping painfully. "Wait for what?" she asked. Maybe he meant *I can't wait for you to have this baby and recover so we can make love.* He probably assumed that they would, she being the *expert* that she was. But she was surprised that he would want to have sexual relations before they were married. Not surprised that he wanted to, but that he had already decided he would! Her mind whirled in confusion.

In response, he pulled away from her, put her nightgown back in place, and sat up. He pulled her to a sitting position at the edge of the bed and dropped to his knees before her.

"Tommy? What's going on? Are we getting kinky? That's fine, but darling, remember that we can't do the actual deed, seeing as this baby is about to pop right out." She threaded her hands through his curly hair, wanting him so badly.

He looked at her and burst into laughter. "Oh, Gabriella, I want to—*get kinky*—very badly, in fact, but that's not what's about to happen."

"It's not?" Her breath caught in her throat and she began to tremble.

"Close your eyes," he ordered.

She obeyed numbly.

"Open," he whispered. She opened her eyes, and there before her was Tommy, holding the gorgeous, sparkling, ridiculously extravagant ring of her dreams, his eyes glimmering. "When I bought this ring, you were in my head; in my heart. I was picturing your hand, your finger, not Bailey's. It never belonged to her, and she knew it, and would never wear it. I bought it for you, Gabriella. I just didn't realize it until—well, recently. Oh, Miss Flores! You are the very best part of me and I want you by my side, every day, every night. Will you marry me?"

"Yes," she gasped. He placed the ring on her left hand where it had belonged all along, and she fell into his arms, her weight sending them both backward until they were sprawled on the floor, laughing, kissing, and avowing their love.

"I'm so sorry it took me so long to ask you, my love. I wanted to find the perfect ring, and then I realized I already had it, but I wanted to find the perfect moment for my perfect lady, and then I realized that every moment with you is perfect."

She laughed and hugged him harder. "You are forgiven."

"When, when? Gabriella, the sooner the better! Will you marry me tomorrow?"

She stroked his face lovingly. "No, love. Bailey must stand up with me. And when we marry, I want to be sleek and trim and ready to have a long honeymoon with my man." She kissed him lingeringly.

When she finally released him, he sat up and pulled her with him. "But Gabriella, I want to give the baby my name. I want him to be born as an Eckles."

"T.J. will be an Eckles. You can adopt him. We know all about that process!"

He looked at her quizzically. "T.J.?"

"Thomas Juan, of course."

He didn't think that he could love her more, but as she placed his hands on their baby, he felt his life truly begin.

Jacob had drug a chair to his window shortly after the evening meal and was staring through the branches of the towering magnolia tree that stood guard there. After spending that first night in the lobby of the courthouse, he had been staying in one of Anton's luxurious guest rooms since he had been back in town, and he despaired at every amenity it provided: a grand, four-poster bed; thick Persian carpet in shades of blue and brown; an indoor water closet seven steps down the hall complete with a claw-foot tub—much bigger than the one at home; silk sheets—really, Anton? Silk sheets?—and most ludicrous of all, a newfangled contraption called a Diehl ceiling fan that kept the room at a quite pleasant seventy-two degrees during this unseasonably sweltering September—hot even for south Texas. He glared at it now as it rotated at a dizzying speed, sending a rush of cool air swirling through the room.

He despised living like a prince while Bailey sat huddled on a hard cot in a tiny, stinking, steaming cell. He knew from Cunningham that she had been transported back to the jail today, and his friend warned him not to say a word to Sheriff McMurray, who had been dragged into the judge's chambers and had his ass chewed clean off. Jacob shoved his hands under his armpits and gripped hard, imagining Rosie staring at steel bars on her tiny window while he watched an abundance of fat yellow roses climb a trellis up to his window. He imagined her sponging herself with lukewarm, dirty water, exposed to anyone who might happen to walk by her cell, while he luxuriated in the largest tub in Texas, a tub built for *three*, Anton had sheepishly confessed. Jacob had refused to sit in it, instead standing stubbornly and washing himself with tepid water and the thinnest cloth he could find. He imagined her eating three-day-old chunks of fatty meat, thin soup, and hard rolls while Anton's cook Libby Berkshire served prime rib, red potatoes and mouth-watering pastries. Worst of all, he imagined her curling up into a miserable ball at night on her hard cot, utterly alone, while he reclined on a plush mattress under the softest blanket he had ever known, hugging a pillow close, imagining it was she that he held.

A thousand times he wished he could turn back the hands of time and take her place in that hotel room, shielding her and shooting that sick bastard himself, which he would have done in an instant and never, ever regretted it. He wished it were he in that jail cell with Bailey safely ensconced at St. Ursuline's. He had wild fantasies of confessing to the crime himself, but knew from Cunningham that evidence that had originally been suppressed for all of these years to protect Adam Hawk had recently come to light, revealed by a police officer looking randomly through cold cases.

Cunningham had warned him to stay away from Bailey; not only would efforts to see her possibly damage his own campaign—not to mention his relationship with Caroline—but it could put Bailey's defense in peril, as the jury had not been chosen yet and public perception was critically important. And so while Eckles, Gabby, Sister Anna, Karl Schwartz, and even Hannah Birchwood were able to waltz into the courthouse and spend time with her, he was left to attend fundraisers, debates, meetings, and suffer through horribly awkward dinners with Caroline and her parents.

Caroline had been very quiet about the whole matter—and he had to admit, she hadn't said a word against his efforts to help Bailey. She had asked a few questions and appeared concerned and supportive, which left him with a curiously ominous feeling. He knew she was jealous of Bailey and highly suspicious of his relationship with her; why hadn't she voiced those concerns? Wouldn't any woman have some questions for her fiancé after he had been quarantined with a woman from his past for four weeks? And yet she had remained silent on the issue, playing the dutiful, supportive, soon-to-be wife. He could detect—probably because he was furtively looking in that vicinity—that she was growing rounder every day. In unguarded moments when they were alone she would stretch, her abdomen thrusting forward, and rub the small of her back, pain flitting across her face, and it was obvious that her stomach was bigger. Apparently she was the type of woman who gained pounds everywhere during pregnancy: her face, hips, arms—every part of her seemed to be fuller. She ate next to nothing at meals, but when Jacob expressed his concern to the cook when Caroline was out of earshot, careful not to clue the woman in on Caroline's pregnancy, the cook had snorted and confided that Caroline raided the pantry at all hours of the day, eating huge quantities of food. He guessed that this increase in appetite was not so unusual: his sister Amalie had a tremendous appetite during pregnancy and always bemoaned the consequences—she could never lose the weight and had become quite fat. He wondered if Caroline worried about that.

He supposed Caroline was worrying about a *lot* of things, and that only added to his misery. She was over four months along—*past four months*! She had not said a word about when the wedding would be rescheduled; he had to give her credit for that. In his own mind, he realized that the situation would soon become impossible for her. The original plan was already quite ridiculous—she would give birth five months after a wedding, and who would believe a baby could survive at five months? If they delayed until after the trial—as he was desperate to do—she could be six or seven months along. At the rate she was growing now, it would be impossible to hide, and then she would give birth a mere two or three months later. But he could not—just absolutely *could not*—get married while Bailey's very life hung in the balance. He imagined her sitting in her cell knowing the very moment he was uttering his vows, committing his life to another woman; he imagined her lying on her hard cot trying not to think about his wedding night. He groaned and let forth with a string of profanity, then shot from his chair, sick of looking at roses and magnolias, and gave the chair a savage kick. No sooner had it crashed to the floor than a knock came at the door.

"Mr. Jacob? Sir? Are you quite all right?" Libby's lilting English accent drifted through the door.

"Yes, Libby! Sorry about that," he called. He strode to the door and opened it, forcing a grin. "I have an issue with tipping chairs. Damn clumsy rancher."

Her troubled glance darted to the chair in question, which had been kicked with enough force to send it end-over-end. "Oh, that's all right. But Mr. Jacob, I've come to fetch you downstairs to the parlor. Your lady is here."

For one split second he pictured Bailey downstairs and his jaw dropped open. Then he realized who she must mean. Libby observed it all with a keen eye: a suffusion of elation followed by a cold dose of reality. Anton had told her about Jacob and that poor girl doctor in jail, and her heart hurt for them both.

Jacob followed her downstairs, dreading what was to come, for he and Caroline had to make some decisions today. He stared at Libby's cheerful blue calico bow bobbing on the back of her apron and wondered how in the hell he was going to initiate this conversation, and then realized, with a pang, that talking to his future wife shouldn't be such an ordeal.

"Jacob! Dear!" Caroline rose gracefully in one fluid motion from a red silk damask French Louis XV settee—yet another of Anton's indulgences—and floated toward him, hands outstretched. Libby curtsied and took her leave, and Jacob and Caroline remained posed in the middle of the ornate parlor, hands clasped, regarding each other: Caroline's expression bright and Jacob's grave.

"Hello, Caroline. How have you been feeling?"

She squeezed his hands and shrugged prettily. "Well, the nausea has passed, thanks to wonderful advice from Dr. Rose, but my back hurts ever so much. But I'll be fine, Jacob! Dr. Montgomery says that we're both perfectly healthy. And I felt the baby move this week! It felt like little bubbles popping in my stomach!" She guided his hands to her abdomen, and he let them rest there, gulping, his heart racing. *My God, this is real. My baby's growing in there.* "I think it's too soon for you to feel movement, but in a few months you'll be able to," she whispered. A soft pink had stolen onto her cheeks, and her eyes held such an expression of desperate love that Jacob's conviction about delaying the wedding began to waver.

Truth be told, he had been hoping that if he could convince her to delay it, perhaps Providence would intervene. He didn't allow himself to think of what that might mean, but the thought of the baby or Caroline dying now made him despise himself. What had he turned into? Was this what Bailey had been trying to warn him would happen? No; there had to be another way with a less sinister outcome. *God, let me find another way to put things on hold,* he prayed.

"Caroline," he began, his voice cracking terribly. "We need to talk about the wedding. We need to have a plan."

She stared at him, the smile still on her face, but her eyes began to frost. He noticed they were the precise color of pale pistachios today. "I thought we *had* a plan."

He pulled her over to the divan and they sat, hands linked. "Have you thought about a new wedding date?" he began. He saw the relief flood her eyes and the frost vanish.

"Yes! I've been studying your calendar. Next Saturday you have a breakfast meeting with Mayor O'Malley. I thought that in the afternoon—two-thirty, perhaps—we could have a small, quiet ceremony at my home, or we could have it here, whichever you prefer." Caroline looked around appreciatively: Anton's home was spectacular, and soon—whenever she ordered him to—she would get the opportunity to sink into that infamous claw-foot tub with her brother-in-law.

Jacob stared at her, the blood draining from his face. *Think, think! There has to be a way to delay this.* "Caroline, I'm going to suggest a different plan." She stiffened and he began to talk faster, grasping her hands in what he hoped was a loving gesture. He was pretty certain he knew what she cared about most, and that was the tack he was going to take. "Do you know what O'Malley and I are meeting about?"

Her brow crinkled in confusion; she hadn't expected that question. "Why, no, I don't," she murmured quizzically.

"It's essentially a transitional meeting. Caroline, something has been largely ignored in the papers due to the news about—well, you know…" He sputtered to a stop and almost lost his train of thought. Bailey's face had been plastered on the front page of every issue of every major paper in the nation over the past week with the words *Child Whore Murdered U.S. Senator 15 Years Ago,* leaving little room for the progress of a mayoral race. Thankfully, his name had not been linked too much with Bailey's, only a few early mentions that she had "quarantined the home of mayoral candidate Jacob Naplava with a positive outcome for all." The press hadn't picked up on his past relationship with her—yet—or his initial efforts to have her moved from the jail, and Sheriff McMurray sure wasn't going to talk!

"A transitional meeting? What do you mean, Jacob? *What's* been ignored by the papers?"

He forced a smile to his face. "The fact that I'm so strong in the polls. Dr. Johnson withdrew his candidacy while I was in quarantine; did you know that?"

She nodded. "Yes, I read that in the paper. But what about Sabine? Wasn't he the big threat?"

"He's still my main competition. Harris, that poor man—I really like him—has so few supporters that I'm surprised he hasn't withdrawn as well. But last week, the day before I got back into the city, Sabine was caught with another man's wife. Apparently he's lost quite a few big backers, but he's not down for the count. He's claiming he was framed and quite a few people are willing to believe that. It's starting to swing back his way, and it's a race to the finish. I need to spend every moment on this campaign, and if I marry unexpectedly, well, folks might guess what the rush is all about and that I may lose those conservative stuffed birds that Sabine has been losing…" He drifted off, realizing that he had been talking much too fast and uncertain of what to say next. Her expression was inscrutable.

"So you believe that having a wedding might hurt your campaign." It was a statement, and when issued in Caroline's quiet, modulated voice, sounded quite ridiculous.

"No, not having a wedding; having a *sudden* wedding."

"It's *not* sudden. It was delayed by the quarantine. It's simply being re-scheduled." She allowed her hands to remain in his, but they had gone quite limp.

Jacob drew forth every bit of rhetorical finesse he had learned in law school. "Stevens—you know the man, he's part of my campaign team—told me that it is critical that I maintain a pristine image during this next eight weeks. Sabine is being painted by the press as a reckless womanizer; I'm the upstanding everyman who is to marry an upstanding, beautiful woman who is highly respected in the community." He was gratified to see a small flush of pride paint her cheeks. "Did you read the society page in the *Express* yesterday?" She shook her head, a look of concern flashing across her normally placid features. Hedelga Jones was absolute poison, and there was no love lost between her and that wretched woman.

Jacob strode to the fireplace, reaching into a basket to retrieve the paper waiting to be used to start tomorrow's fire. "That busybody Jones wrote that since our wedding had been postponed by the quarantine, 'We assume'—as if there's a committee that meets to decide these things—'We assume that the smart couple will delay the wedding until mid-November so Mr. Naplava can put forth all of his efforts to meet his obligations as a candidate for the mayoral race. Lucky Miss Vogler! The lovely woman will have an extra few months to plan what will no doubt be the most extravagant ceremony this pokey town has ever seen.'"

Caroline rose and snatched the paper from Jacob's hands. "'We simply cannot fathom any reason why she wouldn't be delighted with this extension. Can our readers?'" finished Caroline. She gasped and stared at Jacob. "Why, it sounds almost as if she—she *knows* something," she whispered, truly horrified. For the first time, the full ramifications of this manufactured pregnancy were brutally apparent. Manufactured or not; it didn't matter: Jacob thought she was pregnant—as did Bailey—and there *was* a real, live baby on the way—Honey's! Caroline was as good as pregnant. Four months pregnant and unmarried. How could she have ever thought that society would be forgiving? And her mother! Oh, Lord. She must have read this yesterday and said not a word about it. Her father didn't bother with the society pages, but her mother lived for them, and was certain to have understood the subtle insinuation.

She sank back down to the divan, her hands folded in her lap. "Oh, Jacob," she whispered, and he sat down with her, feeling acutely sorry for her and beginning to loathe himself a bit. "What are we going to do?"

"I have an idea," he managed, noticing that his voice didn't quite sound like his own. "But you don't have to go along with it. I'm going to put the decision in your hands." He took a deep breath, understanding that if she chose the second option, he would be getting married next Saturday. "I've thought about this quite a bit, and some parts may sound crazy, but I think it can work to save the election and to save your reputation. So here goes: you could visit Ma at the ranch house this week, and upon your return, take sick with diphtheria—no one would question it. You would be quarantined for at least four weeks, and Dr. Montgomery can extend it and say that the illness damaged your heart, or something along those lines, and you cannot leave your bed."

She stared at him, her face taking on an even paler hue than usual. "What good would that possibly do?" she whispered, not following his line of thought.

"After the election, we'll marry quietly at your home in a private ceremony, and everyone will understand why we're doing it—just in case you don't survive. I'll move you to our home here in the city—we'll purchase a beautiful home—and we'll leak the information a few months later that you are with child, and your health is in even greater danger. You'll give birth in February, but we won't announce the birth until June, seven months after we marry. A baby can survive at seven months; I know, because Rosalie had a baby that early. Dr. Montgomery can release you from an invalid status, but we'll keep the baby out of the public view, citing health reasons. And then a few months later, maybe next August, we can introduce him to the world."

She continued to stare at him, her lips slightly parted with incredulity. "Won't he be a bit large for a two-month-old baby? Since he'll be six months old at that point?"

"I thought of that. I did some research, and did you know that some babies grow unusually fast due to excess thyroid hormones? That can be the health problem I was talking about. No one will question it if Dr. Montgomery backs us up, and we can even get one of those hacks to write it up in the *Express* as a medical miracle."

She just stared, pretty lips parted, a dazed expression in her light green eyes. Finally she spoke. "So you are suggesting that I contract diphtheria, which in turn damages my health, and stay cooped up in my parents' house until after the election? And then cooped up in our home until *next June?*"

"I know it's not a perfect plan. But if you want to give me the best shot for becoming mayor, and for you to give birth without questions about impropriety, it may be our only viable plan. And then who knows? Four or five years from now we could be Washington, D.C. bound!" The words were bitter in his mouth. A career in politics was the last thing he wanted. "But Caroline, I have to tell you, I don't really care that much about becoming mayor. Family has always been my number one priority. We can get married next Saturday as planned, and if it damages my chances, so be it! I know you'd be just as happy living as a rancher's wife back at the homestead, and in the hills no one is going to care if we started that baby a little early." He held his breath, terrified.

The expression of horror on her face told him all he needed to know, and he released his breath, little by little, feeling the pressure in his chest loosen.

She stood and walked to the fireplace, gazing at the logs, unlit on this hot evening. His plan to delay was complicated and brazen and would involve a great deal of duplicity. She appreciated all of those qualities. But she suspected—she *knew*—what was behind it all. Bailey Rose. He did not want to marry her until that disgusting man-girl was released from jail. Perhaps he intended on establishing Bailey as his lifelong mistress. *That would not happen.* Caroline didn't care so much if Jacob discreetly took lovers; she planned to. But not Bailey Rose. *Never her.*

Unfortunately, he wouldn't be able to bring himself to do the right and honorable thing until this matter of the whore doctor was resolved, one way or another. If Bailey were acquitted, she would have to find a way to get her out of the city, forever. She could find someone to seduce Bailey. She had a few connections in Philadelphia, where Bailey's family apparently resided. Or she could convince Bailey to establish a whore clinic back east by appealing to her savior complex. Ultimately, the method didn't matter: she would find a way.

Caroline had hoped with all of her heart that Bailey would hang and be out of their lives forever, but now she wondered if perhaps Jacob would just curl up and die if that happened, and then what good was he? If Bailey were executed, Caroline had to find a way to keep Jacob by her side. The baby! Everything hinged on that baby. The baby would be his salvation, the thing that he lived for. She could even visit Bailey in jail and get her to make Jacob promise to live for the baby.

Honey's baby. Jacob's cockamamie plan actually had a tremendous advantage: it would be so much easier to control Honey if Caroline were living in her own home. When it was time for Honey to give birth, Caroline would go into a very quick, unexpected labor while Jacob was busy with his mayoral duties one day; Dr. Montgomery would simply bring Honey's baby to her house.

Caroline crossed her arms over her chest and clutched herself. She knew Jacob was manipulating her, but what he didn't know was that she was one step—*two steps*—ahead of him. He was stalling, maybe hoping something would happen to change their inevitable course, but it was futile. His plan would only serve to secure his place as mayor and preserve her reputation, just as he said it would. The end result would be the same, no matter how much he dreaded it. They would marry and have a baby together, and Bailey Rose would either be dead or far, far away.

She spun and smiled. "I choose your plan, Jacob. It's a wonderful plan and I love you for thinking of it!" She launched herself into his arms and barely restrained herself from laughing aloud as she felt his arms encircle her. *Enjoy your last few months of bachelorhood mooning over her, love. In a few months' time she'll be out of our lives, forever.*

Jacob returned to his room a few hours later after a walk with Caroline and a long, grueling talk about The Plan. She had taken her leave to go home and pack for the ranch; he would need to send a telegram to his mother announcing Caroline's visit. He cringed on the inside: he knew how Ma felt about Caroline, and he knew she wouldn't relish this impromptu visit. But she would be gracious and accommodating, knowing now that the young woman was carrying her grandchild.

He muttered an excuse about dinner to Anton, scribbled a telegram and sent the stable boy off with it, accepted a sandwich from Libby, and made his way slowly up the stairs, feeling like an old, tired man. He managed half of the roast beef on rye before depositing the rest of it out of the window for the stray cats. He sunk to the floor and gave into it for a few moments: this feeling of utter doom. He had successfully postponed the inevitable: that was the extent of his accomplishment today. Even when holding his future wife in his arms he had been longing for Bailey, and he closed his eyes now, trying to picture what she may be doing at this moment. He quickly snapped them open again, finding the image too painful.

His eyes came to rest on a piece of brown leather peeking out from under his bed. *Her satchel.* He had brought her things from the ranch, clutching them on the train that dreadful day, and had given them to Anton for safekeeping. Seeing them now under his bed elicited a moan. There were two large black satchels, one containing her medical supplies—he supposed he should give that to Miss Flores—and one holding her clothing, and there was a smaller, worn brown one. He crawled a few feet and dragged the satchel out, remembering fifteen years ago when he had hauled it all over the city looking for a bedraggled girl who had suffered at the hands of a bully and molester in front of Jacob's very eyes. His stomach twisted even now in anger and sympathy. So much had transpired since that day a lifetime ago, and yet she was just as much out of reach now as she ever had been—an elusive dream, love unrequited and un-proclaimed, at least on her part.

He reached in and pulled out the volume of Shakespeare, running his hands over the cover with a wistful smile. He pictured her quoting earnestly from this book in the German schoolroom, much to the disdain of most of the students. He had been captivated by her powerful mind even then. He set it aside and drew out another book—*The Green Ray*! Ah, yes, the Verne book she won in a bet from a cocky sheepman. He pictured her laughing by the fire out on the range, giving as good as she got from that rascal Kube while Jacob stewed, vexed with Kube's flirtation. Further down in the soft leather was a journal covered in red velvet, and he resisted the urge to read her private thoughts. There was a handkerchief with *BR* embroidered upon it, and he folded it carefully and put it in his own pocket without compunction. A few odd hairpins—he put those in his pocket, too—a stray bottle of iodine, and that was all. Wait—his groping hand found a folded paper that had slid down into the torn satin lining. He pulled it out and unfolded it, and seeing it was a letter, began to fold it up again, vowing again not to infringe upon her privacy. But something stopped him as his eye caught on the salutation. *My dearest Jake.* She wrote it for him!

He hesitated, understanding that since she had never given it to him, it, too, must belong in that realm of sacred, confidential thoughts. But he heaved a sigh and glared defiantly at the Diehl fan spinning around in circles. "I'm going read it, you son of a bitch," he announced to the fan. "I'm sorry, but she addressed it to me, so it's mine." The fan didn't offer a response, and he stood to pull a chair to the window to catch the fading light of the day. He unfolded the letter again, treasuring the sight of her looping, slightly hurried handwriting. He discerned immediately that she wrote just exactly as her mind worked: with speed, poetic beauty, and gut-wrenching honesty.

August 7, 1891

My dearest Jake,

Could there ever be anything lonelier than a train at night? I find myself clutching the miserable solitude around me like a cloak, glomming onto it like a bereft lover, wallowing in the anguish, for at least the despair is a feeling, and I'm more terrified of the numbness than of the despair.

The cadence of the train is seducing me, Jake. Even as it pulls me farther and farther from you, the rhythm is leaching through my body, cajoling, awakening the memory of you against me, the feel of your hands on me, your tongue speaking in my mouth. I look down at myself right now and watch the movement of the train gently stir my body, and I think about when you pulled me from Death in Glory Creek and held me skin to skin, a boy and a girl metamorphosing into one entity, forever fused somehow. You wept that day, and as you held me, your sobs swayed my body just like this; just like the train moves me now. Funny how that rhythm has become an infinite echo. I will lie down and close my eyes soon and tell myself to sleep, but the train will move me, and the rhythm will become you and I. Your body will move within mine, and I will cry out for you as the train whistle wails into the night.

On the darkest of nights when the ruthless loneliness eats away at me, my body will remember. You are my body, my heart, my soul. My desideratum.

I love you, forever. Only you.

Rosie

For a long while—he didn't know how long, maybe an hour, maybe more—he sat by the window, clutching the letter, tears streaming, his breath coming in jerks, his heart racing. Her passion for him matched his; this, he knew. But she loved him. *Only him.* Forever.
   She loved him.

CHAPTER NINE

Bailey had lost track of her days. For the first week back in her cell she had kept track by scratching marks on the wall, but the act made her feel so sordid that she put a stop to it. She was permitted one visitor each day, in addition to Cunningham, who had met with her three times thus far to reassure her that her case was coming together wonderfully. His effusiveness and self-assurance made her nervous. He acted as though the trial would be an effortless walk in the park. "Just tell the truth," he kept saying as he took her through the questions he anticipated Jennings would ask. "The truth *is* your defense. Trust me." She didn't quite trust him, but she trusted Jacob, and she would smile anxiously and allow herself to be "prepped," as Abraham Lincoln called it.

Thomas, Sister Anna, Karl, Hannah Birchwood, Lindy, and even Marianna—what a wonderful surprise that had been—had all visited her, bringing the warmth and sunshine and life of the outside world in with them, infusing the windowless, gray meeting room with a forced yet welcome cheerfulness. She longed for Gabby's forthrightness—for someone who would just hold her and listen to her cry about living in this shithole and being terrified of never leaving it, someone who would not expect her to smile and be brave *all* of the time—but Thomas told her that Gabby was so near to her time that she was having trouble riding in a carriage. And then came the day when Bailey discovered the precise date: the twenty-third of October. Sister Anna reported that Gabby had given birth to a nine-pound boy and had named him Thomas Juan, delivered without complication by Karl Schwartz. Bailey wept with relief and joy, sending her love to the new parents.

After that the days began to blur again, and there came a stretch of three grim days when no one came to see her, including Cunningham. Every morning she took pains to wet her hair and comb it with the broken wooden comb provided by the matron; she was allowed to wash it only on Saturday nights, and had to lean over a basin with a bar of soap to do so. Every morning she brushed her teeth, the matron snorting and rolling her eyes, muttering that Bailey was the only prisoner who asked for tooth powder in the evening *and* morning. Every morning she anxiously smoothed the wrinkles from her gray cotton gown and sat primly on her cot, wondering who she might see that day. The ten-minute visits, which occurred precisely at ten o'clock in the morning, were her lifeline. The first day that no one called on her she cried for an hour, turning her face to the wall so the matron would not see as she stomped by her cell in her thick black boots. The next day when visiting hour had come and gone she felt a bubble of anger well within her, followed by another hour of weeping. Thomas and Gabby could be excused, of course, but where were the others? Had they forgotten all about her as they moved through the everyday demands and joys of their own lives? Life on the outside moved on, she realized, just as it always had. If she were convicted and her life were spared—*please God, let them execute me if I am convicted*—this is what she must resign herself to: a life as someone who is just a pitiful memory to others, a poor woman growing older each day who must be visited, *but let's just do it on Mondays and get it over with for the week.*

The third day she did not bother so much with her hair, shoving it into a hasty bun, a stony expression on her face. No one came. She did not cry that day; she instead felt a curious numbing sensation as she sat on her cot, hour after hour, staring at the wall, refusing to eat.

She was allowed one book per week, and she forced herself to read at a slow, steady pace so she would have something to occupy her mind for at least part of the day. The books provided to the female prisoners of the Shrimp Hotel were of a decidedly didactic nature, instructing honorable and decent women about the proper etiquette to be used in society and home life. Bailey's least favorite was Emily Thornwell's *The Lady's Guide to Perfect Gentility, in Manners, Dress, and Conversation.* For a solid week she suffered through nonsensical coaching about every miniscule aspect of her life, from how to address her husband in public ("A lady should not say 'my husband,' except among intimates; in every other case she should address him by his name, calling him "Mr."), to how walk properly in public ("A lady ought to adopt a modest and measured gait; too great a hurry injures the grace which ought to characterize her. She should not turn her head on one side and on the other, especially in large towns or cities, where this bad habit seems to be an invitation to the impertinent.") After three days of this she began to talk to Mrs. Emily Thornwell, quite viciously. "Mrs. Thornwell, when I walk with my husband on the streets of San Antonio, I believe I shall skip and prance with joy, my head turning this way and that like an owl, and when I happen upon an acquaintance, I shall say 'Well howdy there, what's shakin' your bacon today? Meet my husband, wontcha? His name is Mr.—oh, never mind, just call him Kissy-Bear; I do!'"

Her voice was strange and hollow in the cell, and she hated the sound of it, so she ceased her conversations with Mrs. Emily Thornwell and read in silence. She longed for her journal. The matrons would not allow her writing materials, stating that a writing utensil could be fashioned into a deadly weapon, and not even Mr. Cunningham could change their minds.

On the morning after the three-day visitor privation, she gave serious thought to skipping the tooth-brushing and hair-brushing. To hell with Mrs. Emily Thornwell and to hell with her friends! She would sit in her filth and become what she supposed she ought to: a slovenly, pale, wild-haired murderess rotting away in a cage. But in the end she demanded the powder and comb and took extra pains with her hair, terrified of what she was becoming. Kindly Mrs. Knittle was her matron that morning, and Bailey ventured to ask her for a mirror. What she saw dismayed her: her cheeks were thin, the one still bruised a bit; there were dark shadows under her eyes, and her hair was lackluster. But she had done a decent job with the braid, and the bruise on her cheek was almost gone, now just a pale shade of yellow-brown. She looked like an exhausted, thin, depressed version of herself. She tried out a smile but it quickly died on her lips: her teeth looked too large for her mouth and the result was ghastly. She really was wasting away; she *must* eat.

As the visiting hour approached she clutched her stomach and braced for the hour to come and go. Today she would not care, she decided. She would stretch and exercise, and rewrite the Thornwell book in her mind with all of the proper instructions. *A lady ought to adopt a carefree and fearless gait, full of the zest for life. She should run wherever her legs will take her, just as fast as she cares to, play tag with children, crawl belly-down in the dirt to follow the path of the busy ants. She should crane her neck to gawk at every beautiful and ugly thing this wide world has to offer; she should experience her world through every one of her senses, gazing until she is lost in the stars, soaking into her very bones the music of the halls and dancing all night, tasting the sugar on her lover's lips after she has fed him a sweet, touching the soft cheek of a baby and the silky ear of a cow, and smelling the sharp scent of her own sweat as she traverses the city at a breakneck speed, and then she must stand still to let it catch her, if it can . . .*

Her eyes were closed when Mrs. Knittle came to fetch her. "Dr. Rose?" she said quietly. The girl looked to be sleeping peacefully, with a faint smile on her face. The older woman was struck by her ethereal beauty, which she had never noticed before. The girl truly looked like an angel! "You have two visitors today, Mr. Cunningham and an older gentleman."

Bailey opened her eyes and smiled. A visit with her lawyers was much, much better than no visit at all! And there would be no guard to stand over them since he was her attorney. She supposed Abe Lincoln accompanied Mr. Cunningham today. She had grown to appreciate his calm steadiness in the midst of Cunningham's rapid-fire energy.

Mrs. Knittle led her down the hallway to the familiar, airless room, and Bailey was seated to wait for her team. Mr. Cunningham soon entered followed by a heavily-bearded man with a wide-brimmed hat pulled down over his eyes; she had never met this lawyer before. Cunningham nodded at Mrs. Knittle, who took her leave, and the two men had a seat in the straight-back chairs. A table had been provided as it always was for these meetings, and Cunningham murmured his greetings as he opened his case and spread his papers.

"I don't believe I've met this member of our team, Mr. Cunningham," she ventured, with no introduction apparently forthcoming. The man's gray whiskers stretched a good ten inches, and she wondered if perhaps he was Cunningham's superior, tagging along to monitor the young lawyer and ensure that he didn't flub the biggest case he'd ever had.

"Oh, I believe you have," he corrected, looking up and smiling at her. Bailey raised an eyebrow and studied the queer old man again. As she watched, he reached around behind his head and fumbled with something, and then the beard fell onto the table. He removed his hat and raised his head, and as a pair of the bluest eyes met hers, a strangled sound emerged from her throat; a cross between a cry and a song.

She didn't remember moving, and she didn't remember him moving, but they both must have stood because the very next sensation was the slamming of his body against hers and his arms hauling her to him before she fell. He clutched her to him painfully, squeezing the breath from her lungs, and she held onto his neck for dear life, her face buried there, feeling his heart pound crazily in the pulse of his throat against her lips. They stood in silence for long moments as Cunningham stared at his papers, wondering for the hundredth time how he had let Naplava talk him into this.

"Just a few more minutes, Jacob, okay, my friend?" he finally murmured. The guard had been suspicious, as "Mr. Snodgrass" was not on the defense list, and he daren't let word get back to Jennings. So much was at stake.

Jacob stiffened and then gently pulled away, taking a long, painstaking moment to look her over, his eyes traveling across her horribly thin face and down the length of her, stopping at the last fading evidence of her bruises and chafed wrists. His stomach clenched: she was in bad shape, worse than Cunningham had let on. His arms fell and his hands encircled her too-tiny waist. "I've wanted to visit you every day, and I have, in my mind," he began, and then shook his head, smiling ruefully. "There's so much I want to say that I don't know where to start."

"It's okay," she whispered. She still had her arms around him and couldn't seem to let go. "What you said, before they took me that day. It's kept me alive." Her eyes filled with tears as she saw the torment in his own.

"I meant it." His Adam's apple bobbed a few times.

"I need to tell you something, Jake." The words were at her lips, ready to burst forth and complete them both. But he shook his head and put his finger to her mouth.

"Not here. Not now. The day you are free; tell me then, okay, Rosie? Let that be our hope."

She stared at him for a long moment, her feelings in turmoil. What if she *never* was free? What if she didn't survive this; what then? How would she tell him? As she was being dragged away by the guards in the courtroom? She let herself imagine it, screaming *I love you, I love you, Jake* as the whole condemning world looked on.

He smiled and tugged on her braid. "Promise?"

She finally nodded dumbly. "Now I know how you felt when I wouldn't let you say it," she whispered. "Like hell."

His grin deepened and he nodded. "Yep. That pretty much sums it up."

Cunningham cleared his throat meaningfully. "Naplava, I'm sorry, friend, but we need to get you out of here."

He hauled her close again. "I brought you a book and there's a letter in it for you. Cunningham told me I couldn't write you one, and then I changed his mind at the last minute and I only had five minutes to write it, so it's pretty rushed."

She nodded wordlessly and kissed his neck, clutching the back of his jacket desperately, sobs building in her throat.

"*I'm* allowed to say it, so I will. I love you, Rosie." They both laughed, verging on tears.

And that was all they had time for, because at that moment there was a banging on the door.

Cunningham swore under his breath. "Attorney client privilege!" he called loudly. "Get your disguise on!" he hissed at Jacob, who reluctantly released his hold on Bailey, dipping his head to kiss her mouth for the space of three seconds, his fingers trailing on her cheek, and she thought she might swoon. A good, old-fashioned swoon: Mrs. Emily Thornwell would heartily disapprove.

Jacob donned the beard and hat just as the guard barreled in.

"What's the meaning of this?" barked Cunningham.

The guard pointed his club at Jacob. "Who did you say you were again?"

"I'll have you know that I am the owner of the firm this young man belongs to! What do you think about that? Now out of my way before I bring suit against you! Obstruction of justice comes to mind, just for starters!"

The guard blanched and put his club away. "I don't want no trouble, Mr. Snodgrass, sir."

"Oh, well you're going to get it, whippersnapper! Damned guards, thinking they know the law! I was leaving anyway, I'll have you know! Now get out of my way! I'm going to find your superior!"

He blustered on and on in a cantankerous, old-man's voice as he ambled from the room, and he was gone in an instant, before Bailey even had a chance to meet his eyes again. She felt simultaneously elated and crushed, and collapsed back into her chair, staring numbly at Cunningham. He sighed and shook his head, regarding her. She looked punch-drunk.

"We're not going to get any work done today, are we?"

She shook her head slowly.

He reached into one of his cases and withdrew a book. The cover was striking: a multi-colored light brown cloth gilt, featuring four dapper gentlemen exclaiming over a magnificent green ray on the horizon while a seated man and woman gazed only at each other. *The Green Ray* she had won from Kube! She had forgotten all about it. And Jacob had said there was a letter inside! She pulled it to her and clutched it to her heart, squeezing her eyes shut.

"They'll never let me have it. I get one book a week and this week is that despicable Mrs. Emily Thornwell," she whispered, knowing she sounded like a loon.

"Take it. I'll clear it with the guard," he sighed again. There was so much to do, and she was clearly lost for the day.

She waited until Mrs. Knittle had gone, until the sound of her heavy boots had died and she had settled herself on the cot, turning to face the wall so no one would be able to see her face. This was the very last contact she would have with him until the trial was over, she knew for certain, and it was a gift, an answer to a prayer.

She found it tucked in Chapter III, and when she pulled it out she saw that he had underlined a passage. *If there be green in Paradise, it cannot but be of this shade, which most surely is the true green of Hope!*

My dearest Rosie,

I only have a few moments. I found the letter you wrote to me on the train, which I'll remember, verbatim, forever. You can't even begin to know what it feels like to finally know that you love me like I love you. The wedding has been postponed until after the trial and election. We are concocting a story about Caroline visiting the ranch, contracting diphtheria and suffering lingering complications to keep her in her home, out of the public eye. I don't have any answers beyond that, but please have faith in me. Read this book; the green ray was not the most important thing after all. We may think our green ray is that big answer that's going to solve everything, but the answer is simpler than that…can't write any more now. I love you.

Always,

Jake

She read it and gasped out loud upon realizing that he had read that intensely personal letter she had written on the train. Oh, mercy, the things she had written! As she recalled it—the rhythm of the train bringing to mind his body against hers, her desire to make love with him, her everlasting love declared—her face flooded with red and she buried her head in her arms, laughing and crying. *He read it! He knows. He knows. He knows.* She read his letter again and again, once she could, and though she did not understand the references to the book just yet, his words kindled a hope in her that acted as a glorious stimulant. Suddenly, everything was possible! It was! How could it not be? After all of this time, all of those years—her whole life since the day she met him—she had spent dreaming of him, yearning for him; finally, they were in the same place together, knowing they loved each other. What else could possibly matter?

She finally put the letter aside and picked up the book, vowing to read slowly to make it last, but an hour later, as she turned the last page and wept, she understand with perfect clarity what he had meant. The heroine of the novel was convinced that she would not know what true love was until she had seen the green ray—the mysterious celestial phenomenon created by atmospheric conditions. And ultimately, when she finally was in position to see it after many adventures and conquering countless hurdles, she deliberately looked away before she could see it, compelled instead to gaze into her lover's eyes. No, they couldn't see the green ray yet; they didn't have the answers to solve everything. But they had their love, and if that came first, then everything else would follow.

Her rational mind tried to reject this romantic outlook, but her heart reached for it and held onto it for dear life.

CHAPTER TEN

The days began to blur together again, but Bailey was happy. *Happy!* She allowed herself to be. There was no logical reason for it: the man she loved was set to marry the woman he had impregnated while she herself stood a fair chance of being executed or serving life in prison for murdering a man, but *Jake loved her!* Every morning she arose and demanded her tooth powder and wooden comb; she sat through her sessions with Cunningham and his team obediently; she read *The Green Ray* seven times. She forced herself to eat and stretch and exercise as best as she could, even though she had not stepped foot outside the courthouse in weeks. She absolutely forbade herself to think of the future beyond each day, to think about the slow progression of the hands of the clock, to think about growing old in her cell or not growing old at all. She had today.

She was obsessed with news of the mayoral campaign, greedily reading the stories in the newspapers Abe Lincoln gave her as Cunningham frowned and tapped his pencil impatiently. Jacob was going to win: Sabine was being portrayed as a buffoon and the men with power in the city had abandoned him more and more with each passing day. Meanwhile, Jacob gave speeches in English, French, German, Moravian, and even Spanish, appealing to the diverse population in the city. The reporters declared his French and Spanish to be shaky at best but gave him acclaim for trying. Her heart swelled with pride.

She was not at all surprised when, on the fourth of November, she had a visitor who was bursting with excitement. Johann Naplava had come to tell her himself that Jacob had won the election in a landslide, and that he wanted her to know he was going to keep his promise to her about the District. She questioned Johann just as fast as she could, hungry for information about where he was when he heard the results (Anton's house), what he said in his acceptance speech (he was going to start with his action plan for reforms the very day he took office on the first of January), what he wore (which elicited a frown of confusion and a helpless shrug from Johann). "I don't know about that one, Bail. You know, clothes, I guess. Pants. A shirt, vest, jacket. Oh, and his boots." Bailey laughed and threw part of the paper at him, causing the guard to growl at her and point his baton.

"Oh, and I almost forgot, Jacob sends his love," he leaned forward and whispered so the guard could not hear, and then smiled his dopey grin. "He's crazy about you, girl. *Never* shuts about you; my *God*, it's annoying! I don't know what's going to happen, but you should know that, I think."

She smiled for a solid week after that visit.

She had a steady stream of visitors, and during the days when no one came to call, she learned to shrug it off and go on with her day. More and more she dwelled inside her mind, building a detailed, glorious life with Jacob. Together they built a house on Feather Hill and went for long walks, discussing everything, *everything* under the sun, as only they could do. They rode the range herding sheep, danced in the barn surrounded with friends and family, greeted the morning with a kiss under the flamingo sky, talked to the trees in Lada's grove, fished in Glory Creek with Wenzel, and made love. Those fantasies grew and blossomed, feeding her hope and providing her with a vital and necessary will to live. In her mind they made love on his very familiar bed in his room, on the floor by the *Jake Loves Rosie* carving, by the creek, on the porch swing, in the cool cellar, in the hot hay mow of the ram barn, under the enormous live oak tree, in the wood shed amongst his incredible carvings, on the wide open range as the sheep meandered by, unimpressed, and—the most intense fantasy of them all—in the green meadow at the foot of Feather Hill, under the light of the moon, as he sang the "Green Meadow" song to her in his voice so true and pure. She remembered the feel of him, the smell and taste of him, with perfect recollection, and for the parts she didn't know, she filled in with her imagination, wondering how close she was to the real thing.

When she began to feel debauched, she would whisper to herself, *this is all of him that I'll ever have. I'll take this much.*

The day before the trial, Bailey was collected from her cell and led to the usual meeting room, and there followed a grueling four-hour session with Cunningham and his team. The questions flew fast and furious, and Bailey strove mightily to retain her focus.

"Hannah Birchwood has fetched you another outfit; it will be delivered to your cell at 7am. You will be allowed to bathe the night before."

"Okay…"

"Do you understand that the first day will only involve jury selection? You just need to sit with us at the defense table and look—well—innocent."

"I underst—"

"Day Two will begin with opening statements, and then the prosecution's case. He will strive to place you in the hotel room, which we aren't disputing. He will be relentless about defaming your character and will most likely have witnesses swearing that you were a prostitute."

"Yes, we've been over all of this—"

"Just remain calm but strive to have a look of injured disbelief, or something along those lines."

She rolled her eyes and didn't bother to reply.

"There will be expert testimony about the cause of death and the condition of the bodies. He will try to represent Mr. Hawk as being incapacitated, for which I will offer a rigorous cross-examination. His witnesses will be prostitutes, police officers, hotel staff, and the coroner."

She nodded. They had been over it dozens of times.

"And then he *may* call you to the stand; just answer his questions and don't worry that he's not allowing you to tell the whole story or distorting your answers. I'll take care of that in cross."

"What kind of questions will he ask again?" She already knew the answer to that one, but felt that since Cunningham was putting so much effort into this, she should show some initiative.

"There will only be a few questions and they will be very specific, and he will object loudly if you try to elaborate. As we have discussed, it's best not to bring up anything about the Vodnik. After all, it really doesn't have any impact on the case what *kind* of monster that bastard was, does it? We know he was one, and that's enough." She blushed and lowered her eyes. It mattered to *her*. Understanding Hawk as a monster in the most tangible manifestation of the word—not just as a metaphor—helped to make sense of something horrible and senseless.

Cunningham cleared his throat and went on. "Jennings' questions will include, 'Were you in the Gaslight Hotel Room #226 on the night of May twentieth, 1876? Was Senator Hawk in that room? Was there anyone else in the room? Did that person appear to be alive? Was Senator Hawk inebriated with alcohol or drugs or both? Did you shoot him? What weapon did you use? Was he seated or standing when you shot him? Could you have run from the room?'"

She nodded again, thoughtful. "For that last question, I really don't know the answer."

"Exactly! And that is what you must say. 'I don't know if I could have run away from him.' That is a key to our defense!"

"Is Jennings really that stupid?" she mused, causing all three men to chuckle.

"Not so much that he is stupid; he just believes that he has an airtight, open-and-shut case. He has no idea what's going to hit him. I've provided him with a list of witnesses and evidence in discovery, of course, but he will be flabbergasted at the truth that emerges."

Bailey raised an eyebrow at Cunningham's effusiveness. "Flabbergasted? You mean he really can't guess about the defense we are going to use?"

Cunningham stretched and gestured to Flanders, the man responsible for rounding up witnesses. "Care to answer that?"

Flanders nodded so emphatically that his round little spectacles almost jumped off his face. "Dr. Rose, I believe that Mr. Jennings will try very hard to establish that the dead woman in the room—oh, I beg your pardon—that she was a prostitute who was there to conduct—well—sexual business with Senator Hawk, and that you also visited the room to conduct sexual business, and that upon seeing the woman in the room, you shot her in jealousy and then shot Senator Hawk."

"Yes…" Really, she had heard it so many times that she was almost numb to it. She hoped that when those words emerged from that little skunk Jennings' mouth, she would have an honest, horrified reaction and not just sit in a stone-faced daze.

He cleared his throat and plowed on. "Well, he won't be expecting us to dispute the so-called fact that you were a prostitute. He'll be expecting us to say that the three of you struggled for the gun and it was an accidental shooting."

There was a silence as she digested this. It wasn't anything new, but honestly, she had her doubts that Jennings was too dumb to guess at their defense strategy.

"Jennings is confident that you've already been convicted by the press— which, by the way, he's *feeding*," added Flanders.

"Dr. Rose," interjected Cunningham softly. "Jennings has fallen into an old trap: he's starting to believe his own press; the fabrications that he himself has leaked. It's a fatal error because it has caused him to prepare improperly for this case. He has been concentrating all of his efforts on how to get you convicted rather than seeking the truth. That will be his downfall."

"Are you telling me that the truth always wins?" Bailey frowned skeptically.

"It sure does, with J.T. Cunningham defending you!" Abraham Lincoln pronounced.

She smiled then: these three men had become much more than her team of attorneys. "You know, I'm going to miss you gentlemen."

"You won't need to. You can visit us in Austin any time you like, and we shall visit you! I've always wanted a tour of St. Ursuline's!"

They were so damned confident. She wished she could feel the same.

She dressed with shaking hands the next day. The costume Hannah had procured for her was not quite so much of a perfect fit as the one for her arraignment: the skirt was acceptable, in shades of dark green bordered at the bottom with a stripe of gold ribbon. The matching jacket, however, featured absolutely enormous puffy sleeves and a ridiculous collar with lapels that were so large and pointy she guessed they looked like wings jutting from her breastbone. The blouse underneath featured a high collar that hugged her throat, and she immediately hated it. And the hat! It was a matching green, with two large, ungainly clusters of bows that left a valley right down the middle. She wondered if she could set something in the center, like a snack for later, perhaps. And Hannah had sent a corset, a firm indictment that she should conform to the proper standards for her important days in court. She stuffed her miserable pillow into it instead, lacing it tightly into a suitable hourglass figure, and propped it up on the cot.

"Wish me luck, Madame Corset," she whispered, and waited by the bars, hoping that Mrs. Knittle would be her matron today. She was wildly nervous.

It was not Mrs. Knittle; it was J.T. Cunningham himself who appeared at her cell, and after a startled double-take at her cot, offered a reassuring grin. "Good morning, Dr. Rose! Are you ready?"

She nodded stiffly, gritting her teeth to stop them from chattering, and waited as the guard unlocked the cage. She followed Cunningham through a maze of hallways, murmuring at what she hoped were the right times as he rambled on and on. He was nervous, too!

"Mr. Cunningham?" she managed to break in.

"Hmmm? Yes?"

"Will Jacob be in court today?"

He turned to look at her kindly. She looked so vulnerable and frightened; if Jacob ignored his wishes and appeared in court today, he would be hard-pressed to keep away from this young woman who appeared to desperately need a strong pair of sheltering arms.

"I have advised him not to be," he replied in a low voice, not wanting the guards to hear. She nodded, her face falling. "But that doesn't mean a damn thing," he added wryly.

They entered the courtroom a few moments later, and Bailey could not keep herself from gasping. The vast room was packed with people—*spectators,* she admitted to herself—every seat was filled, including the gallery! And as she entered, flanked by Cunningham, Flanders and Mooreland, the latter two who had appeared out of nowhere, every head turned and the courtroom erupted in a wave of murmurs. People pointed, mouths open; they gaped at her, the women hiding fascinated expressions behind fans and the men's eyes widening in curiosity. The murmur grew to a swell. Newspaper artists stumbled into the aisle, scribbling madly in their notebooks, attempting to capture her image; cameras were strictly prohibited here. She felt her face grow hot in its usual fashion and wondered if the artists would color her face bright red in tomorrow morning's edition, a special color edition! The red face of the Red Rose! She allowed herself a few seconds to search for a friendly face—oh, how she longed to see his smile—and was rewarded with Gabby's serene expression and Thomas's concerned one, the two of them seated near the rear of the room. Gabby nodded and smirked, as if to say, *stick it to them*!

Bailey began to feel less cowed and shifted her gaze up to the gallery almost defiantly—these folks came to see a show; why not at least let them see her face?—and almost stopped in her tracks in shock. *Charles Duke*! Mr. Duke stood with the other Mexicans and Negroes in the tightly-packed gallery; he was still waters amidst a raging sea of sweaty humanity, and when their eyes met, he raised his fist and shook it once, as if to say, *fight now*! His face was proud and strong. She raised her hand to him, but she lost sight of him at once as Cunningham led her on the long walk down the aisle. Oh, how her head was spinning! Before she had time to process Mr. Duke's presence, somehow she heard her name called within the confused clamor, and her head swiveled to the right: there sat her sister, Hope Miller, with Cordelia and Howard by her side. Hope was waving at her madly. "I believe you," she mouthed, and Bailey's breath caught in her throat. Her sister was here! She had never imagined her newfound family would make that trip!

Cunningham led her onward as the noise in the massive room swelled to a din, and just as she was about to reach her seat in the front row, her head turned to the left and her eyes landed on an entire row of Naplavas. There was Gacenka, looking terribly anxious, and Franticek, looking calm and quite dashing all dressed up in a gray suit. Wenzel gazed at her placidly, his eyes quiet. Next to them were Marianna and Miguel, who both offered a tight smile and a small wave but looked as nervous as she felt; Anton, who tipped his hat and winked, and Alice, who bit her fingernails and appeared troubled. Next to her was Lindy, who smiled genuinely and nodded as if to say, *you can do this*, and Johann, who was frowning and seemingly trying to restrain someone on his left.

Jacob. He was trying to hold Jacob down, who finally put a hand on Johann's chest and pushed him back, none too gently, and rose halfway out of his seat so he could see her clearly.

Her eyes met his for what could have only been two seconds, but it was enough to allow every bit of tension to release from her body. His expression was calm and his lips were tipped up in his ever-present, merry half-grin. Her shoulders straightened and her chin raised, and she felt courage course through her veins. Jacob pointed two fingers toward her then touched his heart, a gesture that was becoming so very familiar to her, and she returned it an instant before she was ushered on by Cunningham, who was swearing audibly. As she was seated at the defense table, her heart pounded in her chest, not from fear, but from elation.

He was here!

Judge Simmons entered a few moments later, pounded a gavel, and glared at the room, which quickly silenced.

"I'll have you know that there will be no hullabaloo in my courtroom! If you have come to watch, you will do so silently or you'll be on your arse on the street!" There were a few titters that were immediately hushed by a fierce scowl. His muttonchops quivered with indignation. "Today we will begin jury selection, and by God, we will finish it today, too."

And then, without further ado and with amazing rapidity, selection was underway. White men in groups of twelve from all walks of life were paraded in and seated in jury seats to be questioned by Jennings and Cunningham. The initial questions were very basic: Are you eighteen years of age? Are you a citizen of the United States? Are you able to read and understand the English language? This last qualifier excused twenty-three of the 152 men who had been summoned. Are you a resident of Bexar County? Have you been convicted of any indictable offense in any state or federal court? This question took care of another seventeen men. This trial is expected to last for at least four days. Is there anything about the length or scheduling of the trial that would interfere with your ability to serve? Thirteen more men were excused. Do you have any medical, personal, or financial problem that would prevent you from serving? Eighteen more men who admitted that they could not afford to lose four days' wages were down for the count.

The juror pool was read the name of the witnesses—many of whom were prostitutes and police officers—and asked if they knew any of them. There followed a rather entertaining dismissal of six men who confessed to knowing Lula or Gretchen or Billie Rae, and with sheepish looks on their faces, were escorted from the courtroom. Thirty-one were excused based on the fact that they had already formed an opinion of innocence or guilt.

For those who remained—a mere forty-four—the rigorous *voir dire* commenced. Bailey had been instructed to face forward at all times and not to turn to catch the eye of family or friends, but she was dying to see a friendly face again: a few of the jurors sat and glared at her as they were being questioned, and of course, those men were challenged by Cunningham. He used his peremptory challenges judiciously and managed to challenge many jurors for cause with a few succinct questions. A brief break for lunch was offered, but Cunningham placed a restraining hand on her arm and instructed her to stay seated.

"Don't turn around," he whispered. "We will eat here at the table."

"Why?"

"This isn't the time to talk to family and friends or let the press near you. We need to keep the spectacle to a minimum."

She frowned. "I'm a spectacle?"

"Not by choice," he sighed, reaching into a duffle and withdrawing a sandwich wrapped in paper and an apple. He offered it to her and she accepted it glumly. "But yes, this is a circus."

She ate silently, wondering if Jacob still sat behind her, wondering if his eyes were tracking her every movement even now. She felt the hairs on the back of her neck raise just thinking about it.

Abe Lincoln leaned forward with a friendly smile. "Just so you know, about half of the courtroom has emptied and I doubt they'll return. Jury selection is a pretty dull business. Why, there goes that new mayor-elect now, that nice young rancher fellow. I hear he has a meeting this afternoon with Jim Hogg, no less!"

Bailey returned his smile, relieved, in a way, that Jacob had taken his leave. And to meet with the governor of Texas! "He shouldn't be here," she whispered.

Cunningham shrugged. "I can't tell that boy anything," he grumbled. "But you're right."

Judge Simmons returned a few moments later and banged the gavel again, and twelve more men were paraded in. The questions went on and on—it was interminable—and Bailey fought to keep the proper expression on her face: innocent, horrified and injured by the charges and imprisonment, a proper lady who has been dealt an unfair hand. She longed to yawn; she was desperate to get up and stretch and rip the tight collar from her throat; she needed to scratch her head where the hat was pinned tightly. Yet she sat straight, perfecting the look of humility and dignity. Her mind began to wander to Jacob, and she was in the midst of riding behind him on the range, her hands encircling his waist and creeping up under his shirt, when the sound of the gavel brought her to her startled senses.

"Very well, that concludes today. The jury has been selected and opening statements will begin tomorrow promptly at nine." He continued to issue instructions to the jury, and Bailey stared at them, marveling at the fact that these twelve men held her fate in their hands. Cunningham nudged her and pushed a note in front of her.

Stop staring at the jury, he had written in a quick hand. She colored and looked at the judge, feeling irritable and downright *pissed off*—one of Gabby's favorite terms—at her lawyer, who seemed to be treating her like a recalcitrant child as of late. Wear an innocent look on your face. Don't look at your family or friends. Don't look at the jury. And Hannah Birchwood sending her a corset! Had Cunningham ordered that as well?

She snuck a peek at the jury just to defy the young man beside her. She had been paying close enough attention to know a little bit about each one of them: the huge, clumsy, kind-looking man dressed in a shabby brown tweed suit in the first chair was, ironically, a schoolteacher, even though he looked like he should be chopping down trees and sending them down the river. She remembered that she had liked his answer to Cunningham's question about presumption of guilt: "I have never presumed anything about anyone; in fact, I'm very deliberate in my judgments." Speedy Simmons had audibly groaned, which had caused a few titters.

The very young man seated next to him was short and fat and clean-shaven; he spoke with a thick Dutch accent and worked in the ticket booth for the railroad. Next to him was another short man, this one slight and thin and darkly handsome, who sported an alarming pair of green and cream checkered trousers, a long-tailed black frock and green bow-tie, and a towering top hat, which he had placed delicately in his lap. He was a stage actor and spoke with a mellifluous voice that carried to the far reaches of the gallery. Bailey was enchanted by his answer to Cunningham's question about whether or not he believed women should be doctors: he had looked directly at her and intoned, "I am no bird; and no net ensnares me: I am a free human being with an independent will." Judge Simmons had quirked an eyebrow in confusion and several in the audience had laughed, but Bailey had beamed: he had quoted Charlotte Brontë! Jennings frantically tried to have the man challenged for cause, having used up his preemptory challenges, but to no avail.

Seated next to the dapper actor was a strapping, middle-aged Irishman with bushy red hair and bright eyes; he was a farmer and was the only member of the jury who avowed to have absolutely no prior knowledge of the case, having been completely consumed with harvest and no access to the dailies; a dream juror for Cunningham and not a bad choice for Jennings, either. Next to the farmer was an older man with a neatly trimmed white mustache and a crisp white collar to match, worn with an immaculate gray morning coat and gray trousers. He was a wealthy banker, and he wore his wealth on his gold pocket watch, complete with a fob, and on his shoes: Bailey had noticed, as he entered, that his highly polished black boots featured diamond-encrusted buckles. He was one of the *glaring goons*. Completing the bottom row of the jury panel was a tall, gangly-looking young man with a bad complexion and a stutter: he was employed as a stable boy at the Menger Hotel and had assiduously avoided looking at Bailey at all, which made her almost as nervous as his scowling neighbor.

The top row began with a fair-haired, thirty-something rough-looking fellow with squinty eyes and a fierce frown: he was also employed as a banker in the city. Next to him was a sparse, elderly gentleman with a gentle expression and a long, gray beard, who was retired from a professorial position at the Agricultural and Mechanical College of Texas. Seated beside him was the juror she feared the most: a dark-haired man, a handyman on a cattle ranch, about her own age with a powerful build and a chilling, flat expression. She was instantly repulsed by him, and when their gazes had collided when he first arrived in the courtroom, his expression said *death*. She had frantically scratched a note to Cunningham, *Not him!*, but her attorney had been unsuccessful in challenging for cause—the man answered all of the questions quite well with a pleasant expression—and as it was late in the day, Cunningham had used all of his preemptory challenges. The next man was a horse wrangler who sported a distinct band of white skin along his hat line and a tough, weathered face and hands. Beside him was a merchant; the suave, stylish owner of a fashionable haberdashery downtown. And the last man was a sheep man, praise be! And a Moravian, to boot! Bailey had never met him, but she was willing to bet that she knew someone from the Hill Country who knew this forty-something man with a calm, take-charge demeanor and an articulate voice almost devoid of accent. This man was named foreman, and Bailey could have sworn he glanced at her and tipped his lips into a smile before quickly looking away.

Twelve men to decide whether she would hang by the neck, grow old and wither away in prison, or walk out of this room, free to live her life. She stared at them openly now, helpless to look away, disregarding the sharp poke under the table from Cunningham. She had avoided men for most of her life, being raised by women—first harlots, then nuns. She trusted so few men, and rightly so. And now these twelve strangers held her fate in their hands.

She squeezed her eyes shut and prayed.

CHAPTER ELEVEN

They were dismissed a few moments later, and she was paraded once again down the center aisle. The Naplavas, minus Jacob and Johann, were still there, smiling at her, Gacenka even reaching a hand toward her and achieving a brief squeeze before her guard nudged Bailey forward with a frown. Hope, Cordelia, and Howard had departed, presumably at the lunch break, as had Thomas and Gabby, who no doubt needed to return home to nurse the baby. She did spot Sister Anna, Karl Schwartz, and dear little Rachel from the clinic, who all sat together near the back and waved to her. One quick look in the gallery confirmed that Charles Duke was one of the few who remained there, and he stood straight and tall and tipped his hat to her, careful not to smile or be too familiar, as the guard in the gallery was already shepherding the loiterers toward the door.

She raised her hand to all of them and felt blessed.

The next morning she arose and dressed in her brown outfit—it was so much more comfortable—and bypassed a hat altogether, choosing instead to clip part of the ribbon from the dress and work it through her hair, which she gathered in a low puffy bun at the nape of her neck. When Cunningham came to lead her to the courtroom he whistled in appreciation. "Dr. Rose, if I may be so bold, you look magnificent!"

She laughed and shook her head disbelievingly. "Maybe for a woman who hasn't had a decent bath for a month!"

He winced. "Well, you must be doing something right because you smell quite nice, I should say."

She regarded him steadily, marveling at the closeness that had developed between them. "You know, you feel like a brother," she confessed. "Sometimes I want to hug you, and other times, I just want to smack you in the head."

"Which is it today?"

She frowned thoughtfully. "We'll have to wait and see. If you pass me any more bossy notes, I'm going to smack you in the head and mess up your pretty hair."

He roared and they made their way down the hall, the jitters effectively under control with their clowning. But when the guard opened the doors to Courtroom #1, it was a replay of yesterday, only twice as congested. People had been packed in like sardines, and reporters were *everywhere*: in the aisles, standing on the benches, hanging precariously over the gallery railing. She strained to see her family and friends, and was rewarded with a glimpse of Charles, Thomas and Gabby, the Millers, and the row of Naplavas. Today Jacob sat on the aisle, and she felt his eyes on her for the duration of her long walk. When she reached him and met his eyes, he reached for her hand, squeezing it tightly before Cunningham pulled her away. She flushed to the roots of her hair and hoped to God that a reporter hadn't witnessed that little scene, but with Cunningham pressed to her side, Flanders directly in front of her, and Mooreland on her very heels, there wasn't a chance. She was keenly relieved that Caroline was confined to her home with her "diphtheria complications." If she would have gotten an eyeful of that exchange, Jacob would have hell to pay.

They stood at the defense table until Judge Simmons entered, sat, and pounded the gavel for order. "Shut up!" he roared, having no patience for elaboration, and the room hushed. "Be seated." There was a shuffle as the crowd lowered themselves; the defense and prosecution teams remained standing.

"I will now read the indictment as prepared by the Grand Jury." He began to read with such a rapid, sometimes unintelligible pace that a few in the audience could not subdue their snickers. "The Jurors for the said County of Bexar of the State of Texas, in their oath present that Bailey Faith Rose, of St. Ursuline's Academy in the town of San Antonio, County of Bexar, on the twentieth day of May in the year eighteen hundred and seventy-six, in and upon one Adam Rutherford Hawk, feloniously, willfully and of her malice aforethought, an assault did make, and with a certain weapon, to wit, a .38 caliber pistol, delivered a mortal wound to the heart, of which said mortal wound the said Adam Rutherford Hawk then and there instantly died. And so the Jurors aforesaid, upon their oath aforesaid, do say, that the said Bailey Faith Rose, the said Adam Rutherford Hawk, in manner and form aforesaid, then and there feloniously, willfully and of her malice aforethought did kill and murder; against the peace of said State of Texas, County of Bexar and contrary to the form of the statute in such case made and prevailed."

There followed a heavy silence that pressed the weight of the world down upon her shoulders. In front of her friends and family she stood accused of murder with *malice and aforethought*. She felt tears prick her eyes and pinched herself hard to stop them. She had heard this indictment read at her arraignment, but for some reason, now the words inspired a heretofore absent sensation of disbelief and rage.

"Opening statement, prosecution," Simmons snapped, and just like that, the trial began. Jennings shot to his feet—no doubt trying to please the judge with his haste—and began to pace up and down in front of the jury. He was dressed in a somber black brushed-cotton sack coat with matching trousers, a gray striped Comstock vest, and the requisite silver pocket watch with a precisely-draped chain tucked into an interior pocket. Oddly enough, he sported a maroon bow tie with tiny yellow dots; a downright *whimsical* choice. She wondered what advantage he believed that would give him: perhaps it was his way of letting the jury know what an affable, fun-loving gentleman he was. The thought of Augustus Jennings engaging in activity that could be considered whimsical or fun made her want to grin, but she kept the grave expression firmly on her face, aware of Cunningham's severe instructions.

"May it please your Honor, Mr. Foreman, and Gentlemen of the Jury," he began in his nasally voice, "Upon the twentieth day of May of the year eighteen and seventy-six—now I beg of you, do not let the passage of fifteen years diminish the import of this heinous crime, for that would be just an egregious and highly negligent crime in and of itself—upon this day, an honorable gentleman, a great man and politician, a Senator of this *United States of America*, one who was steadily making his fruitful journey toward the nothing less than the *White House*, mind you—a young man, full of promise and brilliance and forward-thinking, progressive ideas for this country—this young man, without a known enemy in the world, in his own hotel room, under the cloak of falling dusk in the midst of the activities of a busy, prosperous hotel in this great city of ours, was killed, shot dead, with a bullet to the heart. Today, a woman of questionable social position and reputation and character, is at the bar of this Court, accused by the Grand Jury of this County of this wicked crime."

For all of his quickness of body, Jennings was taking his sweet time with his speech, stretching his words into incessant sentences that wandered and looped back upon themselves until Judge Simmons wriggled with impatience in his chair. The jury, however, appeared to be captivated, and there was not a sound in the courtroom from the gathered masses. Bailey wondered what Jacob could be thinking. *A woman of questionable social position and reputation and character. A wicked woman.*

"There is no language, your Honor and gentlemen of the jury, at my command, which can better measure the earnest significance of this inquiry which you are about to inaugurate, than this simple statement of fact." On and on he intoned, his sharp voice pecking away at the edges of her resolve to remain strong and stalwart. She endeavored to tune him out as he extolled the virtues of the monster that was Adam Hawk and described the excitement of the citizens of San Antonio every time he made one of his surprise—and frequent—trips to the great city. Jennings labored over Hawk's love for San Antonio, his holiday destination of choice, and how this love affair had brought other important men and favorable notice to the city. Bailey glanced at Simmons and noticed he was growing more and more fidgety by the moment. Jennings was doing himself no favors with his long-winded speech. Not until a full fifteen minutes into his monologue did she hear her name mentioned again.

"Your Honor, and gentlemen of the jury, it will be my responsibility and burden to demonstrate to you, beyond a reasonable doubt, that this women, Bailey F. Rose, was raised in a brothel, which is commonly known as and remains known as Fort Allen. She worked there as a prostitute; this fact will be proven beyond a reasonable doubt. She had been pursuing Senator Adam Hawk, and as an honorable gentleman, he had repelled her advances, as she was a young girl. Gentlemen!" He spun and pointed to a juror; the gangly stable boy, who blushed and sank down into his chair. "Do not be swayed by her age at the time! She had reached full maturity and was regularly engaged in adult activities, as will be proven beyond a reasonable doubt. She was of sound mind and a vengeful nature! We all know that children can be capable of wicked deeds; indeed, evil has no age restriction. Children have committed monstrous crimes in this country and have been successfully and rightfully prosecuted for them; why, there are hundreds of precedents for this! Be she fourteen years of age, or sixteen, or eighteen, or twenty-three, what matters, I beg you? If a human being knowingly and purposefully and with malice aforethought takes the life of another, that human being should be made to pay for that crime, I think—I should *hope*—that you all understand that." He glared at a few of the jurors, as if chastising them for not being smart enough to understand a simple concept.

"And now I will tell you about this crime. Miss Rose, as I have explained to you, was engaged as a prostitute in the parlor known as Fort Allen. Senator Hawk frequented that parlor. Gentlemen, I ask you, who among you is not acquainted with a good and honorable man who has, at least once in his lifetime, and possibly more often than that, found himself—sometimes with dim recollection from innocent, celebratory drink, or perhaps in a fog of grief, depression, loneliness, or anger, in a house of ill repute?" He searched the faces of each of the jurors in turn, some of whom were no doubt struggling to follow the long string of confusing syntax to decipher the question. None of them blinked, moved, nodded or vocalized in any way, of course, not wanting to reveal himself or his acquaintances as patrons of vice, and so the question was an incredibly effective rhetorical ploy. The resounding silence seemed to offer acquiescence, and Bailey resisted the urge to groan. Somehow he had just made a visit to a brothel a perfectly acceptable, even inevitable, downright *universal* hobby. Jennings nodded, a kind, understanding smile upon his face.

"Of course, of course. Well, Senator Hawk had found himself in just that position whilst on holiday in our grand city, only to be the object of a girl's crazed obsession. And on the evening of May twentieth, when this young girl discovered that another, older, more beautiful, more experienced lady of the evening had arranged to meet Senator Hawk in the privacy of his hotel room, she flew into a jealous rage! It will be proved, beyond a reasonable doubt, that this girl, upon discovering that Senator Hawk was staying at the Gaslight Hotel, walked to that hotel, entered the hotel and spoke to a doorman to discover the room number of poor Senator Hawk, knocked upon the door, and that when the older prostitute opened the door, Miss Rose shot her through the heart! The poor woman died by the door, and Miss Rose dragged her body to the bed, arranging her in a ghoulish display, leaving trails of blood from the door to the bed! Shot her dead, with one shot straight through the heart, leaving the bed awash in the poor woman's blood!" This last sentence was delivered with a fair amount of histrionics, and the effect was evident on the faces of most of the jury.

Bailey gasped—she couldn't help herself—and the sound ended in a quiet sob. The wave of grief that had been suppressed up to this point with a herculean will threatened to crash over her, and she buried her face in her hands, oblivious to Jacob's attempt to rise three rows behind her, only to be pushed back down again by Johann with a hiss in the ear. Abe Lincoln placed a comforting hand upon her shoulder. Her mother! Her poor, broken mother, dead after having sacrificed herself for her daughter, and this hateful man was leading the jury to believe that she herself had pulled the trigger!

Abe leaned down to her and whispered in her ear. "Chin up, Dr. Rose. All lies, damned lies, and everyone will know it soon. Now be brave; I'll bet your Mama is watching." She took a deep breath and nodded, feeling greatly comforted by his kind words. One glance at Cunningham's face reassured her: her emotional display apparently was in line with his strategy.

"Yes!" Jennings was still going, steam full on now. "And after she killed that poor woman—the identity of whom we will never know, sadly, as no person came forward to identify or claim her body—Miss Rose lay in wait for Senator Hawk. For an hour she waited, crouched by the door, covered in the blood of the other poor woman. And when at last he entered the room, she pulled the trigger and shot him, straight through the heart! And while he lay dying she filled him with drugs in a desperate, clumsy attempt to cover her evil deed. Yes! She did! She left Fort Allen and entered the Gaslight Hotel that evening with one purpose and one purpose only: to kill that lady of the evening who had captured the heart of the object of her own obsession, and then to turn the gun upon Senator Hawk himself, to put a bullet through the heart that refused to bow to her despicable, filthy desires, and to conveniently leave a scene of an apparent murder-suicide."

Jennings turned to stare at her then, his eyes full of accusation and disgust, and she forced herself to hold his gaze. She shook her head, over and over again, unable to help herself. That a man of the law, sworn to seek the truth, could proffer such lies, was devastating.

He turned back to the jury as if he could no longer stand the sight of her. "And then, your Honor, and gentlemen of the jury, she fled from the room, dropping the gun in the hallway in a panic—we strongly believe she meant to leave it in the hands of the older prostitute but did not have time to do so when she heard hotel staff approaching to investigate the shot—and sought refuge in the place whereupon she knew she would never be sought: St. Ursuline's Academy. The good, saintly sisters of this revered institution took her in, never imagining the monster they were sheltering." He paused for several seconds and shook his head at the floor, hands on hips, to show the jury how deeply sorry he was for the poor, deceived nuns of St. Ursuline's. Finally he looked up and began again. "What followed was another travesty, gentlemen. The police officers called to the scene were instructed by a well-meaning but greatly misguided chief, who is no longer living. This chief of police directed the officers to falsify the reports that were released to the newspapers in an attempt to preserve the reputation of Senator Hawk. The falsified report omits any mention of the younger brothel girl—*a girl that hotel staff spoke to and directed to the room!*—only the older woman is included. The falsified report states that the woman died in the bed, with the gun in her hand, and concludes that after she shot Senator Hawk, she killed herself. This was false, as will be proven beyond a reasonable doubt. The true report—preserved and recently brought to light by a courageous young detective—tells the true story, gentlemen. The story of an older prostitute who was shot by the door—of course, when she opened it to Miss Rose—and a hapless man who was then shot as he entered the hotel room an hour later, having no inclination that a deviant was waiting to put a bullet through his heart." The last four words seemed to resound through the cavernous room. He had given them an extra punch, and they hung in the air, ringing in the ears of the jurors, the gathered masses, and Bailey herself.

A bullet through his heart. It was the only part of the dreadful story that was true, and perhaps the only part that would end up counting for anything. She had, indeed, put a bullet through Adam Hawk's heart. She still remembered the sound of it hitting his flesh, the little grunt he made, the way his body jerked and his fists opened and closed before he was still.

Jennings droned on and on about the witnesses he would call, the forensics, and the preponderance of evidence he would provide the court, but Bailey stopped listening. She was back in Room #226, tied to her chair with her red sashes of the dress she had sewn herself to wear to the German school. Her arms throbbed where he had injected her with her mother's drugs. Her head bobbed uncontrollably and there was a bitter taste in her mouth. She was just regaining consciousness, wondering if she were alive or dead, innocent or defiled. She was trying so hard to claw her way out of the fog.

At some point she realized that Jennings had ceased speaking and was taking his seat. She looked up, dazed, and immediately regretted it: the glaring juror was doing his thing, pinning her to her seat with his hateful eyes. The dark man with the flat gaze was looking at her, too, his eyes so completely devoid of expression that she was sure he must be dead on the inside; maybe one of those voodoo zombies Gabby's aunt had always warned them about! The others, however, looked rather, well, *unmoved*. The story already seemed unlikely on so many different levels: why didn't anyone hear the first shot and come to investigate? How would a small girl move a dead body across a room and onto a bed? And would someone who had taken so much time to plan a murder be careless enough to just throw the weapon in the hallway? Those were the questions that bothered her analytical mind, and she suspected that the jurors were grappling with them as well.

She looked at Simmons: he was frowning at Jennings, his muttonchops jumping as he clenched his jaws together. Jennings had stolen a full forty minutes of his day! Abe scribbled a note and pushed it to her inconspicuously. *A horrible misstep for Jennings. Simmons is irate and the jury does not look to be convinced at all. What an idiotic story!* She didn't know if he was right about all of the jury members, but he was dead on about the judge, who snapped to Cunningham to *please* make his opening statement as succinct as possible.

Cunningham rose to his feet with efficient and athletic grace and strode to the jury panel. He cut a fine, serious figure as he stood there for just a few seconds in silence. When he spoke, his deep voice was reasonable and natural, quite unlike Jennings' shrill, overly-dramatic display.

"Gentleman of the jury and Your Honor," he began, talking quickly and urgently but somehow not rushing his words. "What you have just heard is a fictitious account of the tragic events of the twentieth of May, eighteen hundred and seventy-six. An utterly fictitious account." He turned to directly address his next remarks to the jury. "And I believe that many of you are quite keen enough to detect the egregious holes in Mr. Jennings' version of events." He let that sit for a few seconds, and Bailey could have sworn that a few of the jurors nodded almost imperceptibly. "Fact and fiction will war in this courtroom, and the truth will have its day. The truth! The truth will *always* prevail amongst men of honor and intelligence. And so I ask of you, gentlemen of the jury and Mr. Foreman, that you allow the evidence to speak, to tell the story of what *really* transpired in that hotel room so long ago. My duty now is to explain—" here he turned and gave a nod to Judge Simmons—"*briefly*,"—and the audience laughed in appreciation; even Simmons gave a half-snort—"what the evidence will prove beyond a reasonable doubt, even though that is *not* the standard for which *I* am held to! It is, nonetheless, the state of mind that this defense will achieve! You will know, and be assured of, and feel, afterwards, that you have achieved a full exercise of justice, *beyond any reasonable doubt*, after you are permitted access to the evidence my team will present."

He nodded to the judge, the audience, and the jury, and then began again. "The evidence will prove that here before you is a young woman, aged twenty-seven, who, in eighteen hundred and seventy-six, was but a mere twelve years of age." He did not notice, of course, the concerned frown on the face of his good friend Jacob. "She was, indeed, up to that point in her life, raised in Fort Allen, an upscale parlor, or brothel, in what is commonly known as the Red Light District. The evidence will prove that this girl lived under the porch—*under the porch*, gentleman, even on the coldest of January nights—in abject poverty, and was fed only sporadically and beaten often by the proprietress of that establishment. This we will prove, with no doubt in your mind, that this young girl, known as Bailey Rose, did *not* work as a prostitute in this parlor, or any parlor, brothel, cat house or anywhere else on this earth, but instead, was made to labor in the kitchen and laundry of Fort Allen for several hours each day, from the tender age of four years old. We have an *overwhelming number of witnesses* to attest to this fact! Women who worked at Fort Allen and other establishments; patrons of Fort Allen, and the list goes on and on!"

He paused only to take a breath. "This very young girl, small for her age due to malnutrition, survived by her wits and the help of others in the community. Why did she dwell at Fort Allen? Because her mother was a prostitute there. And now let me tell you about this woman, Adele Rosemont." Bailey sucked in her breath and steeled herself; Cunningham had told her exactly what he would say, but she knew she would cry nonetheless. She had become a blubbering, sobbing mess over the past six months. "Adele Rosemont was born into a wealthy Pennsylvania family, and on her fifth birthday, a horrific tragedy befell that family. Out for a ride in her new cart and pony with her mother, her mother was shot in the throat, to perish later that same day, and Adele, the sweet little toddler, was kidnapped for ransom." Several in the room gasped, and a few of the jury members shifted uncomfortably. "She was held for weeks, and when she was finally recovered, she was injured in unimaginable ways." He paused and turned to the crowd. "I would ask now that any women present may want to take their leave, or cover their ears so they might not be subjected to what I am about to say." There was absolutely not a sound in the room. He waited a few more beats to see if any females would take his advice, then nodded solemnly and continued.

"The tiny girl, Adele, who was known as Della, had been violated; subjected to unconscionable sexual abuse. She had been injected with morphine repeatedly, no doubt to keep her quiet and submissive, as had all of the other children who had fallen victim to these criminals." Several women gasped, a few cried out, and three women fled from the room noisily, amidst much murmuring and whispering. Bailey lowered her face into her hands. But Cunningham was not finished. "As you can imagine, the effects of this horror left an indelible stamp on Adele's life. She grew up with no self-worth, her body craving the drugs with which they had filled her, fearful, and lonely, even when surrounded by a loving family. Her society marked her as a pariah and her family was forced to Europe. Eventually she found the drugs again and became impregnated by a heartless, wealthy, supposedly upstanding young man of a banker, who promised to marry her and then *left her at the altar.* Left her! Proving once again, to her, that she was the worthless trash that the kidnappers told her she was. She gave birth and immediately ran away, leaving the care of her daughter to her sister and her family, determined to give that daughter a chance to be a respected member of society, something she could never be again in that heartless culture." He stopped and allowed all of this information to sink in. Bailey could see at a glance that he had commanded the full attention of the jury, and he took advantage of it, making solemn eye contact with each and every one of them so that they could see he spoke the truth.

"She made good in San Antonio, in our great city, gentlemen. She found a position as a dressmaker and, for the first time, began to feel as though she had a clean start. And to enrich her life even more, she was introduced to a highly-respected doctor, a surgeon of the Great War, home on leave! Dr. John Bailey was his name." Twelve pairs of eyes swiveled Bailey's way, and she lifted her chin, profoundly proud of her father. Cunningham listed the battles John Bailey had been involved in, performing the miraculous feat of never once mentioning on which side of the war John Bailey had fought, still a source of intense contention and pain amongst citizens of San Antonio. He painted a portrait of a hero, a selfless, skilled doctor who was known to wade onto the battlefield and find wounded men who could be saved, regardless of the color of his uniform. The eyes of several of the jurors became misty. "And when home on leave, he met the beautiful Miss Rosemont, courted her, and proposed to her. And the day before they were to be married, gentlemen, can you believe what happened? He was called back to his regiment, ordered to report early the next morning. The couple rushed to find a pastor or justice or judge, but no one was available, and so they conducted their own private service, with John's family in attendance. They had one night together, knowing they may never see each other again; and indeed, they were correct gentlemen, for John Bailey died in battle shortly thereafter, leaving behind his progeny."

There followed a breathless silence as the jurors and audience registered what Cunningham was telling them. *John Bailey had impregnated his young, not-*

quite bride. "Yes," Cunningham finally said in a low, mournful voice. "She was alone, *again,* with a babe on the way, all alone on this planet, and once her condition was known, she lost her position and her room and was thrown out onto the street. She was too ashamed to seek John's family, but it wouldn't have mattered: they were being hunted like dogs for their loyalty to the United States of America; she would have been in more danger with them. And so, hungry and penniless and desperate, she was taken in by the sharp-eyed proprietress of Fort Allen. She was spotted by Blanche Dubois sitting on a bench, and this madam knew a refined beauty when she saw one! It didn't take much to reel Adele in, gentlemen: she was hungry and afraid, and Blanche assured her a position in the kitchen, perfectly harmless. But it wasn't long after the baby was born that Adele Rosemont was lured back into the sick, wretched world of morphine and cocaine, and soon after, was working upstairs with the rest of the fallen angels of the night. Her transformation from Adele Rosemont to Addie Rose was complete."

Cunningham had effortlessly established Bailey's mother as a prostitute at Fort Allen: she could see that the jurors—even the scary ones—believed every word of it. And if they didn't, there were so many witnesses lined up to attest to this fact that it really would be incontrovertible. "Meanwhile," continued Cunningham, striding over to Bailey and laying a hand on the table, "her baby was raised in a haphazard fashion, tended to when remembered, spending most of her time under the porch, out of sight of the wealthy, powerful patrons. She spent most of her days on the streets of our city, seeking survival. She never capitulated to drugs or prostitution." He suddenly, swiftly bent over and slammed his palm on the table, making her jump. "Never!" He whirled to the jury. "Mr. Jennings has been misled; he's been lied to. I have multiple witnesses, including leaders of this community, who will swear on this Bible," here he lifted the Bible from the witness stand and shook it at the jury, "that Bailey Rose was never engaged as a prostitute!"

Three rows behind Bailey, the blood drained from Jacob's face. His mouth opened and closed, and his gaze darted to his father, who was looking back at him with a similar, confounded expression. Jacob fought to control his breathing. How could Cunningham claim this? He and his father had heard first-hand, from *everyone* in that damned place on that despicable night fifteen years ago, that Bailey was a prostitute, and furthermore, that she was fourteen years old, not twelve. If Cunningham got caught in false claims, it could mean Bailey's life, and that was an asinine risk since Cunningham could damn well have a solid self-defense claim without the need to prove her purity. He felt helpless.

Cunningham walked back to the jury and stood in front of them gravely. "And now, gentlemen of the jury, Mr. Foreman, and Your Honor, allow me to tell you what really happened on the night of May twentieth, eighteen hundred and seventy-six. Bailey Rose, after spending five days out of the city with a friend, arrived back in the city and made her way to Fort Allen to seek permission from her mother to spend the summer with this family." Bailey was careful to maintain a neutral expression, but on the inside, she was wincing. She failed to understand how Cunningham would ever be able to keep the Naplavas off the witness stand; wouldn't someone have to verify where she had been? Cunningham had assured her that if he had to call someone, he would call Franticek and Gacenka. But his eyes had shifted when he said it. She knew, *she knew*, that Jacob would have to be called, and she had nightmares about the city calling for a repeal of the young mayor-elect.

"But when she arrived at Fort Allen, her mother was not there. A working girl named Lola told her the horrible truth, gentleman. And she's going to tell *you* this truth, too. Lola told her that Senator Adam Hawk had visited Fort Allen looking for a little girl—Bailey Rose. Why was he looking for Bailey Rose? Because he was obsessed with her mother—Addie Rose—and had been rejected, and now his attention had shifted to her daughter, perhaps in genuine interest, perhaps from a desire for reprisal." Cunningham had to tread very softly here: what he was implying was that a respected senator had been pursuing a twelve-year-old girl, and the jury would balk at this without evidence. Already the more skeptical members were frowning. "Lola told Bailey that Addie had followed the senator to the Gaslight Hotel to convince him to leave her daughter alone, and she was there with him now. The girl was appalled: she was afraid for her mother, who was weak and confused from addiction. So what did she do? I ask you, what would *you* do if your mother was in danger?" He paused for effect. "She went to the Gaslight Hotel, gentleman. This little girl ran the whole way, afraid for her mother, wanting to see her again before she—Bailey—fled her horrible life at Fort Allen. Maybe she just wanted to say goodbye."

Cunningham strode slowly back to Bailey's table and laid his hand gently on it this time. He bowed his head solemnly. "When she arrived, she walked right through the front door. A kindly doorman—you will hear from Mr. Jones—directed her to Room #226, and she made her way up, alone. All alone, a little girl in a too-big dress, barefoot, terrified." The courtroom was absolutely silent, holding its collective breath, waiting, waiting for the horrific story to be told. "When she opened the door, a woman did not answer, as Mr. Jennings mistakenly believes. Nothing could be further from the truth. Senator Adam Hawk answered his own door, gentlemen, and when he saw who it was, he yanked her into the room, threw her to the floor, slammed the door, and then yanked her back to her feet again and ordered her to look at the bed." Again, the silence lay like a cloak over the room. "She did not want to look at the bed, because she already suspected what she would see there. When she refused, he struck her across the face and forced her to look. And what she saw was…well, it was her mother. *Her mother*. Dead, on the bed, in a pool of blood." Several of the women who had stayed in the courtroom gasped, and there was a general shifting and murmuring that roused Judge Simmons and spurred him to bang his gavel.

"Quiet!" He roared, and there was quiet.

Cunningham nodded at the judge and continued. "The little girl lost consciousness when she saw her mother, and when she awoke, she was bound to a chair with the sashes of her own dress. Senator Hawk was on the floor in front of her, propped up against the wall, an empty whisky bottle by his side. He was in a faint from drink, asleep with a gun in his hand." He said it so quickly, so casually, that many members of the audience and a few members of the jury thought they may have misunderstood. He looked up and looked around. "Oh, yes. That's what I said. He was passed clean out with a gun in his hand. And when this little girl tried to get up to take the gun away, she realized that she had been injected with drugs: she was very familiar with the smell of morphine from her mother's long-time addiction. She was dizzy and nauseated and she got sick, but she managed to get the gun before she collapsed again in the chair. And then he woke up. Do you know what he told her, Mr. Foreman? Gentlemen of the jury? He told her that as soon as he was able, he would get up and pursue her until he possessed her, in every sense of the word."

Bailey squeezed her eyes shut again, scarcely able to withstand a hot flash of shame. She knew it wasn't her fault, Hawk's sick desire for her, but she felt it nonetheless, a loathing for herself. Cunningham was glossing over some parts, by necessity, of course, but she could only imagine what the jury would do if she swore, on the stand, that Hawk was a Vodnik. Cunningham had expressly forbidden her from bringing that up, and of course she understood why. But there was so very much more to the story than this. Hawk's weeping, his acknowledgement that he was a monster, his explanation of the fight for the gun with her mother and how it had gone off accidentally. The *human* part of him had begged for her forgiveness and asked her to put an end to his miserable life. How much of that truth would the jury hear? None of it would help her claim of self-defense. But it was all part of the truth, and didn't Cunningham tell her, time and time again, that the truth always won out in the end?

"Yes," Cunningham went on, knowing that he needed to wrap this up before Simmons jumped out of his seat with impatience. "As many witnesses will attest, Senator Hawk was pursuing Bailey Rose, and she was well-aware of it; just as aware as she was that her mother lay dead in the bed six feet away from her. And so, gentlemen, your Honor, she did what she had to do to survive. Senator Hawk was awake and was an imminent threat. He had already beaten and drugged her and partially removed her clothing. So she took the only action she could. She protected herself, she *defended* herself, in the only way she could: she shot him, and then she ran in terror."

He strode quickly and stood in front of the judge's bench and turned to address the jury from that vantage point. "And so, Mr. Foreman and gentlemen, without wasting more precious time, we shall ask you to say whether the County of Bexar has satisfied you beyond a reasonable doubt that a twelve-year-old girl stepped into Room #226 that evening with some kind of premeditated intent of causing harm to a grown man, or whether a twelve-year-old girl stepped into Room #226 that evening in order to save her poor mother, and instead, found herself in the terrifying position of saving herself. After you hear our case, gentlemen, you will not only have a *profound* doubt in your mind that she committed the crime for which she has been wrongfully charged, but you will have *no* doubt in your minds that she performed bravely, *heroically*, to try to protect her mother's life, and ultimately, her own."

As Cunningham took his seat, several of the jurors seemed to be on the verge of applause; they were nodding enthusiastically and looking intently her way with open, eager expressions on their faces. A quick glance at Jennings' table told her how brilliant her lawyer's opening statement had been: they looked a bit stunned, and Jennings's fingers were drumming a rapid, frenetic beat on his table. She scarcely had time to process these reactions before Judge Simmons smacked his gavel once again.

"First witness for the prosecution!" he bellowed, and just like that, the testimony was underway.

CHAPTER TWELVE

Jennings jumped to his feet like he'd been shot from a cannon. Today he was wearing a more dignified bow tie in a maroon shade, devoid of any polka dots whatsoever, perhaps to mark the seriousness of the occasion. "Your Honor, the prosecution would like to call Aaron Wentworth to the stand," he snapped in his nasally voice. A big, red-faced man in his late sixties lumbered to the stand, huffing and puffing with the effort. His sparse hair had been slicked down and he looked nervous as hell. As the clerk swore him in, beads of sweat began to pop on his forehead, and Bailey noticed that he licked his flabby lips every ten seconds or so, his tongue venturing forth and disappearing again with a snap like a snake. It became one of those inane idiosyncrasies that fascinated her, like Simmons' muttonchops that seemed to move with a mind of their own or Thomas's habit of pulling his earlobe. The thought of that made her smile, but she quickly wiped it from her face with a poke from Cunningham.

Wentworth completed his oath and lowered himself into the witness stand.

"Please state your name and occupation for the record," said Jennings.

"Oh! Er, I'm Aaron Wentworth. I'm an officer on the police force of the city of San Antonio, Texas," he said slowly and loudly, exaggerating his enunciation and directing his statements to the court reporter. The audience snickered.

"Mr. Wentworth, you may speak with a normal volume and speed," sighed Judge Simmons, propping his chin on his hand, a forlorn look on his face.

"Sorry your Honor," Wentworth muttered, and the audience laughed again.

"Mr. Wentworth, can you please describe to the jury, in your own words, your experiences at your place of work on the evening of the twentieth of

100

May, eighteen hundred and seventy-six?" Jennings was leaving it wide open for Wentworth.

"I sure can. I was called to the Gaslight to investigate a shot fired and two dead bodies."

"And what time was that?"

"That was at 8:12 pm."

"Entering into evidence the police record of the message from the Gaslight Hotel to City Hall at 8:12 pm on the night of the twentieth of May, eighteen hundred and seventy six," announced Jennings dramatically. He handed a slip of paper to the bailiff, who in turned handed it to the members of the jury. They passed it around quickly: it wasn't very interesting; simply a form indicating when the bellhop had arrived in person at City Hall to report the crime.

"How long do you think it took the bellhop to reach the police department from the Gaslight?" Jennings asked.

"Oh, about five minutes or so. He was on horseback and riding with the devil at his heels."

"And you arrived at the entrance to the Gaslight Hotel at what time?"

"About twenty minutes after eight."

"Did you respond to the scene alone?"

"Oh, heck no! I had the chief with me."

"And his name was?"

"Nathaniel Larkwood."

"Is Chief Larkwood still living?"

Wentworth paused to make the sign of a cross. "No, bless his soul. He passed two years ago from a weak heart."

"What happened when the two of you arrived at the hotel?"

Wentworth sat forward, eager to tell his story after so many years of silence. "The desk clerk, feller by the name of Hoss, he had already been up to the room. He was all in a tizzy. He led us upstairs to the second floor to Room #226."

"Up the front stairs that extended in a spiral from the lobby?"

"Why, yes, that's right."

"Did you observe any females descending the stairs or anywhere in the hotel?"

"Well, no sir, but I guess we weren't lookin' for no females right then." The audience chuckled.

"Go on with your account," Jennings directed Wentworth impatiently.

"We got up to the room, Room #226, and right away we saw a gun in the hallway. It was right outside the door, against the wall. Inside the room we saw a man against the wall; it appeared he had been shot in the chest. There was a tremendous amount of blood on his shirt, in his lap, and on the wall behind him. There was another body on the bed, a woman. Her dress was soaked with blood and it appeared that she'd been shot in the chest, too."

"Did you see blood elsewhere in the room?"

"There was a trail of blood from the door to the bed, as though the body had been dragged."

Simmons lifted an eyebrow at Cunningham, but no objection was forthcoming.

"Did you note if the bodies were warm?"

"Yes, the man's body was still warm. The woman's wasn't."

Bailey felt her stomach clench and stared at the table, fighting emotion. Her *mother*. That was her mother they were talking about as though she were a *thing*.

"Did you see anything else of interest in the room?"

"There was a chair in front of the man, about four feet back. There were two red ties—maybe dress sashes—tied to the arms. There were syringes—three of them—next to Mr. Hawk. There were drug vials, too, on a necklace around the woman's neck and on the floor by Mr. Hawk. There was an empty whisky bottle next to Mr. Hawk."

"Anything else notable?"

"Yes, we got down and looked on the floor real carefully, throughout the entire room. There was a hunk of hair on the floor by the chair. Long red hair. Maybe a dozen strands or so, like it had been pulled out."

"Your Honor, I offer the police report into evidence. Bailiff, please hand that report to the witness." Wentworth took the report and nodded.

"Is this the report that was authored by yourself and Chief Larkwood?"

"Yes, sir, it is."

"Is this report a true and accurate account of the placement and conditions of the bodies, the sashes, the hair, the syringes and vials, the bottle, and the weapon?"

"Yes, sir."

"Bailiff, please hand the evidence to the judge and jury." Jennings paused a few moments to allow Simmons and the jury to hand the report around. "Now, Mr. Wentworth. Based on your report, Chief Larkwood and you formed a theory in an attempt to solve the crime. Can you tell us what your theory was, as stated in this police report?"

"Sure I can. At first we thought maybe the woman shot the man and then killed herself until we realized he had just died very recently, but she had been shot some time before him, by the door, not in the bed. So someone had to have dragged her to the bed. Then we thought that maybe he could have shot her by the door, dragged her to the bed, and shot himself later, but that didn't explain the gun in the hallway and the chair with sashes and the long red hair on the floor. We thought that what may have happened was that a third person, a person with long red hair, probably a female, entered the hotel room and either killed the other woman and then the man, or that the older woman killed herself or was shot by the man and then the younger woman killed the man, throwing the gun in the hallway as she fled."

Jennings nodded, allowing the jury to absorb what the witness had just said. "Your Honor, could you please remind the jury that neither of the victims is on trial for murder?"

Simmons glared at him. "Let the jury be informed that neither Adam Hawk nor the unidentified woman are on trial today. And let the jury be informed that Bailey Rose has *not* been indicted for the murder of the unidentified woman."

It was Jennings' turn to glare.

"Mr. Wentworth, would the placement and condition of the bodies, and the placement of the weapon, and the presence of the red sashes and hair support a scenario that the older woman was a shot by the door and drug to the bed at some point around half past six in the evening, and that the man was then shot by the wall at eight in the evening by a third person?"

Mr. Wentworth frowned, hesitating, and the jury looked up from the report, suddenly keenly interested.

"Yes or no, Mr. Wentworth," snapped Jennings.

"I suppose so."

"Yes or no."

"Yes." Wentworth's expression became hard.

"Was this the report that was released to the public and appeared in the newspapers?"

Wentworth's hard expression slid from his chubby face and he swallowed convulsively. "No, sir." His voice had become thin.

"Explain that, if you will."

"Well, Larkwood was paid a visit two days after the crime by Mr. Hawk. The victim's father, you see. He was a former senator and from a real powerful family, of course. Anyway, well, it pains me to say this, but Larkwood took a bribe, a hefty one. Hawk didn't want his family's name drug through the mud, you understand. Well, Larkwood's wife had become terrible sick with consumption and he wanted to move her to the desert, to Arizona, and five thousand dollars would allow him to do this."

"Go on," snapped Jennings.

"So he wrote up another report, a different one, that said the man died first, then the woman took her own life, and that the gun was found in her hand. A murder-suicide by a crazy whore. Oh, my goodness, I beg your pardon, ladies." His face turned red and Bailey seethed.

"Entering evidence," said Jennings, handing papers to the bailiff. "Hand those to the witness, please. Mr. Wentworth, is this the falsified police report?"

Wentworth handled the papers with a thumb and the tip of his forefinger, as though it were infected with something vile. "Yes, sir."

Jennings instructed the bailiff to hand the report to the jury, and there was silence in the courtroom for several long moments.

"No further questions, your Honor."

"Cross?" barked Simmons.

Cunningham rose and approached the witness with a kind, firm smile. "Mr. Wentworth, when you observed the bodies, you realized the man's body was still warm but the woman's body was growing cold, is that right?"

"Yes, sir."

"Did you observe anything else about the bodies?"

"Well, of course, the man was all limp, since he had just been shot, but the woman was pretty stiff."

"Objection!" roared Jennings, jumping to his feet and waving his fist. "Calls for a conclusion!"

"Exception," muttered Cunningham. To every objection each attorney was required to enter an "exception" into the record in the case of an appeal, a tiresome task.

Simmons waved his hand. "Objection overruled. Continue, Cunningham."

"Can you tell us what you mean by 'pretty stiff'?"

"Your Honor!" helped Jennings, who was still standing. "Mr. Wentworth is not a coroner!"

"Sit down," growled Simmons.

"Mr. Wentworth?" probed Cunningham gently.

"Well, you know, once a person has been deceased for a spell, their body starts to stiffen up. We had to move her a bit to look for other evidence. She was getting stiff as a board."

"Have you handled many dead bodies, Mr. Wentworth?"

Wentworth grunted. "I'm a lawman in one of the roughest cities in the west. I handle dead bodies every week."

"And what can you tell us about stiffness? When does it set in?"

"Well, about two or three hours or so after a person has passed, the stiffness sets in, I'd say."

"Have you ever observed a deceased person to become stiff sooner than two hours?"

Wentworth shook his head. "No. And usually it ain't until three hours."

"Now, Mr. Wentworth, allow me to ask you the same question that Mr. Jennings proposed. Does the true, authentic police report entered as evidence here," Cunningham picked it up from the evidence table and waved it, "does this report support the defense's timeline of events? That the older woman was killed around five in the evening—as opposed to a half past six as the prosecution suggests—perhaps by her own hand or at the hands of Mr. Hawk, and then dragged to the bed? And that Bailey Rose, upon entering the room at six-thirty in the evening, was dragged by her hair, tied to the chair, injected with drugs, became unconscious, and forced to protect her life by shooting Mr. Hawk at eight p.m.?"

Jennings shot to his feet and literally shrieked his objection. "Asked and answered! Asked and answered! Is there even a question in that narrative?"

"Exception," said Cunningham calmly.

Simmons winced. "Objection overruled. Approach." The two attorneys approached the bench, Jennings marching, his face red with indignation, Cunningham pleased but actually quite appalled at his adversary's lack of preparation.

Simmons leaned forward to speak in a low voice. "Mr. Jennings, it's not Mr. Cunningham's fault that you failed to vet a witness. If you keep barking objections with no substantiation, you will be *sorry*."

Jennings spun on his heel and took his seat again, his beady eyes snapping.

Cunningham approached the witness stand again. "Can you answer that question? Does the police report support the defense's timeline of events?"

There was a breathless silence.

"Why yes, it does. That scenario fits the evidence even better, I should say."

Jennings' face turned bright red. He shot to his feet, opened his mouth, closed it again, and sank back into his chair.

"Mr. Wentworth, why do you say that my scenario fits the evidence better?"

"Because the stiffness—rigor mortis, it's called—had already started to set in on the woman. If only an hour or ninety minutes had passed, I don't see how it could have. And as for the third person, someone who'd had their hair pulled out and been tied up would seem to be in some kind of danger."

"Thank you, Mr. Wentworth. No further questions." Cunningham took his seat, a mild expression on his face, but Bailey's heart was thumping.

"Re-direct?" asked Simmons, as though he dreaded the answer.

Jennings looked as though he wanted to, but he muttered in the negative. "Prosecution calls David O'Malley to the stand."

Jennings questioned the officer who found the original file, which had been mislabeled and sealed to apparently avoid detection. He described handing the file over to Chief Timothy Sellers, who in turn handed it over to Jennings. O'Malley testified that once the papers picked up the story—complete with the description of red sashes and red hair—an anonymous informant had mailed a letter to the police station with a name of a red-headed prostitute who had reason to hate Adam Hawk. The story was far-fetched but O'Malley himself seemed to believe it. Bailey steamed to think of Jennings leaking all of those details to the press; and who on earth would have read that and connected this crime with her? When Cunningham passed on a cross-examination, she was surprised until she remembered that it didn't matter how they had pinned her as a prime suspect: she had, in fact, killed

Adam Hawk, and they weren't disputing that fact.

The next witness called was William Schaub, the retired coroner who was responsible for the case. "State your name and profession," ordered Jennings after the witness was sworn in.

"William Schaub, M.D., former coroner for the county of Bexar. I am now retired." Mr. Schaub was a slight man with a bald head and spectacles balanced on his pointy nose.

"Mr. Schaub, do you remember the events of the twentieth of May, eighteen hundred and seventy six?"

"Yes, indeed. I was called to the scene of a shooting at the Gaslight Hotel."

"What time was that?"

"A boy came for me at three quarters past the hour of eight p.m. I arrived at nine p.m."

"And what were your duties upon arrival?"

"To determine the time, cause, and manner of death."

"Mr. Schaub, what did you observe when you arrived?"

Schaub cleared his throat. "I observed a deceased man in a seated position, his back against the wall, about halfway between the door and the bed. He had been shot in the chest."

"Where do you think the man was when he was shot?"

"It was clear to me that he died where he sat. That is to say, he had been sitting on the floor with his back against the wall."

"Did you observe anything else?"

"Yes, I observed needle punctures in both arms and I detected the smell of morphine. I suspected that he had drugs in his system. I also observed an empty whisky bottle by his side and empty drug vials."

"In your expert opinion, how long had the man been dead?"

"Perhaps an hour, no longer than that."

"And how did you come to that conclusion?"

"Rigor mortis had not set in. The body was still quite flaccid. The blood was not dried at all. There was a minimum of lividity.

"What is lividity?"

"When circulation of blood ceases, any subsequent movement of this liquid will be gravitational - that is to say, the blood will tend to flow downward. Consequently they will accumulate in capillaries and small veins in dependent parts of the body, and this is manifest as a purple or reddish-purple color on the skin. Lividity is usually apparent within half an hour to two hours after death, fully developing within twelve hours.

"And the other victim in the room? The woman?"

"She also had a gunshot wound to the left chest."

"How long had the woman been dead?"

"I estimated two to four hours."

"Your basis for that estimation?"

Schaub cleared his throat nervously. "The woman displayed profound lividity on the back of the torso and limbs, earlobes and tissue under her fingernails, which is common for a corpse that has been laid on its back. Rigor mortis had set in at that point. Much of the blood had dried or congealed."

There were a few gasps from the few remaining women in the room. Bailey dropped her face into her hands, and behind her, Jacob stared at the back of her neck, aching to hold her. Only now was he beginning to fully understand the horrors of what she had seen on the bed that fateful night.

"Upon autopsy, what more did you discover?"

"I verified my original conclusions. Both victims died from a single gunshot wound to the chest from a .38 caliber weapon, which produces a relatively high-velocity bullet. Both had penetrating wounds: that is to say, there was an entrance wound but no exit wound, which is almost always deadly. Traumatic cardiac penetration of the right ventricle, to be precise, in both cases. The woman's wound had burns and soot marks, indicating she was shot at point-blank range. Both victims had great quantities of morphine in their blood, and the woman, cocaine as well. The man had acute amounts of alcohol in his system. Core body temperature also verified my original conclusion that the woman had died first, at some point between five or six in the evening, and the man had died around eight in the evening."

"Is this the report you submitted to the police?"

"Yes, of course."

"Were you aware that the report had been altered?"

"No, I was not. I was not aware of that until recently, as a matter of fact."

"No further questions."

"Cross?"

Cunningham rose and stroked his chin thoughtfully. "Mr. Schaub, you commented on the state of flaccidity of the man's body, and the state of rigor mortis in the woman's body. Can you explain to the jury, in layman's terms, the definition of rigor mortis?"

"Certainly." Schaub sat up straighter and prepared to expound. "Rigor mortis is caused by chemical changes in the muscles after death. After death, cellular respiration in organisms ceases to occur, depleting the corpse of oxygen used in the making of adenosine triphosphate, thus allowing the corpse to harden and become stiff."

"And how soon after death does this occur?"

"Typically it commences after about three to four hours, reaches maximum stiffness after twelve hours, and gradually dissipates from approximately twenty-four hours after death."

"And does this process happen all at once, instantly?"

Schaub shook his head emphatically. "Oh, no. First, it affects the eyelids, jaw, and neck. Gradually, it spreads to the other muscles, and eventually to the internal organs."

"How gradually does it spread to the other muscles?"

"Not until four to six hours or longer after death."

"And what was the progression of rigor mortis in the female victim as you observed her at nine in the evening?"

"Rigor mortis had set in to her eyelids, neck, jaw, and her arms and legs were beginning to get stiff as well."

Cunningham nodded thoughtfully, a puzzled look on his face as though he were trying to work something out. "Mr. Schaub, you offered a time of death for the man as eight in the evening, and the woman, two to four hours before that time. In your estimation, she died between four and six in the evening?"

"Yes."

"But if she was already experiencing rigor mortis in her limbs at nine in the evening, which you just testified happens at four to six hours after death, that would place her time of death at five in the evening at the very *latest*, is that correct? Not six in the evening or a half past six, but *five in the evening*."

Jennings sprung to his feet. "Objection! Asked and answered!"

"Exception," Cunningham sighed. "I am allowed to ask the witness to clarify his answer."

"Objection sustained. Try again, Mr. Cunningham." Simmons raised a bushy eyebrow.

"Since you testified that she was experiencing rigor mortis in her limbs at nine in the evening, would that place her time of death at what time, at the very latest?"

"Five in the evening would be my best estimate."

"Thank you. No further questions."

"I suppose you have a re-direct?" muttered Simmons.

Jennings rose. "Yes, I do! Mr. Schaub! Are there any circumstances that could lead to rigor mortis happening at a faster pace than normal?"

"Well, yes, I suppose so. Warm conditions can speed rigor mortis."

"Mr. Schaub, in your expert opinion, was the room warm enough that evening to have speeded up the process of rigor mortis?"

Schaub pushed his glasses up on his nose and thought about that for a beat. "It was warm in the room, as I recall. Yes, I guess it could have sped up the process to a degree, although the male had not..."

"Thank you, Mr. Schaub," Jennings interrupted hastily. "In consideration of the fact that the room was warm enough to speed up the process of rigor mortis, is the time of death for the woman of half past six possible?"

Schaub opened his mouth and closed it again.

"Yes or no," reminded Jennings.

"Yes," Schaub finally managed, frowning deeply.

Jennings sat down and waved his hand to indicate he was finished. "Recross," announced Cunningham unexpectedly, and Simmons glared at him.

"Make it quick, Mr. Cunningham."

"Mr. Schaub, you have testified that it is possible that the woman died at six-thirty in the evening. In your expert opinion, is it *probable?*"

"No, no sir, it is not."

"Thank you, that is all."

Jennings steamed and Bailey's heart pounded in her ears. Thus far, Jennings' witnesses had been a disaster for the prosecution. Could her luck hold out?

Simmons abruptly banged the gavel. "Court is adjourned for one hour for luncheon. Clear the courtroom."

Before Cunningham could tell her not to, Bailey spun around to look for Jacob. He flashed a smile and nodded, and she flushed, meeting his eyes, knowing she must not smile in the context of the terrible testimony that had just occurred. She stood with her team and the guard took her elbow, guiding her down the aisle quickly as the spectators gawked and murmured. She just managed to catch Hope's eye, but she saw none of her other family and friends; already the throng had risen and were pushing and straining in a jumbled mass to get a better look at her. She colored and stared at the floor, hating the feeling of being an animal in a zoo.

CHAPTER THIRTEEN

S he spent a quiet hour with Cunningham, Flanders and Mooreland, reviewing the progress of the trial and preparing for Jennings' next witnesses, whom Cunningham informed her would be two prostitutes who used to work at Fort Allen. As she heard the names, her heart sank. How had Jennings managed to find two of the meanest, most hateful girls ever to live at the parlor? Betsy Blue and Lynda Love, both of them as patently false as their ridiculous names. Of course, it must have been Blanche who had tipped Jennings off about whom to find to testify against Bailey.

Flanders, who Bailey now referred to as 'Abe,' even to his face, leaned over and patted her hand kindly, seeing the gloomy look on her face. "Dr. Rose!" he chided. "Why so glum? Have you not heard a word we've said? Jennings is making a terrible mess of things. Why, it's obvious he never bothered to prepare either one of his witnesses. And why he chose not to call Hoss the desk clerk is a very, very good sign for us. Hoss must have something we need."

"Jennings should be disbarred!" muttered Cunningham. "Honestly, it's an embarrassment. He's spent so much time reveling in the attention from reporters that he's failed to prepare his case properly. He assumed it would be an open-and-shut case, prosecuting someone he thinks is a nobody, a *nobody* who killed a *somebody*. I wouldn't be a bit surprised if he was booted from office after this loss."

Bailey looked up, amused. "We haven't won yet," she reminded him.

Cunningham looked at her levelly. "We have. Really, Bailey, it's all downhill for Jennings from here." The man was a fierce optimist, but she was not.

"But some of those jurors hate me."

"That doesn't matter. They will be deliberating whether you are guilty beyond a reasonable doubt, not whether you are *not* guilty beyond a reasonable doubt. If one of the twelve believes you are innocent, you walk free. In my humble opinion, only one or two—possibly three—of the twelve will think you are guilty."

Bailey allowed that to sink in, allowed the hope she felt when Jacob smiled at her to infuse her again.

Cunningham nodded in approval at the change in her expression. "Bailey, we need you to be strong now. Jennings will attempt to discredit your character this afternoon, and we need you to remember who you are. A doctor! A woman of the highest character! A survivor! Keep hold of that today, promise?"

She nodded, but Cunningham's words had only served to make her more nervous than ever. She couldn't even begin to imagine what Betsy and Lynda would say about her, and to have Jacob and the rest of her family and friends hear it was unbearable.

The years had not been kind to Betsy Blue. The haggard woman took the oath, sank down into the chair with a weary sigh and gave her age as forty-five. She was attired in a shabby relic of a gown that was long expired: it was a faded blue chintz, the bustle sagging and the hems frayed. The lace neckline was yellow with age and plunged to reveal a jagged, poorly-healed half-inch scar above her left breast. Bailey recognized it at once as a stab wound from a broken bottle, a popular weapon in the Row. For that was where poor Betsy Blue had landed after all of these years: once a sought-after lady of the evening at San Antonio's finest boarding house all the way down to a shanty in a row, working for a pimp. Betsy's hair was gray and thin now; Bailey remembered it as black and luxurious. Her hand shook as she placed it on the Bible, and Bailey's heart squeezed in sympathy, even though the woman had been very unkind to her all of those years ago. Betsy was a well-known addict, her drug of choice being opium, and she sold herself for drugs and food now, one step away from the street.

"State your name and occupation," snarled Jennings. *Honestly, he treats his witnesses like a piece of offal on the bottom of his highly-polished shoes*, thought Bailey incredulously.

"Elizabeth Agatha Blue. I am a seamstress." The spectators tittered.

"Your place of residence?"

"23 South Concho."

The audience laughed again: Concho was a well-known address for the Row.

"Fifteen years ago, in the year eighteen hundred and seventy-six, where was your place of residence?"

"I lived and worked at Fort Allen," she rasped, her voice a bare whisper from years of smoking opium.

"And what was your occupation at Fort Allen?"

"I was a lady of the evening." She seemed too tired to be offended at the amusement of the crowd or the derision of the attorney.

"While you were there, were you acquainted with Bailey Rose?"

"Yes."

"Can you describe who she was?"

"She was there before I was, actually. Blanche hired me on in sixty-five, right at the end of the War. I was married, you see, and my whole family— my husband, my father, my three brothers—had all been killed. My mother was dead years before. I had nowhere to go and Blanche took me in."

Bailey peeked at the jury and was dismayed to see that several of them looked to be very sympathetic to Betsy. As well they should be; if she was telling the truth, it was a tragic, all-too-common story.

"When I came on, there was a woman working there by the name of Addie Rose, and she had a baby with a funny name, *Bailey*. She was pretty but she was a mess, Addie, high all the time it seems. Most of the girls took care of the baby; just passed her around all day, but not me. I didn't want nothing to do with a baby. I had a lost a baby and it was just too painful." Bailey felt a pull of commiseration against her will. That feeling changed quickly.

"Do you remember whether Bailey worked as a prostitute at Fort Allen when she was older?"

"Yes, she did. She became one of us when she was fourteen, I reckon. Everyone said she was fourteen." It was curious that she had tacked on that last part.

Bailey felt a burning sensation building in her throat. She remembered Betsy very well: a quiet, sneaky woman who was known to spread rumors about the other girls; a true outsider. Betsy was one of the mean girls who had given her as much work as possible.

"Did you see Bailey Rose on the twentieth of May, eighteen hundred and seventy-six?"

Betsy had been at least moderately rehearsed for this question, Bailey could see at once. "Yes I did. I saw her race in the front door and go upstairs."

"What time was that, Miss Blue?"

"That was around six in the evening, I suppose, because I was in the parlor drinking my after-dinner brandy and smoking my after-dinner cigar." The audience snickered appreciatively.

"Did you see her again that evening?"

"Yes I did. I saw her come barreling down the stairs like a bull and out the door at about ten minutes after six."

"Do you know where she went?"

"No, sir. But I had a good suspicion."

"Can you tell us about that suspicion?"

"Well, all the girls said Bailey had run off with a good-looking foreign boy to Boerne. Everyone knows that during shearin' we can get some good work up that way, if you understand what I mean. Lots of lonely men, and she was young and pretty."

Jacob tensed in his chair to rise and Johann grabbed his thigh, squeezing painfully and frowning a warning. "Let Cunningham do his job," he hissed.

"What do you mean by 'good work,' Miss Blue?"

"Well, we all heard she was turnin' tricks up that way, to put it blunt."

"How long was she gone?"

"Five or six days."

"So back to my original question, Miss Blue. Where did you suspect Miss Rose had gone when she fled Fort Allen that evening?"

"Well, I would bet my life that she was going to hunt down Senator and Jezzie."

Bailey's mind whirled in confusion. Jezzie? Jezebel St. John? What had she to do with any of this?

"Who is Jezzie, Miss Blue?"

"Jezzie was Jezebel St. John, that's who she was. One of my dearest friends at Fort Allen, a working girl, like me." Bailey barely managed not to roll her eyes. Jezebel had been the meanest girl at Fort Allen, despised by all, including Betsy! Blanche only kept her around because she was beautiful, multilingual, a divine dancer and conversationalist, and highly sought-after due to her willingness to do for the johns what none of the other girls would. Jezzie liked to whack Bailey whenever she came within range; she remembered the evil woman as quick and powerful.

"And why would Miss Rose would have wanted to 'hunt down,' as you say, Miss St. John?"

"Objection. Mr. Jennings is asking the witness to speculate." Cunningham frowned, not liking where the line of questioning was headed.

"Exception," said Jennings smartly. "I'm simply asking the witness to expound on her own answer."

"Sustained," snapped Simmons, glowering.

Mr. Jennings plowed forward. "Miss Blue, did Miss Rose have any enemies at Fort Allen?"

"Objection. Mr. Jennings is asking the witness to provide hearsay testimony."

"Exception!" blustered Jennings, too rattled now to think of a plausible one.

"Sustained. See if you can get it right the third time, Mr. Jennings," said Simmons blandly. He was in dire need of a cup of coffee.

Jennings closed his eyes and took a deep breath, posturing for the jury, displaying his great patience. "Miss Blue," he finally asked, a kind smile on his face. "Did you ever directly observe Miss Rose fighting, either verbally or physically, with anyone in Fort Allen?"

He turned and held a palm up to Cunningham as if to say, "Was that question acceptable?" Cunningham smiled and saluted, and the audience chuckled.

Betsy took a few seconds to think about that, her lips moving soundlessly, no doubt trying to recall the lines Jennings had supplied her with. "Adam Hawk—we called him Senator, 'cause he was one—Senator liked Jezzie. Bailey was powerful jealous. She was the new girl, Bailey was, and being the youngest, she was used to getting all the attention. So the answer to your question is yes, I saw Bailey screaming at Jezzie on many occasions, warning her to keep away from Senator."

"When you observed Miss Rose leaving Fort Allen that evening, did she say anything?"

"Yes. She screamed that she would make Jezzie pay, that she would make both of them both pay."

It was so ludicrous—so exponentially far from the truth—that Bailey's jaw fell open. It was all complete and utter fiction.

"No further questions."

"Cross, Mr. Cunningham?" Simmons sat back, crossed his arms over his chest, and smiled. This was going to be good.

Cunningham rose and approached the witness stand, smiling at Miss Blue like a gentleman knows how to smile at a lady. Her eyes widened and she smiled back, pleased. He was a handsome young man, precisely the kind of man she used to make love to, unlike the sweaty, dirty apes she serviced nowadays. "Good afternoon, Miss Blue," he said, his voice dressed fine in a layer of silk.

"Good afternoon, Mr. Cunningham," she returned. The audience chortled.

"Miss Blue, you mentioned that you knew that Miss Rose had departed for Boerne for five days in order to 'turn tricks,' as you say. Can you tell the jury how you came upon that information?"

The smile slid from her face and was replaced by a befuddled look. "I don't know. I just heard it from the other girls, I guess."

"Did you see her leave?"

"No."

"Did she tell you where she was going?"

"No, she didn't."

"Do you remember who told you where she was going and what she'd been doing?"

"Well, no, I don't recall."

"Miss Blue, where was Bailey's room in Fort Allen?" he asked abruptly, without pause or change of his pleasant expression.

"What?"

"Her room. You testified that she was a working girl. Where was her room?"

Betsey's cheeks flared. "I don't—upstairs—I don't remember, I guess."

"Did you have many gowns when you were working at Fort Allen?"

"Wh—what?"

"Gowns. I'm assuming you had a luxurious wardrobe? Or maybe I'm mistaken."

"Objection!" snarled Jennings. "Immaterial."

"Exception. I will prove my line of questioning is material."

"Overruled. I'll allow it." Simmons barely repressed a smile.

"Miss Blue, did you own more than one dress at Fort Allen?"

She sat up a bit straighter. "I certainly did. Blanche took care of us. We were the pride of San Antonio. We dressed like princesses, better than any of the society women. I had a dozen gowns!"

"Was it terribly arduous to do all of that laundry? It must have been terrible work for you."

She harrumphed and shot her chin in the air. "No I certainly did not do the wash! Of all things! We didn't lift a finger!"

"Who did your laundry, Miss Blue?"

"That little wild-haired scrub, Bailey Rose!" she rasped, pointing a finger at Bailey.

There was a heavy silence.

Cunningham turned to pace in front of the jury. "Miss Blue. You have testified that Bailey Rose was a high-priced working girl at Fort Allen. Do you expect us to believe that she was also required to do the laundry?"

"Objection! Your Honor! That is a leading question!" Jennings literally stamped his foot, and Bailey wondered if he would burst into tears next.

"Sustained. Rephrase."

Cunningham suddenly swiveled back to Betsy and spoke in a rapid-fire manner. "Was Bailey Rose a boarder at Fort Allen? Was she a working girl?"

"Er—yes."

"Were working girls required to do their own laundry, or the laundry of anyone else?"

"Well, I don't remember."

"Your Honor, would you be so kind as to remind Miss Blue of the consequences of perjury?"

Simmons leaned forward. "Perjury is lying, Miss Blue. You have taken an oath on the Bible to tell the whole truth. If you don't, you'll go to jail."

She gulped and tears sprang to her eyes. Jail meant no opium fixes, and she'd be damned if she was going through withdrawal again. The last time had nearly killed her. "I didn't do my laundry. None of us girls did. Bailey did it all. She did all of the laundry and cleaned our rooms."

"I'll ask you this question again, then. Was Bailey Rose a prostitute?"

She shook her head miserably. "No," she finally rasped. The audience gasped and Jennings grew quite pale. Jacob sank in his seat, his mouth falling open, his brain in a fog.

Cunningham let a few more seconds pass. "Miss Blue. Please give us a description of the stature of Bailey Rose when you knew her fifteen years ago."

"Her stature?" She lifted her teary eyes, confused but grateful to be finished with the subject of whether Bailey was a working girl.

"Yes. How tall was she? How much did she weigh?"

Betsy shrugged. "I don't know. She was small. A scrawny thing. Not five feet tall, weighed maybe seventy pounds, but no more."

"Thank you, Miss Blue. No more questions."

"Re-direct?"

Jennings shook his head mutely, temporarily defeated. The impeachment of his witness seemed to have taken a great deal of the wind out of his sails.

"Well then, Mr. Jennings, call your next witness," ordered Simmons, thoroughly disgusted with the shoddy preparation displayed by the prosecuting attorney of Bexar County.

"The prosecution calls Lynda Love." The audience laughed again, amused at the moniker. A busty woman with curly brown hair arranged in girlish ringlets flounced her way to the stand, garishly attired in a bright blue satin gown with enormous hoops. On her ears and neck were glittering diamonds. Unlike Betsy Blue, Lynda Love had done well for herself: Bailey knew from Gabby that after leaving Fort Allen years ago, Lynda had ascended the throne as madam of her very own brothel: a step down from the splendor of establishments like the Purple Pansy and Fort Allen, but a thriving, clean business nonetheless. Lynda was another girl who had been hateful to Bailey: she remembered her as ambitious and very chummy with Blanche, no doubt learning the business of the trade.

Lynda was sworn in and stated her occupation as owner of a boarding house. Bailey had no doubt that Jennings had threatened her with closure should she fail to testify effectively against her. Lynda would be a tough nut to crack, even though she most likely had no specific grudges against Bailey from so many years ago.

"Miss Love, do you remember Bailey Rose as residing at Fort Allen?"

"Yes. I was employed at Fort Allen when Bailey's mother arrived, pregnant. I remember her well."

"And was Bailey Rose ever employed as a prostitute?" Jennings visibly winced when he asked it. He clearly had ceased to trust his witnesses.

"Yes. Bailey started as a working girl in 1876, when she was fourteen."

"How do you know she was fourteen?"

"Because when Addie—her mother—arrived at Fort Allen and gave birth a short time later, I was just fourteen myself and I had just started at Fort Allen. I helped care for the baby. And when the murder happened, I had just turned twenty-eight, so I know she was fourteen."

Jennings hurried onto his next question as if fearful that Cunningham would object. "Miss Love, had you ever observed Bailey Rose fighting with any of the other girls at Fort Allen?"

"Yes. Bailey and Jezebel St. John hated each other. They had been bickering over a man for a few weeks, Senator Adam Hawk. Hawk was in love with Jezzie and Bailey was jealous, because Hawk was young, famous, rich, and good-looking."

Bailey barely suppressed a groan. It was all so utterly nonsensical. She wished she could see Gabby's face.

"Did you ever directly observe Bailey threaten Miss St. John?"

"Yes, I did. One time, not too long before this, I saw Bailey kick Jezzie in the shin and punch in her the face and scream 'I wish you were dead!'"

Bailey felt her heart drop into her shoes. This testimony was actually completely true. Jezebel had been physically abusive to Bailey, pulling her hair, pinching her, boxing her ears, smacking whatever part of her body she could reach. She strove to make life hell for Bailey, deliberately soiling towels and sheets with food and drink, dumping ashes onto the rugs, smearing food into the upholstery. One day Bailey had reached her breaking point, and Lynda was right: it was just a week or so before she left for Boerne. She was crossing the lobby to return clean glasses to the bar, and Jezzie had sneaked up behind her and pushed her as hard as she could. Bailey had gone flying, landing the broken shards of glass and cutting her arms and hands. As she was writhing on the floor, Jezzie had grabbed her braid and yanked as hard as she could, forcing Bailey's face up, and then slapped her viciously. *You clumsy, stupid bitch!* She had screamed it over and over, laughing like a madwoman, until Bailey kicked her and punched her right in the nose, dropping her to the floor. "I wish you were dead," she had yelled at the hateful woman, and then immediately felt ashamed. She had never wished anyone were dead, and she didn't really mean it. She remembered there were a few other girls in the room: apparently Lynda was one of them. They had applauded, hating Jezzie as much as Bailey did.

"No more questions, your Honor." Apparently Lynda had nothing to offer in the way of the actual night of the crime, which means he called her as a character witness. *He had called a prostitute to testify that Bailey was a prostitute.* She wondered if the irony of it escaped him.

"Cross?" yawned Simmons.

"Yes, your Honor. "Miss Love, you have testified that Bailey Rose was fourteen in 1876."

"Yes, she was."

"Your Honor, I submit the birth certificate of Bailey Rose as evidence."

He handed it to the bailiff, who handed it to Simmons and then the jury. They passed it around and handed it back to the bailiff, who offered it to the witness. "As you can see, Bailey Rose was delivered on the fifth of February, 1864, by a midwife named Theresa Cazella. Mrs. Cazella was known to be an exceptionally detailed record-keeper, and submitted records of all of her deliveries to the county courthouse. Miss Love, since Bailey was born in 1864, how old was she in 1876?"

Lynda Love glared at the young lawyer, her face screwing up as though she had bit into a lemon. "Well, *officially* I guess that made her twelve years old."

Jacob found himself sinking further and further into his seat. *Bailey had told the truth about her age. Blanche had lied to them. What else had she lied about? But how could that be possible? His father had spoken with almost every woman in that damned brothel!*

"*Officially*? What do you mean by 'officially'?"

"Well, we all thought she was fourteen. She lied to us."

"Miss Love, if you remember the day she was born, you should know how old she was twelve years later." The audience chortled.

"Objection!" snapped Jennings. "Asked and answered, and defense is badgering the witness."

"Sustained."

"Miss Love, why didn't *you* start working when you were twelve? Were you not invited by any of the high-class parlors?"

Lynda's pale blue eyes narrowed and her lip curled contemptuously. "That wasn't allowed. Blanche prefers eighteen; she'll allow younger if the girl is mature and sophisticated and a beauty, like I was, but fourteen is the minimum."

Cunningham turned to stare at her, allowing the silence to settle. He could go on impeaching this witness, too, but as he rotated slowly on his heel and regarded the jury, he could see at once that his task was complete.

"Oh! One last thing. Miss Love, how tall was Bailey Rose fifteen years ago? How much did she weigh?"

"How should I know?" Lynda snapped. Blanche was a formidable enemy—maybe even a worse one than Augustus Jennings, and Lynda had made her look a liar today.

"How would you describe her stature at that time?"

"She was petite. Short and skinny. Don't know why the men liked her," she hastened to add, noting Jennings' crestfallen face.

"That is all," Cunningham smiled, and took his seat.

"Re-direct?"

Jennings waved it off. He was in dire need of a drink. "Prosecution calls Blanche DuBois, your Honor."

Bailey felt her spine stiffen and the hairs on the back of her neck rise. She had seen Blanche only a few times from a distance since she had returned to San Antonio; Blanche did not acknowledge her and made it clear that she wouldn't allow Bailey into Fort Allen. It was painfully clear that the woman felt betrayed. And Bailey burned to look at her: here was the woman who had given her a black eye upon discovering she had gone to school; here was the woman who, a few days later, sold a twelve-year-old girl for $5,000 to a drunken, drug-crazed man. She represented everything sordid and ugly and horrific in Bailey's past life, and to look at her was to put one foot into that world again.

Blanche had changed very little over the past fifteen years. She was heavier, the lines on her face were more deeply etched, but she still bore herself like a tall queen, towering over Jennings. She wore a tea gown—a dress meant only to be worn at home to greet callers—and it was no ordinary tea gown. The overdress was constructed of deep red velvet and gold and pink floral brocade. The dress was open with puffed sleeves and a large ruffled cuff lined with velvet and trimmed with lace. As she made her way regally to the stand, the audience was treated to the back of the dress, a scandal in its own right: it was flanked with an inset pleat of deep red velvet and garnished with pink silk roses directly over her rear end, one for each cheek. She wore a mink around her neck, but *her hat!* Her hat was truly extraordinary: it boasted a very wide straight brim with a ridiculously wide crown—Bailey wondered how it fit on her head without covering her entire face—that was tall as well: it rose six inches, covered with pink lace. Plumes of feathers and tulle in shades of red, pink, and mint circled the top like pom-poms and gave the hat its full height of two feet. The hat looked as though it had been created for a giantess, but there it sat on Blanche's head, miraculously staying put. She wore her usual smirk and did not deign to look at Bailey.

She was sworn in and stated her occupation as proprietress of the boarding house, Fort Allen.

"How long have you owned this boarding house, Miss Dubois?"

"Thirty-six years," she said clearly, trilling her R's, her voice quavering with pride.

"When did Bailey Rose arrive at Fort Allen?"

"At some point around 1862. I can't be sure."

"To the best of your knowledge, was Bailey Rose fourteen years of age on 1876?"

"She claimed she was."

"Could she have been younger?"

"I suppose so. I took her at her word because she wanted to start working."

"What do you mean by 'working'?"

Blanche sniffed at the indelicate question. "She wanted to become a boarder."

"Miss DuBois, was Bailey Rose working for you as a prostitute in 1876?"

She drew herself up and rolled her eyes. "Mr. Jennings, my girls are so much more than that—*word*—you use. They are refined, educated companions to the city's most powerful, elite gentlemen. Gentlemen such as yourself, I'm sure."

The onlookers guffawed and it took Simmons three tries to get them quiet.

Jennings face had gone scarlet.

"Your Honor, can you direct Miss DuBois to answer the question?"

"Answer the question," he barked, his patience growing thin.

"Yes," she finally said. And then a curious thing happened. Her face fell into softer lines, and she added softly, "And if she was twelve, I'm sorry about that."

Jennings cleared his throat noisily and hurried on. "Did you observe Bailey Rose arguing or fighting with any of the other girls?"

"She did not get along well with Jezebel St. John." Her answers were wooden and rehearsed. Bailey noticed that her earlier bravado seemed to be waning. And why on earth did Jezzie's name keep coming up?

"Do you have any idea why they did not get along?"

"I overheard them fighting over Adam Hawk." A muscle in her cheek seemed to be jumping.

"Were you present on the evening of May twentieth, eighteen hundred and seventy-six, when Bailey came back to Fort Allen?"

"Yes, but I was asleep in my room."

"Were you aware that Bailey had been out of town for five days?"

"Yes."

"Had you any idea where she had gone?"

"No. There were rumors of a sheep ranch in Boerne, but I can't say for sure."

"No more questions." Jennings seemed happy to be done with her and did not notice the look of triumph flash on Cunningham's face.

"Cross?"

Cunningham rose and approached Blanche, frowning.

"Miss DuBois, who was Bailey's mother?"

"Addie Rose."

"And when did you meet Addie Rose?"

"I told you, 1862."

"What were the circumstances of your meeting?"

"She was knocked up and on the street, and I rescued her," Blanche snapped, her cultured exterior slipping to reveal the rough interior in her nervousness.

"Are you familiar with this city's Blue Book?"

Blanche paled. "I suppose so."

"Can you explain to the jury what the Blue Book is?" The men in the audience murmured and chuckled.

"I suppose so." She seemed to deflate as she spoke. "The Blue Book is the directory of the District that the city publishes."

"The District? Could you explain what that is?"

A spot of color bloomed on each heavily powdered cheek. "The parlors, the brothels, the cathouses, and the Row."

"The houses of ill repute? Where prostitutes are employed?"

"Well, they aren't churches," she growled. More laughter.

"And what precisely appears in the Blue Book?"

She sighed. She knew she was caught. "The names and addresses of all of the working girls."

"Your Honor, I am entering into evidence the Blue Books from the years 1862 through 1866, and 1876 through 1877."

The bailiff accepted them, and the books made their way through the hands of each of the jurors and the judge. Several silent moments passed and Blanche seemed to age before Bailey's eyes.

Finally the books were handed to Blanche. "Miss DuBois, would you please tell me if Addie Rose, Bailey's mother, is listed in the Blue Book for 1862?"

She looked through it glumly. "No."

"How about 1863? Surely she must be there."

She leafed through the pages of the next book, her cheeks flaming. "No."

"Well, let's try 1864, shall we?"

After a cursory look, Blanche announced that she wasn't there, either.

"Will you have a look at 1865?"

"Yes, she's there," muttered Blanche at last, holding the offending book in trembling hands.

"Since these books are published and distributed in January of each year, does it stand to reason that a woman appearing in the book for 1866 was established at some point between February of 1865 and January of 1866?"

Jennings had sunk so low in his chair that his head was barely visible over the back. There was nothing to object to, nothing at all.

"Yes, that's right."

"So, now that your memory has been jogged, can we confirm that Addie Rose did not arrive at Fort Allen until 1865?"

"Yes."

"How soon after she arrived did she have a baby?"

"I don't know. Maybe she already had it. Yes, I suppose she had already had the baby."

Bailey felt a sense of unreality creeping over her. She had *not* been born after Addie started working at Fort Allen!

"How old was the baby?"

Blanche rolled her eyes, but it was clear that she was undone. "How should I know?"

"Was the baby walking?"

The older woman sunk even lower in her chair. "Maybe just starting."

"Was this baby Bailey Rose?"

"Yes." Blanche was close to tears.

"How old was Bailey Rose in 1876, Miss DuBois?"

Blanche gulped and stared at her gloved hands, feeling her empire begin to crumble. "She was twelve."

There was an audible gasp from the galley, and Bailey sensed, rather than saw, a ripple of movement in the jury.

"Miss DuBois. I'm going to ask you a question that I've asked you before, but I'm going to give you a chance to tell the truth. Did Bailey Rose work for you as a prostitute?"

"Objection, your Honor. The witness has already answered this question. The defense is badgering her."

"Exception. With the evidence I have just provided, the witness may wish to change her answer and should have the opportunity to do so."

"Overruled," snapped Simmons.

The courtroom was utterly silent for a full minute.

"Yes," Blanche finally whispered. The stakes were too high. If she told the truth, Jennings would make sure she lost everything. Her home, her business, her considerable wealth, *her girls*, who were her family. Surely he would protect her now that she had perjured herself.

Cunningham shook his head sadly.

"No more questions, your Honor."

"Well, that's enough for today, I should think," announced Simmons. "Court adjourned until nine in the morning." He banged his gavel, the defense and prosecution stood, and the guard gripped Bailey's elbow.

This time, as she was led down the aisle, she trained her eyes to the floor, not even able to look at him. *Jacob.* The thought of him thinking of her as a child prostitute made her stomach clench and her head pound. Three women—well, two, since one witness was impeached—had just sworn on the Bible that she had been a whore all those years ago.

The shame of it, even though it was unearned and fabricated, lay on her like a heavy cloak.

CHAPTER FOURTEEN

"Your Honor, the prosecution calls Franticek Naplava to the stand." It was morning of Day Three, and with Jennings' words, it promised to be the worst day yet. Bailey had received yet another beautiful gown the night before, this one a deep rose color with simple, sweet eyelet trim and breathable, comfortable lines. *He picked it out himself,* Cunningham had whispered in her ear with a grin as they made the short walk through the halls to the courtroom that morning, and the thought of Jacob picking through racks of women's dresses with her in mind made her smile in return. For him to have the freedom to do that must mean that Caroline was indeed ensconced in her contrived quarantine. And it meant that he didn't hate Bailey, even though he may believe that she had lied to him as a child.

But hopeful thoughts dissipated as Franticek was called to testify *against her.* Cunningham had warned her that both Franticek and Jacob were on the potential witness list for the prosecution, but he highly doubted that Jennings would call them, particularly after yesterday's fiasco. Abe scribbled a note and handed it surreptitiously to Bailey. *Jennings' stupidity is boundless,* and she fought to keep the smile from her face. Maybe this would turn out fine.

Franticek was sworn in, repeating the oath in his thickly-accented English. He took his seat and sat utterly still, dignified and sturdy and calm, if perhaps a bit stiff. He wore a hounds-tooth sack coat over a white collared shirt that had been crisply starched, and his smart black bow-tie, slightly askew, made Bailey grin. His thick hair, only now just starting to gray, was carefully slicked back, emphasizing his strong jaw and handsome face, so like his son's. Women of all ages present in the courtroom were quite captivated.

"State your name and occupation," ordered Jennings.

"Franticek Naplava, ranch co-owner."

"Address?"

"Bluebonnet Ranch in Boerne." The jurors looked impressed and Bailey's heart swelled at the name of the ranch. She had named it, after all. God help them if *that* should come up.

"Were you acquainted with a girl by the name of Bailey Rose fifteen years ago, in the year eighteen hundred and seventy-six?"

"Yes."

"What were the circumstances of that acquaintance?"

"She came out with my son to stay at our ranch a few days."

Jennings turned to the jury and quirked an eyebrow. "Came out with your son?" His voice was full of insinuation.

Franticek stared at him, unblinking, silent. He was not a man to be provoked easily.

"Objection, your Honor. The witness already answered that question," Cunningham finally said, if only to decrease the amount of time Jennings stood there with that ridiculous smirk on his face.

Jennings waved his hand. "Withdrawn. Mr. Naplava, how did Miss Rose travel from the city to your ranch?"

"In a wagon," he said shortly. The crowd snickered.

"How long did it take to travel by wagon from San Antonio proper to your ranch in Boerne fifteen years ago?"

"Two days."

"Two full days?"

"Pretty near. Depends on the horses. Depends on the load. Depends on the condition of the roads. Depends on the weather. Depends on the driver." It amounted to a soliloquy, and Bailey stared at Franticek in appreciation.

"What was the name of the son she was traveling with?"

"Jacob." There were many audible gasps, and Bailey made fists, digging her nails into her palms. *Oh, Jake. I'm sorry.*

"How long did it take your son Jacob and Miss Rose to make the trip?" Jennings snapped, irritated at being one-upped.

"Two days." Louder laughter this time.

"Would that include a night?" For a long moment Franticek just stared at him, incredulous at the asinine quality of the question.

"It has been my experience that two days are always separated by a night," he deadpanned, and the audience roared. Even Simmons cracked a smile.

Jennings flushed and attempted to speak over the laughter, forced to ask his next question twice. "Where did they pass the night? I say, where did your son and Miss Rose pass the night?"

The audience hushed; this was getting good. "They stopped where my family always stopped, at the Milans in Selma at Leon Creek."

"Were they chaperoned, to the best of your knowledge?"

"Objection, your Honor. Irrelevant line of questioning."

"Exception," snapped Jennings. "I'm establishing the purpose of the defendant's journey."

"Overruled."

Jennings sniffed and turned back to Franticek. "Were they chaperoned?"

"I don't know."

Jennings' head whipped back around; he had turned to make faces at the jury and he didn't expect this remark.

"What do you mean, you don't know?"

"I mean that I wasn't there. If I tell you that no one chaperoned them, or that someone chaperoned them, wouldn't that be hearsay?"

The audience murmured, impressed, and Cunningham laughed out loud.

"I believe I should offer a tardy objection to that question," he sputtered.

"Exception!" Jennings barely managed to slide in before Simmons opened his mouth.

"Sustained! By God, wake up, Mr. Jennings and Mr. Cunningham! It won't do to have the witness performing your jobs, too!"

Franticek sat expressionless while laughter and murmurs rose in a wave across the courtroom. Jacob felt an acute pang of pride for his father, a truly brilliant man disguised as a humble, foreign rancher. *He should be the mayor, not me.*

"Mr. Naplava! Why did Miss Rose visit your ranch?"

"Am I supposed to say what Miss Rose was thinking? Isn't that hearsay again?"

"Your Honor, permission to treat the witness as hostile."

Cunningham frowned. If Simmons allowed it, Jennings could let forth with as many leading questions as liked.

Simmons sighed. "Let's not do that quite yet. Mr. Naplava, if Mr. Jennings promises to ask questions correctly, do you promise to answer?"

Franticek nodded sternly. "I already took my oath upon the Bible," he reminded the judge.

Simmons regarded him for another moment, admiring the man. *Balls of steel, this one.*

"All right, Mr. Jennings. See if you can ask a question that Mr. Naplava can answer."

Jennings' eyes were snapping with anger. His foot beat a staccato upon the floor. He glared at Franticek for a few seconds before posing his next question. "Did your son, Jacob, or Miss Rose ever explain why Miss Rose had come for a visit?"

"Yes, my son did."

"What was the reason he gave?"

"That she had a wretched life in the city, living under the porch at a brothel, and he wanted to show her clean living and a loving family."

Bailey's eyes stung with gratitude. Most of the jurors' expressions were soft and appreciative. The crowd was murmuring approval. This testimony was not going Jennings' way at all, and he was determined to turn it around, and quickly.

"Were Miss Rose and your son, Jacob Naplava, chaperoned every moment once they reached the ranch?"

"No."

Jennings raised his eyebrows and made suggestive faces at the jury.

"Can you testify that you are absolutely certain that Bailey Rose did not engage in acts of prostitution at your ranch?"

Jacob managed to get halfway out of his seat before Johann on one side and Wenzel on the other yanked him back down. This time Wenzel leaned in to whisper. "That won't help," he said carefully, and Jacob tried to force his muscles to relax. He wanted to beat Jennings in the very worst way.

Franticek gazed at Jennings sternly. "Yes."

Jennings spun on his heel to face him. "Yes? How can you be certain?"

"I have never allowed prostitution on my ranch."

"But you just said that she was not chaperoned every moment she was there. You cannot account for her whereabouts or actions."

Franticek frowned. "I can account for every one of my men. They were all supervised, *every moment*. I run a tight ship."

Jennings flushed again. He was no match for Franticek, and he knew it. He had one more chance to force this impassive man to damage Bailey's character.

"When you returned to San Antonio with Miss Rose and your son and other family and workers, where did Miss Rose go?"

"She went to Fort Allen to get permission from her Ma to stay the summer at the ranch while we unloaded the wagon in Military Plaza."

There were a few gasps from the audience: few had known that Jacob and Bailey had been acquainted all those years ago, let alone that she wanted to live with his family!

"And when did she return?"

"She didn't."

"And so you just left without her?"

"No. We went to Fort Allen to find her."

There was more excited shuffling and rumbling as the story deepened: Simmons had to bang his gavel and bark at the crowd.

"What happened when you arrived?"

"We rang the bell." Titters.

"Will you please tell the whole story, Mr. Naplava?" asked Jennings with exaggerated patience.

"The madam of the house answered, Blanche DuBois, I suppose her name is; the woman who testified. She told us that Bailey wasn't there, but that she had left a letter for us. She went to get it and returned about five minutes later."

"And what did the letter say?"

"It said that she had gone away with her mother and a man, and that her mother wouldn't allow her to spend the summer at the ranch."

"Do you still have the letter?"

"No, I burned it when I returned home."

"What happened next, Mr. Naplava?"

"Jacob didn't believe the letter."

"Was he able to identify Miss Rose's handwriting?"

"He said it looked like her handwriting." The crowed murmured and Bailey's heart fell.

"What happened next?"

"Miss DuBois said Bailey was fourteen, not twelve, and had been working in the brothel for a year. Jacob didn't believe that, either, and he asked me to go inside and look for her, and so I did."

"And what did you find, Mr. Naplava?"

"I didn't find Bailey, if that's what you're asking. She wasn't anywhere to be found in the house or under the porch."

"And did you speak to anyone in Fort Allen as you searched?"

"Yes."

"And can you tell us what you asked, and what they answered?"

For the first time, Franticek hesitated. "I asked if Bailey worked there as a prostitute, and they all said yes."

"No more questions," said Jennings, pleased.

"Cross," barked Cunningham before Simmons had a chance to ask. He strode to the witness stand, eyes flashing. There was no need to question him further about the goings-on at the ranch; Franticek had taken care of that aspect himself. "Mr. Naplava, you mentioned that when you spoke with Miss DuBois, she left you at the doorstep to go retrieve a letter."

"That's right."

"How long did you say she was gone?"

"Five minutes, maybe a few more."

"How long was the note itself?"

"Very short, just a few sentences."

"So it was short enough that Miss DuBois would have had time to write the note herself?"

"Objection!" roared Jennings, too incensed to elucidate what he was objecting to.

"Exception. The witness is being asked a question that only he and his son have direct testimony to address."

"Overruled," said Simmons pleasantly, enjoying Jennings' wrath.

"Yes, she would have had time to do that," Franticek answered.

"And would she have had time to tell a few of the women to pass along instructions to say that Bailey was fourteen and worked in the house?"

Jennings writhed in agony.

"Yes."

"When you searched the house, did you ask the women if Bailey worked there as a prostitute?"

Franticek shook his head, understanding at once where Cunningham was taking this line of questioning. "No, I didn't."

"Did you ask if she was fourteen?"

"No sir, I did not. I was just there to look for her."

"What did you ask the women?"

"If Bailey was there and if they knew where she went."

"And what answers did you get?"

"They all said she wasn't there, they didn't know where had gone, and that she was a working girl at Fort Allen and had gone away with her mother earlier that day."

Cunningham stared at him, then turned to stare at the jury, a frown on his face. Finally he turned back to Franticek.

"Did you find it odd that they all were answering a question you hadn't asked them? That she was a working girl at Fort Allen?"

Franticek nodded. "I'm ashamed to say that it didn't occur to me then, in the confusion of the moment. But now it's quite odd, yes."

"No more questions."

"Re-direct." Jennings hopped up smartly. "Mr. Naplava, did you believe, on that night fifteen years ago, that Bailey Rose was a fourteen-year-old prostitute at Fort Allen?"

Franticek glared. "Yes," he finally muttered, and the audience murmured loudly.

"Thank you," Jennings snapped triumphantly.

As Franticek left the witness stand, his eyes met Bailey's. *Courage*, they seemed to say.

She was going to need every bit of it she possessed, because the next witness Jennings called sent cold spikes of dread throughout her body.

"The prosecution calls Jacob Naplava!"

The audience erupted into loud murmurs and scandalized chatter, and as Jacob stood and made his way to the stand, newspaper artists flung themselves into the aisles to get better angles from which to draw his likeness. Simmons' muttonchops took on a life of their own, springing forth from his face and shaking with outrage as he banged his gavel and called for order.

"I will clear this courtroom if I hear one more peep!" He finally roared, and the crowd hushed almost immediately. Bailey sunk into her chair, closed her eyes, and prayed harder than she ever had in her life. *Please, God. Don't let this cast a shadow on his name. He's a great man. He has a child on the way. Please let him speak quickly and go away from here, unscathed.* She could imagine tomorrow's papers already, *Mayor Elect Takes Stand in Child Whore Senator Murder Case!* When she dared to peek, he was staring right at her, his eyes shining. She looked away, dismayed and petrified for him. Really, he had no fear, and not one counterfeit fiber in his entire being. If he wanted to convey his love to her with his gaze, well then, he would do it, in front of God, the judge, the jury, his friends and family. She would have laughed in sheer admiration if she wasn't so terrified.

Jacob took his oath and his seat, sitting straight and tall like his father, his blue eyes flashing and his jaw set. Unlike his father, he looked to be combustible. Jennings approached the stand slowly as if unsure if this was a wise idea after all. He was striving to besmirch Bailey Rose's character, but if the jury ended up believing that she enjoyed, as a poor, neglected child, an innocent few days with the future mayor-elect and his family in a harmless, bucolic setting, it would be all the worse for his case. It was a risk, but the young Naplava had a temper and he could capitalize on that. "State your name and occupation," he ventured.

"Jacob Naplava, Boerne, co-owner and operator of the Bluebonnet Ranch. Oh, and mayor-elect of San Antonio," he added belatedly without a trace of braggadocio, and the audience laughed quietly, silencing immediately at Simmons' glare.

"How did you become acquainted with Bailey Rose?"

"She attended my school when we were children."

"When was that?"

"In May of eighteen seventy-six."

"How long had you known her before you invited her to your family's ranch?"

Jacob frowned. This was a legitimate question, but it would look bad for Bailey. "About twelve hours."

There was a general murmur.

Jennings paused, clearly conflicted about whether to revisit the whole concept of an unchaperoned two-day trip and deciding against it.

"And once you arrived at the ranch, in what activities did you partake with Miss Rose?"

This was actually a quite well-crafted question: it, too, was legitimate, and served to insinuate that questionable activities were going on between the two of them. A muscle in Jacob's jaw jumped. Best to get it all out there, all at once. "My mother helped her to clean up, first thing. Then we ate dinner. Then she went to bed with my sisters. The next morning she sheared sheep with us. After that—"

Jennings held up a hand. "With us? Who is 'us'?"

"My brothers, my father, and the hired hands, the *pastores.*"

"She wasn't with the women and your sisters in the house that day?"

"Asked and answered," Jacob snapped, and the audience sniggered.

Jennings grew red in the face but said nothing, knowing he would be reprimanded by the judge.

"Why was Miss Rose not spending the day with the women folk?"

"She wanted to shear sheep; I had already promised her on the way to the ranch."

"Were you shearing sheep that day, Mr. Naplava?"

"No. I was packing bags."

"Could you see Miss Rose every moment that day?"

"Not every second, no."

"What do you suppose was the longest stretch of time she was out of your sight?"

"Objection," said Cunningham crisply. "This is irrelevant."

"Exception. I am simply trying to establish whether Miss Rose had any unsupervised time. After all, previous witnesses have already testified to her possible activities at this ranch."

Lord in Heaven, thought Bailey. *He's making it sound as though I were turning tricks in the barn!*

"I'll allow it," Simmons agreed grumpily.

"Mr. Naplava?"

"I don't recall precisely. Probably ten minutes. I put her in the barn to shear a sheep by herself, and it only took her ten minutes. The rest of the day she was working out in plain sight with the rest of us."

Jennings could see he was getting nowhere. "And did you have any unsupervised time with Miss Rose at the ranch?" he ventured, not really hoping for anything.

"I guess you could call it that."

He whipped around, his interest renewed. "Can you explain your answer?"

"Pa sent us to the creek to clean up after shearing and packing wool."

He turned to the jury and raised his eyebrows. "Just the two of you? Alone? To bathe in the creek?" He spun back to see how Jacob would respond.

"Yes." The veins in his neck were bulging now, and he was leaning forward like a cougar about to pounce. Bailey tried to send a mental message. *Don't let him bait you, Jake.*

Jennings leaned his elbow on the witness stand and tipped sideways, tipping his lips up in a knowing smirk, as if he were engaging in manly banter with a friend. All that was missing was the wink. "Mr. Naplava, with the previous testimony established by Miss Love, I have to ask. Did you and Miss Rose engage in any—let's be as delicate as possible here—in any *amorous* activities, and if so, did money change hands?"

Three things happened in rapid succession. First, Jacob leaned forward, grabbed Jennings' shirtfront with one fist, and rose to his feet. By virtue of

Jacob's slightly elevated position on the stand and the fact that he was taller to begin with, Mr. Jennings was soon dangling six inches in the air, his feet kicking wildly, his mouth opening and closing like a fish out of water. Then Simmons began banging the gavel and roaring for the guard as the audience erupted in laughter and cheers. It was utter chaos. And then Bailey stood and reached toward Jacob, panicked with fear for him. "No, Jake!" Somehow, even though her voice surely must have been drowned out by the cacophony, he heard her, and lowered Jennings to the floor.

By the time the guard reached Jacob, he was standing quietly with his hands behind his back, staring at the floor. Jennings had retreated to his chair, clearly unhurt but burning with humiliation at being suspended in front of the audience like a fish on a hook. The guard stood awkwardly, not knowing what to do, as Simmons banged his gavel and roared for silence. At last the room quieted as more of the sheriff's men entered the courtroom and positioned themselves in the aisles.

"Clear the courtroom of all spectators!" yelled Simmons. "All of you animals, out of my courtroom! If you are on the witness list, remain in the hallway. If not, leave the courthouse." There was a stunned silence followed by a noisy shuffling as two hundred people rose to their feet and made their way out of the courtroom, a process that took a solid ten minutes. For the duration of the exodus, Jacob stared at the floor, afraid that any glance at Bailey would damage her case in some way, and that any look toward Jennings would be construed as another attack. So he gazed at his feet, cursing his temper, while Bailey gulped back tears and stared at her hands, clasped tightly together on the table.

At last the room was empty.

Simmons cleared his throat. "Two things," he began, sounding tired. "First, Mr, Jennings, I believe that you intentionally baited Mr. Naplava with an inflammatory accusation in order to get a response. Well, you got it, didn't you?"

Jennings glared at the judge. "This man should be hauled away to jail."

Simmons shrugged. "Are you sure you want to do that?" Jennings frowned, irritated beyond measure. Simmons was right: he needed this witness—he still had questions for him—and putting him in jail would delay the trial for days. Simmons would make him pay for that. Besides, he could always prosecute Naplava later for this assault. He had plenty of time.

"All right. I'll bide my time."

Simmons rolled his eyes. "Let's get on with it, then."

Jennings nodded crisply. "My question about amorous activities was a valid question."

Cunningham snorted. "You asked him if he had paid sexual relations with a child!"

Simmons shifted impatiently. "All right now, shut up, both of you. Let's do this properly for the record. Mr. Cunningham, do you wish to object to Mr. Jennings question?"

"Yes. Objection. The witness is protected by the Fifth Amendment of the Constitution of the United States against self-incrimination."

"Exception! Only if answering implicates him in criminal activity!"

Simmons was about to open his mouth to say "Sustained!" when Jacob waved his hand.

"I'll answer it."

Simmons raised an eyebrow. "Well, all right then, Naplava, get to it, for the love of God."

"No, I did not have sexual relations with Miss Rose for money or any other reason."

Jennings looked like he wanted to go further, but just then he happened to catch Jacob's eye and changed his mind.

"One more question. When Miss DuBois showed your father the letter purported to be written by Miss Rose, did you identify the handwriting as Miss Rose's handwriting?"

Jacob's mind worked frantically, crafting a reply.

"No."

Jennings did a double-take. "I'm sorry? Did you say *no*?"

Jacob stared at him.

"Your father testified that you identified that handwriting as Miss Rose's handwriting."

"No, he didn't."

Jennings blinked a few times. "Court reporter! Please read Mr. Franticek Naplava's testimony regarding the letter from Miss Rose."

The court reporter lifted his fingers from the stenotype machine and shuffled through tape, then began reading the transcript. *"The madam of the house answered, Blanche DuBois, I suppose her name is; the woman who testified. She told us that Bailey wasn't there, but that she had left a letter for us. She went to get it and returned about five minutes later."*

"And what did the letter say?"

"It said that she had gone away with her mother and a man, and that her mother wouldn't allow her to spend the summer at the ranch."

"Do you still have the letter?"

"No, I burned it when I returned home."

"What happened next, Mr. Naplava?"

"Jacob didn't believe the letter."

"Was he able to identify Miss Rose's handwriting?"

"He said it looked like her handwriting."

Jennings sniffed. "Thank you, reporter. Do you wish to change your answer, Mr. Naplava?"

"No. I didn't identify it as her handwriting. I said it looked like her handwriting. *I could have written a note that looked like her handwriting.*"

Jennings' eyes widened with frustration. "All right then, Mr. Naplava, I will rephrase the question. "Did you ever believe the note was written by Miss Rose? Either when you first saw it, or later?"

Jacob's heart lurched. *Damn this crooked lawyer!* "Yes," he said tightly.

"And did you ever believe, either at that time, or later, that Miss Rose was working at Fort Allen as a prostitute?"

"Yes."

"Thank you. No further questions," Jennings interrupted hastily. Jacob risked a glance at Bailey, trying to put every bit of sorry into it, but she was staring at the table, two bright spots of color on her cheeks, looking devastated. He felt his gut twist.

Cunningham stood for the cross-examination. "Mr. Naplava, how many times in your life had you seen Miss Rose's handwriting?"

"Just once. At school the day she came."

"How long of a time did you spend looking at her handwriting?"

"About three minutes, I'd say."

"Are you a handwriting expert, Mr. Naplava?"

"No."

"Do you know anything about garlands?"

"No. I don't know what that refers to."

"How about cascades? Or baseline slants? Do these terms mean anything to you?"

"No."

"Let the record show that Mr. Naplava is not a handwriting expert."

Jennings opened his mouth to object and snapped it shut again.

"Mr. Naplava, you mentioned in your testimony that you had to tie up the sheep for Miss Rose to shear. Why didn't she tie it up herself?"

"She wouldn't have been able to lift it. You have to lift the sheep, flip it on its back, and tie its feet."

"How much did the sheep weigh?"

"At least one hundred pounds."

"Will you please describe the stature of Miss Rose when you knew her in 1876?"

"She was small for her age. Not five feet. Probably about seventy pounds at the most." A memory invaded his brain then: he was pulling her from the creek after she almost drowned: she was so small and fragile in his arms.

"No more questions."

Jennings wisely made no move to re-direct, and Jacob was dismissed from the stand. Cunningham took stock of the expressions on the face of the jurors: amazingly, even though the mayor-elect had actually roughed up the prosecutor, almost every man on the panel was looking at Jacob with respect and admiration. Hell, they probably liked him *more* now. This *was* Texas, after all!

"Mr. Naplava, you may go about your business this morning," advised Simmons, suspecting the young man would take a seat in the courtroom if he didn't say something to the contrary. "I will allow the public back in after the noon hour." Jacob nodded and looked at Bailey as he passed her, but she was still staring at the table, her hands and jaw clenched. *God almighty, I love her.* He put his head down to hide his expression from the judge and jury—it had to be painted all over his face—and quickly strode from the room.

CHAPTER FIFTEEN

"Call your next witness," Simmons sighed.

"The prosecution calls Rufus Jones." The guard had to go fetch Jones from the hallway.

Mr. Jones made his way carefully to the stand, his cane tapping loudly in the almost-empty room, his dark eyes wary and suspicious. His sweet wife had pulled his old gray tweed suit from the mothballs—the one he wore to his own son's funeral after the war—and steamed all the wrinkles over a kettle of boiling water, laying it flat to dry on the kitchen table. She had shaved him and washed his hair in the yard and combed it all out, then slicked it down good with chicken fat she had scented with crushed mint leaves. He was horribly uncomfortable and hot and smelled like a minty chicken, but he had hugged her and kissed her and rubbed her feet. He frowned as he approached the stand. He knew the moment he had talked to that pretty blond girl weeks ago that he had made a mistake; he just felt it in his bones. And now here he was forced to testify against that sweet little Bailey; she *still* was a sweet little girl; he could see that with a glance.

After Jones had established his name, address, and former occupation, Jennings started in: he had one purpose only with this client, to prove that he was too daft or senile to set a definite time of arrival for the Rose girl. "Mr. Jones, on the evening of May twentieth, 1876, describe your encounter with the defendant."

"Well, I was in the hotel, right inside the door, you see, and this little girl came waltzing right through like she owned the place." He laughed fondly at the memory. "Hoo-*hee*! She was trying to be on her high horse, she was; all bluster, bless her heart. A little thing, she was." He shook his head, remembering, and Jennings shifted his feet impatiently.

"Go on," he barked.

"Well, she asked me what room the senator was in, and that threw me a good one. I asked her why she wanted to know, and she told me it was a private affair."

Jennings spun to the jury, his eyebrows raised at the provocative term. "A private affair? Those were the words she used?"

"Yes sir," said Jones uncertainly, not understanding the insinuation.

"And did you accompany her to the room?"

Mr. Jones frowned, confused. "Not all the way, but excuse me, you skipped—"

"Just answer my questions, Mr. Jones. What do you mean by 'not all the way'?"

"I showed her the back stairs and pointed her to Room #226."

"And what time was this?"

"It was half past six, thereabouts."

"You're not sure of the precise time?"

Jones' brow furled again. "Well, I didn't look at my watch, but—"

"Is there a possibility that the time could have been closer to six o'clock?"

"Well, I don't know about that."

"You are just commenting on the possibility, Mr. Jones. You already testified that you didn't look at your watch. Is there a possibility that the time could have been six o'clock? Or just a little after?"

"I s'pose so," he finally said, not wanting to perjure himself.

"Thank you. No further questions."

"I assume you have a cross-examination, Mr. Cunningham?" Simmons said with a heavy voice.

Cunningham nodded and approached the stand. "Mr. Jones, in your best estimation, what time did Miss Rose enter the hotel?"

"Thirty minutes after six," he said immediately.

"And what makes you think it was that time, even though you didn't look at your watch?"

"Well, I remember the clock striking six in the lobby, and that was quite a while before Miss Rose arrived."

"When did you next look at your watch?"

He thought about for a moment, and then his face lit. No one could have mistaken it for what it was: a return of a genuine memory. "About ten or fifteen minutes after Miss Rose went upstairs, I pulled out my watch, because I knew I had a carriage coming for the Wishburns at six forty-five and I wanted to be ready."

"And what time was it when you looked?"

"Six forty-five. I remember because when I saw what time it was, I was scared I missed the carriage, so I ran outside and there it was, just pulling up, right on time."

Jennings slouched in his seat.

"Thank you, Mr. Jones. After Miss Rose told you it was a private affair, did you push for more of an explanation?"

"Yes! I told her she'd have to do better than that! You see, of course, I was going to walk her right back out of the hotel; a little girl shouldn't be in a hotel alone. But she told me her Mama was up there with the senator, and that she wanted to tell her goodbye because she was going away for a spell and didn't want her Ma to worry."

"And did she tell you her mother was Addie Rose?"

"Objection! That's a leading question!"

"I'll rephrase. Did Miss Rose tell you who her mother was?"

"Yes; she said her Ma's name was Addie Rose, and that her Ma was a working girl from Fort Allen."

The jury shifted in surprise.

"And I recognized that name!" announced Mr. Jones unexpectedly.

"You did? Can you explain that?"

Jennings' brow furrowed. He had specifically told Jones *not* to bring this up. Jones had a brother in the state prison, and Jennings had promised to look into getting him released. *That was never going to happen now*, he thought viciously.

"Oh yes. I knew a woman named Adele Rosemont years ago. She worked in the dressmaker shop. I thought to myself, *I wonder if that's Addie Rose*. And now I know that I was right."

"Thank you, Mr. Jones. No more questions, your Honor."

"Re-direct!" screeched Jennings. "Mr. Jones, did you see Addie Rose enter the hotel that day?"

"No, can't say that I did."

"So you cannot testify that Addie Rose was in Room 226?"

"No sir."

"Thank you," Mr. Jennings snapped.

"Next witness," said Simmons. This was moving along quite nicely now.

"The prosecution calls Randall James to the stand."

Randall James was procured from the hallway and sworn in. He was a large, tough-looking man with a gray handlebar moustache, thick gray hair slicked back into a neat coif, and a no-nonsense expression in his dark, snapping eyes. With a deep, gravelly voice he announced himself as the barkeep for the Black Dog Saloon for the past twenty-six years.

"Mr. James, did you observe Senator Adam Hawk on the evening of the twentieth of May, 1876?"

"Yes, I did."

"Can you tell us the circumstances of that observation?"

James nodded tersely. "Yes. Hawk came in for a bottle of whisky."

"Do you remember the time?"

"It was a few minutes after six o'clock. The dinner girls come in to wait tables at six and they were just filtering in. They're always late."

"Did Senator Hawk stay in your establishment to enjoy his beverage?"

"No. He bought the bottle and left."

"Is it customary for customers to buy liquor and take it outside to drink it?"

"Yes, it is. There's a beer garden a block down and there's usually quite a gathering there every night except Sunday."

"Had you ever observed Senator Hawk in the beer garden?"

"Sure, lots of times."

"Is it reasonable to assume he went to the beer garden when he left your establishment?"

"Yes."

"Thank you. No more questions."

Jennings looked downright relieved to have questioned one of his own witnesses who was not disastrous, and Cunningham hadn't bothered to object to anything!

"Cross," said Cunningham quietly, rising. "Mr. James, can you describe the demeanor of Senator Hawk that evening?"

"Yes. He was acting different. Usually he was a nice fellow, polite and smart. But that night he was—I don't know how to describe it—in a daze. He was staring off into space and seemed kind of stunned or something. I just figured he was junked up on drugs. I had heard he did that but I never seen him like that myself."

"Anything else unusual?"

"Well, I don't know if it's unusual, but his hair was wet, like he had just bathed."

"Objection! Witness is speculating!" barked Jennings.

"Overruled," said Simmons before Cunningham had a chance to voice an exception. "Witness is answering the question as it was asked."

Jennings sank back down and muttered angrily under his breath. Cunningham had just been handed a possible piece of evidence on a silver platter: he would make the argument that after Hawk killed the first woman, he bathed to remove the blood. He grappled wildly for a way to undo the damage.

"No more questions," said Cunningham.

"I re-call Betsy Blue to the stand!"

Simmons frowned fiercely. "This better be good. Guard, please escort Mr. James out of the courtroom and fetch Miss Blue."

Mr. James strode from the courtroom without a glance at anyone, and in a few moments Betsy Blue was helped back onto the stand.

"Miss Blue, do I need to remind you of the oath you took?" asked Simmons, and with a frightened look at Cunningham, she shook her head.

"Answer for the record."

"No, sir. I mean you don't need to remind me. I remember."

"Very well. I believe Mr. Jennings has some additional questions for you."

"Miss Blue, do working girls typically bathe after they have—*spent time*—with their customers?"

The question was so unexpected to everyone that Betsy's momentary silence was not even noticed.

"Well," she finally said, speaking slowly and cautiously. "Yes, that happens sometimes." She caught the disgruntled look on Jennings' face and struggled to answer in a way that would please him without perjuring herself. "Jezzie, she was one for baths. She liked to bathe *with* her johns, you see. It was part of her *repertoire*." She hadn't used such a fancy word in a long time, and doing so made her nostalgic for the good old comfortable, secure days at Fort Allen.

"Thank you," said Jennings shortly. "No more questions."

Betsy was escorted from the courtroom and Simmons glanced briefly at the witness list. "Two more witnesses for your prosecution, Jennings?"

"Yes, your Honor."

"Think we can get them done before lunch?"

"Yes, I do," he replied smartly, hoping for points from the judge for expediency.

"Guard, how many folks stuck around today?"

"The hallway is packed tight, your Honor. We tried to make them leave, but every time we order them out of the building, they sneak back in as soon as our backs are turned."

Simmons stroked a mutton chop and considered his options. Truth be told, he didn't mind reading the stories about himself in the papers. He ran a tight, efficient ship here, and he loved sending the dailies to his pompous brother back east, who served as a federal judge in Boston. "Let them back in," he said, and it was another fifteen minutes before the court was packed tightly again, nary a person missing from before, including San Antonio's young mayor-elect, whom the reporters followed around like a pack of dogs.

Simmons read them the riot act and threated to jail anyone who caused a ruckus. "I will have order in my court!" he thundered, and the room became so still that Bailey could have sworn everyone was holding their breaths.

"Call the next witness!"

"The prosecution calls Mary Cantese."

A petite, middle-aged Irish woman was helped onto the stand and took her oath. "State your name and occupation in May of 1876."

"Mary Cantese. I worked as a housekeeper at the Gaslight."

"Are you still employed there?"

"No, sir. I'm retired now."

"Did you work on the twentieth of May, 1876?"

"Yes. I had to work a double shift for a sick girl. I came in at nine o'clock in the morning and didn't leave until midnight."

"Were you responsible for cleaning Senator Hawk's room?"

"Yes, sir. I cleaned it that morning."

"And was he in his room all day?"

"No, sir. He left at ten in the morning and didn't come back until around four in the afternoon."

"Did you speak to him?"

"No, sir. I saw him leave and return because I happened to be in the hallway both times. I was washing and waxing the floor that day, all day, on and off between my other duties."

"Did you see anyone else enter Senator Hawk's room?"

"Yes. A few minutes after five o'clock I saw a woman walking down the hall toward his room. She had come up the back stairs. I know it was five because that's when I made my rounds to collect dirty towels."

"How close were you to the woman?"

"I passed her in the hallway."

"Can you describe her for us?"

Mary put a thoughtful look on her face, but she wasn't fooling anyone: she had been well-rehearsed. "She was a pretty woman with an expensive gown. I assumed she was a lady of the evening because she was not chaperoned, she wore face paint, and she had rings on every finger."

"Did you see the lady enter Senator Hawk's room?"

"Yes. She knocked, and he let her in."

"What happened next?"

"Well, I went downstairs right after that with my towels. I don't know what happened next."

"Mrs. Cantese, did you hear a gunshot at any time between five and six-thirty?"

"No sir, I did not. But there were fireworks going off and I doubt I would've heard any shots anyway."

"Fireworks?"

"Yes, sir. There was a party going on the front lawn, and they'd been setting off fireworks all afternoon. The guests were getting plenty mad about it."

"Did you see Senator Hawk any more that evening?"

"Yes, sir. I was in the lobby dusting when he came down and mailed a letter."

Bailey stifled a gasp; she actually put her hand to her mouth to hide her shock. *He mailed a letter.* A memory came flooding back, so vibrant that she felt as though she had traveled through time. Hawk was propped up against a wall, his grey eyes reflecting horror and grief, and she was bent over in a chair, weak and shivering, a string of saliva hanging from her lip, a puddle of sick on the floor between her feet. The gun was smooth and cold in her hand. *"I wrote you a letter today. After she came. I sent it. I told you to stay away.*

Why didn't you stay away?" He was sobbing. She squeezed her eyes shut as tightly as she could, trying to banish the image, and when she had regained some sense of control, opened them and reached for a pen and paper. *I think the letter was addressed to me,* she wrote in a shaking hand, and pushed the note to Cunningham, whose eyes widened as he glanced at her. He gave a brief nod.

Jennings' continued, oblivious to the drama playing out behind him, only concerned with establishing that his client was engaged in normal activities after the time at which the defense was insisting the older woman had been killed. "What time did he mail a letter?"

"That was ten minutes before six o'clock. I know because at six I had to help with trays, and I kept looking at the clock to make sure I wasn't late."

"Did he seem to be behaving normally?"

She paused and tilted her head, pretending to think about it. "Why yes, I suppose so. He just mailed the letter. I remember thinking he didn't have the lady with him, so I supposed he was going out to fetch food or wine or some such thing, because after he mailed his letter he left."

"When did the fireworks stop?"

"Mr. Willshire finally made them stop around half past six, I suppose."

"Did you see Senator Hawk return?"

"No, sir."

"Mrs. Cantese, did you hear a gunshot at any time during the evening?"

"Yes, sir. I heard a gunshot at eight in the evening."

"How do you know it was eight?"

"The grandfather clock in the lobby had just struck."

"And what happened when you heard the gunshot?"

"Mr. Willshire sent a boy to fetch the police, and then he ran upstairs. He came back down and said that there were two dead people in Senator Hawk's room, and one of them was Senator Hawk. I felt just terrible about it. I had only ever talked to him one time and he seemed like a nice man. Sad, but nice. And then the police came not more than five minutes later."

Jennings cleared his throat. She had said rather more than he had wanted her to say, but overall, she had performed quite well.

"Thank you, Mrs. Cantese. No further questions."

"Cross?" asked Simmons.

Cunningham stood and approached the stand. "Mrs. Cantese, do you feel like you had a good look at the fancy woman who went into Senator Hawk's room?"

"Yes, sir."

"Could you give us the most detailed description you can give?"

"Yes, sir. She was about four inches taller than me, about 130 pounds, I should say. Brown hair. Rather a round face, like a china doll. Very pretty. Her dress was layers and layers of green silk; it looked heavy and hot."

"Can you comment on her demeanor?"

"Yes." Mary hesitated. Jennings might not like what she had to say, but she was a truthful woman, after all. "She looked frantic and kind of crazy."

"Objection!" roared Jennings. "Witness cannot testify to the woman's state of mind!"

"Sustained. Mrs. Cantese, can you please clarify your comments in an objective manner as possible?" Simmons intoned.

Mary flushed. "Well, she was walking very fast and was staring right at the door. Her eyes were very wide open; I could see the whites of them all the way around. She looked scared but fixed on doing something."

Bailey closed her eyes and trained her breathing. They were describing her mother's last moment on earth: to think of her as terrified and fatalistic was shattering.

Cunningham handed an item to the bailiff. "Your Honor, I am submitting this photograph of Adele Rosemont as evidence. This photograph is sworn, through an affidavit signed by Karl Schwartz, to be a betrothal image of Adele Rosemont and John Bailey, taken thirteen years before the day Mrs. Cantese saw the woman in the hallway."

Bailey bit her lips. Her mother hadn't aged too much over time; even though her mind had been ravaged by the effects of morphine and cocaine, her face and body had retained youthfulness thanks to good nutrition and expensive beauty regimes.

The daguerreotype was handed to the judge and then the jury, and at last, to Mary Cantese.

"Mrs. Cantese, is this the woman you saw in the hallway on the night of May twentieth, 1876?"

"Yes, that's her." She had not even hesitated, and the spectators gasped. If the woman in the room had been Bailey's mother, it made her story entirely credible.

"Thank you. No further questions."

"Re-direct!" Jennings had shot from his chair and raced to the stand before Cunningham even had a chance to get out of the way, and the two of them did a humorous do-si-do as they tried to navigate around each other. The audience snickered.

"Your Honor, I'm entering into evidence a detailed description of Jezebel St. John, as verified by affidavit from three women who worked with her for years: Betsy Blue, Lynda Love, and Blanche DuBois." He produced the document with a flourish and it was distributed by the bailiff. Once Jennings had it back, he read from it with his grating tone.

"'Miss Jezebel St. John is approximately five feet, four inches tall, one hundred and thirty-five pounds, with brown hair and green eyes. She has plump lovely cheeks," here he paused, his own cheeks coloring as the audience laughed. "'...and a sparkling, engaging smile. She has an adorable lilting nose." Again the audience chuckled, and Jennings cleared his throat and adjusted his bow tie. "She adorns herself in luxurious French gowns, always silk, and wears rings on every finger and jewels at her throat.'" He glared at Mary. "Mrs. Cantese, does this or does this not sound like a description of the woman you saw in the hallway, right down to the rings on her fingers?"

Bailey groaned inwardly. Almost every girl at Fort Allen wore valuable rings on every finger; it was a sign of status and a hallmark of working at Fort Allen. And Jezzie had borne a strong resemblance to Addie; everyone used to comment on it.

"I suppose it does," she answered uncertainly.

"And tell the jury how many seconds you had a chance to look at the woman in the hallway."

She quailed. "Wh—what?"

"How many seconds? How long did you look at her?"

She stared at him. "I suppose a second or two."

"Can you say for sure that the woman you saw was Addie Rose? Even though you just said that the description of Jezebel St. John fits just as well?"

"Objection. Witness did not say 'just as well'."

"Withdrawn," Jennings said hastily. "Can you say for sure the woman was Addie Rose?"

"No," whispered Mary.

Bailey felt her heart speed up. This was looking bad. She snuck a look at Cunningham and the rest of her team, but they looked relaxed and calm, and she tried to take a cue from them.

"No more questions."

Mary was escorted to the back of the room and Manfred Willshire was called forth, the final witness for the prosecution.

Manfred Willshire was a nervous looking man, quite young for having been the desk clerk of a major hotel fifteen years ago. He had wispy blond hair, starting to thin, and pale blue watery eyes. He was dressed smartly in a striped blue suit with tails and large pointed lapels. There was a red carnation in his buttonhole, and Bailey fixated on it. Willshire kept touching it; every minute or so his hand would flutter to his flower, and after a quick touch, flutter back down again. He was sworn in and repeated his oath in a trembling voice.

"Mr. Willshire, were you employed by the Gaslight Hotel in May of 1876?"

"Yes, sir. I still work there as a desk clerk."

Jennings paused a moment to collect his thoughts, needing to establish a timeline. Everything had been so gnarled by that son of a bitch Cunningham: the jurors might be thoroughly confused at this point. "Can you tell me if anything out of the ordinary happened around four in the afternoon that day?"

"Yes, some of the guests starting shooting off those Chinese fireworks on the front lawn."

"And how did the other guests react to this?"

"They started complaining right away."

"Why didn't you stop the fireworks right away?"

"Mr. Harvey—he was the general manager of the hotel—told me to let that party do whatever they like. They were mighty important folks from Austin."

"I see. Did you see a woman enter the hotel around five o'clock, a woman richly attired, with rings on every finger, with a green silk gown, brown hair, and plump cheeks?" There were a few chuckles.

"No, sir. I didn't see anyone like that."

"Was Senator Hawk a guest in your hotel on that night?"

"Oh, yes. He'd been staying for a week. He was in Room 226."

"Did you see him that day?"

"Yes. I came on to work at two o'clock, and I saw him come in at four o'clock, right through the front door, and go up the main stairs to his room."

Jennings decided to get the question out of the way to take a bit of wind out of Cunningham's sails. "Did Senator Hawk appear to be troubled or inebriated at that point?"

"No, sir. Well, I really can't say, as I didn't talk to him, but I glanced up and he looked normal to me."

"Did you see him again that evening?"

"Yes, sir. He came down just before six o'clock to mail a letter. Maybe five or ten minutes before the hour."

"Did you enter into conversation with him at that time?"

"Not really, sir. I recall that he said, "For the post," and handed me the letter, and I dropped it in the slot."

"Did you look at the letter?" Jennings was mildly curious about the letter, but it seemed to be a dead end and most likely inconsequential.

"No, sir! We are not permitted to look at our guests' mail, of course."

"Was Senator Hawk behaving normally?"

"I believe so; I don't remember anything to the contrary."

"Where did Senator Hawk go after he mailed the letter?"

"Well, I don't know. He went out the front entrance, if that's what you mean."

"Did you see him return?"

"No, sir."

"Is it unusual for guests housed on the second floor to use the back staircase?"

"Not at all, sir."

"Now, Mr. Willshire. Did you hear a gunshot at any time in the evening?"

"Yes, sir. I heard a gunshot at eight in the evening."

"How do you know it wasn't fireworks?"

"Oh, I made them stop at half past six. There were too many complaints from other guests to let it go on. So it was nice and quiet.

"How do you know the gunshot was at eight o'clock?"

"The clock had just chimed; right when it finished, there was one gunshot."

"And how did you react?"

Mr. Willshire leaned forward, licking his lips and groping his carnation frantically. "I was startled, I'll tell you. We don't have these kinds of rough goings-on at our establishment. I know some of the other clerks in town have gunshots every night, but not the Gaslight. We're high-class." He seemed to have lost his train of thought.

Jennings frowned. "What did you *do* when you heard the gunshot?" he clarified irritably.

"Well, I sent a boy after the police. Then I ran upstairs, because I knew it had come from the second floor."

There was a pause, but Mr. Willshire was not forthcoming. "Mr. Willshire, please describe everything you did and saw next," Jennings snapped, exasperated.

"All right." Willshire looked hurt and groped his poor carnation in consolation. "I ran upstairs, like I was telling you. I saw that the door to Room 226 was open. I saw a gun outside the door, in the hallway, by the wall."

"Did you see or hear anyone running from the room, or down the stairs?"

"No, sir. There are only two other rooms in that wing, and they were empty that night. It was quiet as a church."

"Go on."

"I looked in and saw Senator Hawk slumped against the wall. There was a whole lot of blood on the wall and in his lap and on the floor." He paused to shudder. "He looked to be dead; I touched his chest and he wasn't breathing. Then I saw her—the woman on the bed." His eyes darted to Bailey, just for an instant, but long enough for the jury to see it, and Jennings cursed under his breath. "She was covered in blood, all over her chest and all over the bed. I touched her chest, too, and she wasn't breathing, either. They were both dead, in my opinion."

"And then what?"

"I left and went downstairs to wait for the police."

Jennings thanked the witness and sat down, and Cunningham frowned fiercely. Something didn't jive, and he suspected that Jennings hadn't taken the time to thoroughly question this witness, assuming it was a straightforward recounting of events.

"Cross, Mr. Cunningham?"

"Yes, your Honor. "Mr. Willshire, how long did it take you to run up to the room, look at the bodies and check for signs of life, and run back down again?"

"Oh, a few minutes, I suppose."

Cunningham nodded. "Mrs. Cantese testified that you were gone for fifteen minutes. *Fifteen minutes.* Can you respond to that?"

Willshire opened his eyes wide and looked terrified. "I don't think it was that long."

"How long do you think it took you to investigate?"

"Five minutes, maybe less."

"I see. And when you arrived back downstairs, were the police there?"

"No, they arrived about five minutes hence."

"Mrs. Cantese testified that you came back downstairs five minutes before the officers arrived. Officer Wentworth testified that they arrived on the scene at twenty minutes after eight. If you heard the shot and responded at eight, it must have taken you fifteen minutes to investigate on the second floor."

Willshire shrugged, trying to find some courage. "I'm sure it wasn't that long, but I did need to make sure the victims didn't need medical assistance, because it would have been my duty to call for the doctor. I take my duty seriously."

Cunningham switched gears so rapidly that Willshire was taken off guard. "Mr. Willshire, when you arrived in the room, did you see any objects in the room?"

Mr. Willshire paled. "Well, yes. I saw the whisky bottle by Senator Hawk; I believe that's been mentioned, and the syringes by him as well. I saw the red sashes tied to the chair, like the police said yesterday."

I believe that's been mentioned. Like the police said yesterday. What an odd thing to say, Cunningham mused. As if he's trying *not* to say something, making sure he only mentions items already in the court report.

Cunningham stared at him until the blood drained from Willshire's face. He had a death grip on the carnation now. "What else?" he said abruptly.

"Wh—what? Beg pardon?"

"Objection. Witness has already answered."

"Exception. I'm simply giving the witness the opportunity to remember every object he saw."

"I'll allow it, but move quickly, Mr. Cunningham."

"What else did you see in the room?"

"Do you mean—I mean—well, the usual items that are in every room!"

"Humor us, Mr. Willshire. Can you recall those items for the jury?"

He pumped the carnation for courage. "All right. Well. There was a glass on the bedside table. I think it was empty. And Senator Hawk's trunk was in the corner. Let's see; there was a vase of flowers on the table under the mirror."

Cunningham glared at him. "Anything else?"

Willshire panicked. *He knows*, his befuddled brain screamed. *You have to explain it away.* "Well, there were the clothes."

Cunningham allowed a beat to pass, and it was electric. "The clothes?"

"Yes, there was a pile of clothes in the corner."

Jennings snapped a pencil in half.

"What did they look like?"

"Look like?"

"Yes, what did they look like? Were they women's clothes? Men's clothes?"

"Men's clothes."

"Did you recognize the clothes as belonging to Senator Hawk?"

Mr. Willshire's Adam's apple bobbed three times. "Yes," he whispered. He suspected he had made a terrible mistake. Cunningham hadn't known about the clothes.

"I'm sorry, Mr. Willshire. Can you speak louder?"

"Yes. They were Senator's Hawk's clothes."

"Trousers? A shirt? Vest? Jacket?"

"Trousers, yes. And a shirt. That's all."

Cunningham took a slow walk to the jury stand, stroking his chin, and then back to the witness stand. Willshire squeezed his carnation, some of the scarlet petals of which were now sticking to his sweaty palm. "I don't recall Aaron Wentworth, the officer first on the scene, mentioning anything about clothes. Perhaps we should recall him?"

Willshire stared at Cunningham, terrified, and then shook his head. "No, he didn't see them."

"Why didn't Officer Wentworth see a pile of Senator Hawk's clothes in the corner?"

"Objection!" Jennings finally managed, but he was doomed, and he knew it. "Defense is asking the witness to speculate on the actions of another man."

"I will withdraw. Mr. Willshire, did you do something with that pile of clothes?"

A pin could drop in the room. The seconds ticked by: five, ten, twenty.

"Yes," he finally croaked. "I took them to the cellar."

The crowd gasped and Jennings threw his pencil on the floor.

"The cellar? Whatever for?"

"I threw them in the incinerator."

Simmons had to bang his gavel for a solid fifteen seconds.

When order was restored, Cunningham continued. "Why did you throw

Senator Hawk's clothes in the incinerator?"

There were tears running down Mr. Willshire's cheeks now. He had no doubt that he had just lost his position at the Gaslight, and he had five children to feed. "Senator Hawk's family paid me extra to watch out for him."

"Can you explain that, please?"

"To keep him out of trouble. He liked to drink and take the morphine and other drugs; everyone knew it. After he checked in, a wire came to the manager from his family, and it was my duty to check in on him and, you know, clean up after him. Throw away bottles and syringes; keep his name out of the papers, make sure he was discreet."

"I see." Cunningham's voice was gentle and soothing now. "Why didn't you throw the bottle and syringes away that evening?"

"It was pretty obvious he was drunk; he stank of it, and there were needle punctures in his arms. There was no point in throwing them away."

"But what about the clothes? Why not leave them, too?"

Mr. Willshire actually leaned forward and sank his head into his hands, and Bailey felt a tremendous surge of sympathy for the man. He finally lifted his head. "Because they were bloody."

The audience erupted again and Simmons banged the gavel.

"No further questions," Cunningham muttered, and sat down, mind whirling.

"Re-direct!" Jennings hopped to his feet, suddenly energized. "Mr. Willshire! Was the trunk in the other corner locked?"

"No, it stood open."

"And was the blood on the clothing wet or dry?"

"It was dry."

"Does anything you saw or removed from that room preclude Miss Bailey Rose from being the killer of Adam Hawk?"

"Why no, I guess not."

"Thank you. No more questions."

Jennings abruptly sat down. He was grasping at straws: he was going to argue that Bailey could have removed a set of clothes from the trunk and soaked them with the woman's blood to incriminate Hawk. It was the best he had.

"Call your next witness," mumbled Simmons, wincing.

"Your Honor, the Prosecution rests its case."

CHAPTER SIXTEEN

At the lunch hour—spent again in the airless courthouse room with her team—Cunningham immediately asked her about the letter.

"Before I shot him, he told me he had mailed me a letter asking me to stay away. That's all I know." Bailey shrugged helplessly.

"And of course, you never received it?"

"No."

"Where do you suppose he sent it?"

"He knew I lived at Fort Allen, so I suppose he sent it there. But if he mailed it at six, it would never have reached Fort Allen by the time I left, which was just fifteen minutes or so after that time."

"I wonder why he didn't send a boy with it?" mused Cunningham.

"Well, Hawk knew I wasn't home—he knew I was missing from Fort Allen, so maybe he just assumed I would get it the next day or in the coming days. Not to mention the fact that he had just killed my mother and bathed to remove her blood," she added sharply, her nails digging into her palms. "That could be a factor." She was being sarcastic and nasty and she didn't care.

But Cunningham, unflappable as always, just nodded thoughtfully. "Yes, that's certainly true. If the letter was headed for Fort Allen, Blanche must have destroyed it when she arrived. I'll recall her to the stand: it's certainly worth a question or two."

Bailey shrugged. Really, what did the letter matter? No letter would have deterred her from looking for her mother. She was no coward, and she hadn't been as a child, either.

After a brief respite, Bailey was paraded once again into Courtroom Number One. It was time for the defense to begin its case, and she was petrified. Today—or perhaps tomorrow—she would likely take the stand to tell her story, and she wasn't sure she had the strength to do it.

She stared at the ground as she took the long walk down the aisle, refusing to look for family and friends. *For him.* She knew her eyes were red and swollen and rimmed with shadows; she had no desire to cause her loved ones any more anxiety than she already had visited upon them.

She sat with Cunningham and her team after Judge Simmons arrived and called the court to order, and she sank onto her hard bench gladly, for her knees were shaking. In a few moments she would face her former life, in all of its squalor and abject loneliness, exhibited for all to see. Her *true* life, not the fiction created by Jennings. She didn't want anyone to pity her; she didn't care if they were scornful or condemning, but those wretched, pitying looks she had been drawing—she couldn't take much more of that.

"Call your first witness," Simmons growled to Cunningham, hoping the young man's case was more impressive than that idiot Jennings.

"The Defense calls Lola Kramer to the stand."

Lola stood and made her way to the witness stand, her head held unnaturally high. She was proud to be the first witness for the defense, and she only wished that society bitch who had threated her was here to see it. She wore a perfectly-acceptable black crepe high-collared gown with white lace falling in tiers from her waist. Her hands were gloved in immaculate white, and her face, devoid of any makeup save a bit of lip rouge, was attractive, with a pert nose and slightly pouty, bow-shaped lips. Her heavy-lidded eyes were blue, and she gazed out at the crowd with insolence, shoulders back. Her blond hair was piled in ringlets on top of her head, and the only bit of ornament that hinted to her profession were the showy diamond earrings in the shape of large hearts: Bailey had no doubt they were real and could bankroll her clinic for a year. She had taken excellent care of herself for all of these years, and at forty-four, was still one of the most popular ladies at Fort Allen.

Cunningham approached the stand with a nod to Lola after she had repeated her oath and had taken her seat. "Good afternoon, Miss Kramer. Thank you for taking the time to speak with the court today." His manner was so polite and deferent, so different from Jennings' disdain of his own witnesses, that the jury—every last of one of them—looked at Cunningham in surprise.

"Good afternoon," she responded.

"Will you please state your name for the jury, and help us to understand how you know the defendant, Bailey Rose, and for how long you have been acquainted?"

She nodded. "I am Lola Kramer. I met Bailey Rose when she was six years old. She lived at Fort Allen with her mother, Addie Rose, and I came to live there in 1870."

Cunningham showed her the photograph of Adele Rosemont. "Is this woman Addie Rose?"

Lola took it and a look of tenderness came over her face. "Yes, that's Addie, without a doubt. That's her. My, my. I haven't looked upon this face for years and years."

Bailey felt her eyes sting.

"Can you tell us what you remember about Addie Rose?"

"She worked as a companion, upstairs. A nice, nice woman, she was, and we had some good talks, but she was an eater."

Cunningham held up his hand to stop her. "I'm sorry, could you clarify that term, 'eater'?"

"A morphine eater. You know, a dependent. She slept away most of the day. Didn't spend much time with her girl." She shook her head sorrowfully and gazed at Bailey.

Bailey flushed and stared at her hands.

Cunningham nodded kindly and looked regretful about his next question. "Miss Kramer, are you employed at Fort Allen?"

Her chest seemed to puff. "Yes, I am. I have been employed there as a companion since 1870." For some reason, the audience was quiet, perhaps following Cunningham's example in striving to preserve this woman' dignity.

"Was Bailey Rose ever a companion at Fort Allen?" Cunningham retained the euphemism and hoped the jury was paying attention.

Lola shook her head emphatically. "No, she wasn't. Blanche—Blanche DuBois, the madam—she made Bailey clean the place and do the laundry. That's how it had been ever since I arrived to the day Bailey disappeared."

"Did Miss Rose work as a companion elsewhere?"

"No, she didn't. I would have known. I know *everything* about all the girls in this town." This time the audience did chuckle, but Lola smiled, too, displaying straight, white teeth. "I should write a book," she added for effect, and Cunningham had to pause to let the hilarity die down.

"Miss Kramer, did you notice when Miss Rose left Fort Allen for five days?"

"Oh yes, I noticed. It was the fifteenth or sixteenth of May."

"How can you be so sure of the date?"

"Because I keep a diary. I write in it every day, sometimes more than once a day; I've done so all of my life."

"Your Honor, I submit for evidence this diary, which contains information from the year 1876 of the goings-on at Fort Allen." Cunningham handed the diary to the bailiff; as it was handed around, the looks on the jurors' faces was entertaining. Clearly, the small book covered in pink leather festooned with petunias contained a wealth of stories—some of them quite steamy—from a witty, observant writer. Thus, the process took much longer than Simmons would have liked, and sensing the judge's irritation, Cunningham moved on.

"Miss Kramer, can you tell us about the day Bailey Rose left?"

"Sure. Now this is from memory; I'll need my book back to be sure, but Bailey went to the German school on the fifteenth. That week I saw her sewing a dress she cut out of one of her Mama's old gowns; I even helped her with the buttons. I get up early to take exercise—I don't sleep the day away like the other girls—and I saw her walking to school that morning. I saw her come home at noon, and take a beating from Blanche."

Cunningham paused. "A beating?"

"Oh, yes. Blanche was angry with her for going to school without permission. She hit her a few times and sent her back under the porch."

"The porch?" Really, all Cunningham had to do was supply a few clarifying questions here and there: Lola would do the rest.

"Yes. She lived under the porch; Blanche wouldn't let her stay in the house unless there was snow or ice, then she slept by the stove in the kitchen."

Bailey bowed her head, shoulders slumped. She loathed having her childhood deprivation exposed for all to see. She felt naked.

"And she left that day?"

"Now I don't know for sure if she ran away that day or the next morning, but she was gone for sure the next morning. Blanche was in a dither."

"Why was Blanche so angry?"

"Well, this gets complicated." Lola shifted and fussed for a moment as she collected her thoughts. "Addie was a sought-after girl, even though her mind was so ruined by the morphine. One fellow in particular came to see her quite often. We just called him 'Senator,' but he was Adam Hawk."

There was a hum of excitement from the crowd.

"Go on, please."

"He had been coming to see Addie for a few years, but not for—well, you know—*companionship*. He always just wanted to talk to her, and sometimes they would talk for hours, which made Blanche plenty mad until he threw some cash her way. Sometimes Addie would cry and leave him, refusing to talk to him anymore. She wouldn't answer any of us when we asked about him."

"Did Senator Hawk have such friendships with any of the other boarders at Fort Allen?"

"No, but he liked to have companionship with Liza and Nadine. They were both real young. Liza was sixteen, maybe, and Nadine was fifteen at the time. He was a regular of theirs. After Liza left, he always asked for Nadine when he was in town."

Jennings seemed to rouse from a trance. "Objection! This line of questioning is utterly irrelevant and a *waste of time*." Jennings hoped that Simmons would jump at that phrase.

"Exception. It is critical that the defense establish the relationship between Senator Hawk, Addie Rose, and Bailey Rose."

"Sustained!" snapped Simmons, with a look to Jennings that said, *Sit down and shut up.*

"Go on please, Miss Kramer. The original question was why Blanche DuBois cared so much about Bailey's disappearance."

Lola nodded. "Well, Hawk showed up the day after Bailey left, that would be the seventeenth of May. He had a long talk with Addie, who slapped his face, burst into tears, and locked herself in her room. Hawk stayed at our bar and got himself completely toasted."

"Toasted?" The audience laughed.

"Drunk. He was downing shots of whisky like they were water. But then I remember he went into Blanche's parlor and came out a few minutes later, looking pleased."

"Do you know what they met about?"

"Yes, I do. I saw and overheard some of it, but then I heard it from Blanche herself. She came out and told me to find Bailey because she had a job for her the next night. I asked if she was putting Bailey to work, and she said yes. When I reminded her that Bailey was only twelve, she said it didn't matter, that she was ready, and Hawk had already paid Blanche maiden wages for Bailey."

Bailey felt a hot flush of shame consume her body. She sank lower in her chair, her chin on her chest, and wished she could melt into a puddle and escape in a liquid flow between the floorboards. Two rows behind her, Jacob had to bite his fist to squelch a groan; every one of his muscles strained toward her, wanting to envelop her, hide her from prying eyes and scandalized gasps. She had told him a brief version of this story months ago when they met after the debate: she had simply said that a bad man had been after her, and she had to get away. He had no concept at the time what she had meant.

Cunningham cleared his throat delicately. "Miss Kramer, can you explain 'maiden wages'?"

"That's a high sum paid for a virgin. Usually a thousand or so, but Blanche told me that Hawk paid five thousand." More gasps. Jacob felt a burning begin in his skull.

"And Miss DuBois was angry because she could not find Miss Rose, and she would have to give the money back?"

"Yes, and that she'd have to deal with Senator. He was a monster when he was drunk and doped."

"What happened when Miss Rose did not return by the next evening, on the eighteenth of May?"

Lola sighed and shook her head. "All hell broke loose. Hawk started smashing up the parlor. Finally Blanche went upstairs and took another girl away from a john and pulled her downstairs to deal with Hawk. That was Nadine." In the excited flow of the narrative, Lola's carefully-cultivated speech began to revert back to a more informal slang. "She calmed him down and took him upstairs. That was the last time I saw him."

"And where was Addie during this time?"

"She was working in her own room."

"She didn't know about the transaction between Blanche and Senator Hawk?"

"Not that night. But she found out two days later, on the twentieth, at exactly half past four in the afternoon."

"How can you be so sure of the time?" Cunningham asked quickly before Jennings could object.

"I know because *I* told her. I felt like the mother should know. So I went to her room, woke her up, and told her the whole story."

"And how did she react?"

"She was mighty upset. She pushed me out of her room and slammed the door, and a few minutes later, she ran down the stairs and got a rig hooked up and took off."

"Did she say where she was going?"

"No, but I told her that Senator was staying at the Gaslight."

"What time did she leave, to the best of your knowledge?"

"Right around five, probably fifteen minutes before the hour."

"Miss Kramer, did Addie Rose own a gun?"

Lola nodded. "Of course. We all did. Still do."

"What kind of gun?"

"She had a .38, like mine. But hers was pretty. It had pearl grips."

Cunningham picked up the weapon from the evidence table and presented it to Lola. "Does this gun look like the gun Addie owned?"

"Yes, it does."

There was an immediate buzz in the courtroom and Simmons had to bang the gavel.

"Why do you suppose Addie Rose went to the Gaslight Hotel that afternoon?"

Lola stared at the gun in her hand for a long moment. "You know, I've asked myself that question a thousand times. I think she went to scare him. They had a history, those two: I don't understand it, but I think she thought she could probably make him stay away from Bailey, and if he wouldn't, she'd make sure he would with this." Lola waved the gun carelessly, causing several ladies in the audience to gasp.

"Just a few more questions, Miss Kramer. Were you acquainted with Jezebel St. John?"

"Yes. She worked at Fort Allen for a while. She was a witch of the worst kind; Blanche only hired her on because she was beautiful and real smart. She was forever teasing and hitting Bailey; she treated her worse than a dog. And Jezzie was a thief! She had the stickiest fingers in the house, forever palming jewelry and cash. And chocolate! We had to hide our chocolate in the strangest places or she'd gobble it right up. Nothing was safe with her around."

"Was Senator Hawk in love with Miss St. John?"

Lola snorted. "No! I don't think he even knew her. I never saw them speak, and I see everything."

"Did you ever hear Bailey say that she wished Miss St. John were dead?"

"Well, yes, I guess you could say that, but we all probably thought that at one time or another."

"Can you tell us more about that?"

"Jezzie tripped Bailey one day when Bailey was returning clean glasses to the bar. She fell, and then Jezzie pushed her and made her fall right into the broken glass. She cut her hands up pretty good. Jezzie pulled Bailey's hair and slapped her, but Bailey didn't wallow on the floor: she jumped right up and punched that—*woman*—right in the nose, and she probably said something to the effect that she wished she were dead. That's all it was."

"Miss Kramer, did Miss St. John disappear the same night as Addie and Bailey Rose?"

"No, sir. She left about two weeks later, and she had already told anyone who'd listen that she was heading to California."

"Thank you, Miss Kramer. No further questions."

"Cross-examination, Mr. Jennings?"

Jennings gave a terse shake of his head. This witness would be impossible to impeach with her damned diary, and it didn't matter anyway. Why should the jury care if it were Addie or some other whore dead in the bed? Who cares if the whore killed herself, Hawk killed her, or Rose killed her? The fact was Bailey Rose pulled the trigger that killed Adam Hawk in cold blood. All the rest was nonsense and not worth one more iota of his time. Not for the first time, he keenly regretted bringing charges against Bailey Rose. This was supposed to have been an open and shut case, a freak of a woman—an ex-whore turned doctor—killed a United States senator in some kinky sex triangle. An easy win for a busy, overworked county prosecutor. What in God's name were they all still doing here, listening to stories about waifs living under porches and thieving whores? And had he known Naplava was connected to the defendant, he wouldn't have touched it with a ten foot pole.

"Your Honor, I call to the stand Nadine Wrigley," announced Cunningham. A slight woman with chestnut hair and a classically beautiful face approached the stand. She wore an elegant lavender gown with a very deep high lace collar that reached right up under her chin, with bloused sleeves gathered into three wristbands separated by more lace. Her skirt was the modern, elongated trumpet-bell shape, emphasizing her tiny waist, and she appeared to be gliding to the stand. Her brown hair was arranged in a poufy bun with a fashionable fringe; she looked every bit the proper society lady, out for a pleasant afternoon. Her expression was serene and her eyes, although somewhat haunted, were sparkling with good will and intelligence. Bailey stared, delighted. Cunningham had not told her what had become of Nadine.

She was sworn in and perched gracefully in her seat.

"Good afternoon, Mrs. Wrigley. Can you state your name for the jury, and explain how you are acquainted with Miss Bailey Rose?"

She nodded regally. "My name is Mrs. Harold Wrigley—Nadine Wrigley. My maiden name was Brown. I know Miss Rose from the time I was a boarder at Fort Allen."

"And when were you a boarder at Fort Allen?"

"From January to November of 1876."

"Mrs. Wrigley, how old were you at that time?"

"Objection!" growled Jennings. "Why on earth does that matter? This is irrelevant." He knew just where Cunningham was going with this and he wanted to stop it.

"Exception. The relevancy of that question will become clear momentarily."

"Sustained. But don't take your sweet time, Mr. Cunningham."

"Mrs. Wrigley?"

She lifted her chin. "I was fifteen," she said softly.

Cunningham nodded. "Mrs. Wrigley, I'm afraid I'm going to have to ask you some delicate and highly personal questions, but they are critical to this case. Did Bailey Rose work as a prostitute at Fort Allen?" He had considered using Nadine's word, *boarder*, but decided against it. The terminology may be confusing for some of the jurors, especially those whose native tongue was not English.

She didn't seem to be phased. "No, she did not. She cleaned and did the laundry. Her mother was employed there. Her name was Addie Rose."

"Were you acquainted with Senator Adam Hawk?"

"Yes, I was."

"Did you observe him to have a relationship with Jezebel St. John?"

"No, he did not. I don't believe they ever spoke to each other."

"Did you observe him to have a relationship with Addie Rose?"

"Yes, I did. They seemed to be friends; they would speak in the parlor. Sometimes she would get upset; sometimes he would get upset. I don't know anything else about that relationship except they seemed to care about each other."

"Did he ever talk about his relationship with Addie, or did she talk about her relationship with Hawk?"

"Not to me, they didn't; either one. I didn't know Addie well. She kept to her room most of the time."

Cunningham nodded and paced in front of the jury, his mind always working better when he was moving. "Mrs. Wrigley, I beg your forgiveness, but can you explain your relationship with Adam Hawk?"

A splotch of red appeared on her throat, but her face remained tranquil and her voice was steady and quiet. "I was employed as a boarder at Fort Allen, and he was my client." With a glance Cunningham could see that there was no confusion on the part of the jury or the general audience about her role at Fort Allen; many of them looked startled as they gazed at the woman in front of them, who appeared to be of high-born, gentle society.

"On how many occasions was he your customer?"

"Four occasions."

Cunningham kept his voice low and respectful, trying to preserve as much of her dignity as possible. "Was he a violent man?"

"No, never. He was very kind and usually sad and quiet."

"Did he ever try to get you to take morphine or other drugs?"

"Yes, he always said he'd so much prefer it if I took the morphine with him, but I never did. He was quite addicted to them, unfortunately."

"Why do you suppose he preferred to spend time with you when he was in town?"

"Objection! Calls for hearsay!"

"I'll withdraw it. Mrs. Wrigley, did you notice anything about Senator Hawk's preferences in terms of companions?"

Jennings winced: that was even worse, but it was a valid question.

"Yes. He preferred very young girls. Before I arrived at Fort Allen, he had only ever been with one girl at Fort Allen; her name was Liza, and she was sixteen."

"Do you know why he preferred young girls?"

"No, I don't."

The line of questioning was highly sensitive and scandalous, and there was a shuffle as a few women quietly stood and left the courtroom, their faces red. Cunningham paused to let them take their leave.

"Can you describe for the jury the final time you spent with Senator Hawk?"

Nadine Wrigley nodded and seemed to draw herself up; Cunningham had clearly prepared her well and she was ready for this difficult answer. "Yes, I can. I was upstairs engaged with another gentleman. Blanche DuBois came into my room and forced me downstairs. There I saw Adam; he was in the middle of a pile of smashed glasses and lamps. I asked Lola what was going on, and she told me that he had paid a huge sum of money for Bailey Rose, but Bailey wasn't present. I could see that Adam was drunk and full of those wretched drugs he took. I took him by the hand and led him upstairs before he could do any more damage."

"Was Senator Hawk violent with you that evening?"

"No, not at all. I calmed him down; I could do that, for some reason. I would even go so far as to say we were friends." Here she paused, her voice finally wavering, and Bailey was stunned to see a tear glimmering in her brown eye. She was *crying* for that monster!

"How long did he stay?"

"Maybe two hours, no longer than that."

"Did he leave Fort Allen then?"

"Yes."

"Did he say where he was going?"

"Back to his hotel room at the Gaslight. He wanted me to come with him, but I told him no."

"Was he angry that you refused?"

"No, not at all. He just kept apologizing. In fact, I always called him the Sorry Man, just to tease him. He was forever apologizing."

"Were you aware that Bailey Rose was gone from Fort Allen during this time?"

"Yes, but I didn't know where she had gone."

"Did you observe her return on the twentieth of May?"

"No, I didn't. I was reading in my room at that time. I wish I had seen her; I would have gone with her to the Gaslight, and maybe this whole tragedy could have been avoided." Nadine looked at Bailey for the first time, her kind eyes glimmering, and Bailey gazed back, tears of her own tracing down her cheek in spite of her best efforts to suppress them. "I always admired that little girl: she was so fearless. She was so unlike her mother: Addie seemed helpless, and Bailey seemed indomitable. I never saw her cry, *ever*, even though her life was so base." She shook her head in wonder, remembering. "But I see that she's crying now."

The courtroom was an oasis of silence, and Cunningham left it alone, allowing the jury time to realize the import of what they had heard, giving the moment the gravity and respect it deserved.

Finally, after a full minute, he cleared his throat. "Thank you, Mrs. Wrigley. No further questions."

"Cross?" muttered Simmons.

Jennings rose to his feet and strode quickly to the stand, determined to break the emotional spell that had fallen over the crowd. "Mrs. Wrigley, did Bailey Rose have a reason to hate Senator Hawk?"

She stared at him for a few seconds before replying. "Yes, I suppose she did. To find out a grown man had tried to purchase her for sexual favors must have been quite a shock."

Jennings sputtered and turned red in the face. Well, if Hawk was established in the jurors' minds as having a liking for younger girls, so be it. That still didn't exonerate Bailey Rose.

"Mrs. Wrigley, we have already established that Bailey Rose was at the

Gaslight Hotel around six o'clock that evening, asking for Senator Hawk's room. You seemed to have known her reasonably well. Do you think she entered that hotel intending to confront the woman already there and/or Senator Hawk about the transaction that had taken place with Blanche DuBois?"

"Objection! Mr. Jennings is asking the witness to speculate."

"I will rephrase the question. Given your knowledge of the events of the seventeenth and eighteenth of May, what reason would Bailey Rose have had to visit Senator Hawk's room at the Gaslight Hotel?"

This question was still suspect, but Cunningham let it go, giving Jennings just enough rope to hang himself. "To protect her mother."

"To protect the mother who neglected her?"

"Yes."

"Protect her or avenge her?"

"I really couldn't say."

"Had you ever been abused by Senator Hawk?"

"No."

"Had you ever seen him abuse another woman?"

"No."

"So in your opinion, neither Bailey Rose nor the other woman really needed protection against Senator Hawk."

"I didn't say that."

"But you have implied it with your own testimony, Mrs. Wrigley! Now, you cannot have it both ways! Either he was a danger or he was not!"

"Objection!"

"Isn't it true that Bailey Rose went to the hotel that evening to kill him in cold blood, in a fit of hatred?"

"No, I don't believe that is true."

"But you testified that she had reason to hate him even though he was not abusive, Mrs. Wrigley!" He was yelling at full pitch now, his face beet red, while Nadine Wrigley sat calmly, unblinkingly.

"You are twisting my words, sir."

"Objection! Badgering! Please, your Honor."

"Sustained. You are warned, Jennings."

Jennings sat down, a triumphant look upon his face. "No more questions."

Mrs. Wrigley was spared a re-direct and was escorted from the stand, glancing in Bailey's direction with a gentle smile. She appeared to be unfazed, although a deep sadness had settled onto the lines of her pretty face. Her doting husband, a fine-looking gentleman, rose and clasped her hands, guiding her solicitously down onto a bench.

The next witnesses constituted a quick parade of three former Fort Allen girls, all of whom testified that Bailey was never a prostitute and all of whom corroborated the events of the seventeenth and eighteenth of September, testifying to Hawk's booze and drug-fueled rages and his predilection for young girls. Jennings made half-hearted attempts to object but was overruled each time. The last to the stand was Clarabelle Withers, the only former Fort Allen girl Mooreland had been able to locate who had been present on the evening of the twentieth of September when the Naplavas arrived to find Bailey.

"Miss Withers, do you remember Mr. Naplava visiting Fort Allen with his son on the twentieth of May?"

She nodded so vigorously her orange ostrich-plumed hat almost came unpinned. Clarabelle was a short, plump, dimpled redhead with large eyes and thinly-plucked eyebrows that made her seem perpetually surprised. Since the days of Fort Allen she had married a butcher and become a respectable, middle-class woman, and she was none too happy to remember this low point in her life. But Addie had been special to her, and she was fiercely loyal and more than a little brave. "Yes, I remember." Her voice was breathy and girlish.

"Can you recall that event for the jury?"

"Yes. There were only a few of us still on the floor that night, because it was past eight o'clock. Most every girl was engaged with their men upstairs." Unlike the other women, Clarabelle was remarkably candid with her choice of words about her former profession. "There was me, Lynda, Kate, and Josie Rae."

"Where was Bailey Rose?"

"Rumor had it she went to the Gaslight to look for Addie." She dabbed at her eyes with a cream-colored lace handkerchief. She had never gotten over Addie's death.

"Had you spoken to Addie that day?"

"Yes, at lunch. We always ate together. We were friends."

"Had Addie ever told you anything about her relationship with Adam Hawk?"

"No. I asked her, because I knew they were friends and he made her upset sometimes, but she always told me she didn't want to talk about it, so I left off."

"Did you see her after lunch?"

"No, sir. Lola told me later that she told Addie that Blanche had gotten maiden wages for Bailey from Senator, and Addie was furious and took off, then Bailey took off soon after."

"What happened later that night, when the Naplavas arrived?"

"I saw Blanche open the door and heard her talking to them. She closed the door again and came over to me, all frantic. She said some foreigners—do-gooders—were here to take Bailey away from Addie, claiming Addie was an unfit mother, and that we had to lie to protect her. We were to tell the older man that Bailey was older than she really was—fourteen instead of twelve to make it more legitimate—and that she's working here as a prostitute but went away with her mother. If we didn't do it, they would take Bailey away and probably throw Addie in jail." Clarabelle shook her head mournfully. "We were so dumb to believe her, but you know, it had happened a few months before at one of the bordellos: they took a girl away from her mother and put her in the Home, and the mother ended up blowing her brains out in misery."

Bailey paled.

"Go on please, Mrs. Withers."

"Well, he came in eventually to have a look around, and we all told him what Blanche said. And I'm real sorry about that now." This last statement was directed toward Franticek and Jacob.

Jacob bent forward in pain, burying his face in his hands and gripping his hair. His father reached across Johann to squeeze Jacob's knee, his own face full of profound regret. Jacob railed at himself, helpless against the self-abhorrence. *You colossal idiot! How could you have believed those lies about Bailey when she had just told you the truth that very day?* All of these years he had been so sure she was a soiled dove, that she had deceived him and lied to his family and then abandoned him. To think of what she had suffered that night was intolerable. At the very moment they had been at Fort Allen, she had been running through the city, looking for them, just having witnessed her mother dead and having pulled the trigger on Hawk to protect herself. He, Jacob, had failed miserably to protect her.

"No more questions."

"Cross, Mr. Jennings?"

He asked the same question he had asked of all of the witnesses from Fort Allen. "Mrs. Withers, did Bailey Rose, in your opinion, have a right to hate and/or be angry with Senator Hawk?"

"Yes, of course. He was trying to—well, you know—buy her favors. Sexual favors. She was only twelve, you know." She bit her lip worriedly when she saw that Jennings looked pleased.

"How would you describe Bailey Rose in terms of her personality? Was she timid?"

"No, sir. She was feisty and strong-willed. And the smartest person I ever met, even though she was only a kid."

"Thank you." They had all answered the same way, and that was all he needed: a motive for pre-mediated murder.

Cunningham arose. "The defense calls to the stand Miss Gabriella Flores, your Honor."

CHAPTER SEVENTEEN

Gabby was un-corseted, wearing a gown reminiscent of a Greek goddess: if the movers and shakers of San Antonio—those in Thomas's circle—thought his new love would conform to the conservative dictates of dress, they were surely disappointed. The bodice of her gown was silver metallic lace, repeated at the cuffs with sheer sleeves offering a clear view of her lovely rounded arms. A pale peach-colored ribbon rose with embroidered peach rosettes adorned the left side of the square, low-cut neck, with a strip of peach satin to conceal any cleavage. The skirt fell in a shockingly straight line from her bust to the floor like rippling water, the color matching the palest pink-peach of the rose. The effect of the skirt was clingy: it caressed her legs and her post-labor slightly swollen tummy as she walked. She was hatless and gloveless, and a silver ribbon had been worked artfully through her dark hair, which was gathered in a low, loose bun, tendrils escaping. As she approached the stand Bailey took note of the back of her gown, which was eliciting scandalized gasps from the ladies in the crowd: it, too, was sheer, covered with the metallic lace that continued as a drape down her left side, reaching to the hem of the skirt. Bailey smiled: she had no doubt that Gabby was wearing what all of these fussy women would be wearing five years from now—or at least what their daughters would be wearing. She herself felt frumpy in her big skirt and stupid puffy sleeves.

She took her oath in her low, silky voice, and twelve men in the jury stand immediately sat up straighter, a few of them preening. Bailey had a sudden suspicion about Cunningham's decision to call Gabby to the stand, and she hid a smile behind her hand.

"Miss Flores, thank you for being with us today."

She smiled and nodded regally.

"How long have you known Miss Rose?"

"My whole life, as long as I can remember." Her Mexican-accented voice flowed like honey.

"Can you explain your relationship with Miss Rose?"

"We are best friends. We always have been, even in the fifteen years we were separated. She lived at Fort Allen with her mother, and I lived in various places with my mother, who also worked as a lady of the evening." Somehow, with her thick, exotically-beautiful accent, *lady of the evening* lost its sordidness. "We played together, scrounged food together, warded off the evils of the city together, *survived* together." She always had been poetic.

"Did Miss Rose ever work as a prostitute?"

"No, of course not. I saw her almost every day and I would have known. She did not."

"How old were you in 1876?"

"I was fourteen years old."

"Were you working as a prostitute?"

"No. Not yet. I began working at the Purple Pansy when I was fifteen." Her emerald eyes stayed glued to Cunningham, her voice matter-of-fact and unapologetic.

"Can you describe Miss Rose physically at that time?"

"She was very small, about four feet ten inches, a good six inches shorter than I was. She was thin, of course. We were all hungry, all of the time."

"In 1876, were you acquainted with Senator Adam Hawk?"

"No, I had never met him."

"Had Miss Rose ever talked about him?"

"Yes. She was frightened of him. She told me two years prior when she first saw him talking to her mother. She didn't like him spending time with her mother because it always made Addie sad. She also told me that he was the customer of a young girl named Liza, and later, Nadine."

"A previous witness, Lola Kramer, testified that Senator Hawk had paid five thousand dollars for Miss Rose on the seventeenth of September. Were you aware of this at that time?"

"No. I was not aware of it until Miss Kramer testified about it."

"Were you aware that Bailey had gone on a trip to Boerne?"

"Yes. I saw Jacob Naplava looking for her and I told him where to find her. That was on the fifteenth of May, the same day she went to that German school."

"Did you see either one of them after that?"

Gabby turned and looked at Bailey for the first time, and although her eyes were dry, they were full of emotion. "No," she said softly. "I didn't see her again for fifteen years. I thought she was dead."

"You probably knew Miss Rose better than anyone when you were children. Miss Flores, do you believe that Miss Rose was capable of killing Adam Hawk?"

She turned to look at Cunningham again, then at each member of the jury, something no other witness had done. "Yes," she said to them. "But only if she was protecting herself or someone else. She is a survivor, you see." Jacob felt a surge of pride and love.

"Thank you, Miss Flores. No further questions."

"Cross?" asked Simmons, impressed with Gabby's composure.

Jennings stood. "Miss Flores, I will ask you the same question I've asked everyone else who claimed to know Miss Rose intimately at that time. Did she have reason to hate and/or be angry with Mr. Hawk?"

"Yes."

"No more questions."

"Thank you, Miss Flores. You are excused." All male eyes were glued to the stand and she rose and allowed the bailiff to hand her down—the poor man looked utterly bedazzled. She glided past Bailey's table and smiled at her. *I love you,* Bailey mouthed, and Gabby nodded. She made her way to the back of the courtroom, where Thomas stood and leaned down to kiss her cheek, with everyone watching, before seating her. Gabby's heart exploded with joy.

"Next witness, Cunningham." Simmons said distractedly, peeling his own eyes away from Gabriella Flores, whom he thought might be the perfect reincarnation of Cleopatra.

"The Defense re-calls Aaron Wentworth, your Honor."

Sweaty, red-faced, lip-licking Wentworth ambled to the stand, was reminded of his oath, and sat gingerly.

"Mr. Wentworth, I have a few more questions for you today. Can you tell the jury what happened to the clothing, jewelry, and other personal effects of the victims from the night in question?"

Wentworth relaxed: this was an easy question. "Oh, sure. Hawk's personal effects were released to his family. The woman's effects went with her to the morgue. I don't know what happened to her after that: she was unclaimed and unidentified, so I imagine she went to a potter's field."

He issued the statement with such nonchalance that at first, Bailey did not react. Only after a few beats had passed did his words register in her tired, grieving mind. *Unclaimed. Unidentified. Potter's field.* She had never, in all of these years, been brave enough to search for her grave, if there even was one. Her feelings for her mother had been so very conflicted before she understood the tragedy of Addie's life. *Della's life.* She gulped so audibly that Abe heard her and reached for her hand to give a comforting squeeze.

"Thank you, Mr. Wentworth. No further questions."

Jennings waved a cross-examination, and Cunningham called the undertaker to the stand.

"State your name, please, and how you were associated with the events of this case."

"I'm Jerome Mulally, and I was the undertaker they called upon to take that woman's body. I was co-owner of Carter & Mullaly Undertakers; still am." Mullally was a thin, swarthy man with a thick mustache and thick dark hair to match.

Cunningham paused briefly. He could see at a glance that Bailey was upset, and he already regretted what was to come next, but it was vital to make the jury understand that the dead woman in bed had been Addie Rose, not Jezebel St. John or anyone else. Only if Addie were in the room would Bailey have a legitimate reason to be there in the first place. "Mr. Mulally, what happens when you are taking care of a deceased person who is unidentified? What happens to their personal effects such as clothing, jewelry, and the like?"

"Well, generally speaking, any jewelry, money, or other personal effects are stored in a box with as clear label as possible, such as the date the person became deceased and where the body was found—that sort of thing. We used to bury jewelry with the bodies, but I had a family come to claim a body shortly after we started our business, and we had to exhume the body to recover jewelry the family wanted back. I'll never go through that again. So now I remove it all and store it."

"And was the woman in question buried in the clothing she was wearing?"

"No, she wasn't. It was ruined—too blood-stained. We burned the clothing and buried her in a simple—gown—we have on hand for those occasions."

Bailey felt hot prickles of revulsion prick her body, inside and out. Her beautiful mother, buried in a rag. She knew that "gown" meant a simple drape, or even less than that. She found her breathing was becoming labored.

"Did you remove any jewelry from the woman before you buried her? Or any other personal effects?"

"Yes, sir. There was a pin she was wearing at her collar. Several rings; one for each finger, I remember. A necklace with a morphine vial; we see those all of the time. That was all. She didn't have a purse or bag."

"Your Honor, I submit as evidence this box, obtained from Carter & Mulally Undertakers." He handed the box to the bailiff, who passed it along to Simmons and the jury. Long moments were spent looking at the contents, and Bailey bowed her head, desperate to see and to touch her mother's things. Cunningham had promised that once she was acquitted, her mother's things would come back to her.

Finally the box made its way to Mulally. "Mr. Mulally, can you please explain the label and the contents of the box?"

"Yes. The label says 'U/U 20 May 1876, Female, Approx. 30 yrs, brown hair, green eyes, 130 lbs, 5'4", Gaslight Hotel, Room #226, gunshot chest'. 'U/U' means unidentified and unclaimed. I labeled it myself, with all of the information I had available to me at the time." He began to sort through the box. "The contents are eleven rings, one necklace with a drug vial, and one brooch."

"Can you describe the jewelry, in general terms?"

He shrugged. "Well, most of these rings have big rocks! I don't know if they're real or not; that's not my area of expertise." The women in the crowd tittered. He colored and held up a plain gold band and a gold band with a single, small round diamond. "But I reckon this is a wedding band, and a betrothal ring, mayhap."

Bailey's mouth fell open; she had never seen the rings; she didn't know they existed. Had Addie put them on before going to the Gaslight? *Of course she had. She knew she might die there, and she wanted to die wearing John Bailey's rings.*

"And the brooch?"

Mulally held up the item in question, and this time Bailey gasped. The jurors turned to look at her and she clapped her hands over her mouth, unable to suppress her shock. Cunningham had kept this from her! Why? *Maybe to get a reaction just like the one you're giving,* she thought.

For the brooch was identical to her mother's, without question. She was never without it, even if the other girls teased her that it didn't match her dress. The oval setting was gilded silver, and deep red garnets lay nested within in.

There was an answering gasp behind Bailey, and even though she had been instructed not to, she turned to look. Cordelia Howard had her hand over her mouth, obviously in shock as well. She, too, recognized the brooch: it had belonged to her mother, Olivia, and had been passed down to Della. Hope was comforting her, murmuring in her ear, and Bailey realized with a sudden pang how painful these details of Addie's death must be for these two women.

"I ask the jury to have another look at the photograph of Adele Rosemont, which has already been established by sworn testimony to be one and the same woman as Addie Rose. Direct your eyes, gentlemen of the jury, if you will, to the brooch on Adele Rosemont's dress. It is identical to the brooch I hold before you now."

The courtroom was silent as the men handed around the picture and the brooch.

The undertaker was excused, and one by one the former Fort Allen girls were called to the stand to testify that the brooch and the rings belonged to none other than Addie Rose, and that Addie Rose had disappeared the night of the twentieth of May, never to be seen or heard from again. Karl Schwartz was called to the stand and testified that the woman in the photograph was Adele Rosemont, and furthermore, that he accompanied his brother, John Bailey, as he purchased the diamond betrothal ring and wedding band. Finally, a jeweler was called, who identified the brooch as a rare Ashbee piece, extremely valuable, and an exact match for the one in the photograph.

By the end of the day, the identification of the dead woman in Adam Hawk's room was clear: Addie Rose, Bailey Rose's mother, had died in that room that night.

For the first time, Bailey began to believe that she might walk free.

Long-buried memories haunted her all night long: she hadn't slept for more than an hour, tossing and turning, watching Adam Hawk morph over and over again from a man to a Vodnik with hideous scales and drippy, slimy green hair, pushing her onto the bloody bed beside her mother, tearing her clothes away with his long, sharp fingers. She awoke whimpering, her cheeks wet, heart pounding, time after time. When she finally arose and donned the uncomfortable brown costume, she wondered if she might be losing her mind after all. If she were called to the stand today, how would she ever explain her justification for shooting Adam Hawk without mentioning the fact that he was a Vodnik who had tried to kill her once before? Cunningham had told her that she must not mention that, and of course, she understood him: she would be promptly committed to the state asylum. But her whole life long, she had rationalized pulling that trigger to defend herself against a monster—a *real* monster; supernatural, inexplicable, fantastic, but real nonetheless. One she had seen in the form of a stalking wolf and a water— *thing*—that had tried, and failed, to kill her. The fact that Wenzel had believed her made her even more certain that the man she had vanquished had not been a man; or at least *only* a man. He'd been a monster, perhaps possessed, perhaps born that way.

Yes. You are losing your mind. No doubt about it.

Perhaps it was this look of hopelessness and fear that Jacob saw when she walked through the courtroom the next morning, forced to pause several times as newsmen threw themselves into the aisle to get a better look at her, that made him sink back onto his bench ever so slowly, worried beyond measure. "She doesn't look good," he whispered to Lindy, who was seated by him today.

"No, she doesn't. She looks troubled today," Lindy acknowledged. "But she might have to take the stand and tell the story. Wouldn't you be nervous?"

He nodded dumbly and tried in vain to catch her eye, but Bailey's eyes were trained on the floor, lower lip caught between her teeth, her shoulders hunched.

The court was called to order, and once everyone was seated, Cunningham stood again and faced the jury and judge. "I beg your patience today, gentlemen. Mr. Jennings has made some claims that I need to address. He has claimed, in his opening statement, that Miss Rose arrived at Room #226 at six o'clock, knocked on the door, which he claimed was opened by an older woman. He then claims that Miss Rose shot the older woman in the chest and moved her body from the door to the bed, and then waited for ninety minutes to confront Mr. Hawk, who was not in the room. Does that about sum it up, Mr. Jennings?"

Jennings glared at him. Cunningham had already brought the time of Bailey's visit into question, neatly moving it forward thirty minutes to six-thirty, thanks to the testimony of a *negro*, of all things! And he had pretty well established that the dead woman in the room was none other than Bailey's own mother, a fact that Jennings had not even been aware of, thanks to the shoddy work of his team. What in blazes was Cunningham up to now?

Cunningham cleared his throat and moved on, realizing Jennings was not going to answer. "It is therefore my duty to prove the impossibility of Mr. Jennings' claims that a girl the size of Bailey Rose, in 1876, could have moved a woman the size of Addie Rose, nine and one half feet and lifted her onto an unusually high bed."

He gestured toward the guard at the rear of the room, who turned to prop open the gigantic oak double doors. "I enter into evidence this bed, your Honor, gentlemen of the jury, and Mr. Foreman. This is selfsame bed that was located in Room #226 that evening fifteen years ago, and still remains in that room to this day."

And in walked four brawny men, each bearing a corner of an enormous, king-sized four-poster bed. Jennings screamed an objection and the room erupted with gasps of surprise and speculative murmurs.

The blood drained from Anton's face when he saw the bed—this was the very same bed on which Caroline had taken advantage of him—Alice gripped his hand tightly and leaned in close. "Forget it. It wasn't your fault."

He squeezed back, pressing her close.

Simmons banged his gavel repeatedly until the noise finally died. "Your Honor! This is most irregular! It is ridiculous that an entire bed should be drug in here as evidence! This is disruptive!" Jennings' face was red with the effort of being heard over the general chaos. The men bearing the bed placed it at one end of the front of the room at Cunningham's direction and left.

"Exception. I must have the bed to demonstrate the impossibility that my client could have taken the actions of which she was accused."

"I'll allow it, but don't take too much time, Cunningham," Simmons warned, barely managing not to smile. This stunt would make for an excellent write-up in the dailies.

Three of the men returned, each of them carrying a mattress, and as they set up the bed, Cunningham waved a piece of paper at the judge and jury. "This is a sworn deposition from Mary Cantese, housekeeper at the time, that Mr. Hawk demanded three mattresses be put on his bed. She can be recalled if prosecution wishes to question her." He handed the paper to the bailiff and Jennings remained silent. "She testifies that Mr. Hawk preferred to rest several feet off the floor, avowing to a severe fear of rats. The mattresses and height of the bed itself will place a person three feet off the floor."

"Your Honor, I have retained the assistance of young Sherry Davis, who is thirteen years of age, stands five feet tall, and weight one hundred pounds. She is considerably larger and no doubt stronger than was Bailey Rose in 1876. Come join us, Sherry." A hale, sturdy-looking girl rose from the front row of spectators and approached the front of the room. Jennings squirmed with displeasure. "And now I must have a woman to play the part of Addie Rose, whom I have established as the other woman in the room that evening, the poor unfortunate soul who lost her life. I ask Mrs. Heather Reynard to approach, please. Mrs. Reynard stands five feet, four inches, weighs one hundred thirty pounds, and is wearing a heavy silk gown."

A blushing woman in her mid-thirties approached the front of room, patting her dark hair anxiously. She worked as a stenographer in Cunningham's office and had taken the train with her husband all the way from Austin to play her part today; she was wildly excited and nervous.

"Really, your Honor, has the courtroom been transformed into a stage?" snapped Jennings, unable to help himself, so disgusted was he with the whole rotten mess of things.

"The halls of justice have always been, and forever will be, a stage, Mr. Jennings," retorted Simmons with heavy irony, and the crowd laughed appreciatively. He dearly hoped the reporters had gotten that down verbatim—it was a gem; one of his best, really.

Cunningham directed the young girl and the woman to stand nine and one half feet away from the bed—he marked it off precisely with a tape— then he instructed the woman to lie on the floor and make her limbs absolutely limp, playing dead. She did so, much to the scandalized chatter of the ladies in the room.

"Sherry, what I want you to do now is to move Mrs. Reynard from this spot to the bed, and then pick her up and place her on the bed on her back, with legs straight and her hands folded nicely together." The girl nodded but looked extremely dubious about the whole thing. She bent over, bracing her legs, and grasped the woman under her arms. Walking backward, she managed to drag the woman to the bed after several pauses for rest. When she had accomplished that part of the task, she stood and faced Cunningham. She was breathing heavily and her red face was sweaty.

"Might I rest for a moment?" she asked, and several in the crowd sniggered.

"Why, certainly, Sherry. Take your time," smiled Cunningham. Jennings remained silent: the girl had just proven that the woman could, indeed, have been dragged to the bed.

After a moment Cunningham spoke kindly. "Sherry, do you feel as though you could place the woman on the bed now?"

She raised her eyebrows doubtfully. "I'll try," she said. She bent down and tugged at the woman again, grasping her under the arms, but was unable to gain the necessary leverage to get her on the bed. She managed to prop her into a sitting position, but as she grasped her around the waist and attempted to raise her to a standing position, they both fell with a crash to the floor. The audience burst into laughter, but Bailey watched silently, appalled. The woman was supposed to be a stand-in for her mother, and imagining her mother's lifeless body being dragged unceremoniously and manhandled made her ill.

Sherry kept at it, even going so far as to get on the bed herself and reach down to try to drag the woman on, resulting in a painful scrape on Mrs. Reynard's back. The older woman did not complain or even move, minding the strict instructions from her boss to keep as still as the dead. As a last-ditch effort, the girl managed to get the woman propped to a standing, bent-over position at last, with the limp woman's arms over her shoulders, but she was utterly unable to lift her even a few inches off the floor, since the woman's dead weight had to be borne. They both wobbled precariously for a breathless ten seconds, and then crashed to the floor again, the woman squarely on top of Sherry. "I can't, sir," Sherry gasped, the woman's weight crushing her, and Cunningham leapt forward to lift Mrs. Reynard off the poor girl.

After clothing was straightened and propriety was restored, Cunningham thanked them profusely. He turned to the jury. "As you can see, gentleman, even a girl older, taller, and heavier than was Bailey Rose could not begin to maneuver the dead weight of a one-hundred and thirty pound woman onto a bed that is situated three feet off the floor. Have any of you ever lifted dead weight, in which the limbs are completely lifeless? It was impossible, *impossible* for Sherry to accomplish this task." He gestured toward Sherry, who stood panting heavily, her hair plastered to her head with sweat. "And it would have been impossible for a younger, smaller girl to do so as well. Gentlemen, we may never know what happened to Addie Rose in that hotel room, but one thing we do know is that a girl of Bailey Rose's petite stature could not have moved her from the door and placed her on the bed."

"Objection! We cannot possibly surmise the strength of Miss Rose or other tools or leverage she may have had at her disposal. This is all conjecture."

Cunningham did not even bother to offer an exception.

"Overruled. *You* brought this whole scenario up, Mr. Jennings. You should be delighted to have it demonstrated for you."

The audience laughed and Mr. Jennings sat, looking defeated.

"Let's break for lunch," Simmons announced unexpectedly. "Mr. Cunningham, can you wrap it up this afternoon?"

The young attorney nodded coolly. "Yes, certainly."

"Very well." He banged his gavel. "Two-hour recess. I have other business to attend to, believe it or not. We shall re-convene at one in the afternoon."

CHAPTER EIGHTEEN

Bailey was escorted back to her cell by a guard, and she kept her eyes averted as she walked past her loved ones and the rest of throng. She was so wholly weary: she had not slept the night before, and was longing to lie down and close her eyes for a spell.

She had been asleep for perhaps twenty minutes when a guard banged on the bars of her cell with his club. "Wake up, Sleeping Beauty! Your lawyer wants to see you! C'mon, now." She sat up, disoriented and dizzy, and tucked a few frazzled stray hairs into her bun and straightened her dress. Could it have been two hours already? She sure didn't feel rested. She was dismayed to see it was the troll with yellow teeth who had come to fetch her; a truly hateful man.

"No time for primpin' Miss Rose," he snarled.

"That's Dr. Rose to you," Bailey snapped back. "Have some respect."

He yanked her up by the arm and pushed her out of the cell. "I don't have no respect for a whorin' murderin' *woman.*" The word "woman" was obviously the vilest of the three descriptors. Bailey bit her tongue to keep from answering, vowing to have this excuse for a man fired. *A word to Jacob is all it would take*, she thought savagely, then immediately felt small and mean. She shouldn't even consider using Jacob for the power he could wield to exact a *revenge*, of all things!

They walked down the long hallways in silence, and he gave her one last shove into the room before he closed the door and locked it. She stumbled a bit, and when she had regained her footing and looked up angrily, her cheeks burning, her expression changed to astonishment. In addition to Cunningham, Flanders, and Mooreland, Blanche DuBois was in the small room! She was so utterly out of context that Bailey blinked a few times, staring.

Blanche nodded to her. "Hello, Bailey. I see you're shocked to see me here, and I don't blame you."

Bailey cleared her throat and sank into a chair held out for her by Abe. "Yes, I *am* shocked. What are you doing here?"

Blanche's hands ventured upward to straighten her hat: it was more conservative today, a rather simple black affair with one single ostrich feather, clipped short. Her face fell into regretful lines, an expression Bailey was sure she had never seen on this woman's face. "Bailey, oh, my dear. I came to apologize, for one thing. I'm sorry."

"Sorry for what?" Bailey bit sharply.

Blanche shook her head mournfully. "There's so much to apologize for; where do I begin? I'm sorry I allowed Addie to work at Fort Allen. She just wanted to cook or clean, poor dear, but after she had you, I found her one day, when you were just a few months old, passed clean out in Betsy's room, full of morphine. I suspected that she had been an addict before. It wasn't too much longer that she asked to work upstairs—she knew our pharmacist kept the girls fully stocked. I could have got her help and kept her in the kitchen, but I didn't. I knew with her looks and smarts she would bring in the money."

Bailey stared at her, hating her even more.

Blanche stumbled a bit. "Well, and—and dear, I'm sorry for making you clean and do the laundry, and for making you sleep under the porch."

"Is that all?" Bailey finally asked. Blanche's eyes filled with tears. "How about 'I'm sorry for beating you, Bailey, and for refusing to let you go to school, and most of all, I'm sorry for accepting five thousand dollars for your virginity when you were twelve years old. I'm sorry I sold your body to a drunken monster.' That would be a place to start, I suppose."

Blanche exhaled, and it was a sob. She lowered her face into her hands and Bailey could see her age then: her hands were thickly veined and wrinkled and crooked, and trembled a bit now. "I am. I am sorry, for all of it. I'm so sorry."

Bailey pushed her chair back noisily and stood. "Is that all, then? I am exhausted and was hoping to get a bit more sleep before I have to go back in there. Can I be excused?" She directed this last statement to Cunningham, not wanting to spend another second looking at, listening to, or thinking about the pathetic old woman in front of her, the woman who was at least indirectly responsible for her mother's death.

Cunningham rose, too. "Bailey, I think you better sit back down. Blanche brought something that I think you're going to want to read. It's addressed to you."

Bailey stared at him and sank back into her chair, feeling dread and panic bubbling up her throat and making it difficult to speak.

"What?" she whispered dumbly.

Blanche continued to weep, so Cunningham reached forward and handed the envelope lying in front of her to Bailey. Bailey reached forward with a cold hand and turned it so she could read the address and return address. *Bailey Rose, Fort Allen Boarding House, San Antonio, Texas* was the address.

The return address made her whimper and drop the envelope back onto the table as if it were a hot coal. *Adam Hawk, Gaslight Hotel, San Antonio, Texas.*

The postmark was dated 20 May 1876.

The letter. He had sent her the letter, and Blanche had received it, and held onto it all of these years.

She stared at it, mesmerized. Adam Hawk had written this letter after he had killed her mother; she was sure of it. He had killed her, bathed and changed his clothes, written the letter, and calmly walked down to the lobby to mail it before he went out to purchase a bottle of whisky. She tasted bile in her throat and thought she might vomit; she actually bent forward, clutching her stomach, and gagged. Abe put a hand on her back and another on her arm, murmuring gentle things.

She struggled to regain her equilibrium, and finally sat up, still in denial. She found her voice, but it was thin and vulnerable. "He told me he wrote me a letter telling me to stay away. I thought it was just the whisky and morphine talking; I thought he was just babbling, like my mother did when she was gone on the drugs. But he really did. He really did." She shook her head over and over, her eyes dry but wide with shock and grief.

Blanche looked up from her handkerchief. "I got the letter the next morning, and I did inquire at the Gaslight after you, but nobody had seen you. Of course I knew the dead woman was Addie, but I didn't want to implicate Fort Allen, so we couldn't claim her. I didn't know what to do. So I did nothing."

"Bailey," Cunningham interrupted gently. "You need to read the letter. It answers—well—everything. *Everything,* so much more than you could even guess."

Bailey took a deep breath. "I'll read it, but I want to be alone. No— wait. I need Gabby. Please, someone fetch Gabby for me. I need her." The last three words were choked with tears, and she put her head down onto her arms on the table, refusing to look up as the men and Blanche left the room. She waited alone; maybe for only twenty minutes, but it felt like a lifetime. The letter lay in front of her like a serpent about to strike, and at one point she pushed it from her in horror, hating the look of it, the feel of it, the truth of its existence.

At last the door opened, and Gabby glided through, her face as tranquil as ever. Bailey bolted from her chair and flung herself into Gabby's arms, and the two of them swayed for a moment, clutching each other close.

Finally Gabby pulled away and held Bailey at arm's length, looking deeply into her eyes. "So, my friend, Hawk really did write a letter, I hear. Well, you have to read it. Cunningham says it will be entered as evidence; he says it's the turning point, the piece of the puzzle that will set you free. And I don't think he was just talking about the murder case, darling."

Bailey stared at her. "What do you mean?"

Gabby shrugged. "I don't know. But whatever it is, it's a big deal, as they say."

She let go of Bailey and pointed to the chair. "Sit. Open it and read it already. Let's get it over with. Sit up straighter, Bailey." Bailey straightened her shoulders and lifted her chin, feeling some of her spirit return with the help of this strong woman beside her.

Gabby handed her the envelope without further hesitation, and before she could lose her nerve, Bailey opened it, her hands shaking.

The letter had been scrawled on stationery that bore Hawk's official senatorial name and stamp. It was written hastily, almost illegibly, and was rather long. He wrote it in thirty minutes, she mused. Yes, that was possible: he cleaned himself after shooting Addie and wrote the letter, then walked down to the lobby to deliver it just before six o'clock. The date at the top screamed to her. 20 May 1876.

She read it to herself, heart pounding, breath coming faster and faster, and as she read, she felt the world flip upside down.

Cunningham, Jennings, and Simmons had been in the judge's chambers for the better part an hour. Bailey sat at the defense table with Abe and Mooreland, her stomach churning, her insides alternately hot and cold. The team at the prosecution table glared at her, tapping pencils, frowning at each other. Cunningham had requested a private meeting with the judge and Jennings, and that could only mean one thing: there was new evidence, and Cunningham was asking for a dismissal of the charges. The courtroom was abuzz without the judge to keep them in line: the noise had grown to a dull roar by the time he burst through his chambers, ascended his throne, and banged the gavel like a madman, his mutton chops bristling with indignation.

"There will be order!" he roared.

Cunningham took his seat beside Bailey and gave an almost imperceptible shake of his head. That meant no. Jennings had not agreed to dismiss the charges, and now the letter would have to be brought forward. Bailey's breath caught in her throat and she gripped the arms of her chair. It was ghastly what the jury and the audience were about to hear. She felt especially keenly sorry for Hope and Cordelia and wished there was a way to warn them.

The judge ordered the bailiff to bring in the jury, and they shuffled in, taking their seats. Bailey had paid very little attention to the jury throughout the trial, heeding Cunningham's orders. "They'll be trying to interpret every look you give them," he had explained. "It's better not to look at them at all." It had been strange and difficult, but she had managed it, and realized now that she had only a vague idea of how any of them had reacted to evidence. Abe had told her they had reacted in a positive way to the defense thus far, with the exception of the scary, powerful-looking farmhand with the inscrutable expression, and the older banker.

The judge cleared his throat meaningfully and addressed the audience. "New evidence has come to light. This evidence is of a very disturbing and—delicate—nature. I urge the women in the audience to consider leaving the room now. It is most advisable that you *leave the room now.*"

For a moment there was stunned silence, and then several women began to rise, most at the insistence of their husbands. Bailey took the opportunity to turn around; a cardinal sin in Cunningham's book, she knew, but she had to make eye contact with Hope. She found her in her customary spot, and when Hope looked at her, Bailey ever-so-slightly inclined her head toward the door. "Go!" she mouthed, and was dismayed when Hope shook her head. "I'm staying," she mouthed back, and Bailey's eyes shifted to Cordelia. Surely Cordelia would leave, but her aunt just shook her head no, gripping Hope's hand. Howard put his arm around Cordelia and nodded at Bailey reassuringly.

Bailey turned back around, and as the courtroom became a bit more chaotic and noisy, she slowly turned the other way to glance at Jacob. He smiled and winked at her, his eyes gleaming. *You can do this. Be strong.* It was as though he had shouted the words to her, and she turned back around, feeling energized. *He knows what's in the letter.* Cunningham must have spoken to him before he went into Simmons' chambers.

Simmons finally nodded to Cunningham, and the young man stood, letter in hand. "The defense recalls Blanche DuBois to the stand."

Blanche took the stand and was reminded of her oath.

"Miss DuBois, do you wish to recant any statements you made earlier when you testified?"

Blanche nodded. "Yes. Bailey Rose was never an upstairs girl at Fort Allen or anywhere else." She looked directly at the jury. "She wasn't a prostitute," she clarified. Jennings burned with rage. He didn't dare say a goddam word; DuBois could easily testify that he had threatened to close down Fort Allen if she told the truth.

"Miss DuBois, Mr. Willshire testified that Senator Hawk mailed a letter on the twentieth of May. Do you have any idea what this letter could be?"

"Yes, I do. It was a letter addressed to Bailey Rose at Fort Allen. I received it the next morning, and I kept it. I didn't know what to do with it; I felt it was best to leave well enough alone, since Bailey disappeared that night and wasn't seen again for fifteen years."

There were loud gasps from the audience as Cunningham entered the letter into evidence, asking the bailiff to hand it to Blanche instead of the jury. "Miss DuBois, I know this will be difficult, but can you read the letter aloud?"

Blanche wiped her streaming eyes with her handkerchief and nodded several times. Cunningham waited patiently as she gathered herself for the task ahead.

"It is dated 20 May 1876," she began, her voice shaking but carrying across the room, which was now only half full. She took a deep breath, and Bailey's heart sped up to three times its normal rate. Her hands were clammy and her body was suddenly numb.

"Dearest Bailey,

I have a story to tell you. It's a true story and maybe the saddest you've ever heard. When I was eleven years old, I was taken by a tall man and a tall woman. They stole me out of my front yard. I had been playing with my dog, Mr. Jones, and they drove up in a black closed carriage and jumped out and grabbed me. They put a rag on my face that made me fall asleep, and when I woke up, my hands and feet were tied and my mouth was taped shut. The wagon stopped on a street behind a little cart and pony. A little girl rode in the cart and a woman walked behind her, laughing and having a gay time. The man and woman jumped out and I knew what was going to happen, Bailey. The man started talking to the nice woman, and the bad woman—she had black hair like a raven's wings and sharp fingernails like knives—she walked over by the little girl in the cart. I had to warn them! I started banging my head against the glass window. I banged and banged until it started to bleed. I thought if I banged hard enough I could make a hole and get out. I screamed and screamed. The nice woman saw me and cried out and ran toward the carriage, and oh, Bailey, I'm so sorry, the bad man shot her and she fell down, blood gushing from her throat. Then they took the little girl and threw her in the wagon and tied up her hands and feet and taped her mouth like mine, and hogtied me so I couldn't cause more trouble.

We rode for hours and when we finally stopped, they took us into a dark and stinking house, all the way down to the cellar. There were others, Bailey. There were seven others, nine of us in all. They were all asleep, and I thought they were dead. The bad man took our tape off and the little girl was crying. Oh, Bailey, I'm so sorry; that little girl was your mama. They untied us but I couldn't get away: they had guns, and there were two other men there, too. I tried to comfort her. Then the bad stuff started. Two of the men took me to the wagon and made me…" Blanche stuttered and stopped, her face collapsing. "Do I have to read this?" she whispered. "I don't think I can continue; I'm sorry."

Cunningham took the letter and continued, his voice grave and quiet, the letter all the more powerful read in a man's voice. Bailey closed her eyes and could almost envision Hawk telling her the story himself, and she hugged herself tightly.

"Two of the men took me to the wagon. It was parked in back, hidden in brush. They made me undress. Then they undressed and did bad things, Bailey. It hurt and I cried and tried to fight them, but there was always one to hold me down."

As Cunningham read, several people stood and quickly made their way out of the courtroom, a few of them crying audibly, a few of them, men. The jurors were horror-stricken; several of them were covering their mouths in shock.

"Then they brought me back to the main room and tried to take Adele. 'Della,' she said her name was, although you've always known her as Addie. They tried to take her and I fought them. I kicked them and bit them and one of the men punched me in the face. I begged them to take me instead, that I'd do whatever they wanted if they'd just leave her alone, and you know, that worked for the first three days. They thought it was funny that I was her protector. They took me to the wagon a lot. "Let's go to Malachi's wagon," they would say, like it was a trip to the circus. I started to go away in my head when they took me back there. I was a pirate sailing the seven seas, fearless and brave, chopping the bad men to pieces. I wasn't even in the wagon anymore. But on the fourth day they started giving me a sticky white, sweet-smelling medicine called morphine. They shot it right into our arms with needles, and it hurt. Della, too, even though I tried to stop them. I would sleep for hours and hours, and I saw them taking Della to the wagon, but when I tried to stand up I vomited and then passed out. And so it went for a lifetime, Bailey. I'm so sorry. Oh, your poor mother. I tried to protect her with all of my might. Most of the time when they reached for her I could convince them to take me instead. I think they took her maybe five or six times. They took me every day, sometimes two or three times a day. They took the other children, too, but they said I was their favorite. They said we would go back to our families if we were good. I didn't believe them; I thought they were going to kill us off, one by one. I was almost too weak to stand because I gave most of my food to Della when they fed us, which was about once every other day. Bailey, I told Della it wasn't her fault, what they made us do, but I think she was too little to understand. I held her and rocked her like a baby. I tried to protect her but I couldn't. And then they took her away, back to her family, they said. That was the worst two days. They left the other kids alone but they took me to Malachi's wagon a lot and they did new things, you couldn't even imagine, and I can't tell you, because if I let myself write it down, I think I'll lose the last bit of sanity I have. I wanted to die more than I've ever wanted anything. I begged them to kill me, but they wouldn't. And then the police came and killed them all, and took all of us home to our families. I couldn't tell my parents what the bad men did to me, but the doctor told them, and they were ashamed and embarrassed and we never talked about it; it wasn't allowed. I've tried to find those children, for comfort, I guess. Most of them are dead; either by their own hand or they just got sick and died, maybe of sadness. I never could find three of them; they just vanished, and their families didn't know where they were, either. Your mother vanished, but I found her. My sweet Della, and now she's gone, too! She's gone!!

Oh, Bailey, I'm so sorry. I tried to befriend her two years ago; I came to San Antonio to see her when I could, to try to get her to come with me, out of her miserable life, to bring you with her and let me take care of her like I couldn't back then. But she saw through me. She saw I couldn't escape the drug that made us sleep, that made us forget Malachi's wagon with the big spiders in the corner and the rats and the soiled mattress and the smell of urine and vomit and other unmentionable things. She had to have the drugs to keep forgetting, and so did I. And I needed something else: the haven of a young girl. A young girl would heal me, make it all better. Only another child could understand. I'm so sorry about Liza and Nadine. But they weren't the only ones; there was another one, Bailey, not an upstairs girl, either, and I'm so sorry. I'm sorry I need you so badly. I need you, Bailey. You are the only one who can save me. I wish we could run away together. I could be a kid again. We could love each other. I paid Blanche for you. I'm so sorry. Della came to protect you tonight. She brought her gun and said that if I didn't leave you alone, she'd kill me. She pointed it at me, and I told her to put it down. I didn't want her to hurt herself. I loved her, Bailey, just like I love you. I grabbed for the gun; I was going to throw it out the window and talk to her, calm her, like I used to do, but she was stronger than I thought, fighting for you, and we wrestled for it, Bailey, and the gun went off, and I wished it would have pierced my heart, but it didn't. I carried her to the bed and laid her gently upon it and said a prayer, Bailey. And now I'm writing you this letter to tell you to stay away. Even though I need you, right now, in the worst way, in a horrible, depraved way, you need to stay far away from me, Bailey. I can't control what I do, you see. I'm still in Malachi's wagon; I'll never get out, ever. I'm in Malachi's wagon, forever. Stay away. Stay away. I'm so sorry. I'm so sorry."

In the courtroom was a perfect, eerie silence. Several of the jurors wept silently. Simmons stared at his hands, this throat working, thinking that this was surely the most horrific crime he had ever heard of in his entire career. Hope and Cordelia were huddled in the shelter of Howard's arms, shaking. In the balcony, Mr. Duke balled his hands into fists and remembered some of the horrors he and his family had endured, equally as unspeakable. Gabby sat huddled against Thomas, not quite as shocked as the others around her, thinking of the debasing acts she had sometimes been made to perform in her years at the brothel, and many of those at a very tender age. Nonetheless, she had been lucky to have been at the Purple Pansy.

Lindy, Marianna, and Gacenka were all crying, comforted by their husbands. Wenzel sat completely still with his eyes squeezed tight. Anton looked at Alice anxiously: she stared straight ahead, stone-faced. Even more than Gabby, she had experienced much of the same pain and degradation as the kidnapped children. The things Hawk couldn't bring himself to say were an almost daily part of her own story from the time she was eleven, etched clearly in her mind for all time. She had her wagon, but for her, there had never been a home to return to. She had learned to protect herself to an extent, but when a girl was selling herself, even if she was a child, anything was fair game, and there were too many nights to count when she had laid in her cranberry crate afterward, bloody, aching, debased, in shock. Eventually, she, too, had learned to escape in her mind; she had learned how to shut the wagon door. She glanced at Anton, and as she saw the love and agonized worry in his face, she had an epiphany. It was time to open the door and tell him everything; everything she could remember. Maybe she should write it down, too. Maybe she could flood that room with sunlight.

Anton squeezed her hand and leaned over to kiss her cheek and whisper in her ear. "None of it was ever your fault," he said, and she stared at him. "I love you."

"I love you, too," she whispered, holding onto his hand for dear life. She felt the door begin to open, just a crack.

Jacob, who had been informed by Cunningham in a quick whispered conversation of the basic contents of the letter, thought he was prepared to hear the letter read aloud, but he was wrong. He was sick, imagining himself as the boy trying to save Bailey in that situation, and keenly understanding Hawk's wish to die. He longed to reach for Bailey, whose head was bowed, a single red curl escaping down her narrow neck. She was perfectly still, and did not look to be crying, but he knew her heart. She would be shattered.

Bailey was not crying. She was praying. Not for herself, or her mother, or even her sister and aunt. Not for the other children who had suffered so terribly. She was praying for Adam Hawk; for forgiveness for killing him, for his soul to be at peace in Heaven with a Savior who could make him whole again. He was not a monster. He was a victim of abuse of the worst imaginable kind, abuse that made him an addict and a pedophile. *Save him, oh Lord. Save him like he tried to save my mother. Please, forgive him and take him to you.* Could she pray him into Heaven? She didn't know. She wasn't sure what she believed, but the thought of Adam Hawk or her mother having to endure any more suffering was untenable. He had said he believed in God. He had made the sign of the cross before she killed him. Maybe, maybe it was enough.

And while she was at it, maybe she should just go ahead and pray for all of the children suffering on the Row or in the back alleys of this city, of all cities. The magnitude of it stripped her of hope for a dark moment, overwhelming her with a feeling of doom and helplessness. Children still suffered as Adam and her mother had suffered, every day, right here, and elsewhere. *And no one cared, at least not enough to act.*

Jennings at last interrupted the silence. "Your Honor, I question the authenticity of the letter, of course. If I didn't, I wouldn't be doing my job," he hastily added as more than a few glares were thrown his way.

Cunningham nodded briskly. "I am prepared to call a handwriting expert to the stand, as well as members of Hawk's own family."

Simmons nodded. "Very well. We will adjourn for the weekend, which will give Mr. Jennings a fair chance to gather his own experts. Let's plan on wrapping this up on Monday, gentlemen; what do you say?"

Bailey wanted more than anything to go to Hope and Cordelia after Simmons banged the gavel and dismissed the jury, but Cunningham kept her in her seat with gentle pressure on her arm and a shake of his head. The courtroom was cleared before he nodded to the guard and they made their way down the aisle.

"Why did we have to wait?" Bailey murmured, more than a little irritated.

Cunningham and his team shared a look. "You should have seen the press, Bailey. They were waiting, hanging back, hoping to be able to pounce. The guards just now drug the last one out."

"So I guess this trial is still a big deal?" Her voice was smaller now.

Cunningham snorted. "Dr. Rose, I think it's safe to say that you are a national household name at this point."

But Bailey didn't smile in return. She didn't want to be famous, or infamous, for that matter. She wanted to be back at her clinic, helping the women and children who experienced the degradation they had just heard about. She wanted for this to be over so they could all get on with their lives, no matter the outcome. Jacob had been in court all day, every day. What was this doing to his political career? Or to his relationship with Caroline, who was forced to fake an illness in order to hide a pregnancy while her fiancé sent clandestine messages of love to another woman? The absurdity of it all—of her life—struck her dumb, and she plodded along beside Cunningham in a silent funk, the guard applying just enough firm pressure to her elbow to remind her of what she was and where she was going.

She squeezed her eyes shut as she walked, finding that she didn't need vision while she was being led. She was descending into a dark, lonely, terrible place, and she knew why. She needed time to process it, but she knew exactly why the world suddenly seemed to be rendered in muted shades of blurry gray, why each moment seemed interminable and pointless, and why she didn't much care if she awoke the next morning. She knew why. She never was good at self-deception.

All of her life, she had justified killing Adam Hawk because he was a Vodnik—a horrible, real-life monster, an inexplicable ancient beast of some sort, who had tried to kill her in the wagon and in the creek. She *knew* it was him, had believed it with every fiber of her being.

But he hadn't been a Vodnik after all. He had been a ferociously abused child with a ravaged, ruined mind. He had never grown up; he had never left Malachi's wagon. He had been chained to morphine and alcohol; he had quieted the demons only through physical release with other children. He had been twisted, broken; he had wanted to die but could not bring himself to pull the trigger, even after inadvertently aiding in the accidental death of the little girl who haunted his life, Della.

For Bailey believed the letter: she believed everything about it. And she could see now that the type of monster he had become had nothing to do with water sprites or wolves or other mythical, fantastical creatures from her overactive childhood imagination. To remember the wolf and the water thing as anything less than real—so tangible that it almost killed her; *wanted desperately* to kill her—was annihilating. The fact that Wenzel had also heard something evil in the water had always been proof to her that it was real, but maybe—oh God, please don't let it be true—maybe Wenzel was less magical and more troubled than she had perceived him to be.

The letter was the epiphany that would likely exonerate her and save her life, but the unfortunate side-effect was the truth: her rationale for killing Hawk was destroyed. She would never have shot him unless she had believed he was a Vodnik. Guilt and confusion descended on her: it was immense and dark and immovable, and it changed her; shifted her into a spiritless version of herself.

They reached the turn in the hallway which led to the lobby on the left and her cell block on the right. Cunningham began to bid her farewell, explaining that his team had some work to do tracking down folks and shipping them across the country to Texas in the span of two days. Bailey nodded numbly and waved him away, turning to go.

"Dr. Rose! You should be *ecstatic!* This trial is all but over. Jennings made a huge mistake today not dismissing the charges." Abe and Mooreland beamed beside Cunningham, desperate to erase the woebegone expression from her face.

She barely managed a smile in return. She found she had nothing more to say, and turned her back to make her way to the women's wing of the Shrimp Hotel.

CHAPTER NINETEEN

Bailey was surprised when Mrs. Knittle came to fetch her on Saturday morning. "You have a visitor," smiled the matron.

For a moment Bailey's hopes soared wildly. Could it be—*no*, it couldn't be Jake. He didn't dare. But she hastily combed her hair nonetheless, her cheeks red with excitement.

She followed the matron down the familiar hallway to the small room, and upon entering, was surprised at the identity of her visitor. "Hannah!" she exclaimed, reaching out to grasp Hannah Birchwood's hands. Mrs. Knittle allowed it for a few seconds before she gestured Bailey into the chair in the corner.

"Hello, Bailey. I hope this is all right—to come and visit you."

Bailey waved her hand dismissively. "Of course it's all right; I'm so happy to see you! Have you been in court?"

Hannah nodded, and Bailey noticed with her keen eye that the woman looked pale and anxious. "Yes, I have been. I heard them read the letter from Hawk. Oh, Bailey, I'm so, so sorry about your poor Mama."

Bailey nodded and swallowed thickly a few times. "Thank you," she finally managed. "It was difficult to read that letter. I've spent years hating that man, so it's been quite a challenge to—well—to realize what made him the way he was, and that it was the same circumstances that made my mother the way she was." It was an awkward speech, but somehow Bailey felt better having said it aloud. It was the first time she had attempted to give voice to her ambivalent, convoluted feelings.

Hannah nodded but seemed to be only half-listening, and Bailey frowned. "Hannah, what's wrong?"

Hannah glanced at Mrs. Knittle worriedly. "Bailey, I have something to tell you, but it's very—personal. Is there any chance we could have a moment alone?"

Mrs. Knittle cleared her throat. "I'm not supposed to, but I'll give you ladies a moment. Don't tell on me, mind you."

Bailey beamed at the kind woman. "Thank you so much, ma'am."

The older woman flushed importantly and backed out of the room, closing the door softly behind her. She surely did admire that young woman, a doctor, no less! And word had it that she had shot a child molester and drug addict all those years ago; who cares if he was a senator? Good riddance.

"She'll probably be able to give us only a few moments, so you better come right out with it," Bailey said gently. Hannah Birchwood looked extremely distressed; tears were gathering in her blue eyes and two spots of color had bloomed on her pale face.

"Oh, Bailey. I have to tell you something horrible. I'll be quick before I lose my nerve. You see, I knew Adam Hawk when I was twelve; it was just a year before all of this happened. June 12th, 1875; I'll never forget the date."

Bailey stared at her, dread coiled like a snake in her gut.

Hannah's hands twisted in her lap. "He was a friend of my father's; my father was on the city council, and they were in politics together. Hawk stayed at our estate for a week. We all went on a picnic one day, the day before he was to leave, and after we had a lovely lunch, Adam asked me to go riding." She shook her head miserably. "I thought he was courting me, Bailey! He was so handsome and so very kind; I wanted to show off, I guess—show him how mature I was and how well I could seat my horse. I can't believe my parents let him take me; that just shows you how charismatic he was. We went riding for over an hour, and we stopped by the river and tied the horses to let them drink. We sat and talked for a while, and then he pulled out a pipe and asked me if I wanted to smoke with him. Well of course, I said yes, being the sophisticated lady I was. He told me it was opium, but I had no idea what that meant. We smoked quite a bit, I suppose. I was growing quite groggy; everything was so tippy. One of the last things I remember was him leaning toward me and kissing me, and I kissed him back, just like I had seen my older sister do when I spied on her and her beau."

Bailey sat frozen, immobilized with fear. She knew what was coming next, and she wished she could stop Hannah from saying it.

Hannah took a few deep breaths before she continued, pausing to wipe the tears from her cheeks. "I lost consciousness, and when I woke up, my dress was pushed up, my drawers were pulled down, and he was on top of me, having—intercourse," she choked. "It hurt so badly. I tried to push him off but I wasn't strong enough. I screamed at him to stop, but he didn't even seem to hear me; it was like he was in some trance."

Bailey reached for her and gripped her hands tightly.

"When he was done and saw that I was crying, he became very upset. He wept and apologized over and over. He asked for my forgiveness, but I couldn't even speak to him, I was so traumatized. He kept saying that he wanted to die. He begged me not to tell anyone, and that he'd never visit my house again. He asked me if I knew the way back to my parents—I did, of course; it was all our property—and then he just ran away. I never saw him again."

"Hannah," Bailey barely managed. Hawk had confessed in the letter that there had been another girl, and here she was: not a high-priced, consenting courtesan like Liza and Nadine; not a hungry, desperate street girl like Alice. He had raped a high-society daughter of a powerful city official, and gotten away with it. "You know, I think that I have just re-discovered my hatred for him," she said softly, and Hannah laughed shakily, shaking her head *no*.

"Don't do that, Bailey. There's no excuse for what he did to me and for what he wanted to do to you. But there is a *reason*, an evil that drove him to it. You see, I finally forgave him today, after all of these years, sixteen years after he asked me to. And once I did that, the hate was replaced by something else. Pity, I suppose, for the little boy who was so—broken. And grace. I feel a sense of grace."

Mrs. Knittle re-entered. "One more minute," she said softly.

"Bailey, tell your attorney that I will testify. He can put me on the stand if he needs to."

"Oh, no, Hannah! I would never put you through that!"

"It's not up to you. Just tell him, promise? I want to do this, if it's necessary. I won't let you be—" she stopped just short of saying *hanged*, her cheeks flaring again, a look of horror in her eyes. "I won't let you be convicted."

"Time's up now, ladies."

Bailey gave Hannah's hands another squeeze. "Thank you, my friend. Thank you for your bravery. And look what a beautiful life you've had. You didn't let it define you, did you?"

"No, I didn't," Hannah said proudly, lifting her chin. "And George has always known, ever since we were courting. He's very supportive. He sends his love, and he wanted me to tell you that you did the right thing, all those years ago. You stopped Hawk from hurting other girls, too, Bailey. Think about that." She stood and gathered her things. "Goodbye for now."

"I'll tell Mr. Cunningham, I promise." Bailey stood and followed Mrs. Knittle out the door, waving at Hannah and offering a last smile, marveling at the ugliness and beauty to be found in the very same moment. Her soul felt suddenly, infinitely lighter with Hannah's parting words. *You stopped him from hurting other girls.*

When she relayed Hannah's story to Cunningham later that afternoon, his brow furrowed in sadness and anger. "I'm so sorry for your friend. What a brave soul she is to offer to testify for you."

"Do you think we'll need her to do that?"

Cunningham shared a look with Abe. "We would never put her on the stand. You see, rape is very, very difficult to prove. The woman must provide evidence that she fought back—bruises, fractures, torn clothing, other injuries. And of course, there must be an examination by a physician. Hannah cannot provide any of that evidence: it's her word against Hawk's, and to make it even more complicated, he is deceased and cannot defend himself."

"So he just gets away with it," Bailey said dully.

Cunningham nodded regretfully. "Yes, he does. I can put Hannah on the stand to tell her story, but Jennings will have a field day discrediting her. He'll focus on any and every indication that Hannah was a consensual participant—agreeing to go riding, smoking, kissing. It's just pointless to put her through it."

Bailey was simultaneously relieved and disappointed.

"But we don't need her testimony. Mooreland has already tracked down a handwriting expert—the foremost expert in the country—and a member of Hawk's family to testify that the letter was indeed written by him. That in itself is amazing: his brother, Noah, flatly refused to testify for either the defense or prosecution; we both tried for him. But when Mooreland read him the letter over the telephone, he broke down. He wants to help you. And I should let you know that I am likely to call your aunt to the stand to establish that your mother was a victim of the same kidnappers as Hawk."

Bailey nodded; she had expected that Cordelia may be called; The Millers had traveled to attend the trial knowing that it was a possibility.

"I want you to rest and relax this weekend; try to get some sleep, all right? Monday, Bailey. On Monday, it will all be over."

One way or another, she thought darkly, but just nodded and smiled and followed Mrs. Knittle from the room.

No matter the outcome, Hannah's words resounded: *you stopped him from hurting other girls.*

Jacob spent a miserable weekend with Caroline at her parents' estate. To the world, Caroline had been announced as ill with diphtheria weeks ago, and had just emerged that very day from her supposed "quarantine." He found Mr. and Mrs. Vogler to be hostile, thinking he had sent their daughter to his infected home and brought the dreaded disease to their doorstep. Caroline had been bored and cranky, tethered to her bedroom, and pestered Jacob for details about the trial, which was the absolute last thing in the world he wanted to discuss with her. He found it next to impossible to talk about Bailey without betraying his emotions for her, so he spent much of his visit with Caroline with his back turned to her.

"For God's sake, Jacob. What's the matter? You act as though you can't stand to look at me."

He turned to her then. "Can we please talk about something else? I don't want to talk any more about the trial. How about the plans to get our own place? We need to get you moved out of here. I'll start looking right away."

She looked pleased at that prospect and smiled winningly, patting the bed next to her. "Come here, love. Sit down and relax. Will you rub my back? I'm finding that it's aching more and more." She turned her back to him and shrugged effortlessly out of her nightgown, presenting him with bare skin. He was struck with a memory of Bailey sitting in his bed, lifting her hair so that he could unbutton her gown, and he closed his eyes tightly, his hands aching for the feel of her warm skin. He felt a sharp jolt of desire, but it dissipated the instant he opened his eyes and looked at the woman in front of him. Her skin was the whitest he had ever seen, it looked soft and a bit pudgy. He felt a stab of pity; her body had changed so much since her pregnancy. He wondered if she felt badly about herself and imagined that she did; she had always been such an elegant, petite woman. That thought alone gave him the strength to put his hands on her.

But as he massaged her back, she leaned into him, and before he guessed at her intention she had captured his hands and placed them on her wide breasts. He froze with revulsion, thankful that she couldn't see his face. It was ghastly, this sensation of unfaithfulness to Bailey. He felt as though he were cheating with Caroline on his *wife*, Bailey! How any of this would ever be set right was completely beyond his understanding, and he felt a surge of panic.

"Oh, Jacob, I can't wait until we can be together, as husband and wife," Caroline whispered, and then fearful of overplaying her cards, set his hands aside gently and sat forward, drawing her gown closed. She turned to him regretfully. "But you better go now, my love. Find us a place, our home. I can't wait to see it."

He thought he did a fairly acceptable acting job: he smiled, nodded, said the correct things, spent a few more moments, and then took his leave.

But after he was gone, Caroline's head began to pound and her skin began to thrum unpleasantly: she felt as though thousands of tiny insects were working their way from the inside out, and she would soon burst open in an agony of pain. She recognized what was coming and wept, curled in a tight ball, cradling her chubby, un-pregnant stomach. She put her pillow to her face and screamed and screamed until her voice was gone. Then she vomited and called for the maid to bring her seltzer, but it was no good.

She had a pretty good idea what was happening to her—what had been happening to her ever since she was a young teenager. Dr. Montgomery had insisted there was something wrong with her brain; something chemical, or maybe an injury. She did remember a rather bad head knock in a riding accident when she was an older child: she had been thrown from a feisty mare and had been dead to the world for a good three days. But she knew there was nothing wrong with her brain. She knew the cause of the Black. Ultimately, it didn't matter what it was, though. There was no cure. There was nothing for it but to try to ride it out, to not give in to the rage and the voices that told her to drive her scissors straight into her heart.

There was nothing to do but wait for the Black to come and take her for as long as it wished.

For what would hopefully be the final day of the trial—*please, God, let it end today*—Hope had brought Bailey one of the gowns she had given to her in Pennsylvania. She delivered it right to Bailey's cell, having sweet talked a wide-eyed clerk with the unlikely name of Balthazar Nation into letting her access not only the women's block but Bailey's cell. She had to make a dinner date with the red-faced Mr. Nation for that privilege.

"Really, Hope, are you sure this is appropriate for court? Isn't this more of a—*frock*—to wear at home?" They both giggled as Bailey furtively struggled into it while Hope held up the scratchy wool blanket to block Bailey from the eyes of curious passing guards. When the gown was in place, Hope lowered the blanket and gave a whistle of appreciation. The forest green dress with its layers of silk and chiffon was loose, gauzy, and alluring, yet somehow made Bailey appear to be ten years younger. Her long hair was loose and fell down her back in a tangled mess.

"You look no older than sixteen," she whispered. "Those blue eyes of his are going to pop clean out of his head when he sees you today. I hope his brothers get a good grip on him."

Bailey swatted at her, her cheeks reddening. "Hope! Stop it! Now make yourself useful and help me with this horrible hair."

Hope spent the next few moments combing and braiding her sister's hair, *for the first and maybe the last time*, she thought with a catch in her throat, but she laughed and chattered and told hilarious stories of hiding from the smarmy men who pursued her at her aunt and uncle's lavish house parties.

"I have a cowboy for you," Bailey broke in unexpectedly with a grin. "His name is Kube. He works for Jacob."

Hope squealed and spun her around. "What does he look like? Does he wear those blue dungarees? What are they called? Does he wear a Stetson?"

Bailey laughed and nodded. "He's tall and dark and put together with wiry muscle, and he's *very* attractive. He looks like a bad boy until he smiles, and then he looks like the sweet softie he really is. He wears Levis *and* a Stetson! And you are just the woman to tame him!"

They giggled and whispered for a few moments longer until Mrs. Knittle came to fetch Bailey, and suddenly, they were silent.

Hope grabbed Bailey and hugged her fiercely. "I love you, sister. We have a lot of catching up to do, so when you walk out of that courtroom today, come with Cordelia, Howard and me to the Menger, okay? Stay with us for a few days. With your family."

It sounded like heaven to Bailey. She had wondered where she might go if she were freed: she didn't want the relentless newspapermen following her to St. Ursuline's, where so many young girls were housed; she didn't want to intrude on Gabby and her baby, who were still living at the Harding House. She knew where she longed to be: wherever Jacob was. If she were acquitted today, it would take every bit of her resolve not to turn around and fling herself into his arms, because she knew he'd be working his way toward her as quickly as he could shake off his brothers. And that was why she needed to hide for a bit. *If she were free.*

She smiled gratefully. "Yes, that's perfect, Hope. Thank you so much for being here for me."

Hope nodded vigorously, too emotional to answer, and hurried down the hall before Bailey could see her cry.

CHAPTER TWENTY

"Your Honor, the defense calls Cordelia Miller to the stand."

Bailey watched as her aunt repeated her oath and took her seat. She looked relatively calm, but Bailey remembered the attack she had when Bailey had first explained who she was in Pennsylvania, and she jiggled one foot nervously under the table, wishing Hope, whom she had observed to be fearless at just the right times, could have testified instead. Cunningham had assured her that there would only be a few questions, and that Jennings was unlikely to request a cross-examination.

"Mrs. Miller, could you explain to the jury your relationship to Dr. Rose?"

"Yes. I am her aunt. Her mother, Adele Rosemont, was my sister."

Cunningham nodded gravely. "And how did your sister come to be in San Antonio all the way from Pennsylvania?"

With a clear voice, Cordelia recounted the story of the abduction, Adele's abuse at the hands of the kidnappers, her troubled youth, and disappearance when she was seventeen.

"And who were these kidnappers?"

"They were the Leaches; ironic, isn't it?" There were murmurs from the crowd, but nobody laughed, the details of the wicked crime still fresh in their minds. Bailey listened intently: this was new to her. "Alpheus and Malachi Leach were brothers. Alpheus was the leader; Beatrix was his wife. Their mode of operation was to locate a child out for a stroll with a nanny or playing alone, then disable the nanny—they carried rags and chloroform with them—and abduct the child. As we have heard, they also used chloroform on the children. They kidnapped nine children in all: wealthy children from whose parents they could extort grand sums of money. My mother was the only adult killed; she had been trying to rescue a boy tied up in the carriage. We know now that boy was Adam Hawk."

There was a heavy silence.

"Did all of the children survive?" Cunningham asked quietly.

"Yes, or at least that is what the papers reported."

"How long was Adele with the kidnappers?"

"Twenty-three days," answered Cordelia quietly, a tear escaping down her cheek. Her hands, resting on her lap, began to tremble.

"And what was the extent of Adele's injuries?"

Cordelia glanced at Howard and Hope for courage, and briefly closed her eyes. "She had been starved, beaten, and raped."

There were a few gasps, but for the most part, the courtroom was like a vast, sad, tomb.

Tears were coursing down her pale cheeks now and her voice was quavering. "She had been injected with drugs, some of which remained in her system for days. She was incoherent and unable to walk for quite some time."

"No further questions," Cunningham said quickly, abruptly cutting the session short. He could see that the woman on the stand was emotionally frail.

"Cross?" asked Simmons reluctantly.

"No questions," Jennings snapped.

"Your Honor, I enter as evidence newspaper accounts of the crime, police reports, which indicate that both Adam Hawk and Adele Rosemont were two of the victims, and the physician records after Adele was examined." The documents were handed around for several long moments, giving Cordelia a chance to return to her seat and gather herself.

"The defense calls to the stand Ichabod Lehrman."

A tall, thin man with a bald head and spectacles approached the stand, took his oath, and sat briskly.

"Dr. Lehrman, you are being called as an expert witness in handwriting. Please state your credentials."

Lehrman nodded and spoke loudly, his voice reaching to the back of the room. "I am Professor Emeritus at Harvard University. I taught history and anthropology in my career. I currently serve as an archivist for the Smithsonian Institution, specializing in ephemera such as handwritten documents of historical import. I studied with Edgar L. Scurvington, who, as you all know, was the father of handwriting analysis." The jury looked at him blankly and Bailey suppressed a smile. "Well, *ahem*, I have written three books on the subject, and I am often called upon by law enforcement agencies in districts across the country to identify handwriting."

"Thank you, Dr. Lehrman. I would like for you to examine a letter allegedly written by Senator Adam Hawk. Your Honor, I submit for evidence three confirmed documents written by Senator Hawk in the course of his official duties, obtained from his former offices in Washington, D.C." The documents were handed around and finally reached Dr. Lehrman, who was permitted to leave the witness stand to spread the documents in front of him on the evidence table. Of course, he had already examined them, but he made a show of it, pulling out a magnifying glass and bending over the papers for long moments. At last, he straightened and nodded.

"The letter that was allegedly written by Senator Hawk matches precisely with the letters that are confirmed to have been written by him—those confirmed documents are called *exemplars*."

"Can you provide us with a more detailed explanation?"

"Certainly!" Dr. Lehrman launched into a twenty-minute discussion of garlands, threads, angles, arcades, baseline slant, spacing, loops, and pressure points; Bailey tried to follow, but her attention drifted to a covert study of the jury, most of whom looked utterly baffled but duly impressed. Lehrman, at last, concluded his lecture. "Thus, I am positive—there's not a doubt in my mind—that Senator Hawk wrote the letter addressed to Bailey Rose."

"No more questions, your Honor. Thank you, Dr. Lehrman."

"Cross, Jennings?"

"No. The prosecution wishes to call its own handwriting expert, your Honor."

"Get on with it, then."

Dr. Lehrman seemed to be a bit deflated that his moment of fame had come to an end, and the bailiff had to prompt him again to take his seat at the defense table, causing the audience to snicker.

"The prosecution calls Alexander Crabtree to the stand." A blustering older man with wispy blond hair and pink cheeks rose, lumbered to the stand, and took his oath with a growling voice. Cunningham and his team barely managed to refrain from exchanging incredulous looks: Crabtree was infamous throughout the southwest as an expert-for-hire, specializing in everything from bullet forensics to phrenology, a highly-suspect "science" that examined the size of the individual's skull to predict criminal tendencies. Crabtree as a handwriting expert was a new one.

"Mr. Crabtree, please explain to the court about your area of handwriting expertise."

Crabtree droned on and on for five minutes about his degree in Greek and Latin languages, his translation work, and the number of cases he had worked on that involved handwriting analysis. Bailey noticed that Abe was taking notes furiously.

"You have examined the documents in question. Can you please tell the jury what you have concluded?"

"Yes. It is highly doubtful that Adam Hawk wrote the letter addressed to Bailey Rose."

The audience erupted in murmurs.

"Can you tell us why?"

"Yes, I can. First of all, notice how deliberately and consistently Senator Hawk crosses his t's and dots his i's. He also has a distinctive beginning stroke to his L's and A's. All of those characteristics are missing in the letter purportedly written by Hawk. In addition, in the letter, the handwriting has much more of a slant and the letters are spaced more widely.

"Thank you, Mr. Crabtree."

"Cross?" sighed Simmons, knowing what was coming.

"I'd like to re-call Dr. Lehrman," announced Cunningham.

"I'll allow each of you to recall your experts *once*, hear that, Jennings?"

Dr. Lehrman's face lit up like a Christmas tree, and he practically skipped to the stand, much to the amusement of the crowd. Mr. Crabtree scowled his way off the stand and to his seat, sulking like a petulant child.

"Dr. Lehrman, Mr. Crabtree noted that the t-crosses and i-dots, among other characteristics, were markedly dissimilar in the documents verified as belonging to Hawk and the letter in question. In your expert opinion— bolstered by years of training with the founder of handwriting analysis and your own expansion of and publication within the field—" he paused meaningfully, quirking an eyebrow in Crabtree's general direction, making the audience laugh—"how would you answer Mr. Crabtree's analysis?"

Dr. Lehrman snorted. "His analysis is completely and utterly false at the worst and ignorant at best! Any apprentice could tell you that all of the so-called 'anomalies' that Mr. Crabtree identified are not anomalies at all; they can be easily explained by taking into account the speed at which the writer is composing. You see, when any of us writes quickly, certain universal characteristics emerge: hasty and partially-crossed t's, dotted i's, the lack of beginning strokes, and more of a slant and spacing to our handwriting. Any of you could try it!" Here he gestured meaningfully to the jury. "Write a passage at a normal speed, then write the same passage as fast as you possibly can, which I understand to be the case with this letter. You will see all of these characteristics emerge, which is common knowledge amongst handwriting experts." Here he stopped to glower at the charlatan Crabtree. "Furthermore, Senator Hawk had *very* distinctive handwriting, as I noted before. To be identifiable, a questioned handwriting must bear significant, stable and unique characteristics upon which to base an opinion. Those markers cannot be concealed no matter how quickly he writes. The pen lifts are identical to the exemplars, and more importantly, the unusual curls and loops on each and every capital letter is also identical. The letter to Bailey Rose was written by Adam Hawk."

Cunningham nodded. "Thank you again, Dr. Lehrman. No further questions."

Jennings waved off a cross-exam, and after a prolonged flurry of intense whispering with his own expert, he stood and announced, with a scarlet face, that he would not be calling Mr. Crabtree again. The expert in question had sunk about six inches down into his chair and was staring steadfastly at his hands.

"Your Honor, I would like to call Noah Hawk to the stand."

More gasping and quite a bit of ruckus arose as a dapper, middle-aged man made his way to the stand. Simmons banged his gavel and the crowd quieted enough for Bailey to hear his voice as he took his oath. He bore only a slight resemblance to his brother: his eyes were the same peculiar shade of gray, but his hair was dark and he was much bulkier.

"Please state your relationship to Senator Adam Hawk."

"Adam was my brother," he said shortly. His expression was strained; his body language, tense.

"Mr. Hawk, what can you tell us about Adam's abduction?"

Noah's throat worked as he swallowed, and Bailey detected a tremor in his voice now. "Adam was playing outside with our dog. I called him in for dinner and he didn't heed me, so our nanny sent me out to fetch him. He— he wasn't there."

"Was the dog still there?" Bailey thought it an odd question until Noah answered, his voice breaking a bit.

"Yes. He was dead. He had been shot in the head."

There was silence as the multitude imagined the terror of a young boy finding his dog shot and his brother vanished.

"And what happened next?"

"We got a ransom note the next day, and we didn't see Adam for another twenty-five days. Almost a month, it was." Noah's eyes had ceased to focus on Cunningham and were fixed at some point in his distant past.

"Who abducted him, and what was the outcome?"

Noah gestured to the evidence table. "Just like the reports said that you have there. There were three in the kidnapping ring: a married couple and the man's brother. Adam was the last to be released. The police shot the kidnappers when they rescued him."

"Your Honor, I submit for evidence Adam Hawk's physician's report." He handed it to the bailiff and the report made the rounds. Bailey watched the revulsion on the jurors' faces and could well imagine what the report contained.

"Mr. Hawk, can you describe the extent of Adam's injuries?"

Noah just stared at Cunningham for a few seconds, perhaps trying to work up the courage to answer. He took a deep breath and released it. "There was quite a bit of morphine in his system, and some other drugs, too; it's all in the report. They beat him up pretty bad: he had black eyes and a broken nose. His left arm was broken in two places. He had a broken rib. He had extensive injuries—internally—below." He paused and Bailey felt his pain and grief emanating in palpable waves. Not a sound could be heard in the courtroom. "That is to say he, uh, just like all the other children, had been raped as well." He said it quickly and then bowed his head, eyes closed. Testimony about the rape of a child—particularly a *male* child—was unheard of.

Cunningham allowed a few moments of silence as the report traveled through the jury box. "Mr. Hawk, were you familiar with your brother's handwriting?"

"Yes, of course. We wrote to each other every month or so."

"In your opinion, did Adam write the letter to Bailey Rose?"

"Yes," Noah said immediately. "I know he did. But not just because I know his handwriting."

Cunningham's head whipped around; he had not expected this and clearly had no inkling of what Noah Hawk was going to say.

"How else are you sure the letter to Bailey Rose was written by your brother?"

Noah looked at Bailey for the first time, and his expression softened. "Because he had told me about Adele and Bailey. He told me he wanted to rescue them, and that he wanted to bring Bailey to me and my wife, for us to raise her, away from him. And I told him we would welcome her into our family with open arms."

Bailey stared at him, astounded. Adam had been truly trying to rescue her and take her somewhere safe? She had assumed that his "rescue" would include a sexual relationship.

"What do you mean, 'away from him'?"

Noah swallowed thickly and briefly closed his eyes. "I knew that Adam desired young girls. I always felt that he was trapped as an eleven-year-old in so many ways. He really was two people: on one hand he was a normal, well-adjusted young man who went on to Yale and earned his law degree, rose quickly in politics, and was elected to our father's former senate seat. We were all so proud of him, having overcome that—that unspeakable *horror*. But on the other hand he was this lost little kid, you know?" His voice broke and he blinked through tears. "He craved morphine and any other drug he could procure—he fought it so hard, but he always went back to it—and he seemed to need young girls to feel safe. He could never form a relationship with a woman his own age. I think it's because he lost that part of himself forever, when he was a boy."

"The letter?" Cunningham gently reminded him after a respectful pause.

"In the letter he tells Bailey that he wanted to rescue her, and he tells her to stay away, even while he was declaring how much he needed her in an— *unholy* way."

"Thank you for your candor, Mr. Hawk. No more questions."

Jennings waved his hand, lacking a white flag.

Judge Simmons looked at Cunningham hopefully as Noah Hawk made his way to his seat. "Any more witnesses, Mr. Cunningham?" He dearly hoped it was time for closing arguments. This trial had affected him more than any other in his career, and he was longing for a week or two of respite, down at the river, a pole in his hand, his grandson safely by his side.

Cunningham raised his index finger and made his way back to the defense table, leaning down to confer with Bailey in whispers. "It's up to you, Dr. Rose. Do you want to take the stand? You don't have to; I'm sure we have this wrapped up with a pretty bow."

"I want to tell my story," she whispered.

Cunningham gazed at her a moment, wondering if he would live to regret this, then straightened and faced the judge. "Your Honor, the defense calls Bailey Rose to the stand."

The prosecution looked stunned; the jury looked flabbergasted, and the crowd was silent for a beat before breaking out in an excited buzz. Simmons rolled his eyes: it was the very first dumb move Cunningham had made.

Bailey stood and smoothed her tea gown, and the crowd fell silent as she walked to the stand and laid her hand on the Bible. She was a vision in her gauzy green gown: she looked like a delicate forest nymph floating through the courtroom. A few curls had escaped her braided bun and trailed down her back, lending her even more a look of childish virtue. Hope smiled and snuck a glance at Jacob Naplava: his jaw was jumping and a brother on each side had a firm hold of him. She understood how he felt: Bailey should not be taking the stand: it wasn't necessary. What was Cunningham thinking? She thought she might jump up herself and stop her sister!

Bailey sunk into her chair, her oath echoing in her head. *The whole truth and nothing but the truth.* Cunningham had told her the truth would win, every time. Well, this was her chance to tell it, from start to finish.

"Dr. Rose," Cunningham began, wondering how on earth to disarm Jennings before he had a chance to destroy his client. His mind worked frantically, but in the end, he just decided to trust her. "Will you please tell us about the events of the twentieth of May, 1876?"

She nodded and turned to face her jury. "I grew up at Fort Allen, an upscale boarding house—brothel—here in San Antonio, as you already know. I was not a prostitute. I never was. My mother, Addie Rose, was. And you've all heard how she ended up there. Of course, I knew nothing about her story at that time. I was just a twelve-year-old girl who wanted desperately to have a better life. I wanted to go to school, more than anything. I tried to go, on May fifteenth, but it didn't work out so well; some of the other children didn't think I belonged there." She stopped as she remembered Otto and the act he had tried to force her to do, and the way Jacob had come barreling around the corner and launched himself at her attacker. "There was one nice student, Jacob Naplava. He found out that I lived at Fort Allen from my best friend, Gabriella Flores, as she already testified. He invited me to visit his home and meet his family, and since

Blanche—the madam—was so angry with me for going to school, it seemed like a fine idea." She really hadn't planned on telling this part of the story, but she found that the words were flowing effortlessly, and she made no effort to stop them.

"We traveled to Boerne and I spent two lovely days there: the best two days of my life." She paused to look at Gacenka and Franticek and smiled tenderly at them; they beamed back at her, tears coursing down Gacenka's face. Franticek nodded encouragement. "I learned how to shear a sheep, how to administer medicine to a sheep's cuts—that really intrigued me, of course, since I wanted to be a doctor or nurse—and how to bake. Oh! And Jacob's brother taught me how to fish." Her glance rested on Wenzel then, who gazed back at her tranquilly. "They were all wonderful and I wanted to stay. You see, I didn't have much of a family. So when we returned to the city on the twentieth, my plan was to go to Fort Allen to ask Mother if I could spend the summer at the Naplava ranch."

"And what time did you arrive at Fort Allen?"

"About six o'clock. Mother wasn't there, so I spoke with Lola, and just as she already testified, she told me that Mother had gone to the Gaslight to talk to Senator."

"Tell us more about your Mother and Senator."

"Well, of course I didn't know they had been kidnapped together as children; I didn't know that until last Friday. I knew that for a few years he had been coming to see her—maybe four or five times—and they would talk for hours. She would often get upset. I also knew that Hawk preferred young girls at Fort Allen; Liza and then later, Nadine. I was scared of him, because he smashed things and yelled when he was drunk or using drugs. Lola told me he paid Blanche five thousand dollars to—to purchase me. To spend the night with me. And that when Lola had told her that, just about an hour before I arrived back at Fort Allen that evening, Addie had gone to the Gaslight Hotel to stop him from pursuing me."

"What did you do when Lola told you that?"

"I ran all of the way to the Gaslight. It took about fifteen minutes: I was a pretty fast runner. I walked right in; it was six-thirty by that time. The doorman told me I had to leave, but when I told him what I was there for, he told me which room the senator was in." She paused and gathered her thoughts, realizing that what she told next may convict her to hang.

"I went up the back stairs and straight to Room 226. I knocked on the door and he—Adam Hawk—answered it. He appeared to be very drunk. He grabbed my hair yanked me inside, and asked me if I'd ever seen a gun. He told me that my mother had—that she owned one. And then he made me look at the bed. I wouldn't do it—I was afraid of what I would see—and he struck me across the face, knocking me to the floor." The courtroom was silent; the jury, spellbound. "He ordered me to stand up and look at the bed."

"And what did you see?" Cunningham prompted gently when she paused.

She cleared her throat, determined not to cry. "I saw my mother dead. She was covered in blood: it was all over her, all over the bed. Everything just seemed to be drenched in blood. I remember thinking that it was amazing that there could have been that much blood in her body, and now that it wasn't in her body any more, she must be dead. And then I fainted."

Cunningham waited respectfully for Bailey to collect herself. Jacob closed his eyes and died a little bit on the inside. He should have been there, in that room, with her.

"When I awoke, I was tied to a chair. My dress had been removed and I was bound—both my hands and feet—to the chair with my dress ties. Hawk was passed out against the wall, an empty whisky bottle and several syringes around him. There was a gun in his hand: I knew it was my mother's gun. I managed to free my hands and feet, and I took the gun out of his hand."

"Why didn't you leave at that point?" Cunningham was desperate to disarm Jennings however he could.

"I was sick and dizzy; that's when I realized he had injected me with morphine. I knew that smell from years of living with my mother, who was an addict. I almost fainted again; I sat down in the chair and vomited. I was very weak."

"What happened next?"

"He woke up. He admitted that he had injected me with my mother's drugs. He was crying. He said he couldn't help himself, and he asked me to forgive him. Then he told me he had written me a letter telling me to stay away; at the time, I had no idea what he meant, of course. And then he told me how to cock the gun, and I did what he said. I pulled back on the hammer until I heard two clicks. I had never even held a gun before." Bailey took a deep breath and briefly closed her eyes, uttering a silent prayer. She was getting ready to confess, before a jury of her peers, her friends, family, and God, that she had killed a man, and she began to shake in spite of her best efforts to be brave.

"And then he told me what had happened: that Mother had come to tell him to leave me alone, that she had brandished the gun and he had tried to disarm her, that they had struggled for the gun and it went off by accident, shooting her in the chest. He said she was his friend and he didn't mean for it to happen."

"What else did he tell you?"

Bailey clenched her jaw before answering. This was surely the most difficult part to disclose. "He said that he didn't touch me yet, but he couldn't stop himself, and just as soon as he could get up he would put a needle back in his vein and come for me, just like they came for him. That's what he said, "I will come for you just like they came for me."" I knew what he meant to do. He was going to rape me."

There were sounds of crying in the courtroom, and Bailey knew it was Cordelia and Gacenka, her two surrogate mothers, who cried for the child she had been.

"What happened next, Dr. Rose?" Cunningham's voice was quiet and steady, but she found that her heart was pounding and her breathing was coming in gasps.

"He said he was a—a monster now, and he wanted to die, but he didn't want to kill himself." Bailey squeezed her eyes shut. She had thought that he had been confessing to being a Vodnik, but now she understood that he was branding himself a monster of an entirely different kind. "He made the sign of the cross and started praying. He said that I could be forgiven, and asked me to help him; to end it. And so I did."

Cunningham broke the electric silence. "What did you do?"

"I shot him in the chest. And then I ran out, throwing the gun in the hall. It was storming and dark and I ran around the city. I ran to Military Plaza to look for the Naplavas, but I believe they were at Fort Allen at that time, looking for me." She paused to smile ruefully at Jacob, making eye contact for the first time, and almost came undone. His face was gaunt with the enormity of the tragedy and the whims of Fate. "I ended up collapsing in front of St. Ursuline's, and the nuns found me the next morning and nursed me back to health. They kept me when they realized I was—homeless. And I want to make clear that they never knew, nor did the Naplavas, of any of the events of that night."

Cunningham nodded and decided that he must ask one more question.

"Dr. Rose, once you had recovered a bit from being sick and had the gun in your hand, why didn't you run? Why did you kill Adam Hawk?"

Abe glanced at Jennings and noted that he looked deflated; Cunningham was stealing his thunder.

"He had already struck me, undressed me, tied me up, and injected drugs into my arm. He had told me that he would come for me as soon as he could get up. I knew he meant to rape me, and he might strike me again, or drug me. He could easily kill me and probably would kill me, whether he meant to or not. I had to stop him." Her voice was beginning to gain volume and intensity.

"But he had drunk a bottle of whisky and taken drugs himself. Did he look like he would be coming after you any time soon?"

"I don't know. I didn't know what he was capable of. He was awake and moving around. He could have stood up and grabbed me at any second."

"Did you feel as though your life was in imminent danger?"

"Yes. Absolutely! He was two feet away from me; he could have leaned forward and grabbed my leg without even standing. I knew if I didn't stop him, I would die."

Cunningham nodded, relieved and pleased. She had answered perfectly. "No further questions."

"Cross?"

Jennings jumped to his feet and approached the stand aggressively. "Ms. Bailey, did it occur to you, as you were en route to the Gaslight Hotel, that you might have to kill Senator Hawk?"

Bailey flushed but did not hesitate. "Yes."

"You have just testified that you shot Senator Hawk in self-defense. Do you feel that he would have killed you?"

"Yes."

"But why not just shoot him in the kneecap to disable him? Would that not have effectively stopped him from harming you?"

"I don't know what would have stopped him."

"Come now, you are a *physician*. Can a man walk with a shattered kneecap?"

"I wasn't a physician when I was twelve years old," she shot back, and the audience murmured approval.

"Why didn't you shoot to disable? Why did you shoot to kill?"

There was a silence, and Bailey discerned that nothing less than her life was resting on her answer. It wasn't often that a person could recognize such a turning point when it was happening, but she knew with absolute certainty that this was one of those moments.

"I shot to kill so he wouldn't hurt me or kill me at that moment or come after me later." It was the austere, simple truth, and the jury approved, Cunningham could see at a glance.

"Isn't it true that you killed him because you thought he killed your mother?

"No. I believed him when he said it was an accident."

"You believed a man who drugged you, tied you up, and wanted to have relations with you?"

"The word is *rape*. And yes, I believed him."

"That seems ludicrous, doesn't it, this trust you had in him?"

"Objection. That is in no way, shape or form a question. Prosecutor is resorting to badgering the witness because he has nothing else to ask." Cunningham had leapt up and his face was uncharacteristically red.

Simmons opened his mouth to sustain the objection but Jennings waved his hand.

"Withdrawn. No further questions." He sat down with a smug smile.

"Your Honor, the defense rests."

Simmons nodded and the courtroom itself seemed to release a collective sigh of relief.

"Very well. We will adjourn for an hour, and then we will hear closing arguments." He banged the gavel and Bailey slumped with relief as she was handed down by the bailiff. She caught Jacob's eye as he filed out with the rest of the crowd and he pointed at her and put his fingers to his heart, smiling at her. She was amazed to find that her knees went weak. Amidst all of this agony, the painful recollection of memories she had thought would be buried forever, he still had the power to reduce her to a love- struck, swooning girl. She felt her face flame and dearly hoped that no one else had witnessed the exchange.

"You were amazing!" Cunningham whispered in her ear as soon as she reached the defense table. Abe squeezed her arm and Mooreland bobbed his head repeatedly, a silly smile on his face. "And it doesn't hurt that Jennings is an absolute buffoon!" They all laughed and made their way through the now-empty courtroom.

"What happens next?" Bailey asked.

"Jennings will close first, and he'll go on and on. It will drive Simmons crazy. My closing will take about five minutes; that's all we need, Doc! Then Simmons will dismiss the jury to deliberate."

"How long do you think it will take?" She chewed the insides of her cheeks, trying to imagine the anxiety of waiting for the verdict. Live, die, or life in prison. The latter was the worst by far. If she got life in prison, she would be moved to the Johnson Farm, a private cotton plantation near the Huntsville Prison. Women prisoners were housed there and spent their days at hard labor cutting down trees and building roads, and it was common knowledge that the guards whipped the women bloody and took whatever sexual liberties they cared to take. The women of the Shrimp Hotel spoke about Johnson Farm in the most dreaded of whispers.

"I predict they will return a verdict in less than one hour." Abe and Mooreland nodded in agreement, and Bailey let them sweep her up in their giddy enthusiasm, forcing herself to eat a banana and a sandwich, to laugh at their jokes, to look confident and calm as her life hung in the balance.

CHAPTER TWENTY-ONE

Alice Barnes was in a funk, and she walked alongside Anton and the rest of his family with her shoulders slumped. They were to take luncheon at Molly's Place, an upscale eatery in which she had always wanted to dine, but she had little appetite. She had sat through the trial in a distracted state, irked by the fact that she had combed every parlor, brothel, cathouse, and even the Row without finding the girl from the church. She had found many prostitutes that fit the general description, and since all she had to go on was her voice, she had engaged each one of them in conversation. None of them sounded remotely like the girl. It was a dead end, really, trying to find someone whose name she didn't know and whose face she had never seen. Her failure had made her cranky, she knew. Anton thought it was the details of the trial that were getting to her, but he was wrong. She was terrified that Caroline would have Anton under her thumb forever.

The man in question grasped her elbow and leaned in close. "Cheer up, honey! Everyone thinks Bailey will be acquitted."

It was on the tip of her tongue to say *my name's not honey* when something stopped her.

My name's not honey. Honey. My name. Honey.

Her head snapped up and she stopped dead in her tracks, causing Anton to almost trip as she pulled him back.

"What did you say?" she whispered, staring at him with wide eyes.

Anton gaped at her. "I—I said that everyone thinks Bailey will be acquitted."

"No. Before that."

Anton gulped. Alice could be downright intimidating at times. Times like now, when she leaned forward with her hands curled into fists and every muscle in her body tensed. She looked like a panther about to strike.

"I said 'Cheer up, honey.' Alice, what the hell is going on? You look like you're going to kill me. You don't have your blade on you, do you?" He laughed engagingly but the sound trailed off as she continued to pin him with her wide-eyed stare.

"My God," she whispered. "I thought it was just an endearment, maybe a condescending one. But that's her *name*. Her name is Honey!"

It was Anton's turn to stare. "I'm not following…"

Alice was practically jumping with excitement now. "The woman I've been looking for!"

"Oh…" Anton nodded, excited now himself. Alice had told him about seeing Caroline in disguise conducting a clandestine meeting with a prostitute in San Fernando's. It had been such a bizarre occurrence, and he knew how frustrated Alice had been trying to make sense of it all.

Alice moved closer to him so the rest of family, who had now stopped and were backtracking toward them, couldn't hear—especially Jacob. She didn't want Jacob to know anything until she, Alice, knew everything. "Caroline called that girl "honey." She said something like 'Have you been well, honey?' And I didn't think a thing of it, until just now, when you called me that. It wasn't an endearment, Anton! It was her name!"

Anton frowned uncertainly. "But how can you be sure?"

"Because I've heard of Honey! She worked at the Purple Pansy with Gabby Flores, Anton!"

As she spoke his face grew red and he gulped repeatedly. Reluctantly, he nodded. "Yes, I know Honey Lane," he confessed, and was relieved when Alice smiled and reached to squeeze his hand.

"It's okay, Anton. I don't care about any of that if you don't care about my past. We've had this all out, remember? Now try to focus! Is she still at the Pansy?"

"No," said in the barest whisper, for the family was ten feet from them. "I've heard Gabby mention her. She's at Harding House."

They started at each other, confused.

"I have to go," she said quickly. She turned and literally ran back the way they had just come, Anton's family staring at her retreating back, surprised.

"Where's Alice going?" Lindy asked.

"She just remembered an errand she needed to run," answered Anton brightly. "You know Alice; she's a bit mysterious. Let's go eat. I'm starving!"

And somehow he managed to turn them all around with jokes and laughter and his usual tomfoolery, while another part of his brain tried to put together a baffling puzzle.

Alice only knocked once before the door was flung open by a petite Chinese girl with a bulging belly. "Hi, Blossom," greeted Alice. Blossom was everyone's favorite pet: a sweet, shy girl with very limited English who had escaped the deplorable conditions of San Francisco's Chinatown to work for a kindly madam in a clean brothel in San Antonio.

"Mayflower, hello!" greeted Blossom with a thick Mandarin accent, flinging her arms around the taller girl. "You belly, too?"

Alice laughed. "No, ma'am. But I need to see Honey Lane. Is she here?"

Blossom's head nodded repeatedly. "Yes, yes, she here. She's…" she gestured up the stairs, struggling for the words. "I fetch, yes?"

"No. I'll go up. Which room is she in?"

"First left." Blossom bowed two or three times and then melted silently back into the parlor where she had been curled up with an art book. She loved to paint, a secret only the girls at Harding House knew about. Reverend Eckles had procured for her an easel and painting supplies, and when she wasn't painting, she was reading about it.

Alice made her way quickly up the stairs, a hard look on her face. She knew how to get information out of unwilling people, one way or another, and it didn't matter if they were women or if they were pregnant. They would talk. And she needed to know what Caroline wanted from Honey; any dirt she could collect on that bitch would be as good as ammunition in her pocket, and she knew how to use it.

She knocked on Honey's door, and it opened after a pause. At the door stood the girl from the church; Alice was sure of it, even though she'd never seen her face clearly.

"Yes? Can I help you?" she asked, her distinctive accent so very memorable. She was from Louisiana, no doubt about it; one of the Cajun girls. No one sounded like her.

"Hi, Honey," said Alice sweetly.

"Well hi there! I know you; you're Mayflower. What are you doing here? Are you knocked up? Are you gonna live here with us? Wait, aren't you all hooked up with Anton Naplava now? Ooohhhh, lucky, lucky girl!"

Alice gazed at Honey. Her fingers curled around Lucille.

"I don't feel much like answering questions today, Honey. But I have a few questions for you."

They were all seated again in the courtroom: it was more packed than ever, and the air was buzzing with anticipation. The jury filed in and Simmons arrived and banged the gavel, calling Jennings for his closing arguments.

Augustus Jennings was a different man on this day than he was a week ago. Gone was the sharp, arrogant brashness with which he had conducted himself, and in his place stood a sour little man with a bitter twist to his mouth. The case that was to have been a gift, a *cake walk*, had turned into a public relations nightmare. His witnesses had failed him and the jury had turned on him days ago; he could tell that at a glance. Truth be told, he was planning to retire. He had plenty of money and the wife had been hounding him to move to Georgia to be near their grown daughter and her children, and by God, now was the time. He frowned fiercely and decided that brevity was to be his weapon today.

"Your honor, gentlemen of the jury, and Mr. Foreman, over the past week you have heard testimony that has placed Miss Baily Rose at the Gaslight Hotel on the night of May twentieth, eighteen hundred and seventy-six. Two people lost their lives that night, and Miss Rose has confessed to killing one of them. She has confessed to entering that hotel room with the plan of killing Adam Hawk if she was so inclined, and gentlemen, that is exactly what happened. Adam Hawk is not here to defend himself, is he? We will never know what happened in that room that night. Even if you believe that the letter written was authentic—and there's still enough of a question of that to cause reasonable doubt—that does not explain why Miss Rose did not simply leave the room after disarming Mr. Hawk. She could have gone straight to the police station. She could have sought shelter with one of her friends. She could have left the city, or even the state: I think we all see that she had the intelligence and wherewithal to accomplish that. She could have shot to maim him so he couldn't follow. She could have opened the door and screamed for help. The point I am making, gentlemen, is that there are an almost infinite number of things she could have done. *But she chose to kill him.* She chose to pull the trigger and end the life of a man whom many believe was destined to lead this great country of ours someday. A man who, after all that he had suffered as a child, had overcome that tragedy to make something of his life, to have a life of public service. This was a man who even though he was haunted by the demons of his past, deserved a chance to turn his life around, to live. *He deserved a chance to live.*" He paused for effect, and Bailey was dismayed to realize just how affected she was. Jennings wasn't saying anything that she hadn't already tortured herself with for the past three days, but hearing him articulate her own thoughts made them unbearably tangible.

"In the final accounting, gentlemen, your Honor, it matters not whether Bailey Rose worked as a prostitute. It matters not the identity of the other woman in the room. It matters not who killed the other woman. It matters not why Bailey Rose entered Room 226 that fateful evening." Bailey barely suppressed an urge to look at Cunningham. Jennings had basically just dismissed the basis of his entire case. "And it matters not, gentlemen, what Adam Hawk, Adele Rosemount, or even Bailey Rose suffered as a child. What does matter? Why are you here?" He turned to face the jury then and shook his finger at them; probably not a wise move, Bailey mused. "What matters is that Bailey Rose confessed to killing an unarmed, weakened man, and to having a pre-mediated plan to do so. She had the opportunity—she

205

had the duty—to retreat at that moment in time, and she chose not to do so. Gentlemen, let me remind you of the definition of premeditated murder. 'The unlawful killing of a human being by another human being with malice aforethought, either expressed or implied.' Malice aforethought, gentlemen. She shot to kill. *It is just that simple.* Thank you."

He took his seat, surprising everyone. His brevity had been unexpectedly powerful, and Bailey felt herself closing up and becoming numb. She dared not look at the jury, but she was terrified at what she might find if she did so: would they be nodding? Staring at her with accusatory glares? She strove to put a calm, concerned, innocent expression on her face, but she had never been more afraid than she was at this moment.

"Defense?" barked Simmons.

Cunningham remained in his seat for a few seconds, studying his steepled hands gravely, then rose and approached the jury.

"Mr. Jennings was correct, gentlemen of the jury and Mr. Foreman. It *is* a simple decision you will be charged with today. Every piece of evidence— every single witness—the prosecution has attempted to build its case upon has been discredited, has been impeached. His implication that Bailey Rose killed the other woman in the room was proven by forensic evidence to be not only highly improbable, but dismissed by the experts. His accusation that she was a prostitute was proven to be a lie. His misidentification of the deceased woman in the room was a profound error, gentlemen! The fact that Bailey Rose traveled to the Gaslight Hotel to protect her own mother *completely changes the nature of this case*! It *does* matter!" The veins in his neck began to protrude and he slammed his hand down on the jury railing. "A twelve year old girl learns that her virginity—her innocence—her *childhood*— has been purchased by a man whom she has observed to be a drunken, violent, unpredictable monster. She learns her own mother has gone to confront the man to protect her daughter, and she takes it upon herself, this little girl, to protect her mother. She knocks on the door and is yanked viciously by her hair, struck across her face, forced to view her deceased mother who is covered in blood, laid out on the bed as if in a coffin. And when her brain shuts down in shock, this little girl is stripped, tied to a chair, and injected with drugs. None of that is to be understood from circumstantial evidence: all of it is *proven* by forensics! And what happened in that room is further perfectly understood by the letter penned by Adam Hawk himself. Yes, the shooting of her mother was likely an accident, but it was no accident that Bailey Rose had been undressed, tied to a chair, and rendered sick and incapacitated with drugs. And what was she to do, when she awakened to see Adam Hawk with a gun in his hand? Let him wake and kill her, or let him use the weapon to force her to bend to his sick, twisted desires? *Was she to have done nothing to survive?*"

Cunningham was roaring now, his voice echoing, resounding throughout the vast room, in sharp contrast to the calm, controlled tones he had employed throughout the trial. The effect was incredible: the jurors—every one of them—sat straight, wide-eyed, and completely captivated. Even the dead-eyed man and the glaring man seemed to be utterly transfixed by Cunningham's words. Bailey herself felt adrenaline course through her veins: she raised her chin, balled her fists, and felt power surging through her. She *had* survived, hadn't she? No one had rescued her; no one had needed to.

She had rescued herself, and that epiphany was the most empowering feeling she had ever experienced.

"Gentlemen, let me remind you of the law. Mr. Jennings has explained the tenets of murder. Now I shall explain the rules of justifiable homicide, of self-defense. Listen carefully, gentlemen, and apply these rules to what we know happened in that room." Cunningham turned back to the table and picked up a parchment, approached the jury bench again, and began to read, his voice forceful and full of conviction. "The defendant is not guilty of murder or manslaughter and acted in lawful self-defense if she reasonably believed that she was in imminent danger of being killed or suffering great bodily injury such as rape, maiming, robbery, or other forcible and atrocious crimes. She is not guilty of murder or manslaughter and acted in lawful self-defense if she reasonably believed that the immediate use of deadly force was necessary to defend against that danger. She was entitled to use the amount of force that a reasonable person believes is necessary in the same situation. If the defendant had been threatened or harmed by that person in the past, she was justified in acting more quickly or taking greater self-defense measures against that person. A defendant is not required to retreat. She is entitled to stand her ground and defend herself, and if necessary, pursue the assailant until the danger of death or great bodily injury—including rape—has passed. *This is so even if safety could have been achieved by retreating.*" There was an impressive pause as the jury took this in.

"Gentlemen. Let's assume for a moment that you have doubts about Dr. Rose's testimony. Let's consider the other evidence. By his own admission, in a letter proven to be written in his own hand, Adam Hawk was involved in Adele Rosemont's shooting and intent on raping Bailey Rose. The sizable chunk of red hair on the floor supports her testimony that she was drug into the room by her hair. The red dress ties found by the police support the fact that she was tied to the chair. By the testimony of three different sisters of St. Ursuline's convent, Bailey Rose arrived at their doorstep later that night with morphine in her system, needle puncture marks in her arm, and a black eye. All of these facts prove that Bailey Rose took action to save her own life that evening."

He spun suddenly and pointed at the young stable boy. "If your sister were stripped, tied to a chair, drugged, and threatened with rape, would you tell her to shoot?" The young man stared at him, wide-eyed and frozen.

"What about you? What if your mother were in that chair?" He pointed to the young Swede, who flushed ever-so-slightly and shook his head yes. Cunningham spun again and took a big chance: he pointed at the dead-eyed man. "What about you? What if your wife were in that chair? Would you tell her to shoot?" The man's expression didn't change, but he gave a curt nod without hesitating, and Bailey's heart soared.

Cunningham looked at all of the men, one by one, for the next twenty seconds, the silence spinning out. *I would have told her to blow his f-ing head off,* thought Jacob savagely, wracked with guilt at not being there to protect her and bursting with pride knowing that she had protected herself.

Cunningham finally nodded, seeming satisfied, and spoke again, his voice stern and full of genuine earnestness. "The People have the burden of proving *beyond a reasonable doubt* that the shooting of Adam Hawk was *not justified*. If the People have not met this burden, you must find the defendant not guilty of murder, manslaughter, and any other charges brought against her. You must find that the little girl shot the man in justifiable self-defense to save her life. She is not guilty. She is a *survivor*."

He turned and walked back to the table amidst a heavy silence, and Bailey felt as though her heart were about to thump its way out of her chest. Tears were pooling in her eyes and her cheeks were flushed with gratitude. Whether she was found guilty or not, Cunningham's speech had somehow absolved her; had lifted the load from her shoulders that had weighed her down her whole life long, and she found she could breathe again. She looked at him gratefully and he nodded once, his eyes sparkling.

Simmons came to life then, emerging from an appreciative daze. Closing arguments had been brief and powerful—even Jennings had done a marginally-good job—and with any luck, the jury would be out for less than an hour. He cleared his throat meaningfully. "Court will now adjourn for jury deliberations." He turned to the jury and read the instructions before dismissing them, and they rose as one and shuffled their way through a door in the front of the room leading to the jury chambers.

"All parties are free to leave the courtroom or remain for the duration of deliberations. No moving around; stay in your seats if you're staying, or the guards will escort you out, and I don't give a damn *who* you are." He looked meaningfully at a prominent merchant and his wife who had been noticeably chatty throughout the trial. "It could be twenty minutes or it could be twenty hours, folks. You decide." And with that flippant remark, he heaved himself up and disappeared through his door as quickly as he could.

Bailey stared at the door through which the jury had disappeared, swallowing thickly, feeling the elation and bravado from moments before begin to evaporate. The prosecution stood and left the courtroom, pursued by buzzing reporters. No one else budged an inch: over three hundred people waited quietly, murmuring, craning their necks to get a glimpse of the ephemerally beautiful lady doctor, accused murderess of a United States senator, former resident of a bordello, friend of the mayor-elect. The story was impossibly juicy, full of mystery and intrigue and tragedy. No one was going anywhere.

"Should we go?" whispered Bailey to Cunningham, her voice shaking. She was surprised at her level of anxiety, and she forced herself to take a few deep breaths.

"Let's stay," whispered Cunningham with an encouraging smile. "I don't think we'll be waiting long!"

"You're terribly confident. You're almost arrogant, you know." She winked to take the sting out of her words.

"I know," he returned with a smirk. "For good reason."

They waited a few more moments in silence, Cunningham scribbling notes, Abe resting with his eyes closed, and Mooreland reading a law book. "Mr. Cunningham?" Bailey finally whispered after five minutes.

He put his notebook down immediately and turned to her. "Yes?"

"What happens if I—if the jury returns a guilty verdict? What will happen next?" She tried to sound nonchalantly curious, but she must not have pulled it off, because he took the unusual action of briefly squeezing her hand.

"In the very highly unlikely event that the jury returns a guilty verdict—and they have two charges to answer to, murder and manslaughter—the judge will set a date for sentencing. The terms of the sentence will be adjudicated by Simmons—and you will be escorted back to your cell to await that hearing."

"Oh," she managed, staring at him.

"And in the highly likely event that you are found not guilty of all charges, the jury will be dismissed and the trial will be over, and you will be free to walk out of this courtroom, never to be tried again for this crime."

She did manage a smile then, but she still had a pressing question.

"But what about the shooting of my mother? Will Jennings try to—"

She never got to finish that thought, because at that moment, Judge Simmons burst through his door, seated himself on his bench, and banged the gavel. There was an electrified, excited buzz followed immediately by absolute hush: everyone, with the exception of Cunningham, who sat with a beatific smile on his face, was stunned. The jury had been deliberating for less than thirty minutes.

Simmons ordered the crowd to rise, and the jury shuffled in silently. Though she tried mightily not to, Bailey snuck surreptitious glances at each member; none, however, was meeting her eyes, and she felt a chill prick along her spine. That couldn't be good, could it? That they couldn't meet her eyes? She glanced at Cunningham, who had managed to wipe the smile from his face but was looking very pleased nonetheless. She felt herself relax by a degree.

Simmons glared at the jury. "Have you reached a verdict?" he snapped, wasting no time.

"We have, your Honor," replied the foreman smartly. Bailey felt herself begin to panic again. This was too fast! In the next instant she would know her fate: freedom, death, life in prison—she needed more time to prepare! She fought the urge to turn and look at Jacob: how she needed him right now, at this moment!

Behind her, Jacob was experiencing a rush of blood to his head so intense that he thought he may hit the floor. *Not guilty. Not guilty. Please, God, let it be not guilty.* He found he could not swallow, and he gripped the bench in front of him to keep from reaching for her. He stared not at the jury but at the back of Bailey's neck, so delicate, with a wisp of an errant red curl visible.

"What say you?" bellowed Simmons.

Bailey's breath caught in her throat and her entire body went numb.

"We, the jury, in the case of Bexar County versus Bailey Faith Rose, find the defendant not guilty in the charge of murder. We further find the defendant not guilty in the charge of manslaughter."

The rest of his words were lost to the roar of the crowd. Simmons banged the gavel to no avail, then finally gave up after five minutes and yelled something to the effect of "Thank you, jury, for your service today; court is adjourned," and with a nimbleness that defied his size, slipped from his chair and through his chamber door.

Bailey gave a sob and collapsed in a heap on her chair, flanked immediately by her team.

As the crowd rose and surged forward as one body, Jacob found that every muscle in his entire body had turned to jelly. He sank his head into his hands and let out a great, shuddering sigh, feeling the claps on his back from his brothers and distantly hearing Marianna's voice chirping giddily, *Of course she's not guilty! Of course she's not!* Lindy, calm and steady, *Well, they got this one right, didn't they? Now she can get on with her life.* His mother weeping quiet tears of joy. And then a more urgent voice, and a sharp tug on his sleeve.

"Mr. Naplava! Sir! Oh, Mr. Naplava. I'm so sorry to interrupt! You must come quickly!" He lifted his head and recognized Caroline's maid, and his mind whirled in confusion.

"Madge!" He was at a loss of words for a second; she was so out of context here in the courtroom attired in her maid's costume of black and white. "What are you doing here?"

"It's Caroline!" Madge was leaning past Johann and Lindy, practically stretched out on their laps to get to Jacob. "She's been taken to the doctor's. We don't know what's wrong with her. She's had a seizure, the missus said, and she's not conscious. Mrs. Vogler said to come and fetch you."

Jacob shared a terrified look with his mother. *The baby.* And Caroline's mother didn't know she was pregnant!

He stared back at Madge, and then strained to catch a glimpse of Bailey, who was completely consumed by well-wishers at this point, surrounded by a wall of her legal team, family, friends, and reporters. He couldn't even see her, and there was nothing he wanted—*needed*—to do more than to get to her and hold her again. He didn't give a damn who saw.

"We must go, sir! I have a rig right outside. Please!" Madge boldly reached for his hand and tugged on it, tears of panic welling in her rather bulging eyes.

Jacob nodded curtly. "Tell her I'll find her later, will you please, Johann?"

His brother winked. "Of course, my man. Go. You'll never get to her now anyway."

Jacob stood and pushed his way through the tight, noisy crowd, dragged along still in the tight grasp of the fearful maid.

By the time Johann shoved a path to the defense table to deliver Jacob's message, Bailey had disappeared, slipping away quickly through the judge's door with Hope, Cordelia and Howard in order to avoid the relentless press of well-wishers, detractors, and noxious reporters, a heavy ball in the pit of her stomach. She had seen Jacob leave with the maid and suspected that he was being called to Caroline's side; she wondered if the young woman was having a pregnancy-related emergency. And despite her best efforts, another thought occurred.

He didn't speak to you before he left. There is your answer to put an end to your silly dreams. He has other obligations that must always come before you; is that what you want, your whole life long? Time to let go. You are free now!

PREVIEW OF GREEN MEADOW, BOOK 5
BAILEY ROSE, M.D. SERIES

CHAPTER ONE

Most of the frenetic ride to Dr. Montgomery's office was spent in silence. Madge, his fiancé's maid, had come to fetch him alone, and she steered the rig skillfully at a break-neck pace through the city streets, her brown eyes bulging with panic and her bonnet strings flapping. Montgomery's office was on Evergreen Street, about fifteen blocks from the courthouse. In the time it took to travel it, Jacob's mind reeled at an equally frenetic pace, trying to make proper order of the utter mess of his life. He had found his childhood love, Bailey Rose, after fifteen years; the little girl raised in a brothel in the heart of San Antonio's Red Light District had overcome a life of deprivation to become a doctor, returning to serve the fallen women and children. He had found her, but not before one stupid night of drunkenness with Caroline had sealed his fate: he had impregnated a woman he didn't love, and now he was bound to her, for life. He sunk his head into his hands, utterly despondent. Bailey had just been acquitted of murder: it should be a time of rejoicing; she should be in his arms right this minute. She had shot a man fifteen years ago in self-defense, a man who had been revealed to have been kidnapped and horribly abused as a child along with Bailey's mother. Bailey was free now; free to walk out of that courtroom after months in jail, and he needed to be with her! What in God's name was he doing in this carriage? Being trapped in his own miserable life, that's what. He would be marrying Caroline soon; they were having a baby in a few short months, and then he would begin his term as the youngest mayor in the country. And all he desired—all that he *needed*—was to be on the train back to Bluebonnet Ranch, Bailey in his arms.

He sat up then, reminding himself. Caroline was ill; his unborn baby might be in danger. It was time to step back into his life.

"What happened?" he asked gruffly.

Madge whimpered. "I'm sure I don't know, sir. I found her myself an hour ago. I went to her room to take her a tray, and she was shaking on the bed, flopping around like a fish. Scared the daylights out of me. Then she just went limp, and we couldn't get her to wake up. Now, she's had headaches and long days of sleeping sickness before, but never a fit like this, you see. Jerry, the stable boy, got her and her mum to the doctor's right away, and then Mrs. Vogler sent me to fetch you. I suspect it has something to do with the diphtheria, don't you think?"

Jacob gulped, his face flooding. He had never been a good liar, so he said nothing, knowing his omission made him just as duplicitous. And what did Madge mean, Caroline had headaches and sleeping sickness? She had never told him about that.

He was halfway out of the rig before Madge had it completely stopped, and tore into the office. The waiting room was strangely empty, and he wondered what kind of medical office Montgomery ran, being closed in the middle of the day.

"Mrs. Vogler?" he called, his voice echoing. The waiting area looked much like the Rose Clinic, he noticed with a pang. "Dr. Montgomery?"

"We're back here, Mr. Naplava," called Montgomery, and he strode through the waiting room down a narrow hallway, looking right and left into various small examination rooms until he found what he was looking for. Mrs. Vogler sat next to a bed upon which lay Caroline, white and still. Dr. Montgomery stood at the other side, taking her pulse.

"Hello Jacob," quavered Mrs. Vogler. "I'm so glad Madge found you."

He slowly approached the bed, staring at the girl who lay there. Her eyelids were twitching and her chest rose and fell, but the rest of her was absolutely still. Her blonde-white hair had been braided to the side and rested over her shoulder, making her look five years younger than she was. He felt a surge of pity for her and wondered if she had divulged her pregnancy to her mother. Mrs. Vogler's next words put that question to rest.

"I don't know what on earth is wrong with her," she cried. "She's had episodes before where she gets upset and then sleeps for a few days, but nothing like this. It must be the diphtheria." Jacob felt as low as he ever had.

"Mrs. Vogler," said Dr. Montgomery gently. "You've been here for an hour. Why don't you let Madge take you home to rest? Caroline's vital signs are very strong; she's resting now. I have every confidence that she's going to be just fine and will wake up any time now, fully recovered, just like the other times. Let young Naplava here stay with her for a while. We'll send word immediately if there's a change."

It took some convincing, but the elegant woman finally took her leave, assisted to the rig by an attentive Madge. Dr. Montgomery and Jacob followed them out, bidding them farewell in the waiting room. Montgomery then sighed and gestured Jacob into his office.

"What about the baby? Is he okay?" Jacob blurted as they made their way to the small room. Montgomery remained silent, pointing at a chair.

They sat and stared at each other. "She didn't have diphtheria," Jacob began.

Montgomery waved his hand impatiently. "I know. She told me about the plan."

Jacob's face flooded with shame. *The plan.* It sounded so nefarious.

"Then what the hell is wrong with her? And is the baby okay?"

"I honestly don't know what's wrong with her. But you should know that this has happened before. Many times! Caroline has struggled for years with this condition, ever since she and her family came to Texas; since I've known them, anyway."

Jacob stared at him. The doctor wasn't mentioning the baby, which was not a good sign, and a flush of dread began somewhere in his chest and spread to the rest of his body.

"The baby. Is he dead?"

There was a crash as the entry door in the waiting room was flung open with enough force to drive it into the wall behind it, jangling the bell jarringly. They both jumped.

"Hello?" called a woman's voice, and she sounded familiar.

"Hello there? Where's the doctor?" she called, and Jacob had it. Alice! Anton's Alice! He jumped to his feet and ran to the waiting room, followed by Dr. Montgomery.

They both stopped in their tracks, shocked into immobility for entirely different reasons.

Alice Barnes stood with her feet spread wide, one hand clamped firmly around the wrist of another woman who appeared to be just a few years' Alice's senior. The other girl stood sobbing, her golden hair coming loose from a bun and hanging in strands around her face. It looked as though a struggle had occurred and Alice had come out on top.

Dr. Montgomery uttered a sound that could have been "No!" or a moan of pain. He began to back up, his eyes bulging with fear, but Alice pointed at him.

"You might want to think about not moving another step," she hissed, and Jacob gaped at her.

"Alice! What the hell is going on? This is Caroline's doctor! And she's sick—she's back there laid out on a table, unconscious!"

Alice's expression softened as she regarded Jacob. He was her favorite Naplava boy by far, except for Anton, of course. She considered herself an excellent judge of character, and this man was as good they came. "Oh, Jacob, I think we all better sit down," she said gently, and still with the angelic smile on her face, shoved the girl roughly into a chair, then lowered herself gracefully beside her.

She pointed at Montgomery again. "Sit," she ordered, and he sat, as did Jacob, who was beginning to realize that this was perhaps the strangest day of his life thus far.

Alice took a deep breath and looked at each of them, her eyes finally resting on Jacob. She shook her head admiringly. "I've never in my life seen a man with prettier eyes," she said unexpectedly. "Everyone moons over Anton—and he *is* pretty—but I think you might be the looker in the family." He stared at her, flushing, and could not think of a thing to say.

"Alice," he finally managed after a terribly awkward pause. "What is going on?"

"Well, this is all quite simple, really. Brace yourself, Jacob. Ready?"

He stared at her, wondering if she had lost her mind.

"All right then. Jacob, Caroline Vogler is not pregnant."

The words fell into the room like a hard rain, drenching him in icy fingers, robbing his breath. Montgomery produced a guttural sound and sunk his face into his hands, and the other girl's chin dropped to her chest in shame.

"I'm sorry. Alice, what did you say?" he finally managed after several long seconds, his voice choked.

"Caroline isn't pregnant and she never was. She lied to trap you into marriage. Montgomery here is in on it. And so is this sorry girl, Honey Lane. Caroline disguised herself as a matronly older woman, Mrs. Hall—she wore a wig and stuffed her clothes and everything, I saw her with my own eyes, Jacob—and she gave Honey a thousand macaroons, with the promise of a thousand more upon delivery. You see, Honey here is expecting a baby, and Caroline's been paying her to get her checkups with Montgomery. When the time comes for her to deliver, Caroline was just going to come here and pretend to go into labor and *oi-la*! There's a baby!" She flipped one hand in the air to demonstrate the simplicity of the plan.

Jacob stared at her, the blood draining from his face and settling somewhere deep where a hot ball of rage had begun to form.

"I saw Caroline meeting with Honey at San Fernando's a month back and I didn't have the whole story yet, Jacob, or I would have told you. Caroline was in disguise—oh, it was a good one, and I never would've known it was her until I heard her speak and followed her home and saw the dark wig and clothes and stuffing in the carriage. But I figured it all out and tracked down Honey at Harding House. You see, Honey was going to adopt that baby out anyway, and for two grand, it was just so easy to say yes, wasn't it, Honey?"

The girl sobbed louder and shook her head violently. "I told you, I changed my mind. I was trying to get the money back she gave me so I could tell her no. I want to keep my baby! Oh, can I, Dr. Montgomery? I don't have to give it to Mrs. Hall—I mean, Miss Vogler, do I?"

Montgomery groaned again, apparently incapable of forming an answer, his eyes bugged with fear. He was certain that the big Naplava boy would kill him.

There was another long, strained silence, Jacob trying to remember how to breathe, the girl sobbing, and Montgomery groaning.

"No, Miss Lane," Jacob finally said with a kind voice. "You don't have to give your baby to Miss Vogler. You keep your baby, and don't worry about paying back that money." He smiled gently at her, even as the ball of rage expanded, pushing against his heart and making it pound with a furious rhythm.

"Oh, thank you, Mr. Naplava! Thank you! I'm ever so sorry. I didn't know she was tricking anyone. I thought she was a nice older lady who just wanted another baby and couldn't have one. And she's not even married!" She ended on a wail, and Jacob grimaced, feeling the ball pushing everything else out of the way.

He stood, balling his fists. "Alice. Would you please take Honey back to Harding House and make sure she's fine? There will be no charges filed against her, and if she chooses to tell Reverend Eckles, that's up to her. None of this is her fault."

Alice stood, yanking Honey with her, not quite ready to relinquish her prisoner. "Why, of course I will, Jacob, but are you sure?"

He nodded tersely. "Yes, I am certain. I'm indebted to you, Alice. Really, I am. Thank you." He took a step forward and gave her arm a squeeze, smiling into her eyes, and she was surprised to feel her heart flutter a bit. She'd have to confess to Anton that she had just a tiny crush on his younger brother. She was pretty sure Anton had just a tiny crush on Lindy, so they'd be even!

She smiled and saluted. "At your service! Anything for a brother of Anton's, of course." She whisked out of the office, pulling Honey with her, endeavoring to be a bit gentler now that the drama was over and Jacob seemed to be most forgiving.

Jacob did not feel forgiving—well, maybe toward that poor hoodwinked girl, but not toward the blubbering man in the chair behind him. And certainly not toward the serpent who lay coiled in the bed down the hall. He felt murderous.

He turned to the doctor; Montgomery was full-on weeping now, sure that he was about to die. "How did she get you to do it?" he finally said, his voice deadly quiet. "Was it money?"

The doctor only shook his head, unable to speak. For long moments the only sound was his sobbing, punctuated by hiccoughs and snorts.

"Did she pay you?" he asked again, his voice gaining volume. He heard a roaring in his ears from the rage and failed to notice quiet sounds from the hallway beyond.

"Y—y—yes," Montgomery finally blubbered.

An onerous thought occurred to Jacob and he ground his teeth together so fiercely he felt shooting pains in his jaws. "Did she pay with *favors*, too?" he forced himself to say, and leaned forward to pull the man to his feet by the lapels. "Did she?" His whole body was shaking now, from the inside out, the ball of rage pushing at his skin, his face, contorting his features, lending him strength beyond his considerable norm.

"Yes," wailed the doctor, and Jacob threw the man with such force back onto the chair that he tipped backward and fell to the floor with a crash, and lay there, unmoving, the toes of his boots pointing at the ceiling, still whimpering. Jacob crouched down and put his face one inch from the doctor's.

"You will be gone by tomorrow morning. Get out of this city, forever. Get out of the state. If I ever see you again in the state of Texas, I'll kill you. Do you understand?"

Montgomery's head bobbed on his shoulders like a floppy doll, relief rendering him limp.

Jacob straightened and tried with all of his willpower to stem the rage surging inside of him. He failed. Every muscle in his body was on fire: his blood surged, his heart raced, his eyes bulged. He needed to hit something before he walked back into the room down the hall. He turned and put his fist through the wall with such force that his knuckles traveled through several layers of paint and plaster. He gasped and pulled his hand out of the wall, sinking to the floor and cradling it for a moment. It was broken for sure, and bleeding like a son of a bitch.

He bowed his head and let the fury wash through him in wave after sickening wave. Caroline wasn't pregnant. She had tricked him, all this time, using the vilest means imaginable, exploiting others to get what she wanted, and he had been the colossal dumbass who had fallen for the oldest trick in the book.

He allowed himself a moment to think about what might have been. Bailey, his sweet girl, his one love, with him in the hen house the night of the barn dance, *oh, Lord*. If not for Caroline he would have been on his knee that night proposing to Bailey, begging her to marry him. She would have said yes. And right now, already—because he would have walked her to the church within a week, *the next day*, if she would have let him—he would be her husband. *Bailey's husband*. That's who he had been born to be; he was more certain of that than he had ever been of anything in his life. How unforgivably he had hurt her, loving her, making her love him, all the while intending to marry Caroline. Even today, he had left her. My God, what did she think of him now? Where was she now? He felt a primal need to get to her. But there was something he must take care of first.

He drew a bolstering breath and got to his feet. Montgomery still lay in a heap on the floor, but with a sharp command from Jacob he leapt up and scuttled out the front door, still blubbering. "Leave your rig," growled Jacob after him, and the man squeaked like a mouse and ran on foot from the building.

Jacob turned to look down the hallway, his anger sufficiently dissipated. All it took was to think of Bailey, and the world regained balance and made sense again. *Just get it over with.* He straightened and strode quickly down the hall; he would wake her and tell her he knew everything. He would give her the same ultimatum he had given Montgomery: leave this city. Leave this state. Remove yourself from my sight or I will ruin you. Ruining Caroline would not involve lifting a hand against her, which of course, he would never do, no matter how tempted. He would send Alice with a story to Hedelga Jones for *The Express,* and Caroline's life in her precious high-society world would be over. He would give her one day to get out of town or she would suffer a social death.

He took a deep breath and entered the room.

She was gone.

ABOUT THE AUTHOR

Jenny Haley is the author of the *Bailey Rose, M.D.* series. As a writer, she was shaped by the works of LaVyrle Spencer, immersing herself in compelling stories of strong women in authentic and relatable situations within rich historical settings. Jenny's genre is tricky to define: historical magical realism paranormal romance, perhaps. You will not find bodice-ripping stories with helpless, flawless protagonists in her books, but stories that deeply resonate, featuring courageous, imperfect women and the men who love them.

Jenny makes her home in the American Upper Midwest where she lives with her husband, teenage daughter, her young adult son close by, and two retired racing greyhounds. In her spare time, she works as a college administrator and writing instructor at a public university.

Jenny loves to hear from her readers! Visit her website at www.jennyhaley.com, where you can watch the latest book trailer, read her blog, and connect via email. If you enjoyed this novel, the nicest way to say "thank you" is to leave a favorable review online!

Made in the USA
Las Vegas, NV
04 December 2021

36080413R00132